THE LAST COMPANION
A NOVEL OF ARTHURIAN BRITAIN

BOOK ONE OF THE ALBION CHRONICLES

Patrick McCormack

ROBINSON
London

Constable & Robinson Ltd
3 The Lanchesters
162 Fulham Palace Road
London W6 9ER
www.constablerobinson.com

First published in the UK by Raven Books,
an imprint of Robinson Publishing Ltd in 1997

This revised edition published by Robinson,
an imprint of Constable & Robinson Ltd 2005

A copy of the British Library Cataloguing in
Publication data is available from the British Library

ISBN 1-84529-150-6

Printed and bound in the EU

2 4 6 8 10 9 7 5 3 1

DRAMATIS PERSONAE OF ALBION

Aelle King of the South Saxons in Arthur's day; died at Badon.

Aescwine The first king of the East Saxons. Wiegu was his rival.

Agricola, or **Aircol** High Lord of Dyfed in Arthur's day, father of Vortepor.

Ambrosius The Elder and the Younger. Father and son who opposed the policies of Gworthigern and refused to acknowledge his authority.

Anir Arthur's son, killed by him.

Arthur At first Warlord and later Emperor or Amherawdyr of Albion.

Atlendor One of Arthur's Companions.

Beanstan Saxon serving in the City Guard of Lindinis.

Bedwyr One of Arthur's Companions. He and Cei were Arthur's oldest friends and chief Companions.

Beli (1) Fisherman from Eurgain's village.

Beli (2) Character from legend: in the tale told by Teleri at Caer Cadwy one of the seven survivors of the expedition to rescue Gwair.

Bieda West Saxon rival to Cerdic; died at Camlann.

Bran (1) Boy from Eurgain's village.

Bran (2) Character from legend: in the tale told by Teleri at Caer Cadwy one of the seven survivors of the expedition to rescue Gwair.

Budoc A hermit. Formerly one of Arthur's Companions, he survived Camlann and became a monk in Brittany before returning to Dumnonia.

Cadwallon Lord of Gwynedd during Arthur's later years, father of Maelgwn.

Cadwy Legendary hero of Eastern Dumnonia.

Caradoc One of Arthur's companions. Heroic leader who fought against the Roman invasion.

Caswallon Legendary hero.

Cattegirn Son of Gworthigern, fought against the Saxons in defiance of his father.

Cei Called 'the Long Man' because of his great size. With Bedwyr, the chief of Arthur's Companions. Slain by Gwydawg mab Menestyr.

Ceolric A young Saxon, son of Wicga.

Cerdic King of the West Saxons or Gewisse.

Cian Leader of the settlement on the east shore of the Hyle estuary.

Cuchulain Legendary Irish hero.

Cunedda Ancestor of the rulers of Gwynedd.

Cunrig Saxon, leader of Cerdic's warband.

Custennin, or **Constantine** High Lord of Dumnonia in succession to his father Kynfawr.

Degaw Wife to Talorcan and friend to Mab Petroc at Arthur's court. A Pict, of the tribe of the Creones.

Dovnuall Follower of Eremon.

Drust mab Erp Semi-legendary leader of Pictish Federation in Gworthigern's day.

Dyfnwal Ruler of Strathclyde in Arthur's day.

Dyfyr Eurgain's sister.

Edar Boy from Eurgain's village.

Enoch Bishop at Arthur's court.

Eochaid Founder of the ruling dynasty of Dyfed; ancestor of Vortepor.

Eremon Outlaw of Irish descent. Foster son of Gereint and nephew of Lleminawg.

Erfai Gorthyn's father, foster father to Nai. Killed by Dovnuall.

Eurgain A girl from the village near Budoc's hermitage, on the western shore of the Hyle estuary.

Fergus mac Erc With brothers Lorn and Angus the most vociferous of the Scotti raiders along the north-western coast in Arthur's day. Granted the peninsula of Kintyre by Dyfnwal of Strathclyde.

Fingal   Older adviser to the young Vortepor of Dyfed.

Folcwalda, Frodi's son   Saxon, Captain in the City Guard of Lindinis.

Garmund   Saxon serving in the City Guard of Lindinis.

Garulf   A Frisian. As a young man served in the City Guard of Lindinis; as an older man was steersman of the *Sea Stallion*.

Garwen   Mab Petroc's dead wife.

Gereint   Minor lord in Dumnonia, served by Gorthyn and Nai. Also, common name in Dumnonia.

Glewlwyd   Arthur's Gatekeeper.

Goronwy   One of Arthur's Companions, accompanied mab Petroc to Lindinis.

Gorthyn   Dumnonian warrior, member of Gereint's warband. Foster brother of Nai.

Gwair   Character from legend: in the tale told by Teleri at Caer Cadwy he was stolen away at his birth and rescued by seven heroes. Gwair was his childhood name: he later became Pryderi or Peredur of Prydein.

Gwalchmei   The Hawk, one of the Companions and kin to Arthur. Died at Peryddon in Gwent.

Gwenhwyvar   Wife to Arthur.

Gworthigern the Thin (Vortigern)   'The High King': Vitolinus, who first invited the Saxons under Hengest to Britain, to help fend off the attacks of the Picts and the Scots.

Gwydawg   Son of Menestyr, killed Cei.

Gwyl   Woman from Eurgain's village.

Heilyn   Gereint's bard.

Hengist   Leader of the original Saxon mercenaries invited to Britain by Gworthigern.

Heuil   A pirate and reiver along the western coasts of Britain, particularly Dyfed.

Hussa   Saxon serving in the City Guard of Lindinis.

Iddawg   Once one of Arthur's Companions, opposed him at Camlann, and died there.

Jago   Fisherman from Eurgain's village.

Kynfawr, or Cunomorus   Ruler of Dumnonia in Arthur's day, father of Custennin.

Llacheu   Arthur's son, killed by Cei.

Lady, The   Character from legend: in the tale told by Teleri at Caer Cadwy the mother of Gwair.

Lleminawg   The Dancer, one of Arthur's Companions,

descended from Irish settlers along the River Oak in Dumnonia.

Mab and Mac   Respectively the British and Irish terms for 'son of'. I have varied my usage depending on the speaker and the person addressed. For example, Gorthyn and Nai think of Eremon as a Briton of Irish descent, so call him *mab* Cairbre; Vortepor, on the other hand, and Eremon's Irish followers, call him *mac* Cairbre.

Mab Petroc   One of Arthur's Companions, leader of the expedition to Lindinis.

Maelgwn   Lord of Gwynedd, son of Cadwallon. Young rival of Vortepor of Dyfed.

Magnus Maximus, or **Macsen Wledig**   Roman General of Spanish origin. While serving in Britain he declared himself Emperor of Rome in 383. He invaded Gaul, and was defeated and executed in 388. Many later British rulers claimed some connection with him.

Medraut   Once one of Arthur's Companions, opposed him at Camlann and died there.

Melwas   Formerly betrothed to Gwenhwyvar.

Menestyr   The name of a clan of tattooed men from the far north, the Sons or Children of Menestyr, and of its leader: Pedrylaw Menestyr 'The Skilled Cupbearer'.

Menw   One of Arthur's Companions.

Morgant   Adviser to Gereint.

Moried   One of Arthur's Companions, close friend of mab Petroc.

Myrddin   Character from legend: in the tale told by Teleri at Caer Cadwy one of the seven survivors of the expedition to rescue Gwair.

Nai   Dumnonian warrior, member of Gereint's warband. Foster brother of Gorthyn.

Nudd   Character from legend: in the tale told by Teleri at Caer Cadwy one of the seven survivors of the expedition to rescue Gwair, though wounded in the thigh.

Oesc   Son of Hengist, and king of Kent.

Oswine   Saxon serving in the City Guard of Lindinis.

Pedrawg   Boy from Cian's settlement on the east shore of the Hyle estuary.

Pedrylaw   See Menestyr.

Peredur, or **Pryderi**   See Gwair.

Pwill Character from legend: in the tale told by Teleri at Caer Cadwy, the Grey Man, who stole the baby Gwair.

Rhodri Eurgain's father and head of their village.

Scatha Warrior woman in Irish legend who trained the great hero Cuchulain.

Serach Follower of Eremon.

Seradwen Woman once loved by Nai.

Sigebeorn, Sigeferth's son Saxon, Captain in the City Guard of Lindinis.

Sigemund Legendary dragon slayer.

Taliessin Character from legend: in the tale told by Teleri at Caer Cadwy one of the seven survivors of the expedition to rescue Gwair.

Talorcan One of Arthur's Companions and friend to mab Petroc. Husband to Degaw, and like her a Pict.

Taran Character from legend: in the tale told by Teleri at Caer Cadwy one of the seven survivors of the expedition to rescue Gwair.

Teleri Female bard loved by mab Petroc

Teyrnon Character from legend: in the tale told by Teleri at Caer Cadwy, Lover of the Lady and father of Gwair.

Vitolinus See Gworthigern.

Vortepor High Lord of Dyfed, son of Agricola.

Wicga Saxon. Ceolric's father, and Captain of the *Sea Stallion*.

For Dion

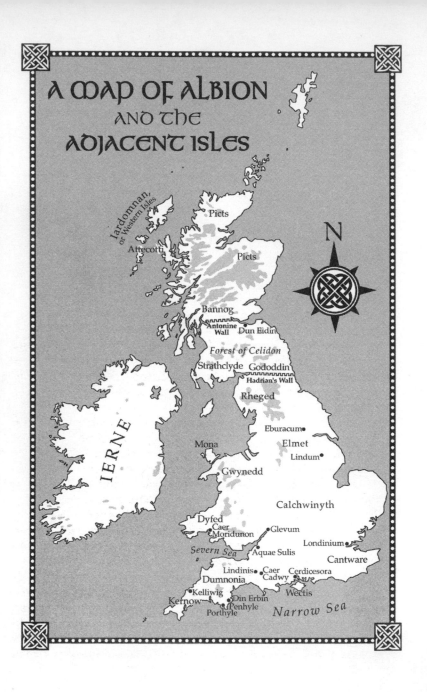

A MAP OF ALBION
AND THE
ADJACENT ISLES

N

Iardomnan,
or Western Isles

Picts

Attecotti

Picts

Bannog

Antonine
Wall   Dun Eidin

Forest of Celidon

Strathclyde   Gododdin

Hadrian's Wall

Rheged

Eburacum

Mona   Elmet

Lindum

Gwynedd

IERNE

Calchwinyth

Dyfed
Caer
Moridunon   Glevum

Londinium

Aquae Sulis

Cantware

Lindinis   Caer   Cerdicesora
Cadwy
Dumnonia   Wectis
Kelliwig
Kernow   Din Erbin
Penhyle   Narrow Sea
Porthyle

Severn Sea

PROLOGUE

Budoc was alone now.

He had been alone with his memories for a long time.

And sometimes he dreamed of Camlann.

In the distance horns are blowing, hooves are drumming. Medraut is come, Medraut who never shirked a fight nor feared to speak his mind, Medraut whom no king in all the world could refuse, on account of his beauty and his wisdom.

Medraut the traitor.

The horsemen withdraw, regroup. Their steeds are blown, no longer proud and high prancing. The greasy grass has been churned to mud, and the horses slip and slide as wearily they re-form around their leader. These are the Companions, the teulu *of Arthur the Battle Emperor of Albion, and though their numbers have dwindled they are undefeated in war.*

They ride like shadows through the mist, the men of Medraut, and when they see the tiny band on tired horses which are all that remain of Arthur's Companions they couch their spears and charge, knowing victory is theirs.

This is the moment. This is why Arthur has entrusted the early stages of the battle to the first and last of his lieutenants, to the one man he can trust to think and act as he would, to the only man other than himself who could have reined back the teulu *when they defeated Iddawg's horse, then pulled them back a second time when they had destroyed the Saeson infantry, rallied*

I

them so that they would be sitting there helpless when Medraut arrived.

Medraut cannot resist. His men sweep across the churned ground and fall upon the Companions, whose exhausted steeds can barely muster a trot, whose arms are so tired they can hardly raise their weapons to defend themselves.

Then the reserves appear, walking their horses over the crest of the hill, and at the forefront is a man in a purple cloak, who lifts his sword to the sky and shouts:

'We ride!'

And the voices thunder in reply: 'We ride! We ride! Amher-awdyr!'

There is nothing Medraut can do as Arthur stoops like a hawk, mowing through his ranks like a red reaper, nothing he can do but wait and hope that enough of his followers survive to strike back once Arthur's charge loses its momentum.

Which it does, eventually, though not until many saddles have been emptied, and Arthur has fought his way through to his lieutenant's side, greeting him with a grin, and the two of them turn together to meet the traitor's men in this, the last battle.

And so one by one the heroes of Britain fall, dying in the rain and the mud as the mist thickens and the darkness grows, dying unseen and unsung. And with them dies the hope of the island.

The dreams were becoming more frequent. He found them disturbing, in that they reminded him of things he would prefer to forget, things from which he had been fleeing these past ten years.

At first he had enjoyed wandering through the countryside, glad to be home after years in exile in Lesser Britain. But gradually he came to realize that his wanderings were forming a pattern, that he was being drawn to a particular place. So that when he dreamed of trees, of great oaks and beeches and ashes, of long glades separated by fringes of bracken and bramble, and rays of honeyed light lancing through the foliage like shafts of gold piercing through water, he knew that they were real woods and that he must find them.

So he had turned south, towards the lands he had known as a boy, and at last he came to a tiny fishing village on a promontory between an estuary and the sea. The locals greeted him as though they had been expecting him. Deep in the heart of the woods above the village he found the place which had called him: a clearing ringed by ancient oaks with a stone basin at its centre. The oaks had been old when the Romans first came to conquer Britain, old when Christ died upon another tree, old when Julius Caesar retreated from these shores. They had had their beginnings in the dim past when gods walked the earth and goddesses chose mortal men as lovers, when the world was unnamed chaos and enchanters strove to give it form. Here was a place where he could find the healing not even the monastery in Lesser Britain had been able to provide. Here he could pass his remaining days in peace, waiting for the end.

Soon the locals forgot that he was a newcomer. And he was happy to lose all sense of himself as an individual, to become what they expected, indistinguishable from a hundred other such figures tending chapels or holy sites across the land.

Walking now in the summer dawn three years later, he knew the time of peace was coming to an end. Night after night his sleep had been disturbed by images from the past, images he had pushed aside.

The water sluiced over the side of the basin, cold enough to chill his teeth as he drank. He splashed a little over his face and head, and poured some onto the grass as a libation to the spirit of the place.

'Help me, I beg you,' he said aloud. 'Show me what comes.'

Then he sat back on his heels and stared into the basin, letting his mind go clear as he concentrated on the surface, opaque now as the rays of the young sun angled through the trees and struck the basin in a flash of silver light, and gradually he saw:

A cloak of worn purple, face fat and pockmarked, talking and listening to . . .

Tall, with long fair hair bound back in a braid, shabbily dressed in a worn leather cuirass stained with sea salt, face hard, a madness in the eyes . . .

A mask in the shape of a white speckled bird, long trailing wings fluttering in the wind, something moving behind the eyeholes, something that felt Budoc's presence and turned to seek him . . .

He broke the contact, every limb trembling uncontrollably. This had never happened to him before. Scrying was a chancy business at best, more likely to reveal one's own fears and doubts than to show real events, but never before had any part of the vision shown any awareness of his existence.

The man wearing royal purple – to which he had no right, though it was clever of him to wear an old cloak with the implication that the colour was faded through long and habitual use – was Vortepor of Dyfed, Overking of the lands across the Severn Sea, son and heir to Agricola who had been Arthur's faithful servant while he lived. But Vortepor was not the man his father had been; though Budoc would have trusted Agricola with his life he did not trust Vortepor at all. It was Vortepor who had secretly bribed the Saesons of the south to march to Camlann in alliance with Medraut, knowing precisely what the consequence would be.

The second man Budoc did not recognize. A pirate, from the sea stains on his leather armour, a robber and raider preying on those weaker than himself.

The mask he did not understand. He knew it was part of the regalia used by the druids in their magic ceremonies. But to the best of his knowledge there were no true druids left in southern Britain, unless one counted a handful of people like himself who mixed the best of the Old Religion with the best of the New. The only surviving druids came from Ireland or the Western Isles, from the domains of the tribes loosely known as the Scotti.

Could the fair man be one of the Scotti? His gear had looked right: the sword slung at his side had been of Irish workmanship – Irish swords tended to be smaller and lighter than their British counterparts, though no less deadly. The man had been a stranger, and yet something about him had reminded Budoc of someone, someone he had forgotten . . .

Budoc knew now that the feeling which had been pressing upon him for days, the feeling of some great change being in the air, was a warning of danger.

The wood was a place of power, one of the few left in this part of the world. It was a sanctuary in more senses than one: a holy place in that here dwelt a part of the Mystery; and a place of refuge and healing for weary souls like himself. It could not be allowed to fall into the malevolent hands of whoever wore the bird mask.

To defend it he would need help. The fair man would bring others of his kind, warriors with swords and spears against whom the local villagers could not hope to stand.

*   *   *

4

Again he dreamed of Camlann, but this time not of the battle itself; nor did he dream of the great deeds wrought upon the field; nor even of the end, when all order was gone and the shield walls were broken, when all was confusion and chaos.

He dreamed of the aftermath, when the Lords of Albion lay dead upon the field and the scavengers gathered, the wolves, the ravens, the kites and the crows; the slinking grey shapes and the great black birds that ripped and tore at the dead and dying. And he dreamed of lying there helpless, unable to move, the groans of his fellow fallen in his ears, seeing again and again the blue-grey blade swooping on the unprotected head, seeing again and again Arthur's long slow topple from the saddle, the final fall from which he would never rise. And he dreamed of hearing singing, and the sounds of lamentation, and of dark wings fluttering . . .

Of all the battles in which he had ever fought, Camlann had been the worst. Partly because so many faces on both sides had been familiar, even among the Saxons – large numbers of them had followed the centuries-old tradition of their people and hired themselves out as mercenaries to the Amherawdyr – and it is a terrible thing to find against men who were once your comrades. And partly because the slaughter had been on such a vast scale, so frightful that men said a generation had died there.

It had been a battle nobody had won. The leaders of both sides were killed. The Amherawdyr's men remained in possession of the field, but that availed them nothing, for Arthur left no heir.

A few years ago, not long after he first arrived in Lesser Britain, he had heard a bard singing of the Seven Survivors of Camlann. Sandeff Angel Face escaped on account of his beauty, Morfran the Ugly on account of his hideousness, Kynvelyn on account of the speed of his horse, Cedwyn on account of his luck, Derfel on account of his great strength, Geneid on account of his fleetness of foot. The seventh name had been his own, and he had escaped because of his skill with a spear.

He had wept then, wept because already, not ten years after the event, Camlann and those who had fought there were passing into legend.

Lying alone now in his truckle bed, with fever raging through him, the memory of it made him weep afresh.

*　　*　　*

The next few days passed in a blur of delirium. Sometimes it seemed to him that Teleri sat at the end of the bed, smiling at him sadly – only her hair, which had been dark, had somehow become a reddish gold. Other times he talked with his long-dead friends: great-hearted Cei, cured of the failing sight which had caused his death; young Llacheu, to whom Cei himself had given the final blow as an act of mercy; sweet Gwalchmei the Hawk with his golden tongue; Cynon who had guarded his back until the battle of Agned; Moried who had done so thereafter; Degaw of the Creones, who had been his friend until her husband Talorcan fell fighting Hueil; Lleminawg the Irishman, Lleminawg who had died on an expedition to the North, to the Lands at the back of the world, the islands, coasts and sea-lochs of the Iardomnan . . .

As the days and nights passed in seemingly endless dreams of death and darkness, he came to understand that it was not Teleri who sat on the end of his bed and sometimes held a bowl to his lips, feeding him sips of water or broth. It was two of the children from the village, Eurgain and her sister Dyfyr, sent by their mother to watch over him.

They were no longer children, he realized. The older girl, Dyfyr, would marry soon, have children of her own, and the younger would not be far behind. Both were fast becoming beauties, as their mother must once have been, and in a way he was sorry, for in these unsettled times beauty in a woman was more often a curse than a blessing.

Eventually the fever broke, leaving him weak and lethargic, and the children – the girls, he should say – visited him less often.

Every morning he performed his practice exercises as he had done every day since he was a child, even in the monastery. He still believed his exercise was not undertaken in order to mortify the flesh but rather to enhance it so that mind and body could work together in harmony. Even now, when every limb trembled after the slightest exertion, he believed it.

He turned to the basin, his limbs steadier now, and concentrated on the surface of the water. Setting his mind drifting, drifting . . .

. . . *drifting through visions of the sea breaking on white sands, of moonlight falling on land and sea alike, of half-hidden shapes running and fighting, of a small group making a stand against men with lime-washed shields and snarling faces . . .*

. . . *a wooden longship, a Saeson ship, slipping bare-masted down a river on a cold grey morning with the mist writhing all around, oars lifting and falling . . .*

Scowling, Budoc came out of the trance. He breathed deeply, letting the quiet of the sanctuary enter him, fill him. Around him, the leaves rustled in the breeze: a familiar, soothing sound. The water in the basin played on, a merry, tinkling tune with no end and no beginning. Then the surface clouded, became opaque, a misty background on which shadows moved . . .

A big man, deep chested and strong thewed, demonstrating the use of sword and shield to a line of nervous boys . . .

Another, dozing on a hillside in the summer sun . . .

PART I

CHAPTER ONE

1

'Move the shield up and down, boy, *up and down*! Don't waggle it from side to side.' A heavy sigh of exasperation. 'Use it, by the Trinity, use your shield! It's a weapon, as much as the knife!' Nai, the heat of the sun on his face and the bark of the tree cutting into his back, screwed his eyes tighter, trying to shut out the sound of Gorthyn shouting instructions to the lads at sword and knife play.

The sun was not so warm now. He could feel evening coming on, and the hint of a cool breeze.

'Why do we have to do this?' somebody whined, and Nai smiled. In every group there was always one, and he could have spoken Gorthyn's response himself: 'Because one day you might need to know how.' A moan of protest came from the group and Gorthyn's voice rose to a bellow: 'And if that is not enough for you, *then because I say so*!'

He did not need to open his eyes to know how Gorthyn must look at this moment: three times the boys' size, his massive chest puffed out to its full extent, his face grim, apparently in the grip of an enormous rage.

'Try it again!' shouted Gorthyn. 'Make the blade sing in the air! Keep those shields moving up and down!'

Nai could smell cooking, drifting from the kitchens by the Great Hall, and his dry mouth watered at the thought of food, though he was not a greedy man.

He nestled lower, jumped as a bee buzzed beside his ear. One hand came up to cover the scar at his throat and he slipped away into sleep . . .

'Nai!' bellowed Gorthyn. 'Wake up and come over here!'

He jerked awake and opened his eyes.

It was late. A faint haze hung in the shadows when he looked towards the lowering sun, and there was a paling of the sky above the hills on the horizon.

He pulled himself to his feet, massaging his back where the trunk had cut into it.

Everything seemed washed out, all the colours bleached from the landscape. Blinking, he turned towards his friend, feeling dizzy, and staggered drunkenly in the direction of the training ground.

'Too long in the sun,' roared Gorthyn. 'Come on, wake up!'

The boys were collecting their bits and drifting away in small groups, some going to the stream to drink, others racing past him to the fort, shouting and yelling.

Gorthyn was standing in the middle of the training ground, a shield slung carelessly over one shoulder, his scabbarded sword clutched in his right hand, the belt dangling in the grass. There were two older men with him, one a spare figure with cropped grey hair, the second a stout man wearing a puffed leather cap that rose to a pointed tip.

At the sight of them Nai came properly awake, his minor discomforts forgotten as he wondered what had brought their lord and master Gereint to seek them out rather than summoning them to his presence.

'Sleep well?' Gorthyn enquired wickedly. 'I was going to send one of the lads to wake you, but you looked so peaceful lying there I lacked the heart.'

Nai nodded, and dipped his head in salute to Gereint, who acknowledged absent-mindedly.

'A Saeson ship* has been sighted sailing in this direction,' said the stout man, Morgant. He removed his cap and wiped his balding crown. 'It worries me.' He replaced the cap and frowned.

'Only one?' said Gorthyn.

'At the moment. It coasts westwards at a leisurely speed. A medium-sized vessel from what we can gather, with a crew of perhaps forty.'

* Please see map in prelims and glossary at the end of the book.

'So?' said Gorthyn. 'A raiding party.' He glanced curiously from one to the other. 'Where is the difficulty? We have dealt with them before.'

'One hears rumours,' Gereint said carefully, scratching in the dirt with a toe. 'Cerdic Elesing is an old man now, and his followers grow restless. You know that he declared himself king of the West Saesons not long ago? *Cyning*, they call it.'

'Until recently he was an *Ealdorman*,' added Morgant.

Gorthyn shook his head. 'I do not understand barbarian titles. A *Cyning* is a higher thing than an *Ealdorman*?' He stumbled over the unfamiliar words.

'Yes,' said Morgant. 'An *Ealdorman* is a chieftain, but a *Cyning* is a ruler over chieftains.'

'In their tongue,' Gereint said with a thin smile, 'I would be called *Ealdorman*, and Custennin my overlord would be called *Cyning*.'

Gorthyn thought about this for a moment, then shouted with laughter. 'But Custennin rules this huge sea-girt peninsula of Dumnonia, while Cerdic rules a few hides of marshland opposite the island of Wectis. I doubt he controls as much land as you, Gereint.'

'There is no limit to the vanity of these Saeson savages,' Morgant said petulantly. 'None at all. And by declaring himself king, Cerdic has angered many of his neighbours, who consider themselves his equals not his subjects.'

'What disturbs us,' said Gereint, 'is that some of these neighbours may decide the time has come to leave their present lands and find new ones out of Cerdic's reach. And Cerdic is, I think, too old to stop them.'

'Leaving him king of an empty kingdom,' Gorthyn said drily. 'But surely, if they do move, they would move inland? Towards Aquae Sulis, or further east towards the valley of the upper Thames where they already have kin?'

'Some might.' Gereint rubbed out the pattern he had drawn in the dust of the training ground and began again. 'Others might sail westwards along our coast.'

He glanced up and his gaze met Nai's. 'What do you think?' Nai inclined his head.

'All too possible, is it not?' Gereint kept his gaze on Nai, speaking directly to him. 'We fear this ship may be a forerunner of a larger fleet, like the first swallow of spring. I doubt if this one will go much further west – they will want to be beyond Cerdic's immediate reach, but not so far away they cannot call for help if necessary.' He rubbed out the second pattern and sighed. 'I want you to ride the coast road looking for signs that the Saesons have landed.'

'How far do you want us to go?' asked Gorthyn.

'As far as the Tamar if necessary – but I do not think it will be.'

'Our guess,' Morgant said gloomily, 'is that they will try a landing at somewhere like the Porthyle estuary. Good shelter for the ship, a long way from the nearest stronghold, not many people, wonderful farmland – I might try it myself in their position.'

Nai smiled to himself at the thought of the portly Morgant leading a crew of Saeson pirates.

'There is a second matter I want to discuss,' said Gereint. 'This is not to be mentioned to anyone else. It is the reason I came to find you out here, where nobody can overhear us.'

'Ah!' Gorthyn cocked his head to one side. 'I thought there must be more.'

Gereint ignored him, concentrating on Nai. 'My kinsman and overlord, Custennin of Dumnonia, sent me word of a meeting which took place a few days ago. Vortepor of Dyfed, our neighbour to the north across the Severn Sea, had brought to him in great secrecy a man of the Scotti. This man spoke our tongue with the accent of Dumnonia, and called himself –'

'Eremon mab Cairbre,' growled Gorthyn with sudden understanding.

Nai's hand slipped to his throat and began to finger the ragged mass of scar tissue, aware of the others looking anywhere but in his direction.

'Vortepor has been sending messengers over the sea to Ierne for some time,' Morgant said gloomily. 'One is forced to conclude that he has been trying to find Eremon, and Eremon alone.'

'Our first thought,' explained Gereint, 'was that Vortepor is trying to raise an army of warriors without ties in Dyfed, an army he could use to subdue his more independent-minded subjects. But Vortepor has kin in Ierne, and he would turn to them first. If he has sought out Eremon, it is because Eremon has some special skill or knowledge that he needs.'

Nai frowned. The conclusion was obvious, but he could not see the motive behind it.

'Eremon knows these waters better than any man alive,' mused Gorthyn, echoing Nai's thoughts, 'but what use is that to Vortepor?' He tapped his teeth with a blunt forefinger.

A gull mewed overhead. Nai tracked it with his eyes as he remembered the cold autumn day when he had last seen Eremon the renegade, grinning over the point of a spear with the mist and the rain gathering behind him, the droplets of moisture flying from the mane of the exhausted pony as its master flogged it into one last gallop. The gulls had been wheeling overhead on that day too, gulls and black carrion birds waiting for the men to leave and the feasting to begin.

'Nai?' Gorthyn's voice startled him back to the present. 'What could Vortepor of Dyfed want with this small and unimportant area of Dumnonia?'

He looked from one to the other, all eagerly awaiting his pronouncement: Gereint faintly annoyed that Gorthyn had dared to call his lands small and unimportant (which of course was why the big man had done it); Morgant fiddling worriedly with his cap, face furrowed with concern; Gorthyn – solid, reliable Gorthyn – waiting for him to give them the answer.

'I do not know,' he said, and the sound of his raw and ruined voice made the others start, even though they were expecting it.

2

The stallion struggled as Wicga led it down to the water's edge, and Ceolric could see the muscles in his father's arms bunching with the effort of keeping the beast under control.

Behind him he heard somebody mutter 'Not willing!' and he turned to scowl at whoever it was, hoping to frighten them into silence before the god could hear and reject the sacrifice. Instead he found old Garulf the Frisian standing at his shoulder, staring at the scene before him.

'Pay no heed, boy,' said Garulf out of the side of his mouth. 'There's willing and willing, and I've seen a lot less willing than this one.'

Wicga wrestled the stallion to the place where the river waves lapped at the muddy shore. With one hand he held it still, its forefeet in the water, himself nearly knee-deep in the clinging mud; with the other he fumbled in his belt for the ceremonial knife.

Ceolric shuddered. He would be glad to leave. Nothing here was as he had expected, not even the stallion, which was supposed to be white and was really a dirty grey colour, with an oddly shaped head that made it look small and stunted.

Everybody knew the story of how Cerdic Elesing had swept inland with five keels and fought against the Britons at the place now called Cerdicesora in his honour. Hearing the tale as a child in Cantware, Ceolric had always imagined Cerdicesora as a place worth fighting for, a fair haven at the head of a beautiful estuary, a natural landing place for a born leader.

It was nothing of the kind, and twenty-five years of settlement had not improved its appearance. By the standards of Cantware or the lands of the South Saxons, the village was miserably poor. The huts were like those of the meanest peasant or slave, and the people were no better, even those who claimed to be well born. The stink of the marshes hung over everything like a dark cloud, and he could see why the Britons had not fought very hard or long to keep Cerdicesora.

Wicga had finally brought the stallion under control. The breeze dropped and the waves stilled, so the ripples from the horse's forelegs travelled out across the grey water as the animal stood shivering, patiently waiting for whatever came next.

'Don't watch the horse,' whispered Garulf. 'Watch the people.'

Ceolric tore his eyes away from the heavy-bladed knife in his father's hand, and glanced around him at the crowd.

There were more people gathered together in one place than he had ever seen before. He had been told his father's hall in its heyday could hold fifty if everybody squeezed up on the benches, but he was too young to remember it properly, for they had left after his mother died when he was barely old enough to walk.

A few years ago they had visited Londinium and he had seen the vast numbers of people eking out an existence in the ruins of the city, but not all together, like this. It seemed that every farmer of the Gewisse must have given his household a free day to come and watch the offering, that every loaf-eater and slave in the lands of the West Saxons was gathered on the river bank.

Off to one side where they had a clear view were the forty crew members of the *Sea Stallion*, looking bewildered by the noise and crush. He doubted if they formed more than a fifth part of the whole.

The murmur of sound which accompanies any large group gradually died away. All the faces, whether they belonged to people he knew or to strangers, had a similar look to them: an expression of eagerness and excitement. Nearly every mouth was open. There was no movement, and every gaze was intent. Some were grinning, some pale, some flushed.

Ceolric could tell the moment of the strike from the sigh of pleasure which went up from the crowd, as if everybody had been holding their breath and only now dared release it. The faces changed: lips were licked, brows mopped. The hum of talk began again, together with the coughing and sniffing.

'Remember this,' Garulf whispered in his ear.

Ceolric nodded, knowing he had learned a lesson today even if he was not sure what it was, and swung round to view his father's handiwork.

Wicga had made a clean kill. The blood was gushing into the dirty water and the stallion was sinking slowly to its knees as its eyes dulled, seeming not to understand what was happening, the long muzzle dipping to meet the spreading cloud and its own reflection.

The horse toppled forward into the water, spraying Wicga with a mixture of mud and blood.

'Wotan!' shouted Wicga. 'See my offering! I, Wicga son of Wermund son of Witta son of Wihtgils son of Wegdag son of Wotan, give you, my first father, this fine stallion. Send us a good wind, I beg you, a wind to waft us westwards to new lands . . .'

Even as he spoke a fresh breeze sprang up from the north, ruffling the surface of the river, a steady blow with no sudden gusts, a sailor's wind.

The crowd cheered, and Ceolric looked round him at the grinning faces and wondered that people could be so easily pleased. He knew from listening to his father and Garulf discussing it beforehand that the timing of the sacrifice had been very carefully chosen: the wind often veered in the late afternoon, and since it had been blowing from the west for several days a change was long overdue.

'Let us hope it holds,' Garulf muttered. 'Cerdic's men are eager to see us gone. If it does hold, we leave in the morning.'

Leaving the body of the horse where it lay on the margins of the water, Wicga waded free of the mud, pausing to rinse his hands and arms, and strode towards his son and shipmaster, a great grin splitting his bearded face.

'We sail with the dawn!' he said, raising his voice to be heard. 'Out and down the estuary, through the channel by the island of Wectis, then westwards, ever westwards, along the coast beside the tall white cliffs –' his hands described them in the air '– until in the

17

afternoon they give way to long beaches of shingle shelving to the sea. Then towards evening will come more cliffs, of a lurid blue you will not believe until you have seen them for yourselves. Somewhere there we shall find a quiet cove and pass the first night.'

He looked at his listeners, his face alight and dancing. In that moment Ceolric admired his father more than he had done for years.

'On the second day we shall pass hills pared vertically by the sea, as if by a knife stroke, to reveal their red cores; and then great escarpments of many colours, a mixture of greens and browns and pinks. I tell you, this will be a voyage of wonder such as you shall boast of to your grandchildren!'

He flung one arm round Ceolric and the other round Garulf, and drew them close, hugging them into his body as he talked.

'And all the while we shall be coasting towards the empty lands where live only a few harmless peasants and fishermen; rich land, crying out to be mastered by good Saxon farmers; beautiful land, waiting for us. We shall find the sheltered place Garulf remembers, beach our ship, and found the kingdom of the Sae-ware, the Sea Folk!'

As always Ceolric was moved by his father's words, though he had heard them or something similar many times before. For as far back as his memory went his father had had a head filled with schemes: schemes for a new life with himself the master of a great hall surrounded by fertile farmland, an *ealdorman* in fact as well as title, dispensing mead and gold to his warriors.

Before Ceolric was born his father had arrived in the corner of Britain called Cantware, and sought to make himself a place among the followers of Oesc son of Hengist the First Comer. Wicga had wedded a native girl (a princess, of course) who had borne him three sons and two daughters, all now married and holding lands of their own except Ceolric the youngest. And always Wicga had felt he was not receiving his due, so that after the princess's death he had gathered a rag-bag group of men around him and set out for the lands of the East Saxons.

For five years he had fought and flattered his way to some kind of dominion over the scattered groups of kinsmen settled around the remnants of Londinium, and at the end he had been thwarted when Aescwine his rival had declared himself king. So they had fled westwards to the territory of the Gewisse, the loose alliance of natives and newcomers in the area around the old Roman harbour opposite Wectis, and here Wicga had seen the error of his ways. What he needed was not to dominate an existing settlement, but to start from the beginning, well away from the other Saxon kingdoms to avoid envious eyes, yet not so far away he could not recruit from them as necessary.

During the journey to the lands of the Gewisse they had fallen in with Garulf the Frisian (or he had fallen in with them), a man knowledgeable in the ways of the sea. Garulf had told them of a voyage he had made long ago when he was young to the far western waters of Britain and the islands beyond, and of a certain anchorage where the voyagers had passed a night.

Listening to him, Wicga knew that he had found the place he sought: a neglected peninsula cut off from the rest of Dumnonia by the long arms of the sea, where he could establish his new kingdom without fear of attack by the natives.

And now he had his wind, and tomorrow they would sail.

3

They slid along the waves, the three leather curraghs, swimming up the crests like beasts of the sea, then rolling easily down into the troughs, the slim ash masts bending and creaking with the weight of the sails that bulged under the force of the wind.

It was quiet aboard the leading craft, with most of the crew trying to snatch some sleep after running all night before the strong west wind: quiet except for the rattle and slap of the sails as the gusts caught and released them.

Eremon could feel the curragh twisting and flexing with the swell, alive to every motion of the sea. She lay low in the water, so there was no more than the length of a man's arm from elbow to fingertip between the gunwale and the surface of the sea, which meant that every wave loomed above her until she began her slow and ponderous climb to its top. Her companion vessels appeared and vanished on the crests and troughs of the waves like fleeting reflections, their flaxen sails catching the sunlight before they disappeared behind the glittering green billows.

The stink of leather and wool grease was so familiar Eremon was no longer aware of it, any more than he noticed the permanent dampness of his woollen tunic. He squinted towards the blue blur of the coast, feeling the boat shift and change its shape beneath his feet as it moulded itself to the actions of the waves.

In his wilder moments he claimed to know every cove between the Promontory of Belerium in the west and Moridunum in the east, but at present he could see nothing he recognized. For a moment he wondered whether to stand further in to the shore, but almost at once dismissed the idea. If the wind veered slightly he could easily find himself caught against the coast, and though the prevailing currents were running with him now, the tide would soon be on the turn, reversing the flow, so that even with all hands working the oars he might not be able to claw free.

Sitting beside the steering paddle was the man in the bird mask, mumbling quietly to himself as he had been doing ever since they left the coast of Ierne. If asked, the man would have said he was keeping the wind blowing from the west, but Eremon privately suspected he was praying for an end to the voyage and these cramped and crowded conditions.

As if he had sensed Eremon's gaze upon him the man raised his head. The feathers were bejewelled with spray, so the mask seemed to have a nimbus all the colours of the rainbow, while the eye holes were black pits, unfathomable as the deeps below. Eremon felt a cold shiver run down his spine, even though it was he who had chosen to bring the man aboard.

The man in the bird mask represented his vengeance upon them all, all the ones he had hated these last five years or longer: on Custennin of Dumnonia and Custennin's lapdog Gereint, who had been for a time Eremon's foster-father; on Gereint's followers, Nai now called the Silent and Gorthyn the Strong, who had once been his comrades if not his friends; and finally, if Vortepor of Dyfed was to be believed, on the last of that older generation which had betrayed his uncle Lleminawg the Leaper, the dancing one, the fated one, to his death.

Eremon checked the mainsail, eased a cord, tightened another, raised a hand to wave at Dovnuall as the larboard curragh crested a wave at the same time as themselves, so that for a brief moment they both hung suspended between sea and sky before the endless green swallowed them again, glanced to his right in the hope of seeing Serach in the third vessel and caught a glimpse of a white sail.

'How long?' shouted the man in the bird mask.

'Not long, not long,' he called back regretfully, the wind stealing his words and whirling them away. 'It will be soon, now.'

'Good.' The man's voice was muffled by the mask, hard to hear against the renewed shrieking of the gulls. 'This is not my realm. This is the realm of Manannan and Tethra, the realm of the Fomoire, the people-under-the-sea. Here my powers can help you but little, Eremon mac Cairbre.'

Eremon grinned mirthlessly and wiped the beaded spray from his beard.

'It was not for this that I brought you with us. The sailing of curraghs, the wielding of arms, the taking of slaves – three things in which I am skilled. But the holding of land . . .' He shook his head sadly. 'There I do not fare so well.'

The man in the bird mask grunted and settled back against the gunwale. The steersman flinched away as if frightened to touch him, ostentatiously concentrating on keeping the curragh on course, pretending not to notice the bird mask by his leg.

Eremon stretched and yawned. Under his feet he could feel the bulkheads protesting at the strain to which they were being subjected, groaning and creaking as they shifted in opposite directions, stretching the leather skin of the boat as they moved.

His fingers were covered with grease, thick and black under his blunt nails, ground into the grain of his skin. It came from the boat, from everything one touched, and was so much a part of life afloat he rarely noticed it any more. During construction the leather hides which formed the hull had been thoroughly soaked in wool fat, for without some form of protection they would eventually rot and dissolve in the sea water. The grease kept them flexible and, even more important, waterproof. Now the curragh was nearly four seasons old, and in the spring she had been re-treated, a long laborious process which involved heating the grease and then applying it by hand, to every part of the boat. It was this fresh treatment that had left everything covered with a fine film of fat.

He wiped his hands on a rag, then ran the rag down the cold blue blade of the sword in his lap. There was a spot of rust forming near the point, a hollow brown ring marring the grey perfection of the steel, and one cutting edge was just beginning to discolour, like a tooth showing signs of decay.

It was the salt water that did it, he thought to himself as he busied himself with rag and whetstone. However careful one was, the salt ate away metal, which was why the curragh used very few metal fittings, and those it did have were buried under layers of protective grease.

This sword was one he had taken in Ierne not long after his exile began. What he thought of as his own sword, the original blade his grandfather had given him when he became a man, had been lost on the shingle during that last frantic scramble for safety as Gereint's warband pressed down upon him five years ago.

This blade, according to the markings on the tang, had been made by the royal smith at Temair of the High Kings – if he read the Ogham script aright, and reading was not and never had been his strong point. The symbols looked like chicken scratches to him, all right angles and slashes like nicks in a knife edge. It was a lighter and smaller weapon than the one his grandfather had given him: the length of a man's arm with wickedly sharp edges and a sudden taper to the point.

Some people swore by Saeson blades, longer and heavier than Irish or British work – the better for battering down your opponent's shield, said those who liked them. He preferred a weapon he could wield all day, like this one, and his face slipped into an easy smile as he thought of the havoc he would wreak when they made their landing in the Porthyle estuary.

A shadow fell across him, blotting out the light. The bird mask bobbed as the man sat down beside him, eyes gleaming within the deep holes.

'You feel your sword,' said the man, his voice muffled.

He frowned, not following. 'I live by it. I am a warrior, and this my chosen weapon.'

'Your sword is precious.'

Again it was a statement, not a question. Eremon realized the man was not referring to the physical value of the blade, but he was not sure he understood what he did mean.

'Vortepor of Dyfed gave you gifts,' said the man, seeming to change the subject. 'The hounds that lie tangled with your crew.' He gestured towards the shelter near the bow where men and dogs snored in a jumble of limbs. 'Another gift he gave you, Eremon mac Cairbre: a guide to the object he wants you to find.'

'He did,' agreed Eremon.

'Yet you decided you did not need that guide.' The faintest intonation indicated that this was a question.

'Indeed,' said Eremon, turning his most winning smile – still powerful enough to charm most people – upon the bird mask.

'What happened to the guide?'

'What happened to him? Why, my friend, he decided to leave

us long before we touched upon the coast of Ierne and found you to take his place.'

Eremon finished cleaning the sword, sheathed it and laid it aside, warming to his story. 'A terrible thing it was. We were not far out from the beach in Dyfed where we had landed so I might meet with Vortepor, when this guide he had given us began to moan and protest about the motion of the waves. All afternoon he demanded we turn around and set him ashore again, until we were sickened by his endless whining.

'The night was beautiful. The wind had almost dropped, and the sea was calm. There was us, and the stars, and the crescent moon climbing to cast her silver light upon the water. It was a perfect night, a night of such peace and utter tranquillity as one can only have at sea, and then but rarely – save for one thing only, and that the Pict and his complaints.'

Eremon shrugged ruefully. 'I confess it. I lost my temper. Overboard he went in a sprawl of dark limbs like a great spider, landing in a spray of white water. We must have been moving much faster than I thought, for by the time he surfaced, struggling and kicking and spluttering, he had already dropped astern.

'We threw him a rope and he caught its end, floundering and cursing, marring the smooth track of our wake with his struggles. Perhaps a stronger man could have pulled himself aboard, but it was all the Pict could do to hang there, slowing our passage like a sea anchor, while we laid wagers on how long he would last.

'I think at first he did not believe we meant it. He was thinking we would soon tire of the jest and haul him up like a great fish on the end of a line. But I had no use for him, and nor did the others. By moonlight and starlight I could see his face, the tattoos invisible at this distance, could see the changes come over him as he passed through anger to fear then anger again, and finally despair as he realized the truth.

'I did not see him let go, but I felt it. The curragh surged forward as if released from a great weight. I glanced back, and saw him swallowed by the darkness under the foam, slipping away like a waterlogged piece of driftwood. Once he was gone, I could not even be sure of the place where he had been.'

'And Vortepor?' said the man in the bird mask after a while. 'Do you not fear his wrath?'

'No,' said Eremon, and turned his attention to the rocking of the curragh as she swam with the waves.

CHAPTER TWO

Like most contemporary strongholds, Din Erbin nestled within the remains of a much older fortification. The hill on which it stood overlooked both the estuary of the River Oak and the open sea, and was thus only easily assailed upon the landward side. At some stage, so long ago nobody could now say when except that it was before the Romans came, a pair of concentric earthen ramparts with ditches had been dug around the hilltop. Over the years the outer bank had dwindled, its soil washing down into the ditch, until neither provided more than a minor obstacle.

But the inner bank and ditch had been refurbished in the time of Gworthigern the Thin by Gereint's great-grandfather – or by *his* father: the generations passed and memories blurred – and had been kept clear ever since. Now they provided a formidable defence: the ditch the depth of two tall men, and the bank with its wooden palisade the height of three.

Nai peered at the wall, wondering, as he often had before, how one would set about taking this place. Fire, he supposed, though if you had plenty of tree trunks you could use some as platforms to cross the ditch and others (with the nubs of the branches left uncut) as ladders to scale the wall. But the losses among the attackers would be enormous. It would be easier to starve the place out, and there again of course your problem would be the feeding of your own people while you waited. Easiest of all would be to bribe someone to open the gates.

'What are you thinking about?' asked Gorthyn as they entered.

'Bribery.'

The big man grunted, lowered his voice so Gereint and Morgant could not hear. 'If Custennin keeps spies at Vortepor's court, I wonder where else he keeps them? There is no great love lost between Custennin the wily and Gereint his cousin.'

At this time of day Din Erbin was crowded. Slaves and bond-peasants coming in from the outlying fields mixed with warriors like Nai and Gorthyn back from the practice ground. Less fortunate were the craftsmen, forced to fight against the flow as they came down from their workshops in the north-eastern corner of the fort (placed there so the prevailing winds would carry away the fumes; on days when the winds blew from the north the whole fort reeked).

The crowd swept around them, and they allowed the throng to carry them aside between the slave quarters and the peasants' huts set against the palisade.

'Saesons from the east and Scotti from the west,' said Gorthyn.

'The Saesons,' said Nai. 'Gereint and Morgant know too much.'

'You think they have an informer among Cerdic's followers?' Gorthyn tugged at his beard. 'No reason why not. The lands of the Gewisse are full of our people, our distant kinsmen.'

He began thrusting his way through the crowd with the born arrogance of one who expects others to give way, forcing Nai to take long strides to keep up.

'You doubt the ship has sailed yet,' he said over his shoulder. 'That is what you mean, eh, Nai? Thinking about it, the wind has been wrong these last few days. They would have difficulty leaving Cerdicesora.' He slapped a thigh triumphantly. 'Which is why Morgant said the ship was coasting westwards at a leisurely pace. And why Gereint was in no hurry for us to leave.'

'Porthyle estuary,' said Nai, massaging his throat to help him speak. 'Could land anywhere.'

Gorthyn nodded. 'Morgant did seem very sure it would be the Porthyle. And I agree. It lies on the very edge of Gereint's territory, bordering a part of the country Custennin rules directly – which means it is neglected. If the Saesons could gain a foothold there, it would be like the hinge of a door – a weak point which could allow them access to the rich farmland further inland.'

'Cerdic.'

For a moment even Gorthyn was lost, accustomed though he was to interpreting his friend's cryptic remarks.

'Cerdic?' he repeated, drawing Nai through the gap between two huts and out into the open space on the other side. 'Whew! That is better. The stink was starting to reach me.'

They stood on a piece of waste ground rank with weeds and nettles that ran behind the slave quarters like a moat dividing the huts from the better parts of the fort.

'You mean Cerdic himself may have told Gereint the ship is coming?' Gorthyn frowned, trying to work out the ramifications of what his friend was suggesting.

'Cerdic is Cyning.'

'And fears his subjects may desert him.' The big man nodded slowly as understanding dawned. 'So one ship leaves, sails west, and meets with disaster because we are forewarned. Word filters back to the Gewisse, and they decide to stay where they are, because however much they dislike Cerdic and his over-weening pride, better the devil they know than death on a strange shore.'

They found a path between the houses and followed it up the slope. The slanting rays of the sun illuminated the whitewashed walls, revealing the imperfections where the plaster had been daubed on too thickly. The walls were repainted every autumn, before the gales began, so the wash was beginning to show its age, flaking away or blackening with mould where the damp had caught it.

'The treachery of kings,' said Gorthyn softly. 'I do not think Gereint would sacrifice us without due cause, but Custennin his overlord would not hesitate to do so if he saw some advantage for himself.'

'Rather than his own.'

'Exactly, cousin. Why use your own followers when you can use those of your underling? Whatever game Custennin plays with Vortepor of Dyfed – and I confess I do not understand it, nor do I see why Vortepor needs our old friend Eremon mab Cairbre – we are not likely to trouble Custennin's sleep if it becomes necessary we should die.'

'And Gereint risks little by sending but two,' said Nai.

Gorthyn smiled without humour. 'Gereint has ever had a way with promises. He promises help if we discover the Saesons or the Scotti landing in force, but the help will take a while to reach us, and meanwhile where are we? If Dumnonia and Dyfed play games of power between themselves while the Saesons take a third hand on another part of the board, it is an ill time to be a mere token edged towards the very hub of the action.'

'When we were boys . . .'

'Oh yes, when we were boys we longed for glory and would have leaped at such a chance. Now we are boys no longer, cousin, but seasoned warriors too wise for the world in which we walk.'

They mounted the hill, climbing towards the Great Hall which stood at the heart of the fortress. It was a long timber building with a high hipped roof around which swallows and martins were diving and squealing, feeding off the clouds of midges.

Around the Great Hall like minnows around some monster of the deep, were the sleeping quarters of Lord Gereint and his warriors, small whitewashed houses akin to the homes of the craftsmen.

Gorthyn and Nai shared one of these houses with three other widowed or unmarried men. Since they spent most of their waking hours out of doors or in the Hall, the system worked well enough; and it was only rarely all five of them needed to sleep under the same roof at the same time.

Nai pushed open the door, saying over his shoulder: 'Why Eremon?'

The room was empty, but Gorthyn lowered his voice before replying.

'I do not know. They seem unlikely allies, Vortepor of Dyfed and Eremon mab Cairbre. As I said earlier, Eremon knows these coasts and waters better than any other man, but how does that affect Vortepor?'

He stacked his equipment in one corner then splashed his face and hands with water from the ewer the household servant had set ready for their return.

'Of course, none of it may be true,' he said as he towelled himself dry. 'If you are right and the message about the Saeson ship comes from Cerdic himself, it may be a trick to draw us west while the real attack comes in the east. Even if it does not, there is no certainty they will land in the Porthyle estuary. And likewise the business with Eremon may be moonshine. Vortepor may have wanted him for some other purpose altogether.'

'Gereint sends only us,' said Nai.

'So he risks little.' The big man grimaced, shook his head. 'What do you really think?'

'Bad,' grunted Nai, and into that single word he put all his doubts about what Gereint wanted them to do: the difficulties of two men alone trying to watch a long expanse of exposed coastline; his mistrust of the treacherous Custennin, their nominal overlord; the time it would take Gereint to respond to a message for help . . .

'I think so too.' The big man laid the towel aside and ran a comb through his hair, wincing as it dragged through the knots. 'Whatever the risk, it would make more sense to send a full troop, a force with teeth. Even if you and I do find the enemy, it will be too late to help the locals.'

Nai shrugged expressively.

'I know, I know,' said Gorthyn. 'They always bear the brunt, the little people. But every year another farm is abandoned, another craftsman is killed without training an apprentice. Every year we draw in a little more upon ourselves, huddle a little closer around our fortresses.'

But the unfortunate truth of the matter, thought Nai, which you know as well as I do, is that Gereint cannot send a full troop west without weakening his defences elsewhere.

As for the farmers and the fishermen, they have not been safe since Arthur's day, and nor do I see any hope for them. The dream of a peaceful land ended ten years ago on the field of Camlann.

They cannot see it yet, not Custennin with his ambition, not Gereint with his sense of duty – not even Morgant, with all his fears for the worst – but Albion is finished. The land is lost, and the song is ended.

All he said aloud was: 'We do what we can,' and the truism made Gorthyn smile and clap him on the shoulder.

'We shall,' said the big man, not understanding. 'We shall.'

There was no feast tonight, none of the extravagance of lit tapers or glassware on the tables. They dined on common fare, on stewed mutton and oat cakes lightly smeared with honey, washed down with plain water or the vinegary red wine the Steward had been trying to dispose of for the last year or more.

As befitted men of their age and reputation, Gorthyn and Nai reclined on couches near the High Table where Gereint and his chief advisers sat. Below were the younger men, noisy and boisterous as ever, eager for the fighting the summer was certain to bring. The women sat at their own table, placed so they could discreetly withdraw on feast nights when the warriors had drunk too much.

When they had finished eating and the slaves had cleared away the worst of the debris, Gereint gave the signal for the mead to be brought out, much to Nai's surprise. At the same time Heilyn the Bard rose to his feet and struck a chord on his harp that rang from the rafters and brought silence to the Hall.

'Listen to the elegies of the men of Gereint, the generous Prince, the horseman of hosts, the dragon of battle; listen to the elegies of those who fell fighting the treacherous one, the betrayer of friendship, the ill-fostered one, Eremon the False.'

At Heilyn's words Gorthyn sat up in his seat, nudging Nai.

It was a clever move, thought Nai. Five years was a long time and the memory of the pirate and renegade Eremon mab Cairbre would have dimmed in the minds of these youngsters, especially as the story of his downfall reflected no great glory on any of those involved.

'*First to die was Erfai, Amren's son, of glorious lineage,*' said the bard, and played another chord upon the harp.

The women in the Hall bent their gazes on Gorthyn mab Erfai, and Nai, sitting beside him, saw the colour rise to stain his weathered cheeks above the line of his beard.

'*Hard did Dovnuall Frych torment him with hot irons, but not a word of Gereint's plans came from mab Amren, not even at the end,*' said the bard.

He played a few notes, the sound rippling through the empty hall, and sang:

> '*The pillar of battle, the feeder of crows,*
> *A true friend was Erfai, still truer a foe.*
> *In the Hall he had drunk deep of Gereint's mead,*
> *And he did not betray him now in his need.*
> *Slaughter on slaughter on the foemen he wrought,*
> *Bitter his blade, till at the last he was caught.*
>
> *Green grows the grass on Erfai's grave.*'

Nai remembered Gorthyn's father well, a man almost as large as his son and renowned for his massive strength. After Nai's parents had died in one of the endless epidemics which regularly swept across the land, Erfai, a kindly bear of a man much loved by children, had taken him in and raised him as his own.

Gorthyn's face was a frozen mask. While the bard sang he sat still as stone, a wooden cup clenched in one great fist. As Heilyn reached the refrain, the fist tightened, the knuckles standing out white and the veins smoothing into the taut flesh of the back of his hand. The cup shattered, spraying mead across the scrubbed pine table.

'Dovnuall Frych,' he muttered, so low only Nai could hear. 'Dovnuall Frych.'

He frowned, looked with surprise at the widening pool of pale liquid like a man wakening from a dream, and gestured impatiently for a cloth.

Heilyn told how, having failed to learn anything from Erfai, Eremon and his followers had fled westwards along the coast, hoping to outrun Gereint's vengeance. The warband had caught them on the cliffs near the Black Pool, and a messy, indecisive, running fight had developed, with Eremon's men still trying to escape to the west and the warband struggling to bring them to bay.

The fighting lasted from mid-morning till late afternoon. It had been a wet day, cold and blustery with the rain driving in from the sea in horizontal sheets, blinding the men and the horses. One by one they had fallen, a few at a time, and all the while they rode westwards, now at a walk, now at a trot, now at a gallop, till the ponies were foundering.

> 'On the long sands he fell, on the white pebble
>   beach,
> After he glutted the grasp of grey eagles' beaks.
> Like the tide coming in was his wrath in the battle,
> Tegfan herded the foeman as he herded the cattle.
> By the hundred he drove them, the spoils of war,
> With his blue-bladed spears he drives them no more.
>
> Green grows the grass on Tegfan's grave.'

Nai bowed his head. He remembered them all, all those whose deeds and deaths Heilyn was now celebrating, whose hope of immortality lay in their exploits being recalled in song down through the ages of the world.

The poem was a long one. Although Nai knew it was an easy trick, one to which none of the great bards would have stooped, he still found himself moved by the constant refrain: 'Green grows the grass on so-and-so's grave.'

The youngsters in the hall were less affected. Some were openly chattering; others, though pretending to be interested, were stifling yawns. Gereint frowned from his High Seat, signalled for the mead to be passed round again, for the cups and horns to be replenished.

Heilyn took the hint and brought the song to a close with a description of Eremon's flight and Gorthyn's pursuit along the shore beneath the cliffs as the tide was coming in, the floundering past each headland as the water foamed and gushed around their waists.

(Nai remembered none of this. He had been lying unconscious with a crude bandage round his throat at the place where the last of the ponies had foundered, driven past the limits of even their hardy endurance.)

Eremon had escaped out to sea, while the pursuers, trapped by the tide, had been forced to scale the cliffs in an ignominious end to the day.

Now that Heilyn was talking about somebody they knew as opposed to shadowy figures they only half remembered, the youngsters quietened, settled to listen to the final verses. Gorthyn was popular among them, known as a good teacher of weapon play and as a fair and generous man under all the shouting and bluster. His strength also was much admired, and it was by his strength he had brought those with him alive up the cliff from the shrinking beach.

> 'This was the tale of the Men of Gereint,
> And I Heilyn sang it, alone in my grief,
> Green grows the grass on the graves of the heroes.
> May their souls be welcome in the land of Heaven.'

They pounded the tables and shouted and whistled, toasted the bard in mead, their earlier boredom forgotten.

'Give us "The Hunting of the King Boar",' someone called, and the cry was taken up by others, for it was a good rollicking song with a good rollicking beat and plenty to laugh at in the words: a cheerful song to dispel the air of solemn gloom that had come over them at the thought of all those people dead half a decade earlier when they were boys.

Heilyn laughed and began to play, his fingers moving quickly on the strings and his audience sang along with him, humming where they could not remember the words.

Gorthyn rose with a grin on his face and marched across to where the women sat. He pulled the prettiest to her feet and started to dance, moving with a horseman's grace. Others followed suit, and in no time the mood of the hall had changed.

Nai stayed on the couch, watching the swirl of colours as crimson and purple cloaks mingled with checks and tartans, stripes and spots. The sadness still gripped him. Most of these people would be dead before their hair turned grey: the boys in battle, the girls in childbirth and its associated illnesses. He was no more than five or six years their elder, but already Gorthyn and he, by dint of their survival, had more in common with greybeards like Gereint and Morgant than with these youngsters.

Listening to Heilyn's song, he had realized that of those who had been his fellows in the Boys' House, learning the lessons which would one day make them warriors worthy of their mead, only a handful were still alive. There were Cadlew and Addonwy, and great-hearted Gorthyn himself; and then, he supposed, there were Eremon mab Cairbre and his two companions, Dovnuall Frych and Serach the Tall. Seven in all, and three of them now landless renegades doomed to a life of piracy and plundering until somebody made an end of them.

'Save seven, none came home from the Spiral Castle.'

The line from the old song ran through his head as he made his way towards the door and his bed. He paused on the threshold for a last glance at the crowd: Gorthyn towering above the rest, head flung back in laughter as he whirled his partner around him; and Gereint, brooding among his advisers at the High Table, one hand cupped behind an ear as Morgant sketched another of his schemes.

'Three shiploads of Prydein we went on the sea,
Save seven none returned from the Castle of Death.'

CHAPTER THREE

1

It was a cold grey morning, not at all the stuff of great beginnings, not at all the way Ceolric had imagined. In the stories the heroes always sailed in bright sunshine. They strode from the mead hall to the wave strand, their armour and weapons glittering splendidly in the light, watched by an envious crowd, every one of whom wished to be going with them.

They did not sneak before dawn from the hovels they had been reluctantly granted, unwatched and unwanted, moving without talk so as not to wake the natives, treading awkwardly around the middens, blindly following the man in front.

A few cooking fires burned among the huts, the smoke mingling with the river mist. A dog growled. There was nobody about, or if there was they were staying out of sight until the strangers had gone.

It was the silence Ceolric found the most unnerving. Even Wicga seemed subdued, walking at the head of his crew with his shoulders bowed like a much older man, his face under the tousled beard pale with lack of sleep.

The stench was worse this morning. Everything reeked of decay and damp and rot, with the smoke and the mist hanging over the moss-green thatch like a great grey blanket, holding down the smells.

'I hate this place,' Ceolric said to Garulf.

The older man nodded. 'I shall be glad to be gone myself.'

On the river the mists twisted and curled, pale white wraiths coming and going in the gloom before dawn, the surface of the water black and murky where it was not altogether hidden.

The *Sea Stallion* was too large to bring in at the landing stages, which were flimsy wooden platforms running out into the mud and mist. Wicga and Garulf helped themselves to the boats moored along the platforms, dividing the men into small parties. Ceolric, as one of the youngest and least important members of the crew, was in the last group to be carried out to the ship. No sooner had he touched her wooden sides than his father, eager to show no favour, gave him the task of returning the boats, now lashed together in a long chain.

His hands were cold and clumsy on the oars. He could feel the weight of the other craft dragging on his own, could see the curved line slowly straighten as he pulled for the shore, which was much further than he had thought.

Aboard the ship they were making ready, their voices echoing across the water. He pulled faster, suddenly and unreasonably afraid of being forgotten, of being left behind in this dreary village.

The boat hit the landing stage with a thump. A moment later the second boat collided with his own, then the third with the second, and so on down the chain.

'Come on, boy!' his father's voice bellowed through the mist.

He jumped out and squinted in the direction of the *Sea Stallion*, almost lost now in the grey coils writhing and swirling across the face of the water (like steam in a cauldron, he thought hungrily), and saw the long bank of oars poised ready to drive her down river to the sea.

He lashed the lead boat to the platform then he raced the length of the platform and leaped from its end.

The shock of the cold hit him so hard he thought his legs would refuse to work, but somehow they carried him on, half wading, half running, until he was deep enough to swim. Old teachings returned to him as his arms began to strike out in rhythm with his legs, and so the river and his own skill bore him to the long oak shaft held outstretched for him, and the friendly hands of his companions were waiting to haul him aboard as he scrambled up the oar.

'Well done,' growled his father. 'Find a change of clothes and rest a while. We shall have need of you on the oar bench later.'

Despite the gruffness, Ceolric knew his father was pleased with him, and hastened to his sea chest, pulling out a fresh tunic and trousers. Before he had stripped the sodden clothing from his body they were under way, sliding down the river between banks of grey and featureless scrub.

Running down the stream before the true dawn was risky work, but Garulf was eager to catch the tide. Out here in the middle of river the surface of the water was invisible, buried under a thick blanket of mist which cut off sight and sound, so the oars seemed to cleave only vapour with a muffled churning.

The grey scrub gave way to grey wooded marsh. The sky was brightening in the east, and the wind was freshening, thinning the mist and carrying with it the promise of the sea.

As the sun rose it burned off the mist, enabling them to travel faster and revealing more of the dreary shoreline. Again Ceolric wondered what had possessed Cerdic Elesing to make his landing in such an unlovely place, then remembered the old rumour that some of Cerdic's forebears had come from the region.

When the *Sea Stallion* left the shelter of the estuary and headed west towards the narrow channel between the mainland and the Isle of Wectis, or Wight, Garulf ordered the oars brought in and the sail raised on its ropes of greased hide. The ship accelerated so rapidly that the less experienced hands like Ceolric were almost jerked from their feet, obliged to grab a shroud or brace themselves by leaning forward as her speed increased. Faster and faster she seemed to go, and Ceolric found himself wanting to dance with delight, going about his duties with a fixed grin on his face until the instant he first sighted the Needles and what awaited them at the mouth of the channel.

The Frisian spat on his palms and renewed his grip on the steering oar. There seemed to be white water boiling everywhere, a confused jumble of waves, short steep seas with breaking crests.

The *Sea Stallion* began to shake under the buffeting. Spray broke over the bows and sides in great sheets, drenching and blinding the crew. The ship rolled, fighting against the cross-currents, battered this way and that by the turbulence, then she was out into the steady swell of the open sea, out and still running before a fast wind, flying along in all her glory, wind-whetted, white-throated, the gulls shrieking and mewing around her mast.

After that, things were calmer. They sailed and rowed their

way westwards, never hurrying, keeping as close inshore as they dared – which sometimes was so far out to sea that the land became a blue-grey blur on the horizon.

Looking back, years later, it was Garulf that Ceolric remembered best from that long voyage. Wicga had welcomed the Frisian to the crew, reckoning himself lucky to find a man with his experience, for at that time there were few among the English who knew the waters to the west, along the coasts of Dumnonia.

Some part of that experience Garulf now tried to pass on to Ceolric, giving him lessons in navigation and ship-handling which were to stand him in good stead when he was older, although the method of teaching tended to be fierce and painful.

'Listen,' said the steersman, pushing Ceolric's head towards the bulwark during that first day. 'Listen to the waves beating on the hull.'

At first Ceolric could hear nothing unusual, just the water thundering against the planks as it had done ever since they set sail, the sound greatly magnified by the wooden hull.

'Listen to the rhythm!' commanded Garulf.

His neck was beginning to hurt. The older man was squeezing hard, keeping him at an awkward angle. From the corner of one eye he could see his father watching with obvious amusement.

'Hear the counter-surf?'

Buried behind the hiss and roar of their passage was something else, faint at first, until he concentrated on that alone and tuned out all the other noises: a pattern of sounds not unlike the grunting of a pig as it wallows in mud.

'Do you hear the sucking? Like a large body struggling to free itself from marsh?' Garulf smacked his lips in imitation. Wicga laughed aloud, but the older man ignored him. 'And running with it, a series of grunts – *unk unk unk*?'

'Yes,' said Ceolric.

Garulf released him. The youth straightened, rubbing his neck.

'And what did I tell you we called this headland?'

'Pig Point.'

'And will you remember it now? If you hear it again, late at night, with the wind pushing you towards land and the rain streaming down your face so that you're cold, miserable and frightened, will you recognize it?'

Ceolric nodded.

'Good. Because although other headlands may sound similar,

none of them sound exactly like this one. You must train your ear, lad, train it to distinguish between the varying sounds of the sea on the shore.' He paused, studied Ceolric intently for a moment, seemed satisfied with what he saw. 'Now see how the wind is falling off? What we need is more breeze, or else we must break out the oars and start rowing – and you know how the men hate that. Never use your oarsmen unless you must. Keep them fresh, for the moment when you need a burst of speed. So, find me a wind!'

Ceolric scanned the waves, looking for the darkness that would signal a breeze. 'There!' he said, and pointed.

The Frisian clouted him hard enough to hurt. 'Don't just stand there. Do something about it. Take the steering oar and bring her round.'

With his ears still ringing from the force of the blow Ceolric wrestled with the rudder, coaxing the *Sea Stallion* onto her new course, trying to ease her round without either touching the sail or ordering the crew to break out the oars. Garulf claimed this was the mark of a real seaman: any fool, he said, could alter course by using the oars to spin the ship; only a true master with a feel for his vessel could do it using the rudder alone.

When the wind filled the sail and the *Sea Stallion* began to plane across the surface of the waves, her timbers thundering and her throat white with foam, then Ceolric forgot the pain in his ears and laughed aloud, and even Garulf smiled with approval.

'We'll make a sailor of you yet,' he laughed.

On the first night, after they had eaten and before they slept – most of them were too excited at the thought of the great adventure ahead to sleep – a man who had joined the crew at much the same time as the Frisian said jokingly:

'Garulf, is it true you once fought with the Emperor?'

'Against him,' corrected the steersman. 'Though once I did save the life of one of his Companions.'

'Which emperor?' demanded Wicga.

'There was only ever one Emperor in this land during my lifetime,' said the Frisian. 'The Emperor Arthur, of course, the Warlord of Britain.'

Wicga raised an eyebrow, thinking upon this, while Ceolric moved closer, anxious not to miss a word.

37

'You saved one of his Companions?' said the captain after a while. 'When was this? What made you do it?'

'I had taken service as a Federate in the city of Lindinis,' said the Frisian.

'Why?' asked Wicga.

'I was young and hungry. Things had gone badly with me.' Garulf glanced around, gauging the mood of the company.

'Tell us, Garulf,' said the man who had spoken first. 'Tell us the story.'

'It is not a tale that does me great honour. For much of the time my loyalty was torn between the different people who had a call upon it. So if I tell you what happened, you must remember the person to whom it happened was very young, new to the ways of the world.'

'Nobody would hold the follies of youth against a man of your repute,' Wicga said formally. 'You are well known along these coasts as a man whose word is good whether in counsel or in the swearing of service to a captain. Whatever you tell us we shall think no less of you.'

The fire crackled and spat. Garulf stared into the flames then began to speak.

'It was thirty summers ago. I had gone raiding with a man called Cunrig, an Irishman whose forebears had settled here in the days of the High King – his nephew of the same name now leads Cerdic's warband. We were a mixed crew: some Irish, some Frisians like myself, some Yutes, with barely a language in common between us, and we spent most of our time quarrelling among ourselves. Everything went wrong. It ended when we were caught in the open by a party of British horsemen.'

He shuddered at the memory, and Ceolric shuddered too, suddenly seeing in the dancing flames the shapes of riders hacking down fleeing men.

'Only a few of us made it back to the ship, and still fewer survived the voyage home. It was a hard sailing, with wounds to lick and no booty for all our efforts. We ran into a summer storm before we sighted safety, and several hands were lost overboard.

'After that I vowed to give up the sea, and try seeking my fortune on dry land.'

Wicga leaned close to the fire, flung another log into its heart. A shower of sparks flew upwards and vanished in the summer night.

'You were Cerdic's man in those days?' he asked with studied neutrality.

Garulf frowned wearily. 'We had come home empty handed, as I told you. Cerdic's grip on the land was not strong in those days, whatever he may claim now that he has crowned himself king. Thirty years ago he was one among a host of petty lordlings, and the owners of the homesteads had little time for him. He sought to bolster his power by giving gold rings and keeping the drink flowing in the hall, that men might think him mightier than his rivals.

'To do that he needed treasure. And we were supposed to provide that treasure, on our foray to the west. Instead we had lost more than half our crew. We seemed ill fated, and Cerdic did not look upon us kindly when we returned. He released me from my oath to him, cast me adrift in the wide middle-earth.

'A few years earlier Arthur had destroyed a generation of our warriors at Badon Hill. Since then there had been minor fights, skirmishes and raids like the one from which I had just returned, but none of our people had dared face him in open battle.

'Likewise there was peace among the Princes of the Britons – or at least, as much peace as there can be between that quarrelsome race. Arthur had imposed it upon them, forcing them to unite against us, and against the seaborne raiders from the north and east.

'Arthur was therefore the greatest power in all this island. Since Cerdic no longer wanted me, I took my spear and shield and made my way westwards, meaning to take service with Arthur.'

'Did you see him?' demanded Ceolric. 'What was he like?'

Garulf smiled, stared blankly into the depths of the fire as somebody threw on another piece of wood and made it flare.

'A big man, well built, with auburn hair going grey. I suppose he would have been ten years younger than I am now, though there was an air of agelessness about him. He had that power – Cerdic has it to some extent – of making it seem as if you're the most interesting person in the world. I would have followed him anywhere, if he had asked me.'

His voice trailed away and there was a moment's silence.

'Though he was a man, it would not have surprised me to discover he was more . . . You know they say he did not die, at the end, that he went to be healed of his wounds and sleeps somewhere under the earth . . .'

The Frisian shook himself like a man waking from a dream.

'This land is old, very old. It was old before the Romans came. Everywhere you go you find signs that somebody has been before you: mounds and barrows, the grassy rings of ancient camps, tumbledown field walls, stones arranged in rows and circles. The woods and streams and hills are full of spirits, of little gods and big, of ogres and elves and shades. If one of those ancient powers had clothed itself in human flesh and walked among us, then I think it might have been like him, like Arthur.'

'Yet he fell at the end,' said Wicga, his voice sounding petulant. 'Is that not the Weird of all men, to die? Is it not better to win fame before death, so that one's deeds may live on?'

'You were there at the end? You were at Camlann?' somebody asked from across the fire, eyes eager in the hungry flames.

'I was. But that was fifteen, twenty years later, and I was on the other side.'

'Tell us first how you came to save one of the Emperor's warriors.'

'In those days he was not yet the Emperor,' said Garulf. 'He was the war-leader of Britain. Different groups called him by different names. To the hill tribes of the west, if they loved him, he was the Warlord or the Battle Emperor. To the people of the lowlands who supported him he was Magister Militum, Commander of the Armies of Britain, Heir to Ambrosius. To those who hated or feared him he was the Tyrant, the Usurper, a soldier grown over-powerful.'

The Frisian's face was sad in the flickering light. He was silent for so long that Ceolric began to fear he meant to say no more, but then suddenly he roused himself and began to talk, hesitantly at first, then more fluently as the memories took hold.

'Arthur was no fool. Men like me he put to work on the western shores, guarding against raiders from the island of Ierne, the Scotti, kin to Cunrig. If somebody like Cunrig took service with him, he gave them the eastern boundaries to ward, so that they would never have to fight against people who might be hearth friends or kinfolk.

'I went north and west from Cerdicesora to Caer Cadwy, Cadda's Burg, the great fortress city where Arthur was most often to be found. It was late summer by this time and all spring and summer dozens of other youths had been doing the same thing. By the time I reached Caer Cadwy, Arthur had no need of yet another untried boy.

'But he and his men were kind to me. They fed me, and sent me on down the great paved road to Lindinis, the old city which lies not far from Caer Cadwy –'

'I want to hear about this warrior,' protested a voice from the far side of the fire.

'Be still, and you shall,' said Garulf. 'For soon I was to meet with him, one of the greatest of Arthur's men, though it was a long while before I knew who he was.'

2

The City Fathers of Lindinis wanted strong arms to defend their walls and they were keen to have me. I joined a company of men much like myself: hard men with not a native born Briton among them, for cities are not the place for warriors. There is something about living all hugger-mugger like ants in a hill that turns men fat and soft.

Once Lindinis had been a thriving place, the chief city of this part of the country, standing proud where the road to the old ports of the Severn Channel crosses the mighty Fosse Way.

But it was dying now, dying a long, slow, drawn out death. The sick smell of age and coming doom hung over it all. Parts of the town were very old, cunningly built of stone and made to last, but often the timbers which had held the roofs had turned to powder or cracked under the weight of the red tiles, so great sections stood open to the skies, and the rain and the snow wrought havoc in what had once been snug rooms.

The outer areas had been abandoned first, though a few farmers still clung desperately to the tired soil. The people huddled together at the heart of the city for the sake of light and warmth and company, and who can blame them, when no man knew what fell creatures might stalk through the ruins after dark?

Like all cities, Lindinis was the fruit of magic, the work of giants or wizards in the days when the middle-earth was young. Men could not have built such a place, and certainly those who now lived there did not have the art. How else, except by magic, could the Romans have cut stone as we cut wood, finding its grain and sawing across it to make the blocks they piled together? And the mortar they mixed must have held the blood of many sacrifices, human as well as animal, for it bound the stones together in a marvellous way, more firmly than any other mortar I have ever seen. But even magic wears thin after a while and the years had taken their toll.

I stayed through the autumn and the winter, which was a bad one, bitterly cold. Even when spring should have been on its way the ground was still frozen, and the sea marshes to the north-west were rimmed with ice. At night the wind howled around the walls, bringing flurries of sleet or more snow, and we guards on the ramparts huddled deep into our thick woollen cloaks and blew on our mittened fingers to stave off frostbite.

Like so much else these walls were semi-ruined, long stretches of them made unsafe by loose stones. A great section of wall around what had been the main north-east gate had fallen down and been replaced by a timber palisade, now itself grown old and frail. In the middle were two stumps of masonry, and hanging from them the wooden gates, which stayed open during daylight. Behind them was a rough barrier of rubble and hurdles which we used to limit passage into the city – anybody coming in, you see, had to pay a small toll.

We had a small guardhouse with a brazier where we kept warm while one of us stayed on watch, and when a traveller was sighted we all dashed out and lined up behind the barricade.

That was how I saw him first, from over the rim of a shield as I crouched behind a hurdle. My place was at one end, out of harm's way, for I was little more than a boy, and from there I had a clear view of all that happened.

He was in the lead on a brown horse, sitting comfortably in the saddle like a man at ease, well wrapped against the cold of the afternoon in a heavy hooded cloak, his fingers encased in thick leather gauntlets.

There was a quiver filled with throwing spears hanging from his saddle, but he made no movement towards them as he passed through the gates at a trot, nor did he reach for the shield slung at his back.

He reined in his horse, signed for the riders behind him to halt, and stared at us, his gaze passing along our line and holding when it met our captain, Folcwalda son of Frodi, a grim South Saxon who had fought with Aelle at Badon Hill. Folcwalda stared back, his spear held level and steady, the hatred written all over him. He was a big hard man wearing mail under his cloak, a man that even now I would hesitate before trying to face down, but this *weala*, this Briton, suddenly surged forward on his pony, bringing it right to the edge of the barricade, crowding Folcwalda, daring him to make a move.

'In the name of Arthur,' said the horseman, his voice soft and even.

Folcwalda spat. 'What do you want?'

'I have business with the City Council. Clear the way.'

Slowly the captain turned and waved to us, and with equal slowness – to prove that we at least were not impressed by the name of Arthur – we dragged the hurdles aside so there was room for the horses to pass.

The leader rode through, keeping his eyes to the front and the pony to a walk, though he must have been able to feel the hatred and hostility of my fellows beating at his back.

'You will need a guide,' growled Folcwalda. 'You, boy!'

He beckoned to me and I ran forward, my feet slipping on the icy cobbles.

'Escort these *wealas* to the City Fathers,' he said in our tongue.

The horseman turned and looked down at us. 'It is not we who are the foreigners,' he said in the same language. 'Not in this our own country.'

'Soon you will be gone,' snarled the captain.

'We shall see, Saeson.' He gestured to me. 'Lead on, lad.'

It was a strange place, Lindinis, half empty and haunted with ghosts. Others, wiser than I, had told me it was dying because the reason for its existence had died. There was no longer much trade between Dumnonia and the lands across the Severn Sea; what trade there was took place at a local level. With few travellers, there was no custom for the craftsmen who had once sold their wares in the market.

But the centre of the city still had some signs of life, even on an afternoon like this: people who scurried about their affairs with their heads down, barely sparing our party a glance, as if Arthur's men were such a common sight on the streets that they no longer aroused any curiosity.

These streets were one of the oddest things about this odd place. They ran straight as spear shafts, with no shelter from the wind: some from north to south, others east to west. Thankfully, many – though not all – of the lesser lanes were more natural, paths a man's feet might gladly follow, wandering hither and thither with the lie of the land. Between the roads, lanes and alleys were the buildings, like islets in a many-channelled river where it flows down to the sea, and this was what those who dwelled within them called them: islands, or insulae.

I had been inside a few of these insulae. Often the walls had magic pictures on them of dark-eyed gods and goddesses, so every room became a temple. If that were not strange enough, the magic pictures were on the floor as well, prettily laid out in pieces of coloured stone. The old ones, the wizards and their servants who lived in these houses when the middle-earth was young, must have taken strange and roundabout routes from one point to another, to avoid treading on their gods.

Most of the houses at the heart of the city were still lived in, and there were rows of shops open for business, running right to the crossroads around which Lindinis had been built, where the Fosse Way – known within the walls as the Cardo Maximus – crossed the road to the Severn Channel – called the Decumanus Maximus inside the city. This crossroad was dominated by the market place with the town hall behind it. Nearby was the inn, the oldest building in the city, and, from the outside at least, still one of the best preserved.

The leader of the horsemen had smiled at me once in friendly fashion, then ignored me while I trotted at his side. All the way I had stolen quick glances at him, wondering who he was. I ran through the list of Arthur's Companions in my head. Not Cei, who was a blond giant famed for his great strength. Not Bedwyr, who was famed for having only one hand. Not Lleminawg, who was an Irishman and was said to speak with a lilt this man lacked. Gwalchmei, perhaps, or Caradoc, or Anwas Fleet Foot, or Erim, or Atlendor . . .

Whoever he was, he reined in at the market square and gave his orders, speaking so rapidly I was hard put to follow him.

'Moried, take half the men. Visit the City Governor and tell him what we are doing. Demand the use of a reasonable-sized house for the night, somewhere we can defend if necessary.'

A young man in a tartan cloak sketched a salute and wheeled his horse aside, the pennon on his spear flapping in the icy wind.

'The rest of you follow me to the south-west gate.' He turned

44

and looked at me, a long cold measuring gaze. 'You have done your duty, lad. Come or stay as you wish.'

I told myself that Folcwalda would want me to stay, but the truth was it was I who wished to see more of these strange and half-magical beings.

'If the Saeson dogs get in our way?' somebody asked hopefully over my head.

The leader smiled a very different smile from the one he had given me earlier and deliberately loosened his sword in its sheath before urging his pony across the cobblestones. I followed, hearing behind me laughter amid the clatter of hooves as the men divided into two groups.

By the time we reached the wall the weak sun was sinking fast and darkness was gathering in the narrow streets. This gate was also garrisoned by mercenaries, and like my fellows on the far side of the town they stared at us without speaking as we approached.

'I am Arthur's man,' said the horseman, keeping his words simple so they would understand. 'We are here to meet an embassy from Agricola of Dyfed.'

'An embassy?' said the captain of this guard, lowering his spear. His eyes passed over us, widening a little as he saw me.

'A group of riders. Horsemen, like us.'

'Yes, yes,' the captain said impatiently. His name was Sigebeorn and, unlike his counterpart, grim Folcwalda, he was a good-humoured man. 'I know what is an embassy. One was here earlier, asking about them. A man of the North, a painted man.'

Sigebeorn twisted a finger above his cheek to indicate the characteristic tattoos of a Pict.

'Did he say what he wanted with them?'

The captain grinned, his yellow teeth eager under the tangled beard. 'He offered us gold to tell him where they sleep this night. You will give us more gold not to tell him, hey?'

'No.' He swung himself from the saddle, shivering slightly in the cold wind. Now that he stood on the ground beside me I could see he was not so tall as I had thought. 'You tell him whatever he wants to know.'

Sigebeorn snorted, beat his spear butt on the pavement. 'Come, cold out here. There is a fire inside.' He indicated the guardroom beside the ruined gatehouse.

The Briton nodded and followed Sigebeorn through the door.

His men looked doubtful, but they went after him, all save one who stayed behind to hold the horses. I waited a moment then trailed after them, slipping quietly into the room and finding a place among my own people.

The British sat on one side and we sat on the other, as if this were some great council at which the fate of whole races would be decided. I could see the horsemen trying to hide their disgust at the reek of bodies and bear-fat in the confined space. (Thirty years ago many of our people dressed their hair with fat or clay if they could find it, and if you were not used to it the smell was powerful.)

'What is your name?' demanded Sigebeorn, proffering a bottle full of cloudy liquid.

The horseman sipped, found it to his liking and took a hearty swig.

'Mab Petroc,' he said, returning the bottle.

The captain frowned. 'Strong son?'

'If you like. It is a name, no more.'

When it came to my turn I drank deep, not wishing to seem less than my companions, and almost choked. It was sour beer strengthened with strong spirit, and it burned my throat.

'With us too a name sometimes means something, sometimes not. I am Sigeferth's son, Sigebeorn of the Secgan. Victorious warrior, that would be in your tongue.' He grinned. 'Sa, Sa. I am alive, and my foes are dead. That is victory of a kind, I suppose.'

'The Secgan? Who are they?'

'We are hearth friends to the Ingwine, the East Danes. A small people, with poor land.'

'But hospitable sons,' said mab Petroc as the bottle came round again. 'Are you all of the Secgan?'

'No, no.' Sigebeorn pointed round the room at his men. 'Beanstan is a Bronding, Garmund and Hussa are of the Angles – the youngling Garulf is a Frisian.'

'So none of you are Saesons?'

Sigebeorn laughed. 'In this land we are all Saesons, hey? Or how do you say, *Eingl*.' He shrugged his heavy shoulders. 'It makes no odds. We are all People of the Knife.' He touched the sax hanging at his belt, the single-edged war-knife from which the name Saxon is said to come.

'And what brought you here to Lindinis?'

'Myself, I killed a man with wealthy kin. The others, much the same.' Sigebeorn leaned forward, dropping his voice, and I saw mab Petroc flinch away slightly from the smell of drink on the big man's breath. 'Arthur. The Magister Militum –' he stumbled over the words '– does he need men?'

'Always. And he is more generous than the City Council. Come to Caer Cadwy, when you are free of this place, and say that mab Petroc sent you.'

'Thank you. I do not like this town.' He shuddered, his face serious. 'Too many ghosts.'

The door opened and Moried came in. He saluted, formal in the presence of strangers, and said:

'The embassy are in sight, my lord. I have arranged the use of a house with the Governor.'

Mab Petroc nodded. 'Well done. My friend here tells me a Pict was asking after the Dyfed men.'

'A painted man,' Sigebeorn said helpfully. He rotated his finger above his cheek again. 'The paint was a line, going round and round – I do not know the word.'

'A spiral?' Mab Petroc drew in the dust of the floor. 'Like that?'

Sigebeorn nodded, pleased the Briton had understood. 'A spiral, yes. I had not seen such a shape before, on a man's face. On rocks, yes, but not on flesh.'

'A labyrinth,' said Moried, peering over mab Petroc's shoulder. 'Curious. It means nothing to me. And why would a Pict be looking for the embassy from Dyfed?'

'He did not say. But he promised us gold to tell him where they sleep.'

Moried glanced worriedly at mab Petroc, who waved a hand impatiently.

'Well? Where are we sleeping tonight?'

'Off the Decumanus Maximus.'

'Come on. I want the Pict to find us. Tell my friend Sigebeorn where we are staying.'

'In the fifth insula.'

Sigebeorn brightened. 'The big house. I know it.' He turned to mab Petroc and said earnestly: 'Do not trust the staircase. My friend Wulf nearly fell through it when he was there.'

'We shall be very careful,' mab Petroc said gravely.

He rose from the bench, brushed off his cloak, and patted the Secgan on the shoulder. 'Do not forget. Come to Caer Cadwy when you have finished your time here. You will be welcome.'

'I shall,' said Sigebeorn, and stood until all the Britons had shuffled out into the cold.

When they had gone the room seemed empty. We waited in silence until Sigebeorn had seated himself, waited for him to speak.

'I like that man,' Sigebeorn said at last. 'He did not try to bribe me.'

'Not with gold,' said Beanstan. 'Instead he offered you a place with Arthur.'

'Only when I asked.' He sat back, belched happily, his thumbs hooked through his belt and a grin on his face.

'We have a choice, my friends. We can sit here and do nothing. We can take the Pict's gold and join his attack on the house tonight. Or we can help mab Petroc.'

'Who is he?' demanded Hussa.

Sigebeorn chuckled. 'Do you not know?'

Ever since the horseman named himself I had been thinking hard and long. I had never heard of mab Petroc, but from the pride with which he had spoken I did not believe he had given a false name.

The captain was enjoying his moment of knowing more than the rest of us. 'Think!' he said. 'It is hot in here, yet he never removed any of his clothing. Not his cloak, not his gloves – he did not even push back his hood!'

Hussa shrugged. 'I took it he wished to stay hidden. Most of us have fought Arthur's men in the past. Perhaps he feared a blood feud –'

'That man never feared anything in his life!' snorted Sigebeorn, and I agreed, sitting quietly in my corner.

'I say we should take the Pict's gold but help the Briton,' Beanstan said suddenly.

The others growled their approval. I think we had all been impressed by mab Petroc, even the doubters among us.

'What of Folcwalda?' I asked hesitantly.

'What of him?' Hussa's voice was rough and filled with contempt, for he did not like the South Saxon.

'If the Pict offers him gold to fight he will take it. He hates Arthur's men.'

'He hates everybody,' said Beanstan, and the others laughed.

'As the City Guard we swore an oath to keep the peace within the walls of Lindinis,' said Sigebeorn. 'Our duty is clear. If

Folcwalda turns oath breaker for the sake of Pictish treasure then he must pay the price the gods demand.'

There was bad blood between Sigebeorn and Folcwalda. Where one was grim and dour, the other was sunny and light-hearted. Both were big men, strong and dealers of hard blows whether with weapons or bare hands, and the rivalry between them surprised no one.

'Are you with me, Garulf?'

Sigebeorn fixed me with iron blue eyes that gave the lie to the smile on his face, and I knew that had I answered other than as I did my life would have been forfeit. Yet the answer was the one I wanted to give and no threat would have changed it.

'Then go, youngling, and keep with the *wealas* for as long as you can.'

Outside it was bitterly cold after the close heat of the guard-room. I drew a breath and felt it sear my lungs; coughing, I tasted again the raw alcohol with which Sigebeorn had bolstered his beer.

'There they are, my lord,' Moried was saying, pointing down the road.

Far off, almost on the horizon, a group of horsemen came on at a slow pace.

'Why did you want that Saeson to tell the Pict where to find us?' asked Moried, his face creased with worry.

'Better here than on the road tomorrow,' he said. 'Besides, it may be something quite innocent.'

Moried grunted dubiously.

Wet flakes were gathering at the base of the barren walls in thin white drifts which melted away while I watched, leaving dark patches of damp on the grey stones. The wind was rising, whistling through the streets, cutting through my cloak and making the Britons huddle in the lee of the ruined gatehouse.

Mab Petroc and Moried stayed where they were, exposed to the growing force of the storm.

I crept out behind them, shivering and beating my hands together to bring back some feeling to the numbed fingers. Moried sensed my presence and turned with a scowl, but mab Petroc laid a gauntlet on his arm.

'Leave him be. We may be glad of him later.'

Mab Petroc peered anxiously through the storm, hoping for some sign of the riders. While they kept to the road they would be safe enough, but in this blizzard it would be easy to go astray. There was nothing to be seen except the snow, and he shook his head, indicated with a lift of his chin that Moried and I should follow him into the meagre shelter of the ruined gatehouse.

A shape loomed through the gateway, a blurred and bent shadow huddled atop a shivering pony. The horse took a few steps and then stopped, as if it had decided its task was over now it had reached the city. More riders followed, crowding through the arch, their cloaks wet with snow, faces hidden by hoods and scarves, heads hanging like men who had come to the end of their strength.

'Vortepor of Dyfed?' shouted mab Petroc, stepping out into the full force of the storm. 'Welcome to Lindinis!'

The newcomers were scarcely able to speak. All were exhausted, and the warriors among them bore signs of recent fighting. Their horses were cut and bloody, their wooden shields were hacked and splintered, and many of them rode awkwardly, as if their heavy cloaks hid bad wounds. Near the end of the column were several saddles with bodies slung across them.

'What befell you?' demanded mab Petroc.

Vortepor of Dyfed pushed back his hood. He was a young man, not much older than I, his plump face marred with blotches that stood out red and angry against skin made pale by the cold and his tiredness.

'An ambush. In the hills below the moors.' He spoke slowly, dully, every word a great effort.

'Shut the gates,' commanded mab Petroc. 'Form up and escort our guests to the house.'

His men hurried to do his bidding, closing around the new-comers so any attacker would have to pass through them before reaching the Dyfed men. In the failing light they seemed mena-cing, dangerous, and I backed away against the crumbling wall of the gatehouse, knowing they would see me as a spy.

But the man who called himself mab Petroc beckoned to me.

'Follow behind, boy. I would know if anyone else is interested in our presence.'

I did as I was told. The streets were empty now, the townsmen driven to shelter indoors by the wind and whirling snow. The Britons set off at a goodly pace, hastening against the fall of night from the grim sky, and I skulked along behind them, constantly turning to see if I was being followed.

Lindinis was a frightening place after dark. The Britons cut through the narrow side alleys, seeking the shortest route to the house they had been given. The buildings loomed above me, on one side blank walls with only the occasional tiny square window to break the monotony, and on the other neglected timber balconies supported by stone columns, in whose shadows an army might have hidden.

Soon I lost sight of the riders. The wind was pushing at my back, and whenever I turned to look behind me the snow stuck to my lashes, blinding me. But the churned track of the horses was easy to follow, and I could still hear the clattering echo of hooves not far ahead. Sometimes they scraped and slid on the ice laycring the cobbles, so that I expected at any moment to round a corner and come upon the bulk of a pony lying in the alley, for the Dyfed horses had seemed close to foundering.

They must have been stronger than they looked. Every corner showed the same gloomy view of dark walls half hidden by the swirling snow, and the tracks leading on, deeper into the city.

When the tracks led out from the narrow alley onto a broader thoroughfare I had been blindly following them for so long that I was caught by surprise, and staggered out into the middle of the road. To my right torches flared. I picked my way towards them across the icy ruts and found mab Petroc sitting on his horse outside a small gate through which the others had already ridden.

'Anything?'

I shook my head.

'Well done. My thanks.'

He tossed me a token of silver, waved a hand in farewell and passed through the gate, leaving me alone in the road.

My mouth opened to shout after him, to warn him of the coming attack, then closed again. It was none of my affair. I had offered my spear to Arthur and had been refused.

After a while my feet began to freeze, and I began to move, aimlessly at first, not knowing whether to return to Sigebeorn or to Folcwalda.

I had not gone far when something struck me in the middle of the back, driving the rim of my slung shield into my flesh with bruising force. I staggered, dropping my spear. My legs were kicked from under me and I fell into darkness.

*   *   *

51

It was the cold that brought me back to life. It had seeped deep into every bone, the kind of chill which is the mark of fever. My body shook and my teeth rattled, and as I woke I heard myself moaning.

I was in a small dark room, filled with smoke from a fire smouldering in one corner. Coughing, I sat up, feebly beating my arms against my sides in an effort to drive out the cold.

'He is awake,' growled a familiar voice.

Folcwalda Frodi's son and another man squatted beside me. A taper guttered in a sconce on the wall, casting flickering shadows across their faces. Folcwalda was as grim and forbidding as ever, but the other was a creature out of nightmare – worse even than the ghosts with which I had terrified myself as I crossed the town.

He was a stocky man, well built – not so tall as the son of Frodi, but then few men were. He had a shock of dark hair which would have seemed unkempt had not a slim plait hung down on either side of his face, making the wildness of the rest appear deliberate. His skin was dark and a green spiral was tattooed on each cheek. This in itself was frightening enough, but worst of all were his eyes.

They were the deadest eyes I have ever seen, like black pits, with not a flicker of emotion in their depths.

I knew him then for one of the night walkers, a troll child, a creature of the dark: something from the high moors and fells, from the wolf-slopes and windswept headlands beyond the lands we know.

'Question him,' he said to Folcwalda in thickly accented Saxon.

Folcwalda frowned, not liking the way the tattooed man gave the order, but he made no complaint. He leaned forward and grasped my shoulders.

'What were you doing in the street?'

'Sigebeorn bade me follow the *wealas*,' I stammered, sick and dizzy.

'The leader, what did he give you?'

'Nothing.'

His grip tightened on my bruises and I yelped. Behind him I saw the tattooed man smile.

'A token,' I said, 'a silver token. In my pouch.'

'Why?'

'It was payment for guiding them across the city.'

Folcwalda's eyes narrowed. 'You guided them from behind? Do not lie to me, puppy.'

'I led them to the City Fathers. Then I took half their party to the south-west gate, which Sigebeorn keeps. The horseman gave it to me in mockery, I think.'

'Sa, sa,' hissed Folcwalda. 'And Sigebeorn? What does he do?'

I pretended surprise. 'Captain, I do not know. He told me to follow the *wealas*, to be sure they went to the house. I do not know his plans.'

The tattooed man had busied himself with finding a new rushlight and fitting it into the holder before the old one went out. Without bothering to turn round he spoke, his voice harsh. 'You lie. Tell us the truth, or my curse will be upon you.'

He swung to face me, the light behind him. 'There was another boy once who did not tell me what I wanted. I put my curse upon him and the flesh was blighted from his bones in the space of a single night.' He licked his lips hungrily. 'I remember he kept me awake with his screams.'

I stared in horror at Folcwalda, who nodded slightly.

'All Sigebeorn plans is to take your gold and tell you where the *wealas* are sleeping. That is all I know. He did not tell me anything else.'

There was a long silence while they both stood over me. I was still cold, though by now the shivering was caused as much by fear. The tattooed man terrified me, and when he spoke of curses I had no doubt he meant exactly what he said.

'What do you want?' I cried to the son of Frodi. 'Have I not always been loyal, worthy of my mead? I do not understand what is happening.'

'He knows nothing,' Folcwalda growled to the tattooed man. He released me and stood back, giving me room to rise.

'An innocent,' muttered the tattooed man. 'Send him to join the rest of your men. We must talk alone.'

Folcwalda opened a door and thrust me through into a place of light and warmth.

It was a larger room than the first but so crowded with men it seemed cramped. Everywhere I looked tattooed faces stared back, hostile and inhuman, with cold sly eyes. At first sight all seemed alike, with the same shocks of dark hair and slim braids dangling beside the green spirals. Most were busy honing war-knives and spear blades or checking their shields and harnesses.

In one corner was a different group, holding themselves aloof from the Picts. I pushed a path through the throng, careful not to jog any of the workers or to meet their eyes, and was greeted by my comrades from the City Guard.

'What is happening?' I demanded. 'Where are we?'

'We wait,' said Oswine, a man not much older than myself. 'We wait for orders from Folcwalda, then we fall upon the *weala* like a thunderbolt.'

'Who are these people?' I waved an arm at the Picts.

'Hearth-friends and allies from the far North. They are on a holy task, to recover a relic stolen by the Lords of Dyfed. It is a rightful cause, and we are oath-bound to aid them.'

Then he added quietly with a grin: 'Besides, Folcwalda hates Arthur and his men. The Northerners will attack first. We, the Guard, will hear the noise but arrive too late to stop the slaughter.'

I looked around the room. There were about a dozen of us and perhaps twice that of the Picts. I tried to remember how many warriors mab Petroc had brought with him – fourteen, fifteen? The Dyfed men would not make much difference.

'They will guess you are coming.'

Oswine raised an eyebrow. '*We*,' he said. 'They will guess *we* are coming.'

'I have no weapons.' I spread my arms wide.

'In the corner. Folcwalda brought them in after the Picts knocked you down.' He ran a hand through his beard, of which he was proud, for it was thick and full. 'We have twice our foemen's numbers. The Dyfed men are finished – the Northerners have been whittling away at them ever since they landed in Dumnonia.'

'Why did they not take them before they reached Lindinis?' The question seemed obvious, though I had not thought to ask it before.

'Because the Northerners did not have their full strength. Little by little they have slipped into the country, some by land and some by sea, and they only met together earlier today.' He glanced round the room, lowered his voice: 'They are not easy to disguise with those marks on their faces. If they had come as a troop all the world would know about it.'

I nodded, seeing the sense in this. But the movement hurt my head, and I sat down on the floor until the pain passed.

*   *   *

54

Much later Folcwalda and the Pictish leader came into the room. Beside the son of Frodi the Pictish leader with his scored face and wild hair seemed like a creature of the night. I knew that nothing but pure greed, the lust for gold, drove Folcwalda to side with him.

The Pict spoke to his followers, his words fast and slurred so I found them difficult to understand. (In those days I had not yet discovered that the best way to learn a new tongue is from its girls, at ease under their bedcovers during the long winter months.) But I understood enough to tell he was not talking of a sacred relic. He mentioned a woman, often, though what woman and why she mattered I could not make out.

When the tattooed man finished speaking he gave a signal, and all the lights were doused. We waited a few moments in the darkness, then the bars were drawn back and the huge doors were flung open.

It had stopped snowing and the moon was up, riding among the stars like a ship of war running before a strong wind.

The Picts went first, loosening their blades in their scabbards, clutching their throwing spears. They moved silently, like huntsmen stalking a boar, managing to cross the snow with scarcely a sound. Folcwalda let them go a little way then led us after them, striding firmly in their wake, trampling the ice underfoot.

The wind howled along the alleys. Avalanches of snow slid rumbling from the roofs, covering our tracks. Doors or shutters creaked and banged in the distance as the city went through another spasm in its long dying.

Soon we came to the wall around the yard of the house in which the British slept. From the yard the staircase of which Sigebeorn had spoken rose to the upper storey. Once we crossed the wall it would not be hard to gain entry to our foemen's lair.

The Picts spread out, ready for the signal. We stood in reserve, waiting to see where the danger lay before making our move. For a moment there was silence. The wind dropped, as if the gods held their breath.

Then came the scream.

It ripped through the air like the wail of a vixen in heat, fading then regathering strength, seeming to last for ever. Beside me Oswine dropped his sword, unmanned by the sound. Even Folcwalda, grim Folcwalda the veteran of Badon Hill, flinched and made the sign of the Hammer.

Whatever had caused the noise, it must be something inside the house.

Bolts rattled and doors opened. Torches made circles of light on the snow. Voices called as the house awoke. A man ran up the wooden steps, the dull echo of his feet carrying to us where we watched from the darkness beyond the torchlight. He shook the latch, banged on the door, shouted to the men below:

'Nothing passed me, my lord. It came from up here.' He beat on the door with his spear butt. 'Open, in the name of Arthur!'

I stared at the group gathered around the foot of the stairs. Some – the ones who had been on watch when the scream came – were fully dressed, with mailshirts and winter cloaks. Others wore nothing but simple tunics, and carried whatever they had snatched in their haste – a sword, a war-knife, a spear.

Mab Petroc was one of these. He stood bareheaded and bare-armed at the heart of a ring of men, lacking even a cloak, though oddly his hands were still hidden by the heavy leather gauntlets, peering up at the guard on the landing.

'Break it down, Goronwy!' he shouted.

Goronwy turned, as if he had not heard what mab Petroc had said above the drumming of his spear on the wood. He leaned over the rail, and in that moment the javelin struck him. Its force threw him against the door, and the thud echoed flatly round the court-yard. He dropped his spear and swayed upright, one hand reaching behind him to grope at the shaft in his back, and then blood gushed from his mouth like vomit, and the wooden rail broke under his weight as he toppled head first from the platform.

The Picts were swarming over the wall before Goronwy's body had hit the ground, hurling javelins as they went. Some of the British fell, and the rest flung their torches from them, realizing the light made them targets. The torches hissed and guttered in the snow, but many kept burning, throwing a red glow across the yard and casting strange shadows.

Mab Petroc leaped forward to meet the attack, shouting, 'To me, to me!' He hacked the legs out from under the leading figure, spun and nearly collided with a second, blocked the swing of the man's war-knife with his forearm to the other's wrist, shortened his grip on his sword and pushed it home in the Pict's belly.

For a long moment he seemed to stand alone, drawing the Picts to him like moths to a flame, lacking even a shield to protect himself.

Beside me I heard Oswine's breath go out in a hiss of admiration for the man's courage: admiration, and sorrow, for no one man could last more than a few heartbeats against so many.

Then mab Petroc began to fight in earnest and I forgot everything – the bitter cold, my aching head, the rivalry between Folcwalda and Sigebeorn – while I watched him use his sword. Suddenly I saw why Arthur's men were said to be unbeatable in battle.

He did not move fast. Others among Arthur's Companions moved quickly, I knew – Lleminawg the Dancer was said to have the speed of a striking snake – and I had always thought they must all be of the same kind, trained to fight in the same fashion.

He moved slowly, so slowly I could not at first see how he kept his feet when all around him were Picts raining down blows on his unprotected body. Yet somehow he was never there when they struck, so their blades hissed through empty air or they tripped over one another as they tried to reach him.

'They are afraid of him,' said Folcwalda, 'and their fear makes them clumsy.'

He raised his sword. 'Stay together in a wedge. Use your spears to keep the *wealas* off. We go for the main door. *Now*!'

We vaulted the wall and trotted towards the house, our shields locked and our spears bristling. Two of the British tried to bar our way, but the wedge trampled them down.

We were perhaps halfway across the yard and I was frantically trying to decide whether to throw in my lot with Folcwalda or simply to slip away, when a great voice bellowed:

'Hold!'

My heart leaped within me at the sound. Sigebeorn had arrived at last, and with him a dozen or more of our people.

The wedge faltered as those of us at the rear turned towards the new threat.

'I am for Sigebeorn,' I muttered to Oswine, and I broke from my place and ran to the newcomers, holding my shield away from my body so they could see I was not making an attack.

'Oath-breaker!' somebody – it might have been poor Oswine – called after me. I ignored the taunt, for Beanstan and Hussa were pounding my back, welcoming me to their ranks.

Now Sigebeorn was speaking, stern for once, he who was usually so light-hearted.

'It is not Garulf who is the oath-breaker! We are the City

Guard of Lindinis, not the servants of savages. These people you attack entered the city openly through its gates, like men about their lawful business. Those you defend sneaked over the walls like thieves or housebreakers, hiding their dishonesty under the cover of darkness.

'Folcwalda! You are not fitted to lead us. Put up your sword. The rest of you, fall in with my men.'

For a moment it seemed it might work. Folcwalda's followers shuffled their feet, glanced nervously from one to the other. They had no stomach for fighting their comrades.

Then the son of Frodi gave his answer.

'Sigebeorn of the Secgan, your lust for power knows no end. I lead here, not you, and I carry out the will of the City Fathers. Like you, Arthur's men grow overproud. They must be shown they are not the masters here – as must you!'

Sigebeorn snarled and rushed at him, sword held high, hoping, I suppose, to end the quarrel quickly. Folcwalda sidestepped, launched a blow that sent pieces flying from the Secgan's shield. Sigebeorn staggered, and before he could recover the son of Frodi swung the giantish blade full into his torso, shearing through mail-rings and flesh alike. Sigebeorn fell to his knees. Folcwalda swung again, bringing the great sword down on the son of Sigeferth's unprotected head.

It was over so soon and so easily that the rest of us stood there gaping like fools.

Folcwalda straightened, sword dripping with blood.

'I lead the City Guard,' he said. 'Do any dare gainsay me?'

'Yes!' cried Beanstan, and he hurled a javelin at the big man.

Folcwalda swatted it aside with his shield, but it acted as a signal to the two groups. Within moments we were at each other's throats, pushing and shoving with spear and shield. I saw poor Oswine go down, the beard of which he was so proud slick with his own blood, while the press held Hussa upright at my side long after he had taken his death wound. At last the huddle fell apart into two lines of men leaning on their spears, exhausted by the struggle. In the churned snow between us lay several good warriors from both sides.

Most of the Northerners were down, and the handful still alive were trying to escape over the wall. The man who called himself mab Petroc was walking towards us, with Moried and a few others carrying torches beside him. In the red-gold light his face seemed tired and drawn, much older than when I had first seen him.

'Finished!' he shouted in our tongue. 'Is finished. Your weapons put away and go home in peace. Sigebeorn is with you?'

Nobody spoke. Then Folcwalda stepped into the space between the two lines and kicked one of the bodies.

'Here, *Weala*. He is here. I killed him myself. Would you join him?'

'Go home, Saeson,' mab Petroc said wearily. 'Go home.'

Folcwalda drew himself up to his full height, swinging the giantish blade back and forth so it keened and sang through the air.

'I *am* home.'

Mab Petroc's gloved hand dropped to the hilt of his own sword. Moried caught his arm, and for an instant they were frozen like figures in one of the god-paintings the Romans put upon their walls when the middle-earth was young.

The great sword rose and began to fall.

I do not believe Folcwalda intended any treachery. I believe his pride and anger had mastered him, and that he struck without thought.

Nor did I think. The warning that came from my mouth surprised me as much as it surprised everybody else.

At my cry mab Petroc shoved Moried aside, out of the sword's path. He drew his own blade, but he was caught wrong-footed, and when Folcwalda's heavy linden war-board banged into his ribs he gave ground, staggering, his feet slipping and sliding on the ice.

Remember, he was still without mail or leather coat, shieldless, with nothing save his sword to protect him from the son of Frodi's wrath. Remember also that he was tired, war weary, for alone he had borne the brunt of the Pictish attack. Then too, Folcwalda was a wily fighter, the veteran of many a hosting. He had dealt easily with Sigebeorn, himself no mean warrior.

So we watched, waiting for the son of Frodi to strike down the smaller man. The giantish blade hissed and howled as it sought its prey, struck sparks from the stones of the yard where it carved through the snow.

The fighters turned, circling in their search for victory. I saw Folcwalda's face, grim behind his war-board. Then I saw mab Petroc's face. He was laughing, alive with the joy of battle, and he was still laughing when he finished the fight with a single thrust that split asunder Folcwalda's war-coat and buried itself in his belly.

Mab Petroc twisted the blade and pulled it free, stepped back a pace. Folcwalda stood rocking on his feet, not believing he was dead, swaying like a stricken tree in a gale. Then he came crashing forward, as the oak comes crashing forward when the woodsman's axe bites deep, and hit the ground so hard it seemed to me it shook under the impact.

'Who shouted?' demanded mab Petroc.

His hair was matted with sweat and his chest was heaving, but to me – I was very young then – he seemed like a god, a god of battle, like great Tiw the warrior come to middle-earth.

My comrades drew aside, leaving a space around me.

He smiled. 'My thanks, guide.'

Moried, who would have died with his lord under Folcwalda's blade had I not cried warning, put an arm on his leader's shoulders. 'Your silver was well spent,' he said, urging mab Petroc towards the house.

'Not for that,' I protested to their backs as they walked away. 'Not for the silver. Never for that.'

Thirty years later the memory still burns within me – that Moried believed I had been bought.

3

'So?' said Ceolric, unable to wait any longer. 'Who was he? What happened to the leader of the Picts? Why were they after the people from Dyfed?'

'What was the scream that roused mab Petroc before the Picts launched their attack?' demanded someone else. 'Come, Garulf, you raise more questions than you answer.'

'Is that not the way of life here on middle-earth?'

'Who was mab Petroc?' repeated Ceolric.

Garulf smiled, a smile such as Sigebeorn the doomed Secgan must have given when asked the same question. For the first time Ceolric saw what his father did not like about the Frisian: a smug secretiveness, a way he had of hugging knowledge to himself. (And yet that was not fair – Garulf had not stinted in the lessons on navigation and ship-handling.)

'The answer lies in the tale. Think about it and you will see.' Garulf stretched and yawned. 'As to the rest, I do not know for sure. The Dyfed people had some treasure the tattooed men did not want in Arthur's hands, but what kind of treasure I cannot tell you.'

He drank from the horn again, his long-sighted seaman's gaze shifting from face to face around the fire.

'What I can tell you is this. Not long afterwards Arthur sailed north with a band of his most trusted Companions. He was gone for a while, so long that it was rumoured he was dead. When he came back men began to call him Emperor – Amherawdyr in the British tongue.'

There was a moment's silence, while the wind sifted the ashes of the fire and sent the smoke swirling around the cove. Above them the stars glittered and the waxing moon shone on the empty sea. A wolf howled, far away inland, and the men stilled to listen.

'Mab Petroc was like a god, you said, like Tiw himself.' Wicga spoke slowly, as if he had been thinking on this long and hard.

'I did,' agreed Garulf. 'That was how he looked to me after he slew Folcwalda Frodi's son.'

'Ah,' said Wicga, nodding to himself. The Frisian watched him with quiet amusement, and Ceolric watched them both, not understanding.

'Tell us about Camlann,' cried a voice.

'Aye, tell us of Camlann and Arthur's fall,' cried another.

The Frisian yawned and shook his head. 'Not tonight. I need my sleep, for we must wake early with the tide. Tomorrow, if you still wish it. Tomorrow I will tell you of Camlann.'

CHAPTER FOUR

Once his right hand had been renowned for its strength, famed for a grip fit to match with even Glewlwyd of the Mighty Grasp, who had been Arthur's Gatekeeper when the world was young.

(His left hand, of course, was a different matter.)

Looking at it now as he dragged himself back towards the hut was enough to make him weep. The blue veins stood out in knots; the pale flesh had fallen away from the bones, leaving the knuckles swollen and prominent. Even his wrist was thin and spindly.

He was an old man, and this bout of fever had come closer to killing him than he had realized.

The girl was waiting at the top of the slope, her hair burnished by the setting sun. When she saw his halting approach she ran flying down the hillside, and took his arm, letting him lean on her.

The scent of her filled his nostrils, sweet and wholesome, reminding him of summer evenings and the swallows swooping around the Great Hall of Caer Cadwy.

She was talking, cajoling him into taking the next step, scolding him for having walked too far, but he was not listening, lost in his dream of the past . . .

'Budoc! Let us sit and rest.'

The urgency of her voice, her hands pressing on his shoulders (thin and bony, the muscle wasted away by his illness), all of it was happening a long way off, at the far end of a long dark tunnel.

'Eurgain,' he said suddenly. He blinked, and the world sprang back into place around him. 'My dear child.'

He looked around him, recognizing the gorse bushes as those which clustered around the hollow where the hut lay.

'I went to the wood,' he said in explanation.

'Mmm,' she said disapprovingly and frowned, her expression intent as she studied him with all the seriousness of the professional surgeons who had served Arthur and the Army of Albion, her gaze travelling from his head to his feet and back again. His lips began to twitch.

'Why are you laughing?' she demanded suspiciously.

'Because I am alive,' he said, and he could hear the wonder in his voice because it was true; he was alive, and he was glad.

She watched him uncertainly, and then seeing the joy in his face she let her own composure fall away and herself dissolved into laughter.

'Thank you for your many kindnesses,' he said after a while, wiping his eyes with the hem of his tunic. 'Will you thank your sister for me as well when you go home? Without the two of you, I think I might have died.'

Eurgain nodded, then flushed bright red right to the roots of her hair. 'It was our mother. She told us to come.'

'I dare say she did,' he said calmly. 'But the care the two of you gave me when I lay helpless and burning with fever, that was your own, given freely and not of another's bidding.'

'Ah well . . .' She plucked at the grass, embarrassed.

'I am truly grateful,' he said gently.

They sat in companionable silence, savouring the last of the sunlight and the breeze blowing in across the clifftops from the sea, the crash of the waves on the one side of them and the hiss of the trees on the other.

'In my fever,' he said, 'did I call out?'

'Yes, often. You thought Dyfyr and I were somebody else. And you kept talking to people we could not see.'

'Did I use any names?'

She tugged at a stray lock of hair, wrinkled her face in thought. 'Many names. Hawk was one.' She spun the strands around her finger. 'No, I cannot remember.'

'Teleri? Did I mention Teleri?'

'Yes!' She clapped her hands in triumph. 'That was who you

thought we were.' She glanced sideways at him. 'Was she your wife?'

'No.'

She flinched at the stark denial, fearing she had offended him by asking too personal a question. He saw the movement, remembered she was very young, softened and added:

'Had things been different she might have been, I think.'

CHAPTER FIVE

1

Eremon mac Cairbre, close now, so close to all he had desired
these past five years, watched the spindrift floating past the
bow of the curragh, then turned to study the jut of the
cliffs.

His glance fell upon the man in the bird mask huddled by the
steering paddle. Had he been right to throw the Pict overboard?
Should he have kept Vortepor's guide with him at least until they
had landed?

He laughed aloud.

Vortepor's spy.

He had known there was something strange about the Pict with
the spiral tattoos from the moment he had first seen him sitting
alone in Vortepor's hall between the warband and the local
farmers, shunned by both. (Just as the man in the bird mask
was shunned by his crew.)

He had known too that for all his vaunted cunning Vortepor
had made a mistake if he thought Eremon would allow a Pictish
spy to interfere with his plans.

The cliffs were drawing closer. One more major headland
and they would be in the final sweeping bay with its
yellow sands, almost within touching distance of their destina-
tion.

He did not need Vortepor of Dyfed.

He did not need anybody or anything except his curraghs and his crews.

Vortepor . . .

2

He was a fat man, Vortepor of Dyfed, with small hard eyes almost lost in the sags and creases of his face. His breathing was heavy and raw, shallow in his lungs, and the perspiration glistened on his olive skin as he forced his ungainly body to cover the few paces from the stuffy hall to the bench outside that looked across the valley with its orchard to the haze of the sea beyond.

Two guards walked at his side, ready to catch an arm if he should stumble. They were strong men and well built, but Eremon following a few paces behind wondered whether even their muscles would be enough to arrest the fat man's fall once it had begun.

Vortepor collapsed onto the bench, puffing and wheezing, and raised his face to the late afternoon sun. The two-toned cry of a buzzard rang in challenge across the heavens, holding and fading on the second note. Somewhere behind them a cock crowed.

'You came,' said the fat man. The wind ruffled his thin white hair, a breeze filled with the scent of apples and new-mown hay underlain with the tang of the sea.

Eremon nodded. 'I hold your son hostage for my safety.'

'I have many sons,' said Vortepor. His voice was pitched higher than one would expect from such a squat and fleshy shape, pitched to carry across a crowded hall. It was a performer's voice, a trained voice: an unnatural voice.

A cold fist thrust within Eremon's chest. However fast he moved he could not escape from this place alive, but if he were quick enough he could strike with the heel of his hand to the base of that heavy nose, driving it up into the fat man's forehead before the guards sank their blades into . . .

'There is no need. If I wanted you dead you would be dead.'

The fat man was smiling, his teeth yellow and broken, worn down like those of an old dog.

'Sit you,' he urged, patting the bench beside him. 'Fetch us wine, then leave us,' he said to the bodyguards.

Cautiously Eremon eased himself onto the bench, the thick

66

slate cold against the backs of his thighs. Though he overtopped the older man by a full head or more he felt small and puny beside his bulk. He could smell him too: the odour of stale wine and old sweat partially disguised by a sweet and sickly perfume.

'If I wanted you dead you would be dead,' Vortepor repeated with a hint of satisfaction.

'What then? What do you want?'

'I want your help.'

Eremon looked around him, at the neat orchards running down to the sea, at the fields on the sides of the hill, up at the eaves of the hall above his head – and this estate was among the least of the Lord of Dyfed's personal holdings.

'Mine?' he said, putting all his doubts into the single word.

'Yours,' said Vortepor, accepting the beaker of wine offered by one of the guards, and waving the man away with a pudgy hand on which rings glittered like cold fire.

'Yours, because of who you are and what has happened to you.' Eremon heard the creak of the wooden armrest as the heavy form slumped lower.

'As to who you are: you were born the heir to Cairbre of the Hundred Battles. You were born Eremon of the Eoganacht Maigi Dergind i nAlbae, Eremon of the lands of the Children of Eogan in the Plain of the River Oak in the island of Albion.' The words rolled from the fat man's tongue like an incantation. 'Your ancestors came to this land in the days of Gworthigern the Thin, who called himself High King of Prydein, just as mine came a generation or so earlier at the behest of the Emperor Magnus Maximus, whom men call Macsen Wledig.'

Eremon smiled to himself, for this was not the version of the tale he had heard.

'But whatever you were born, now you have nothing.'

The smile vanished from Eremon's face as the heavy head turned in his direction. He could see the large pores in the unhealthy skin, dimpled with sweat, and the ancient scars of youthful acne stretched and distorted by the flesh the man had gained over the years.

'I have my ship and her crew,' he snarled.

'And you eke out a precarious existence as a pirate and a raider along the coasts and creeks of Britain. A young man's game, and though you are still young, the years pass, Eremon mac Cairbre, the years pass faster than you can imagine at your age.'

Eremon swallowed, stared at the cluster of old craters along Vortepor's jawline where a few grey whiskers sprouted that had escaped the barber's razor.

'When you are my age – if you live so long, which is doubtful – you will be too old to spend half your time afloat and the rest battling for plunder. Then you will wish you still had your lands beside the River Oak.'

'Already there is not a day that I do not wish that,' Eremon said quietly.

'And do you curse yourself for a fool for losing them? Be honest!'

'Ye . . . es,' he admitted reluctantly. He hesitated, pulled at the long braid dangling over his shoulder, twisted the yellow hair round and between his fingers. 'What do you want of me?' he demanded.

Vortepor belched loudly. The mound of his belly shook with the force of the eructation, and one heavy arm rose to pat his chest (lost somewhere within the shapeless heap of his slumped body). The loose flesh of his forearm quivered as the sleeve of his tunic slipped back to the elbow. Fingers fiddled with the ornate buckle of his belt, heaved titanically to draw in the leather band and release the pin. The belt came free, and the great bulk subsided with a sigh of relief.

'I want to talk with you. A while ago, when you thought you had entered a trap, that I would be content to trade my son's life for yours, you debated killing me.'

Eremon tugged at his braid, the hair coarse and harsh under his fingers.

'You have a falcon's proud eyes, with madness burning in their depths,' said the fat man. It sounded like a remark he had made before, to someone else.

The breeze sifted the dust where countless feet had worn away the ground around the bench, parted and combed the grass, set the leaves of the apple trees dancing in the long light of late afternoon.

'There was a man once, called Lleminawg, who was one of Arthur's Companions,' Vortepor said.

'My father's older brother,' said Eremon.

'Yes,' said Vortepor. 'How much of your family history do you know?'

Eremon contemplated his thumb, chewed a piece of dead skin from the quick, spat it out. 'Not much.'

'And what do you know of the past sixty years?'

He shrugged. 'Very little. What the bards sing.' He assumed a sing-song voice in imitation of the less successful storytellers. '*Once upon a time there was a king who was wise and noble and good* . . . Tales for children. Beyond that, nothing.'

The fat man hauled himself upright on the seat and drank greedily from his beaker, spraying a shower of droplets to join the drying stains on his tunic.

'I hated him,' said Vortepor. 'Hated him from the first time I saw him, hated him with a fierceness that was all the stronger for being in a sense quite unwarranted.'

'Who?'

'Arthur. The Amherawdyr. Arthur the Battle Emperor of Britain.'

'Why?'

The fat man wiped his face, smearing the beads of moisture across the oily skin. 'I saw him first three years after the battle of Badon Hill, where he crushed the Saesons in the culmination of a hundred years' constant fighting.'

Vortepor's stomach rumbled. The fat man shifted his position on the bench. 'These are crude and barbarous times.' He coughed, belched loudly, massaged his belly. 'Every petty lordling with an armed following styles himself *Brenhin*, or *Rex* if he has in his service a priest who writes Latin. We adopt the customs of the Irish and give ourselves titles the more grandiose for their lack of meaning. We resemble the Sacsons, who do the same thing, calling themselves *King* or *Ealdorman* if they have three armed retainers. Titles to appease our vanity!' He hawked and spat a gob of green phlegm.

Eremon frowned, not following him.

'I have been High Lord of Dyfed for nearly twenty-five years,' said the fat man with fresh animation. 'Now I grow old, and enemies are all around me. To the south, across the Severn Sea, Custennin of Dumnonia flexes newly found muscles. To the north, Maelgwn the Tall sits in the Isle of Mona expanding the web his father wove across the mainland, forcing his unruly kinsmen, the heirs of Cunedda, to admit his supremacy. Custennin and Maelgwn are young men, ambitious men, recent heirs to well-established fathers. And I am caught between them, I who have acknowledged no superior since Arthur fell at Camlann.'

Eremon shook his head. 'I do not understand. What has this to do with me?'

'There is nobody I can trust.' The jowls sagged, writhed with a life of their own. 'My kinsmen harbour ambitions of their own. My sons wait for me to die, that they may quarrel over my carcase.' The small eyes blinked. 'Do you know how Lleminawg died?'

'Lleminawg? No . . .' A faint memory from childhood came to him: lying beside a warm hearth in a dark and draughty space while adult voices rumbled overhead. 'It was after Badon, I think. The Emperor went north to the Western Isles, the Iardomnan, to destroy a nest of pirates, and Lleminawg was killed in the fighting.'

'In those days Arthur did not call himself Emperor. It was not until *after* your uncle's death that Arthur claimed sovereignty over all Prydein. Until then he took no title save that of war-leader, Magister Militum per Britannias, like Ambrosius before him.'

'I do not understand.'

'No, why should you? You are the child of these ignorant and fragmentary times, in which, as I said, every petty lordling calls himself a ruler of men. While Arthur was at war he did not need a title. It was only after he had defeated the Saesons he dreamed of being Emperor. The poets, the praise singers, had taken to calling him *Amherawdyr llywiaudir llawur*, by which they meant no more than that he ruled the battle – both in the sense of leading the war host of Prydein and in the sense of being always victorious.'

'In a way it was my fault.' The baggy, swollen features creased anew. 'Arthur had won the war, and now he needed some means of winning the peace. Who wants a warlord when the war is over? Not the Princes of Prydein, I can assure you. They would happily have gone back to their long and bloody rivalry from which the struggle against the Saesons had been no more than a brief respite, a mere interlude in the battle to determine which of them should replace Gworthigern the Thin as the pre-eminent power in the island.

'By accident I set Arthur on the road to mastery.'

He blotted the sweat from his brow with the loose fabric of one sleeve.

'I was used, of course, used by others more cunning than myself. And I thought I was so clever! Ah well, I was young then.'

The mountainous form heaved, the bench creaking under its weight. One of the guards, who had remained nearby though out of earshot, leaped forward to help, but Vortepor waved him aside. The crumpled face tautened, a pulse beat wildly at the temple, and the tendons sprang to prominence through the sagging flesh of the neck. The stumpy legs fought for balance and found it, the feet turning outwards to brace against the pull of the belly, and the body rocked back and forth while the chest heaved for air.

'Come,' said Vortepor – or so Eremon interpreted the sound, though it might have been no more than part of the battle for breath.

The body rocked forward to the point where it seemed it must fall, and the legs moved to compensate. Suddenly Vortepor was walking, alone and unaided, taking tiny steps at great speed like a man demented, his face a mask of concentration. Eremon was hard put not to laugh at the sight, though at the same time he recognized what a feat of strength and will it was for a creature so gross to move at all.

Vortepor halted by the entrance, clutching the door posts while he let his eyes adapt to the gloom. Eremon waited beside him, not knowing whether he should offer an arm as a prop.

'Lleminawg died that Arthur might become Emperor,' said Vortepor. 'Your uncle was sacrificed to further another man's ambition.' The black eyes glared at Eremon, daring him to challenge the statement. 'What do you think of that?' The question snapped like whiplash.

Eremon shrugged lazily. 'It was a long time ago, before I was born. They are all dead now, the Companions of Arthur. What does it matter why they died?'

'Are they all dead? Are you certain?' A thin trickle of saliva ran from the corner of Vortepor's mouth, dangled like a spider on its line, lengthened and broke away to fall into the dust.

'If any were still alive they would be very old by now.' As soon as he had spoken he remembered that they need not be any older than his host, and some might have been younger. 'Besides, the best of them fell before Camlann,' he added in an attempt to redeem himself. 'Cei, the Long Man, died years before the end. Gwalchmei the Hawk was killed in a skirmish in Gwent. Gereint the Older was slain at Llongborth.'

'Yes, yes,' Vortepor said impatiently. 'I know the tales as well as you, if not better. For years every wandering bard has regaled me with episodes from the Emperor's life.' His expression changed, became cunning. 'They do not sing to me of Camlann.

They do not sing to me of the Emperor's death, because they know I had a hand in it.'

He chuckled, his body rocking back and forth in time with his laughter until he had gathered enough momentum to totter across the hall in his curious splay-footed shuffle.

Eremon followed, puzzled, for he had never heard that Vortepor had played any part in Medraut's rebellion. Although Lleminawg and Gereint the Older had died before he was born, while Cei and Gwalchmei had fallen during his childhood when he was too young to care about such distant far-off things, the great battle of Camlann had taken place in the year he reached manhood. He could still remember the disbelief with which they had heard the news that Arthur was gone – Arthur who had always been there, Arthur the rock on which the petty intrigues of the lesser lords had broken and dissolved away like so much harmless froth, Arthur the centre and linchpin of Albion.

And he could remember no mention of Vortepor or Dyfed, which had been at that time a marginal place on the western edge of Britain. (Things had changed since: with the collapse of the centre, the margins had assumed an importance they had never before known, until Vortepor could justly claim to be one of the most powerful rulers in the south and west.)

Which made him wonder how far he could trust the old man's recollections.

Vortepor quick-shuffled the length of the hall till he came to the great seat at the far end: a massive throne made from heavy slabs of oak, decorated with stiff and lifeless carvings of the beasts of the chase.

He lowered himself into it while one retainer placed a cushion behind his back and another fussed with the seat covering. After a time his breathing came under control, and he began to fiddle with one of the pegs in the joint between the arms of the throne and its base.

'It comes apart,' he said. 'I take it with me wherever I go, now that I am too heavy for lesser furniture.' He wheezed laughter, his eyes vanishing inside the folds of flesh, then suddenly sobered and shouted:

'Fetch him a seat! Christ on the Cross! Must the Protector's guest stay standing till dusk?'

A slave darted forward with a folding stool and placed it in front of the throne.

Eremon sat and waited. He could hear the swallows and martins feeding outside, shrieking and chattering as they swooped around the hall, and further away, so faint the sounds seemed almost ghostly, the clatter of the cooks preparing food.

Vortepor had called him his guest, which in some places would have meant his safety was assured. But he had no faith in the fat man's hospitality – any more than he would have had in his own had positions been reversed – and though the Lord of Dyfed seemed friendly enough at present, he guessed the man's mood could change very quickly.

'I want you to find something for me,' Vortepor said after a time. 'It would be of no use to you, though it is of great value to me. If you succeed, I will reward you with lands of your own in Dyfed and a place in my warband.'

'And if I fail?'

The fat man waved a pudgy hand. 'Even if you fail, I might still reward you.' He slumped deeper in the throne, merging into the shadows so his high voice seemed disembodied.

'Three years after Badon I visited Arthur's court for the first time. My father, Agricola Protector of Demetae, Aircol Long-hand of Dyfed in the vernacular, was a man renowned for his loyalty to the old ways. You know the tale of my ancestors? You know why we Dyfed lords are called *Protector*?'

Eremon nodded, but either Vortepor did not see the gesture or else he chose to ignore it.

'When the Spaniard Magnus Maximus, Macsen Wledig, de-nuded Britain of troops to fight the usurper in Rome, he knew Dyfed would be lost unless he found strong arms to defend it in his absence. My ancestor Eochaid mac Artchorp, chieftain of the Dessi of Ireland, was the mightiest of the pirates then raiding the shores of Dyfed, so Macsen Wledig thought to set a thief to catch a thief, and gave to him the Lordship of Dyfed, binding his loyalty with great oaths and still greater gifts. Macsen took Eochaid's sons with him as part of his bodyguard, and thus they were awarded the title of Protector, which was a very great honour and a sign of the trust the Emperor Maximus placed in them.'

Eremon had heard they were nothing more than hostages for their father's good behaviour, whatever fancy titles Macsen might have given them to ease the hurt. Still, to be fair, it would not be the only time hostages had adopted their holder's cause so thoroughly that both sides forgot the original reason for their presence. It was said that Gwalchmei had first gone to Arthur's court as a hostage, but by the time of his death he was among the Amherawdyr's most trusted friends.

'Over the years we proved our worth. For a hundred years we stayed loyal to whatever central power remained in Britain. First Vitolinus of Glevum, who called himself High King, the man remembered as Gworthigern the Thin. He it was who first invited the Saesons into Britain, just as Macsen invited my ancestors and with much the same motive.'

'But Hengist was too clever for him.'

The rings glittered in the gloom as the old man waved a hand. 'It was complicated. We were busy here in the west fighting the depredations of the Scotti pirates out of Ireland – plunderers like yourself, Eremon mab Cairbre. What happened in the east was no concern of ours.'

He spoke as if he himself had been there, which was impossible. Although Eremon's grasp of events was vague, he knew Vortepor must be describing things that had happened a hundred years or more ago. At times he found the old man hard to follow: Vortepor's British had an accent quite unlike that of Dumnonia where he himself had been raised, and the fat man liberally sprinkled his speech with Latinisms, words whose meaning Eremon had to guess.

'Then the house of Ambrosius came to the fore. We supported them, sent them troops we could ill afford to spare from our own battle with the Scotti. At that time the Lords of Prydein stood united, ranged against the common enemy, but as the years passed it became obvious the Saesons were too numerous ever to be expelled entirely from the island. The eastern Lords came to accept their new neighbours, to make alliances with them in pursuit of old feuds – '

'You mean that at one time the British hoped to drive the Saesons overseas?' interrupted Eremon, interested in spite of himself.

'Certainly.'

'But Arthur never tried it?'

'No. In his day the best we could hope for was to confine them to their territories in the east.' Eremon saw the flash of yellow teeth in the shadowy mass on the throne as the old man grinned. 'Besides, there were Saesons who fought *for* the Amherawdyr, just as there were British who fought *against* him.'

Eremon whistled softly. 'I did not know that.'

'No. It is something the bards do not mention in their pretty songs. But then there is much the bards do not mention in their songs of battle.'

The younger man nodded, remembering how sick he had been after his first skirmish, vomiting till he thought his heart would come up. (But that was long ago, before he had discovered the pleasures to be found in another's suffering.)

'At all events, my father Agricola continued to support Arthur, accepting him as heir to Ambrosius. We made many sacrifices in order that the Warlord might have troops from Dyfed at his side when he fought his nine great battles. After Badon, when the Saesons were defeated once and for all, it seemed not unreasonable to us that some payment might be made for those sacrifices.'

'Payment?' said Eremon.

'We had helped the Lowlands against the Saesons. Now we wanted help ourselves against the Scotti who raided our coasts.' Vortepor let loose a great wheeze of air in a long sigh. 'And of course we feared our neighbours to the north, the Sons of Cunedda, an ambitious clan. My father was ageing and I was his heir, but you know how vulnerable a kingdom becomes at the time when power passes from one generation to another. Some sign of Arthur's support would protect me from their predations when my father died.'

Eremon shifted uncomfortably on the stool. It was stuffy in the hall, despite the open doors behind him.

'You want to know what this has to do with you,' said Vortepor, seeing the movement. 'Be patient, and you will understand.'

'My men will begin to worry if I do not return soon,' said Eremon. 'They did not trust your offer of safe conduct.'

'Despite my sending a son for them to hold against your return?'

Eremon shrugged expressively in reply.

'Send them a message.' Vortepor's tone was dismissive. 'You must have agreed some code, some secret word or phrase, which would let them know you remain here of your own free will.'

The younger man grinned in acknowledgement. 'I did.'

Vortepor clapped his hands. Suddenly the hall came to life around them as Eremon's message was recited and memorized, and directions were given for the finding of the ship and the manner in which it must be approached to avoid precipitating the execution of the prince who was a hostage.

By the time this business had been completed the servants and slaves had prepared the hall for the evening's feast. The long trestle tables had been dragged from their places by the wall, and the benches and couches drawn out from their daytime storage. The tapers were lit, casting a soft glow over the shabby building, showing it at its best. Vortepor's warband and the workers on the estate strode or shuffled in from outside to find their seats. A procession of servitors carried a variety of dishes in from the kitchens, while others poured mead or ale into the waiting vessels of wood and horn and glass.

All the while the noise grew louder and louder, as the warriors in the middle of the hall laughed and drank and ate. Only down by the still open doors was it quieter, for there sat the farmers, craftsmen and labourers who lived and worked on the estate, and they were cowed into silence by the proximity of the rough and boastful warband which they saw no more than once or twice a year, when Vortepor made his rare visits.

Sitting at the High Table, at the right-hand side of the Protector – the place of an honoured guest – Eremon felt a twinge of nostalgia for the time when he too had eaten every night in a civilized hall. Not since the disastrous series of events which had resulted in his exile had he dined in the company of a Christian – or nominally Christian – lord and his retinue.

The last few summers he had spent at sea, eking out a precarious existence raiding and pillaging the western and southern shores of Britain – an area which had been so thoroughly looted over the last two centuries that there was very little left worth having within easy reach of the sea. The winters he had spent in Ireland with his distant cousins – never the same one twice – bartering what little wealth he had amassed during the raiding season for the safety of a hall in which to sleep while the wind wailed and the wolves howled outside.

It was the long winters he hated the most. Despite his ancestry, despite the blood of Irish kings which ran pure and unsullied in his veins, he was not a true Irishman, not to the inhabitants of Ierne. To them he was a halfbreed, a renegade Briton, a foreigner from over the water: one of the Cruithne, which was what they called the inhabitants of the neighbouring isle.

Yet to the British he had always been an Irishman, one of the Scotti, an interloper in their midst.

To both groups he was a stranger. At least in Britain he had been a person of some importance, before the series of events which had led to his exile. In Ireland he was an importunate beggar who appeared with the autumn gales, a beggar whose limited wealth was based almost entirely upon the slave trade – because for all the fine talk of gold cups and gold rings, the most common booty from his raids was not treasure of a material kind, but captives whose bodies could be used for work or sex.

He looked around the hall. Vortepor's retainers were richly dressed in gold and purple robes that he could not help comparing with his own sea-stained garments, almost colourless with age. Most of them were bedecked with jewellery, with rings and arm bands and brooches, while his own fingers and arms were bare of all ornament, and his cloak was held in place by a bronze brooch from which all the gilt had long since vanished.

Scanning the long tables Eremon could see only one person who did not seem to belong with either the warband or the local community. This person sat in the no-man's-land between the two groups, eating hungrily with his head bowed, ignoring the noise around him.

'Who is that?'

Vortepor glanced up from his food, chin shiny with grease. 'The one by himself?' He drank, belched enormously. 'He is a Pict.'

Eremon frowned, toyed with a slice of venison. 'What is he doing this far south?' he asked when it was clear no more was to be forthcoming.

The fat man laughed. 'There were Picts in this tale from the very beginning,' he said. 'Listen, and I will tell you of my first meeting with Arthur. Then perhaps you will understand.'

3

I was not always fat (said Vortepor, while his warband feasted around them). Though of a stocky build, in my younger days I was agile enough to be no mean warrior. For five years I captained my father Agricola's warband, leading it out against the Scotti pirates who came raiding our shores.

At first those raidings seemed random, but more and more often we found ourselves in the wrong place, lured there by a feint, while a fleet descended on some unprotected part of our coast.

Soon we came to realize there was an intelligence behind these attacks, that the disunited bands had found themselves a leader who plotted the timing and disposition of their assaults.

I told you my father was a loyal man. All his life he kept the faith, like his ancestors before him, with whatever central power remained in Britain, balancing the local needs of Dyfed with the needs of the island as a whole.

Then came the news of the great victory of Badon Hill. At first we did not dare hope. The savages had been defeated before, yet always after a year or two they regrouped and began again their relentless drive for mastery of the rich lowlands.

Gradually, as the months passed and the Saesons remained pent in their eastern reservations, or fell to fighting among themselves, we understood how momentous a defeat Badon had been.

(And it is true that from that day to this, thirty years later, the Saesons have stayed within the bounds ordained.)

My father and I took counsel together. By this time Agricola was past his prime, an old man worn down by the cares of kingship. Increasingly the responsibility for making decisions was mine, and I knew it would not be long before my father finally took the step he had been threatening for so long, and retired to a religious community, naming me Protector in his stead.

Although Arthur owed much to Agricola and Dyfed, he owed me personally nothing – if anything, he had reason to dislike me, since I had always argued against the sending of our best to die in his wars. So I had no reason to think he would assist me against my foes when I came to assume the Overlordship of Dyfed.

I needed Arthur's support to hold my throne against the machinations of the Sons of Cunedda in the north, a rapacious crew, ever eager to expand their influence.

But did Arthur need me? For months I pondered, trying to think of some way in which I could put the Warlord in my debt.

My father had long since given me this very estate as my own, a private place where I could practise the arts of governance in miniature, a preparation for the day when I would rule all Dyfed.

78

I used to hold court here – a small court, admittedly, but one unrivalled for the diversity and imagination of its entertainments.

Thirty years ago Britain was more civilized than now. It was also a safer place than it is now, despite the depredations of the Saesons. It was still possible for a bard to travel the length and breadth of the country without being set upon by thieves.

One such came to me, here in this hall, late in the winter of the third year after Badon, when the snow still lay thick in the mountains and few were out and travelling. This bard had been born on an island to the north and west of Britain, one of that long chain which protects the exposed flank of Prydein from the full wrath of the ocean. The Iardomnan, some name them: the Western Isles at the back of the world.

This island had since become the haunt of a great pirate and raider, who called himself a sea king: Hueil mab Caw. It was this Hueil who had united many of the disparate bands of Scotti adventurers under his command. The bard wanted me to lead a counter-raid upon the island, but to my mind it seemed wiser to travel in more strength than could be raised in Dyfed alone.

Those were strange waters, the waters of the Isles, dangerous and uncharted except by the native fishermen, prone to sudden tides and great races as the seas sweep through the narrow channels. Even with the bard to guide us, we would need skilled shipmen, and there were few such in Dyfed. Besides, one did not know how many men Hueil could summon to his aid. Those islands are close to the northern coasts of Ierne, and there have always been strong links between the two – just as Dyfed has always had strong links with southern Ierne.

So it seemed to me wiser to make an appeal to Arthur.

In retrospect, I realized that this was what the bard had wanted all along, to lure Arthur to the Iardomnan. But at the time it was also what I wanted, for by making an appeal I was both acknowledging the Warlord's superiority and signalling that I wished to continue the relationship my father had begun.

To succeed, our assault had to catch Hueil in his lair. We would need to strike at the very beginning of the sailing season, which meant there was not a moment to be lost.

With my father's permission I took a small party including the bard to seek Arthur's aid. We intended to go overland, east to the crossings over the Severn, then south and west to Caer Cadwy.

On the first day, before we had even left Dyfed, we were set upon by a force of tattooed men.

They caught us in a valley – I confess I was careless, being still in what I regarded as a safe region – and mauled us badly. We had no alternative but to return home, licking our wounds.

The attack made no sense to me. Tattooed men, Caledonii, Pehts, Picts – call them what you will, they had no quarrel with me or Dyfed that I knew about.

We roused out the warband under one of my brothers and put it to scouring the countryside. Meanwhile I sent messengers overland to Arthur, saying that I was coming, and took the gamble of hiring a ship to cross the Severn Sea. You know better than I how great a gamble it was, in late winter. Whatever God or gods there are must have been with us, for we had a brief spell of fine weather which did not break until after we had landed in Dumnonia.

Then we ran into trouble. We traded horses from one of the lords of the hill country and started riding. The blizzards began the next night, and we spent two days trapped in some nameless village with nothing to eat except what we were carrying. I have never been so cold.

At length the storms lessened and we were able to move again, but half a day's ride from the city of Lindinis the tattooed men ambushed us a second time. How they had found us was a mystery to me. Nor did I know what they wanted, except that it seemed to involve killing us all. Somehow we fought them off, and limped into Lindinis at nightfall, in the teeth of another blizzard.

To my relief Arthur had sent an escort to meet us, led by a man who called himself mab Petroc.

Mab Petroc quartered us in the upper storey of an old house, while his own men kept watch at ground level. This upper level was cold and damp, the plaster falling from the walls, the timbers black and brown with age. There was mould growing in the corners, and one had to be very careful where one put one's feet on the rotten floorboards.

We had a single brazier to keep us warm. Although the men had managed to find some wood in the outbuildings, it was not enough to keep the fire going all night, and the flames soon sank to a dull red glow.

I rolled myself into my cloak and curled up on a clean part of the floor, but I had gone beyond the point of being able to sleep.

Even as a boy I had not liked old cities, and as a man I hated them. In the country, I knew an owl, a wolf or a fox, the wind in the trees, but in the city every rusty hinge and loose roof tile sounded like an army quietly surrounding the house.

This night was worse than most. It was unlikely the City Governor would allow anything to happen to Arthur's men and an embassy from Dyfed, not if he valued his future, but there were always hotheads eager to make themselves a reputation, even this close to Caer Cadwy.

And then there were the Picts, somewhere out there in the night. They had tried twice. If their purpose was to prevent us reaching Arthur, they did not have long in which to try again, for we would be with him by midday tomorrow at the latest.

I drifted into an uneasy nightmare in which the wind unpeeled the roof like the skin from a hazel wand, and cold snow blew inside to cover me deep under a wet cold blanket that muffled my cries for help. Then I fell again into a long drifting dream in which the wind howled around the cold house where I slept with my companions, waiting for the dawn.

The scream echoed through my dream, flung me bolt upright reaching for my sword. I was halfway across the room before the others had begun to move, freeing the blade from its sheath with a flick of the wrist that sent the wooden scabbard spinning into a corner.

The sentry turned at my approach, shaking his head.

'It was nothing, my lord Vortepor. The bard was having a nightmare.'

I realized he was right, that the scream had come from within the room. Old Fingal was already trying to comfort the bard, who was sitting up, still swathed in a heavy travelling cloak and hood. A series of long deep notes echoed from the walls. None of us could believe those sounds were coming from a human throat.

It is said that Cadwy, the great hero of the eastern Dumnonians from the time before the coming of the Romans, the hero who gave his name to so many places in the south-western parts of Prydein, once faced a host of warriors and druids with only a small band of companions. Undaunted by the odds against him, he gave voice to three great shouts. The first broke his opponents' weapons in their hands. The second reduced their chariots to kindling and unhitched the horses. The third slew every one of the druids stone dead where they stood.

Until that night I had never believed this story.

There was an antique tumbler I used to take with me on long journeys, a pretty thing of thick green glass with bubbles of air trapped inside it. I had placed it on a ledge near where I slept, filled with water lest I felt thirsty after the wine I had drunk before coming to bed. It began to resonate with the sounds, giving back a low-pitched hum.

By now somebody was beating on the outside of the door, but none of us could tear our gaze from the green glass.

Suddenly the glass shattered, spraying fragments and liquid across the room.

It was as if we had been released from a nightmare. The bard lay down again, seemingly unaware of the excitement. I found my shield while the others armed themselves, and then I would have flung open the door and sallied forth to join the fight, had Fingal not restrained me.

'Steady, Vortepor, steady,' he said, his white beard red in the light of the dying fire. 'We have fought long and hard once already this day. Let Arthur's men carry some of the burden. Time enough for us to join them if we are needed.'

Reluctantly, I admitted the wisdom of his words. The Picts wanted to prevent me reaching the Warlord. To thwart them, all I needed to do was stay alive, and that was best achieved by keeping out of the battle.

I peered through the rickety shutters overlooking the court-yard. The yard was covered with snow, and a handful of torches sputtered yellow and red against the white where they had been tossed aside. The moon flitted through thin wisps of cloud, casting a cold light on the scene.

The leader of Arthur's men, the one who called himself mab Petroc, had dashed out into the middle of the Picts. Clearly the man was either mad or in the grip of a death-wish.

I am not greatly interested in swords and war-knives and shields, in techniques of fighting. But, as I told you, I had trained as a warrior, and had become proficient enough to lead my father's warband without making a fool of myself.

So while I cannot claim that I was ever a great warrior, I was sufficiently knowledgeable to appreciate what was happening down below.

He was slaughtering them.

He moved like a poem with not a syllable displaced, not a line out of balance – with perfect rhythm, purposeful and unhurried.

He had no shield, no armour, no protection at all, and he made it look effortless.

I suppose one tends to think of great warriors as being big men, like Cei or Arthur himself – or you, come to that. But mab Petroc was of average height, no more. He was well muscled, sinewy, but not excessively so. Yet every blow he struck sheered through flesh and bone as if it had a giant's power behind it. His timing was perfect.

All the same, I think it was his own death rather than that of his enemies which he sought in the weapon play. While I watched, a group of Saesons climbed over the wall and looked to join the fray on the side of the Picts. A second group followed – these I recognized as mercenaries employed by the citizens of Lindinis to guard their gates – and after the usual exchange of speeches these Saesons always seem to need to nerve themselves to combat, they fell to fighting each other.

By now the Picts were finished, either dead or in flight. Mab Petroc and a few others strolled over to the newcomers, and before I could blink he was engaging the largest of them in single combat – quite unnecessarily, so far as I could see.

He killed him, of course.

In the morning we rode for Caer Cadwy.

Arthur had built it himself, and for that reason he favoured it above all his other fortresses, so that when one thinks of him one thinks of him in the Great Hall there, holding court with his warband and their ladies all around him.

I knew what it looked like, of course: everybody did. I had heard tell of the hump-backed hill towering above the surrounding plain like a whale breaking the surface of the sea. I knew the hill had been fortified since time immemorial by a series of ramparts and ditches following the contours of its steep sides. I knew that from the summit one could see for miles in every direction except the east, where rolling hills formed the limit of the plain. People had told me of what it was to look to the north-west, where the great landmark of Ynis Witrin was clearly visible, rising from the lagoons and sea marshes like the breast of a goddess, with the inlets of the Severn Channel shining in the distance beyond, and they had described to me how it was to stand with the wind in one's face, gazing south and east across the great vale of Lindinis to the Durotrigian hills in the background.

As a defensive site its advantages were obvious. It was also strategically well placed: neither so close to the debatable lands that it would be in constant danger, nor so far distant that its garrison could not march to quell any threats.

Arthur had rebuilt the innermost rampart. First his engineers raised a dry-stone wall above the old bank, braced by great timbers. Then they added a wooden breastwork with an inner walkway, tying it to the timber frame of the wall, so that from the outside one was faced with sheer battlements, but on the inside the defenders could move easily from one place to another. The finished wall stood several times the height of a man, and was some twelve hundred paces in length, enclosing an enormous area.

These defences were pierced by two gates, one in the south-west corner and one in the north-east. Above each was reared a mighty tower, modelled on those of the great northern Wall which the Romans built to keep out the barbarian Picts, so the road ran under the tower in a kind of tunnel through the rampart.

Within the walls was a small city filled with craftsmen and skilled workers – whitesmiths and blacksmiths and armourers; potters and weavers and leatherworkers; carpenters and masons; jewellers and doctors – besides the warriors themselves with their grooms, servants and families. The surrounding countryside was filled with farmers raising grain for the horses and food for the fortress, secure in the knowledge that their lands lay under the protection of Arthur's Companions.

It sounds impressive, yes?

It was. Believe me, it was, especially when you saw it full of life and bustle as I did. The rich cloaks of the warriors, the fine horses prancing up the main street, the creak of carts laden with produce, the smell of cooking fires . . .

I have no idea what it is like today. I would imagine the walls are crumbling back into the ground, that nettles and weeds have filled the ditches, that the roofs have fallen in and the wind and the rain have begun the work of decay.

After all, it is ten years since anybody lived there.

They say Gwenhwyvar waited on the battlements for news of the fight at Camlann, and when word came that though Arthur had once again defeated his enemies he himself had fallen in the last charge, she came down from the ramparts, looking neither to right nor left, and rode away through the great gates into the dusk of evening, and no man ever knew where she went or what became of her . . .

But I digress. At the time of which I speak all that lay nearly twenty years in the future.

I remember how we rode across the cold and barren landscape, the ice crackling under the horses' hooves, the snow lying thin and pocked across the plain, the weariness deep into my bones as if I had not slept at all the previous night, feeling naked and exposed under the great grey arch of the sky.

We rode in pairs. All of us were wary, half expecting an ambush to burst from behind each bush, and I noticed that some of mab Petroc's men rode with javelins at the ready in their gloved hands.

It was an open road, slightly raised on an embankment, running straight and true across the flat land, and from the tracks and ruts on the broken surface of the road it was obvious this route must be well travelled, even in winter, but there were no signs of people. The farmsteads were cleverly built to take advantage of the lie of the land or hidden behind windbreaks of trees, and with that gale blowing there were no telltale traces of smoke.

We were out of sight of the city walls when the hail began, otherwise I think we might have turned tail and fled for their dubious shelter. The great lumps stung our faces and made the ponies shy, rattled against our slung shields and rebounded from the stones of the road.

'We must find shelter,' shouted mab Petroc, and pointed to a low hillock crowned with slim black trees a bowshot to our right. The company broke for the meagre cover.

'Perhaps we should have waited a while in Lindinis,' muttered Fingal, dismounting stiffly and stamping his feet to bring them back to life. He peered angrily at the road, at the white ice gathered in the ruts, then stared out across the flat countryside with its thin covering of snow.

'The fleas would have eaten us alive,' I said. 'Besides, it did not seem to me a restful place.'

'Why such haste?' mab Petroc plucked at the fabric of his own cloak, drew it tighter around him.

'We seek Arthur's aid before the Scotti begin to raid our coasts again with the coming of spring,' said Fingal, beating his arms against his sides in an attempt to get warm.

'Besides,' I added, 'there is one among us who insists we must not wait.'

Fingal scowled at me, but Mab Petroc followed the direction of my gaze. All save one of the embassy and the escort had followed our example and dismounted, gathering at a respectful distance. The solitary rider towered above the rest, shapeless in a grey robe, features muffled by a long hood.

'This is the one who knows where these pirates have their stronghold?' asked mab Petroc, speaking softly so we three alone could hear.

I nodded. 'Yes, and more than that. The bard claims to know many things which will be of interest to the Warlord of Prydein.'

The storm lessened and we rode on. I hunched into the saddle, my hands hidden inside their leather gauntlets, my face numb with cold. My mind drifted away, became concentrated on the road itself, which went on in the unnaturally straight way of roads built by the Romans. If one followed it for long enough one would come to Caer Vadon, which the Romans called Aquae Sulis, the Waters of Sul, and thence onwards across the width of Albion, running always to the north and east, until at last one would reach the Northern Sea beyond Lindum. This was a source of great wonder to me, then as now, how one might step out along a road and find oneself caught up in its going as in the current of a river, led on and on through the land to strange places of which one had never dreamed.

But in the meantime I was cold, and felt horribly exposed. The ground on either side had been growing steadily marshier for some time, and the embankment had gradually risen as its foundations thickened, so that now the road was raised up on a causeway several feet above the surrounding mire.

This part was in better repair: the mud and other muck that had accumulated on the surface had been scraped away and fresh gravel laid in the potholes, so the horses' hooves rang on stone as they had not done for several miles.

'Soon we turn south,' called mab Petroc, his voice loud in the emptiness.

A low range of irregular hills filled the southern horizon, much closer than they seemed. One among them loomed higher and more massive than the rest: I could see the shapes of the buildings on its summit, and the dark line of a track winding through the snow-covered embankments.

'Caer Cadwy!' he said.

It was not at all as I had pictured it, though the descriptions fitted well enough. I could see why people had said it was a hump-backed hill, and indeed they were right. It was just that it was an entirely different sort of hump from the kind I had visualized.

'It is vast!' I exclaimed naïvely, forgetting for a moment that I was Prince of Dyfed and not easily to be impressed.

Mab Petroc smiled. 'It is Arthur's,' he said simply.

The hill grew taller as we approached. Now there were signs of life: a small settlement of huts clustered around the base of the hill, a tiny village that predated Arthur's refurbishment of the fortress. The track ran through the village, then made a sudden turn, swinging up the steep slope in a long curve.

There were – and are – several places named after the hero Cadwy. I can think of two others without trying: Din Cadwy, the monastery founded by Saint Congar in the days of Gworthigern the Thin; and the deserted hillfort north of the great city of Isca, with Cadwy's Wood close by.

But only one place was called *Caer* Cadwy: the fortified town of Cadwy.

In all Albion there was nothing comparable. Many princes, such as Kynfawr in western Dumnonia and Cadwallon Long-hand in northern Gwynedd, had reoccupied ancient hillforts, but their defences huddled in a corner of the old ramparts, like a hut built in the ruins of a palace. Only Arthur dared refortify the whole perimeter, for only he had the forces with which to hold it.

I could not help but be impressed by the defences. The old outer ditches had been re-dug, so that the hillside was a steep maze of slippery inclines and exposed hollows where an attacker would find no shelter from the missiles of the defenders. The trees that had grown up around the slopes had been felled, leaving the rotting stumps behind as more obstacles to be negotiated by the assaulting troops, and a series of brushwood entanglements reinforced the places where the slope was not so steep.

Then there was the inner wall. I suspect my mouth fell open when it came into sight. The walls of my father Agricola's court were built of stone, quarried from the local hills, but they were crude by comparison with these.

Nor had I ever seen such skilled carpentry as that of the timber palisade which topped the wall, every joint fitting snug to its mate, the wood well seasoned and treated with some preservative so that it might have been set in place but yesterday.

As for the great gate, it took my breath away. I stopped my mount and sat staring at the tower.

Mab Petroc nudged me, pointing to the open double doors. At the entrance to the tunnel running under the tower stood a smiling man almost as broad as he was tall, waiting patiently. He stepped forward, bowing his head in greeting, and proclaimed in a great voice:

'Welcome, Vortepor son of Agricola, to Caer Cadwy and the court of Arthur the Magister Militum, Commander of the Armies of Britain, and welcome to all those with you. I am Glewlwyd the Gatekeeper, and the Lord Arthur bids me lead you to the guest house, that you may clean the dirt of travel from you and refresh yourselves before your audience with him.'

As the broad man spoke I knew we were highly honoured, though I suspected it was more for my father's sake than my own. Glewlwyd of the Mighty Grasp was one of the legendary figures of Arthur's court, and it was only rarely that he himself deigned to greet visitors. Indeed, it was said that he performed his office only at the three great annual festivals, Midwinter, Easter and Pentecost, and for the rest of the time his duties were carried out by deputies.

He had originally been gatekeeper to Gwenhwyvar's father, and thereby hung one of those strange tales which gathered about the Warlord like iron filings drawn to a lodestone – proof, if any were needed, that Arthur was no ordinary man, for this was a story which followed a familiar pattern and had been told since time immemorial about various heroes. (And yet for all that I believe it happened, if not quite so neatly as in the polished version told by the bards.)

In the days when Arthur was an impecunious follower of Ambrosius, not yet named his heir, he glimpsed the Princess Gwenhwyvar across a crowded hall and decided this was the woman who would become his wife. He wooed and won her heart, then sought her hand from her father, but her father would not give it, saying she was betrothed to Melwas Lord of the

Summer Country. So Arthur came to her wedding feast in disguise, and was admitted by Glewlwyd Mighty Grasp even though Glewlwyd had recognized him and guessed his reason for being there. When Arthur stole Gwenhwyvar away from under the very noses of the assembled company, Glewlwyd was disgraced and flung into prison; but in later years, when Arthur's fame and reputation exceeded that of all other men in Britain, he had Glewlwyd released and raised him up to be his own Gatekeeper, Gatekeeper to the Warlord of Prydein.

I find it difficult now to recapture the sense of wonder which attended my first visit to Caer Cadwy. All of these people were heroes to me – and to themselves, one suspects. It did not surprise me that mab Petroc had slaughtered the Picts the previous night: one expected nothing less of Arthur's Companions.

We dismounted, stretching stiff limbs. Servants took away our ponies and our goods, carrying them up the hill to the guest house.

Glewlwyd led us through the town by a roundabout route. Despite my tiredness, I was fascinated by the display of Arthur's power and wealth. Although there were many houses in Caer Cadwy – not to mention the stables, barns and workshops – the fortress did not feel cramped or crowded, unlike any other fortress I had ever seen.

This was a new place, no more than ten or twelve years old. Few of the timbers were weathered, and at every turn one was reminded of this freshness, this newness.

'What think you?' asked Glewlwyd as he brought us towards the guest house at last.

I shook my head, at a loss for words.

'It is Arthur's dream of what might be,' said the Gatekeeper. 'We take the best of the Roman, spice it with a dash of the native British, and borrow whatever is good from the Saesons. We who live here are very proud of Caer Cadwy.'

'With reason,' Fingal said smoothly, 'with reason.'

The guest house proved to be a sturdy hall in miniature with room enough for three times our number. Ewers of hot water stood waiting for us, with towels laid out beside the basins. A bright fire burned in the central hearth, and bread and meat and fresh honey cakes were set upon a table against one wall.

'Refresh yourselves!' said Glewlwyd with a wave of his hand. 'If there is anything for which you wish, the servants will fetch it.

When you are ready, the Lord Arthur awaits you, but there is no need for haste.'

I washed the dirt from my hands and face with the steaming water, relishing the warmth against my skin, and changed into fresh clothing. Around me the others did likewise, and for a time I was too busy to pay attention to my companions.

'Will you not refresh yourself, sir?' I heard one of the servants asking in the background.

I turned and saw the hooded figure of the harper standing by the door in a small knot of serving men, like a stag brought to bay by a pack of hounds.

'Let the lady be,' I said. 'Perhaps you might find her some privacy in which to change?'

There was a moment's shocked silence, and then the apologies began.

We had agreed it would be safer to keep the bard disguised until we reached Caer Cadwy, though to my mind she was not an attractive woman, and in any case our journey could scarcely have been made more dangerous by her open presence. Still, that was the plan, and we had kept to it. I confess I enjoyed the expressions of stupefaction.

Eventually the servants stopped grovelling and led her away through an inner door. For a time the room was empty of Arthur's followers. I glanced round me, then whispered to Fingal:

'They seem friendly enough.'

'And why should they not be? Is this not the heart of Arthur's power, and is your father not a man who has proved his loyalty a dozen times?'

I said uncomfortably, 'They must be aware that I have argued long and hard against the sending of our best to Arthur's warband.'

Fingal gazed at me with steady eyes. 'It is true we come from the borders of Britain, from the hill country the Romans never really conquered. And it is true our ancestors were once pirates raiding the shores of Dyfed, until Magnus Maximus, Macsen Wledig, thought to set a wolf to catch a wolf, and gave the Lordship of Dyfed to the mightiest of the pirates, Eochaid mac Artchorp, chieftain of the Dessi of Ireland.'

'My grandfather's grandfather's father.'

'Even so. Your father Agricola is the fifth ruler of Dyfed since the time of Macsen, and through all those years our people have kept the faith, even when it seemed the ancient unity of Britain had crumbled. That is a thing of which to be proud, and it is not to be wondered at that Arthur and his servants welcome us as honoured guests.'

Fingal's smile broadened. 'And do not forget that numbered among them are more than a few of our own people. Not all in Arthur's hall are strangers to you.'

I pulled on the spare red cloak from my baggage and fixed it in place with a circular brooch of finely wrought silver.

'You look like a prince,' said Fingal.

'Like a prince of an ancient land,' echoed a voice from the inner doorway.

We turned, and saw her framed there: a tall woman with thick black hair flowing past her shoulders, wearing a gown of blue as deep and dark as the sky at twilight, ornamented by bronze clasps and silver buckles that flashed and sparkled like miniature suns and constellations of stars.

'Lady Teleri,' I said, and repeated it again, so struck was I by the transformation in my travelling companion.

When she had first appeared at my court in Dyfed she had seemed very ordinary to me, not worth a second glance. She was a good performer – as a bard, I mean; I had no urge to test her abilities in other directions – and female bards were sufficiently unusual to have a rarity value. But when she was not playing or reciting she was plain and almost shy, and did not stand out among the women of my court, who have always been chosen for their beauty. Had I been older I might not have been surprised – I might have begun to guess that she was one of those women who can change not only their appearance but their whole nature as easily as their gown, that the subdued Teleri I had seen until now was no more the true Teleri than I was the dutiful son of Agricola I pretended to be.

She moved into the room, amusement showing on her strong-boned face, and said: 'Remember, Lord Vortepor, that Dyfed is a land as old and as proud as any part of this island of Albion. Remember that while Arthur's need was upon him Dyfed never asked for aid, but rather kept a steady stream of her best flowing unbegrudged to his warband. Now the final victory has been won and the Saeson dogs sent cowering to their kennels, Dyfed asks for help against her old foes, the Scotti of the Western Ocean.'

'And remember also,' added Fingal, 'that the descendants of

Cunedda in the north, Cadwallon Longhand of Gwynedd and his cousins, have almost freed their lands from the infestation of Irish settlers. Once that work is done they will turn their attention southwards to Dyfed.'

'Yes,' said Teleri. 'They are a hungry dynasty, the Sons of Cunedda, and will gobble up Dyfed as they have gobbled much else unless Arthur makes clear his support for your father, and your father's successor.'

'So we need a sign, my Prince,' Fingal continued eagerly. 'A sign from Arthur that he believes in Dyfed and its present dynasty. A sign to the Sons of Cunedda, saying "Keep your distance!"'

'Very well!' I raised a hand. 'I know. I understand.'

I was overwhelmed by everything: by being here, in Caer Cadwy, with its luxury, splendour and size; by the famous names surrounding us and the prospect of shortly meeting the most famous of them all. The change in Teleri, who had suddenly turned from a mouse into a roaring lion with a strong grasp of statesmanship, was just one more strange factor among many.

The chief servant coughed and came forward from where he had been standing out of earshot. 'My Lords, Lady. If it pleases you, the Magister Militum awaits your pleasure.'

'My harp,' said Teleri, disappearing into the inner chamber.

Fingal stared after her with narrowed eyes. 'I wonder,' he said. 'We thought she came with us at our behest, but I think she is here by her will, not ours.'

The Great Hall lay at the very heart of the city, on the high point of the plateau, dominating the other buildings as a cow dominates her calves; a rectangular building over twenty-one paces long and eleven wide; its high roof covered with wooden shingles; its lines broken on either side of the long walls by porched entrances.

It was a place of light and glory. Everything seemed to glisten and gleam, even the walls, which were hung with fine needlework and gleaming weaponry, with whitewashed shields and parade armour of blue iron or polished bronze.

A row of hearth-pits ran down the middle of the hall, between the long tables where the warriors sat for their feasting, and a series of hanging lamps were suspended from the great beams that supported the roof. These lamps were bronze bowls, richly decorated in red enamel, filled with oil and a floating wick. With the hearth fires burning and the lamps lit, the light was reflected back and forth, up and down, and the bronze bowls shone with a golden glow like miniature suns.

The tables were laid with polished drinking horns, with vessels of green glass, with goblets of silver and gold, all sparkling and lustrous in the light of the flames. Parallel with the tables ran great benches or couches covered with white fleeces, and on these sat or lolled a host of richly dressed and jewelled warriors: men of all the many tribes of Albion.

It seemed to me like a Hall of the Sidhe, the Lordly Ones who live under the hills.

A small group near the door had marked our entry, and these now began to pound on the table and stamp their feet on the floor, shouting and chanting: 'Dyfed, Dyfed! Vortepor of the Demetae! Gwortepor mab Aircol!' (Aircol is the way they say Agricola in the dialect of Dyfed.)

Many of the warriors twisted in their seats as I passed, and the murmur of 'Demetae' (which is the old Roman name for the people of Dyfed) followed me like a wave.

These were men of Gwynedd and its satellite territories, lands ruled by the heirs of Cunedda: Cadwallon Longhand, his brother Ewein Whitetooth, and their cousins Kevyr, Meilir and Yneigr. Some were small and dark, typical hillfolk of a kind to be found in Dyfed itself; others were tall with fair or red hair, like the Sons of Cunedda themselves.

Then I forgot about the men of Gwynedd. There before me upon the dais was legend come to life: the Saviour of Albion, the Warlord of Prydein; the victor of the fights at the fords of the Clearwater and the Blackwater, the conqueror of the River Bassas and the Caledonian Forest, the captor of Fort Guinnion and the defender of the City of the Legion, the master of the Speckled Shore and the Hills of Agned by the ruins of Bravonium, the champion of Badon Hill; the unrivalled one, the invincible one, Arthur Magister Militum – Arthur the Master of the Soldiers of Britain.

He was a tall man, Arthur, and well built. His hair was auburn tinged with grey, cut short in the Roman style, and he wore a tunic of imperial purple. He was clean-shaven, handsome with a strong but open face.

That tells you nothing.

Let me say this. Standing on one side of him was a giant of a man with long yellow hair shot through with white, the biggest man I have ever seen. On the other side was a younger warrior with a hawk face and fierce proud eyes. Either of this pair (they were Cei and Gwalchmei) would have drawn the gaze in any crowd, yet I did not even notice them at first, for all my attention was on Arthur.

I disliked him on sight.

Somehow I coped with the protocol of greeting, saluting in the Roman manner, the way my ancestors had learned to do when they served with Magnus Maximus. Then, my throat dry, I began to speak, striving to keep the Dyfed accent out of my words so they would be comprehensible to everybody:

'Greetings, Master of the Armies of this Island. And be this greeting equally to all those present, so that there be none without their share in it. And may you never be less mighty than you are now in this hour, and may your glory never fade, you who are the defender of this land against all ills.'

Arthur inclined his head and replied: 'Be welcome, Vortepor son of Agricola; be welcome, you and all your company.'

His voice filled the hall and echoed from the shadows of the rafters, yet still managed to sound far more natural than my forced tones.

'Come, join us,' Arthur added more quietly, smiling to put me at my ease and waving me up the step onto the dais.

Seated upon a great throne was a golden lady, and it seemed to me in that moment that she was the most beautiful woman I had ever seen or heard of, more beautiful even than the legendary Fflur, for whose sake Caswallon son of Beli travelled to Rome in the guise of a cobbler when she was stolen away by Julius Caesar.

'Lady Gwenhwyvar,' I said, and she smiled and indicated a chair beside her.

Sometimes I wake in the middle of the night and lie sleepless wondering if she still lives, and if she does, what time has done to that golden hair.

I hated Arthur, hated everything he represented, but I could not hate Gwenhwyvar.

That fool Medraut put it about that she was unfaithful, which is a lie, but men like to believe these things. It brings her down to their level, lessens both her and Arthur, who would otherwise be as far above the common herd as the stars above the earth.

No doubt it seems strange to you that I should speak of them, Arthur and Gwenhwyvar, in such terms. But I came close that first afternoon to falling under their spell, and something of it remains with me so that even now, though it was I who sent the gold and silver which bought the Saeson foot that fought at Camlann, I am not entirely free of their magic.

I delivered my appeal for aid, and watched Arthur giving it his consideration. I could tell that Gwalchmei was keen while Cei was more cautious, and I knew that the matter would need to be debated in Council before any decision was reached. But I also knew it was Arthur's opinion that counted: if he thought it was practical, Heuil's nest of pirates would be destroyed.

If Arthur said a thing could be done then it *was* done. For half a century Ambrosius and his father before him had struggled against the Saesons without ever achieving any lasting success. Arthur had announced it would take him fifteen years to pen them on their reservations, and lo, it was accomplished.

I listened to the three of them, fascinated. My part was done now, my presence temporarily forgotten. Gwalchmei would throw out an idea, Cei would argue, Arthur would suggest a modification. I had heard that they did this, Arthur and his closest Companions, sat together round a table and talked. I could not imagine my father conducting his affairs in such a fashion, nor is it a method I have ever used myself, but all the same it was interesting to observe.

In the body of the hall a harp began to play, the notes spreading into an ever widening pool of silence as the warriors hushed to listen.

'You think it worth it?' said Arthur.

Gwalchmei nodded, a broad grin spreading across his face. 'We have not moved towards the North since Cat Coit Celidon, the battle of the Caledonian Forest.'

'And that was in the lowlands,' said Cei. 'If we do strike at the Isles, it will remind the inhabitants that you are the defender of all Britain, not just the South.'

Arthur nodded. He turned to me and summarized their conclusions: 'We think the idea sound in principle. A punitive raid into those northern waters would remind the chieftains of the Iardomnan that the Magister Militum has a long arm. But I will need to be convinced that the action is feasible, and that your source does indeed have useful information about the stronghold of your enemy.'

I opened my mouth to speak, but thankfully Arthur waved me into silence. My head was beginning to spin from trying to follow their conversation. Although I had some grasp of affairs of state – I could scarcely avoid it, as a future Lord of Dyfed – this was all on a much greater scale than anything I had ever envisaged, and all so casual.

'Let us listen to the harper,' whispered Arthur. 'We will talk again later. She is good, this girl you brought with you.'

Startled, I looked towards the source of the music.

Teleri had come out into the central aisle and begun to play, pacing slowly towards the dais, and as she moved the men fell silent and remained silent in her wake.

The blue gown shimmered in the warm glow from the fires and hanging bowls, and her jewellery flashed and glittered as she strolled from light to shadow.

I heard an intake of breath beside me. 'She is beautiful,' murmured Gwalchmei.

Frowning, I looked again at this strange woman, this uncompanionable travelling companion. I could see that she was striking, perhaps even attractive in a strong-featured sort of way, but it was not my idea of beauty. It was the clothing and grooming that gave her distinction, not her face and form. (Now Gwenhwyvar . . . Gwenhwyvar would have been beautiful even if she were dressed in a piece of old sacking and caked in farmyard dirt from head to toe.)

'Who is she?' asked Gwalchmei.

'Her name is Teleri. She is our guide to the Iardomnan.'

While Teleri played, the lesser ladies of the court came out from the room beyond the partition wall and found their places, and the eating and drinking began with scarcely a word being spoken – a thing I have never known before or since, in that hall or any other.

At last she stopped, and the hall echoed to the rafters with the roars of applause. When the noise died down a little she raised her eyes to Arthur, and cried out:

'My lord, I beg a boon of thee!'

'Then a boon thou shalt have, if it be reasonable,' Arthur replied in the same formal style.

'Reasonable it is, lord, and no great hardship in the granting of it.'

'Speak on,' he commanded.

'The boon I ask is this. That after the feasting is finished, when the drinking horns and goblets are replenished with pale mead and blood-red wine, when the entertainers come forth to amuse this great assembly with their antics, then I may be permitted to tell a tale I have heard, an old tale from the very dawn of time.'

'A heathen tale?' asked Arthur, with the hint of a smile on his lips.

She bowed her head, the long black hair cascading around her shoulders.

'It may be, my lord.'

'So, so,' he said. 'It will not be the first time a Christian gathering has heard a heathen tale. And no harm in that, for there is sometimes a wisdom hidden in these stories of our ancestors.'

'It is in my mind that this is such a tale, lord.'

'It is in mine also,' he said gravely. 'I grant thee thy boon.'

She bowed and returned to her seat by the door.

'Who is she?' asked Gwalchmei.

I shook my head. 'Truly, I do not know.' (And I did not any more, though I had thought that I did.) 'She comes from the far north, from the islands and sea lochs of the Iardomnan, but she is not of the Scotti.'

'A Pict perhaps?' said Cei.

'She speaks with a faint accent, but it is not one I have heard before.' Gwalchmei frowned. 'I thought I knew most of the accents of Britain.'

'You have travelled much?' I enquired politely, in an attempt to turn the talk away from the subject of Teleri's origins.

Cei laid a heavy arm across my shoulders and nearly deafened me with laughter. 'Of course he has, boy. This is Gwalchmei you are talking to. He may look like a sweet innocent, but he is Arthur's Captain of Horse, the fourth most dangerous man in Caer Cadwy (and thus all Prydein) after Arthur and Bedwyr and myself.'

'Hush, Cei,' said Gwalchmei. He turned to me. 'You must remember there are men and women from every part of Britain at Arthur's court. People from here in the west, landless folk from

97

the east, driven out by the Saesons, people from the midlands, and some from the northern kingdoms – even a handful of Picts from beyond Bannog. I can hear most accents without even leaving my seat. Listen!'

Through the babble of the hall I traced and held the different strands: the sing-song voices of Gwynedd; the sweet burr of Dumnonia; the low and Latinized pitch of Calchwinyth of the limestone hills; the flatness of Elmet; the hard tones of the bleak North; the guttural bark of Saesons.

'But this Lady Teleri,' said Gwalchmei. 'I have never heard a voice like hers, though I catch touches in it of the Irish, and hints of the Pictish. I do not think our language is her native tongue.'

'So who is she, lad?' demanded Cei.

Suddenly I was very aware of the fair man's size, of the long left arm stretched lazily across the back of the couch, an arm that could all too easily break my neck.

'I know very little about her,' I said unsteadily. 'She came to me a month or more ago, saying she had the solution to our problem with the Scotti . . .'

'Why you? Why not your father?' he said sharply.

'I . . . I suppose because my father is old and I am his heir . . .'

'You are his sole heir?' asked Gwalchmei.

'Yes. We do not divide the inheritance between sons, like the Men of Gwynedd. With us, the designated heir takes everything.' I was babbling, and knew it. 'When my father dies – may it not be soon – I shall become Lord of Dyfed.'

'Thus avoiding the fratricidal wars which periodically rend Gwynedd,' said Gwalchmei.

'Fascinating,' Cei said with heavy sarcasm. 'Tell me, why do you not wish to talk about this woman?'

I choked on a mouthful of meat.

'She terrifies you for some reason.' The big man's eyes were shrewd and hard. 'Or is it that there is some secret about her you do not want us to discover?'

I was saved for the moment by Glewlwyd of the Mighty Grasp, who rose to his feet in the body of the hall and in his booming voice demanded silence, that the Magister Militum's boon might be fulfilled.

Eremon opened his eyes when the fat man's voice at last fell silent. The fires had burned low, and Vortepor's warriors were drunkenly making their way to their sleeping quarters. The farmers and labourers had already gone, slipping quietly out through the doors before the heavy drinking began, knowing they would become the butt of rough horseplay if they stayed.

The slaves were clearing away the couches and the tables, replacing them with skins and bolsters for those who would be spending the night in the hall. Vortepor sat brooding in his chair above the remains of his meal, gazing at the activity.

'What of my uncle?' said Eremon.

The massive head swung in his direction and the small eyes studied him.

'Your uncle?'

'I thought . . .' Confused, Eremon wondered whether he had dozed more deeply than he realized, and somehow missed the meat of Vortepor's long tale.

The fat man grunted. 'Lleminawg the sacrifice. Yes.' He snuffled through the bones on the table in front of him, found one with some shreds of flesh left on it and began to suck and chew.

'The woman cast a spell over them. She foretold the whole thing, except the need for a sacrifice.' He snorted. '*That* she kept quiet.'

A slave girl leaned across to start clearing the debris. Rings flashed in the failing light of the fires as Vortepor's swollen hand hoisted her skirt and buried itself deep between her thighs. She gasped and fell forward against the table. His fingers moved, writhing like plump worms feeding on their prey.

She was very young, the girl, scarcely more than a child, but when she turned her head (all the while making little sounds of pleasure) Eremon saw that her eyes were wise and knowing beyond her years. He was not a man with any care for the thoughts or feelings of others, but something about her expression made him feel sick.

In that moment he reached his decision. He would agree to whatever Vortepor planned, swear whatever oaths the fat man wanted. And the moment he escaped from this place he would do anything in his power to thwart Vortepor's ambition.

'The tale Teleri told,' said the fat man as if the girl were not present and his fingers were not doing what they were doing. 'It was an incantation. It was an invitation. When she had finished it was inevitable that Arthur would sail north to the Iardomnan and destroy Hueil and his alliance of raiders. It was inevitable that he would return and claim the Sovereignty of Prydein.'

The girl moaned and convulsed. Vortepor pulled his hand free, sniffed his fingers and thrust them at the girl to lick clean.

'He brought something back with him. A talisman, a symbol of his right to rule. The most preciously guarded secret of Arthur's long career. After his death it vanished.'

'Like Gwenhwyvar?' said Eremon, dimly beginning to see.

'Like Gwenhwyvar, riding out of Caer Cadwy with not a backward glance when she heard that Arthur had fallen.'

He pushed the slave girl aside, sending her sprawling in the dust of the floor. She lay there for a moment, winded, then scrambled to her feet and scuttled to safety.

'Gwenhwyvar knew it was over,' he continued, ignoring the girl. 'Arthur had no heir. His sons were dead – Llacheu at the hands of Cei, Anir at the hands of Arthur himself. Medraut had proved too impatient, and tried to snatch prematurely what would have been his in the fullness of time. As for the rest of us, those who already ruled some part of Prydein, we hated each other and would never have allowed one to dominate the rest. With Arthur and Medraut dead, there was nobody we would have accepted as our master.'

'You want me to find this talisman?'

The fat man belched, shifted his vast bulk. The carved throne creaked alarmingly.

'No, not find it. I know where it is. I have known these past three months. Not long after Camlann a man entered a monastery in Armorica. At that time he was calling himself Budoc. This Budoc left the monastery about three years ago, saying only that he was returning to the land of his birth to pass his final days in solitude. Now, if he is the man I think he is, then he was born not far from the River Oak – where you used to live before you annoyed the good Gereint. My servants have scoured the area, seeking word of a hermit or holy man who arrived within the last three years.

'My servants did not find him at first, because when they asked how long the holy man had been at the Sanctuary some fool of a peasant answered *always*!'

'The Sanctuary?'

'The *nemeton* beside the Porthyle estuary. The holy wood.'

'I know it.'

The fat man snorted. 'Of course you know it. That is one of the reasons why you are here, because it is familiar ground to you.'

He clicked his fingers, summoning more wine, waited until it had been poured. 'This hermit's name is Budoc, and he is of the right age. He practises a mix of Christianity and paganism, which is exactly what I would expect.' He drank, spilling droplets down his tunic. 'The Budoc of Sanctuary Wood is, I am certain, the same person as the Budoc who joined a monastery in Armorica after Camlann.'

'And who is he?'

'The man to whom Arthur and Gwenhwyvar entrusted the secret brought back from the Iardomnan. The man who now has in his keeping the key to the Sovereignty of Albion. The man I once knew as mab Petroc.'

CHAPTER SIX

1

The last day of the village began much like any other.

Afterwards, what Eurgain remembered best was her older sister Dyfyr skirmishing with their mother over whose turn it was to carry the washing down to the stream.

The fight ended, as such fights usually did, with Dyfyr flouncing out carrying a wicker basket of dirty clothes, and with her mother sighing as she raked out the old ashes from under the fire.

'Eurgain, when did you visit the hermit last?' Even her voice sounded weary after one of these battles with Dyfyr.

'Yesterday evening. I took him the porridge you had made.'

'Of course, you told me,' said her mother, shaking her head in self-reproach. Will you visit him again this evening? I do not like to think of the poor old man being ill up there all alone.'

'Yes, I'll go. It's a pretty walk through the woods.'

'Good girl.' Her mother smiled, suddenly much younger. 'And did you bring back some corn?'

Eurgain nodded.

Eurgain and her mother spread an old hide on the floor and sat down. Each took a sheaf of corn and set fire to the ears with a splinter of burning wood from the fire. As the flame took they seized up a stick and, at the precise instant the husk burned, they beat off the grain, which fell onto the hide. When they had finished they swept all the grain into a pot and toasted it.

Wiping the sweat from her forehead, Eurgain's mother said: 'You clear up the mess and I'll grind the corn. The bread will be ready by the time the men are home. If you like, go and see if Gwyl wants any help with the children. You could take them for a stroll along the shore and gather some seaweed. We've nearly run out of laver bread, and I expect Gwyl could do with some.'

Her mother grinned mischievously. 'Just don't go near Dyfyr, or she'll complain.'

That was the last time Eurgain saw her mother.

It was a beautiful morning. She collected the two children from a harassed Gwyl (Gwyl was always harassed these days) and took them along the beach, steering well clear of the stream where her sister would be dancing on the clothes to shake loose the dirt. (Dancing with her long red hair unbound, dreaming of a household of her own, she who would be dead by the time the tide turned.)

They gathered handfuls of the pink seaweed, and Edar found a crab in a rock pool, and Bran gorged himself on mussels until he was sick, and they dammed one of the little streams on the beach to make the water back up and flooded a great plain, drowning all the farms so the people had to escape in a big boat like Dwyvan and Dwyvach when the Lake of Floods burst its banks and swallowed all the world . . .

'My daddy has a boat,' Bran boasted. 'He says when I'm a bit older he'll take me out fishing with him.'

'And me, and me,' shouted Edar, hopping from one foot to the other and accidentally kicking down the dam so the flood drained away.

'Not you,' said Bran contemptuously. 'You're too clumsy.'

'Look!' Eurgain pointed at the estuary. 'Isn't that Daddy's boat now?'

The round coracles were coming home from the morning's fishing, and they could hear voices calling across the waves as the men compared the day's catch.

'There's Daddy.' Bran, who had sharp eyes, pointed. 'On the left. And that's Grandpa behind him, paddling slowly. Can you see them, Edar?'

The little boy squinted against the glare. 'Yes,' he said doubtfully.

Eurgain picked him up and put him on her shoulders. He was a fragile child, not strong like his brother, and he did not weigh very much. They had thought they were going to lose him last winter, of the coughing sickness, and though he recovered it took a long time for the colour to come back into his cheeks, and even now he was not so quick as he had been.

'I can see him, I can see him! Daddy, Daddy!'

His thin voice was lost in the sound of the surf on the beach, but one of the men looked up and waved, then called across to the boys' father and grandfather. They changed course, making for the place where Eurgain and the children stood watching, the little oval boats low in the waves.

'Eurgain!' called Beli as he came into the shallows. 'Landed with the brats again then? I'm grateful to you, and so's Gwyl. I don't how she'd cope if you and Dyfyr didn't keep helping out.'

He backwatered with the paddle to prevent the light craft from beaching.

'We enjoy it. They're fun to be with.'

'You'll not say that when you have some of your own,' he said, but the grin on his face belied his words. Certainly neither of the children, both of whom had run out into the surf at his approach, seemed in the least worried.

'Dad and I thought we could give them a ride home. Give you a bit of peace like.'

'That's kind of you,' she said, playing the game, knowing how much he wanted to show off his children.

(And afterwards she was glad, so glad, that at least they had had this last ride home together.)

She waded out into the water and lifted Edar into the seat beside his father. It was a squeeze, though the boy was small. Coracles were not built to take two, and the floor was heaped with fish, their silver scales dulling as they dried.

Bran had already scrambled further out and clambered aboard his grandfather Jago's boat, making it bob frantically.

'Sit still boy!' roared Jago, easing his heavily burdened craft out into the chop of the estuary. 'You'll have us over if you keep fidgeting!'

It was quiet on the beach without the boys. She carried the seaweed down to the shore and washed off the grains of sand that had got onto it when Edar kicked down the dam, then loaded it into her bag, cramming it tight.

She sat back on her haunches, fascinated by the cream of the froth lapping at her toes, by the tracery of foam on the deep gold into which her feet were slowly sinking . . .

A voice thundered, so sudden and so loud she lost her balance and toppled backwards on the bag of seaweed.

Get away from the shore!

Her head hurt. She rolled over onto her hands and knees. Something odd had happened to her vision: the world had broken up into a mass of tiny dots, though she could still feel the sand crunching under her knuckles, could still hear the wavelets hissing on the beach.

Get away, get away, get away!

It was a woman's voice, but she did not recognize it.

Great wings beat about her head, buffeting her ears. She felt sick, as if she had lain in the sun too long, and filled with dread.

The voice came again, fainter now as if from much further away: *Run! Into the trees and hide!*

Eurgain knew then that it was the goddess who spoke.

She staggered upright, swaying drunkenly, leaving the bag of seaweed where it lay. She ran, awkwardly at first, whimpering softly deep in her throat, ploughing clumsily through the sand, tripping on the nest of driftwood marking the line of the high tide, almost falling into the shadow of the trees behind the shore.

Hide! the voice had said. She cast frantically around, panicking when no obvious place at once suggested itself, fled deeper into the woods.

A bird sounded a warning from further in the forest. She froze, listening with all her being: heard the uneasy ticking of a robin in the distance.

Something was approaching, something terrible. She could feel its passage through the forest, could sense the pressure building as it came closer.

A blackbird flew overhead, screaming '*zinc zinc zinc*'.

She dived into a thicket of hazel, forcing her way between the stems, wriggling deep into the cover on her hands and knees. Once safely inside she lay still, trying to bring her ragged breathing under control, peering through the thick foliage for some sign of whatever was stalking through the trees.

One moment she was looking at a patch of dappled shade, the next a man was standing there, a man dressed in a dark robe that merged into the shadows. He came into a patch of sunlight, snuffling the air suspiciously as if he knew he was being watched.

When he turned in profile she saw that his skull was oddly shaven in a wedge from ear to ear. The hair behind the line fell in greasy black locks to his shoulders; that in front formed a wispy fringe. His face was thin and vicious, and the bald part of his scalp seemed a mass of ugly bumps and bony protrusions.

He stared directly at her, nostrils flaring. She could hear him sniffing, scenting the air like a hound, and then he was gone.

She waited, not daring to move.

The blackbird shrieked again.

Eurgain had guessed that the man in black was not the thing that had frightened the birds: he had moved far too quietly, slipping between the trees like the Lord of the Stags. He was a forerunner, scouting ahead of a larger company.

Now the others came into view.

Leading them was a large man with golden hair and a brown beard. His cheeks were riddled with old scars, reddened craters from some skin disease. He wore a shirt of mail, the rings silver in the sunlight.

Behind him came a company of lesser creatures, to her eyes skinny and half starved, carrying spears and small round white shields high on their arms, their tunics ragged and much darned. Some walked barefoot.

They passed, moving clumsily. One or two at the back stumbled so often she thought they must be ill. She waited, trembling with fear, her mind numb, torn by indecision.

Were it not for the man in black she would stay here. She was fairly confident he had not seen her – surely he would have said or done something if he had – but she was not absolutely certain.

He was the most terrifying person she had ever seen.

She had to move, find a better hiding place. And she had to know what happened in the village. There was always a faint chance the strangers were on their way somewhere else.

Eurgain crawled out of the thicket and stood up, brushing off leaves and bits of twig.

She still did not know what to do, and without having reached any conscious decision she found herself following the trail left by the strangers, keeping a little off to one side, making use of every patch of cover, tracking them as she might have tracked an animal for the pot.

Their path led, as she had known it would, straight and true to the edge of the wood. She held back, slipping from trunk to trunk, trying to find a place from which she could see without being seen.

She worked her way forward into a stand of bracken in the lee of a big oak. Cautiously she parted the last slender ferns.

The strangers had spread themselves out along the great bank which divided the fields from the forest. It was topped by a thorn hedge, and they had stationed themselves at intervals behind this hedge so that they would be hidden from the village. A small group had gone further up the valley to block the track leading down from the ridge; she could just make out the blur of their white shields.

The air shimmered above the roofs of the huts where it was distorted by the heat of the cooking fires. Some of the older children were playing catch: one of them might have been Bran, though it was difficult to tell at this distance.

Two figures were strolling towards the coracles drawn up on the strand. Another was sitting with something dark hanging from his lap; from the movements of his arms, Eurgain guessed that he was repairing a net.

She could not understand why nothing was happening. Why did the strangers not attack now that they had more or less surrounded the village? Why were they waiting?

If she stood up and shouted, waved her arms and made as much noise as she possibly could, her family might be warned in time.

(*In time to do what?* said the voice in her head.)

There was a big black crow in the branches of the oak. As she lay trying to summon the courage to do something it shouted then hopped into the air, flapping across the fields.

The fisherman with the net had risen and was staring at the creek. The other two joined him, gesticulating wildly. Eurgain pushed aside a few more fronds, careless of the noise she was making in her haste to see what they were looking at.

Two ships had rounded the mouth of the inlet and were racing for the shore, sails furled and oars sweeping, seven to a side, with a man in mail standing in the stern of each, urging the rowers on with whoops and cries.

The youngsters who had been playing ball ran down to the water's edge, eager to find out what the fuss was about, turned and fled in all directions as they saw the boats. People appeared in doorways, ducked back inside as they realized what was happening, reappeared carrying babies or valued possessions. Men shouted, women shrieked and children screamed, dogs barked and chickens squawked, the sounds mingling and rising to the place where she lay.

The crow, which had perched on a rooftop, took flight along the valley, following the line of the track, swerving aside when it reached the party of armed men.

The leading boat shipped oars and glided through the surf to the beach, its crew already leaping overboard as it slid across the sand leaving a great track in its wake. The other followed close behind.

The mailed warrior was the first ashore. Two of the villagers ran at him, perhaps hoping that if they could bring down the leader at once then the others might withdraw. One had a spear, the second (she thought it was Beli but could not be sure) a scythe.

They came at the warrior together. He sidestepped, hacking the spearman across the back of the neck as the latter staggered on past, then casually turned to cut the legs from under the second man before he had time to raise his scythe.

He left them writhing on the ground for his crew to finish, strolled towards the village, cleaning his blade on a piece of rag.

An older man, white hair blowing in the breeze (she was almost certain it was Jago), stepped out of a hut with a bow in his hands. The warrior did not break stride, even when the old man bent and loosed. Instead – and this seemed incredible to Eurgain, who after all could not see the flight of the arrow – the sword licked through the air like a tongue of grey flame and the warrior kept walking. The bowman clearly could not believe he had missed at such short range, for he made no attempt to string another shaft but stood there waiting until the sword swung again, biting through bowstave and body alike.

The people fled, running at full pelt along the track leading inland.

One of the boys outdistanced the pack, rounded the curve and realized what was waiting for them. He checked awkwardly, glancing behind him. Something flashed in the sunlight. The boy fell over backwards, his legs kicking spasmodically, his heels drumming on the turf.

The next villager reached the body, hurdled it without looking up to see the white shields waiting for him, and ran right onto their spears.

The rest scattered, scrambling over the field banks and spreading out across the hillside in a ragged line, careless of the standing corn, the wisest of them sprinting directly for the cover of the trees.

The group blocking the track leaned on their spears and watched, talking and laughing among themselves.

The fugitives panted up the slope, heads down, all their energy concentrated on running, seeing nothing until the long line of men suddenly rose from behind the hedge.

Nobody escaped.

Not the men, not the women, not the children.

The man in black stood on the earthen bank dividing the fields from the forest, arms folded, satisfaction in every line of his body, supervising the slaughter.

Fragile Edar was lucky. He was seized by one of the mailed men and swung by the heels, swung against a rock so that his head was dashed open. The man was laughing as he cast the body aside.

Granny Afan, too old and lame to leave her bed, was carried from her hut still wrapped in a blanket and tossed in the air, flipped higher and higher till she flew above the roofs, and each time they tossed her the men chanted a count. When they reached ten they dropped the blanket and let her fall.

Gwyl's brother Rhun, uncle to Edar and Bran, was cornered by three men, each with a long spear. They pricked and goaded him, making him dance, driving the spears deeper and deeper as his strength failed. When he could no longer stand they beat him with their spear butts, and the sound of the blows carried to Eurgain where she wept on the hillside.

When she could bear to look again she saw her sister Dyfyr, long red hair tangled about her face, threading a way through the stampeding cattle, using them as cover. But the cattle would not go where she wanted. Eurgain could see her flailing at the flanks of one cow, trying to drive it up the slope towards the woods. The beast broke free, bucking and plunging, mad with terror, turned and raced towards the village.

Dyfyr abandoned the cattle and sprinted for the bank, arms pumping as she fled across the open pasture, running directly for the safety of the woods though she must have known the way was barred.

The men on the bank watched her come. The figure in black

barked an order. Three of the raiders rested their spears and shields against the hedge and leaped down into the field, spreading out to intercept the girl. One rubbed at his crotch and called an invitation; Dyfyr swerved towards him, making the others shout with laughter. At the last moment she sprang aside, leaving him fumbling the empty space where she had been. The laughter turned to cries of rage.

The girl reached the hedge, no more than thirty or forty paces from where Eurgain lay hidden. She boosted herself up the bank, vaulted the barrier of thorns, stumbled and stood upright for an instant, her body silhouetted against the light.

Suddenly she fell forward, rolling helplessly down the bank and into the shallow ditch at its foot, a spear shaft tangled between her legs.

The mailed man with the pockmarked face strode towards her, wrenched her into the air with one hand. Eurgain could hear the sound of tearing cloth as Dyfyr's tunic parted under the strain.

The man flung the girl up the bank, still using one hand, and jumped after her. He raised her to her feet, though from the way Dyfyr lolled Eurgain knew she had been winded by the fall, and ripped the tunic from her body before casting her back to the ground.

A cheer went up from the others at the sight of the long brown limbs and the pale breasts, and they rushed forward to watch and help the mailed man as he dropped his breeches and pushed himself into the girl. Dyfyr cried out once, and then was silent.

Afterwards they dragged her back to the huts with the other young women and flung her down in the space where the children had played ball. The remaining men took turns with her, continuing long after she had ceased to move.

And this too Eurgain saw from her hiding place among the ferns, watching dry-eyed because she had no more tears left, until at last the horror of it rose up and engulfed her.

2

They followed the winding road down the cliffs, the big man talking and laughing as they threaded between the drifts of pine trees, his monologue punctuated by the creak of leather and the rumble of the ponies' stomachs.

'It must have been near here you took that spear in the throat,' he said as they reached level ground. 'I remember we chased Eremon and his crew down the bluffs and caught them on the plain, but the rest is a blank. How long ago was it, Nai? Five years, more?'

On that day five years before, Nai remembered, they had fought in the morning, on the high ground behind them, and the Irish horse had finally broken and fled, abandoning the foot to their fate. Gereint had led a part of his warband in pursuit, the youngest and fittest of his warriors, and they had ridden through the long autumn afternoon, the ponies foundering one by one, the chase punctuated by little flurries of action when they snapped too close to the Scotti's heels.

At the last the Irish had been brought to bay, here on the narrow strand. Nai had been in the forefront of the British charge – lumbering horses urged into a feeble canter, tired men striking at each other with a dreadful slowness – and had come face to face with Eremon the Irish leader, a man he had known since childhood.

He shuddered. He could still see the spearpoint, dull with somebody else's blood, could remember how he had flung himself sideways in the saddle, how the spear had followed and he had known this was his death, there was nothing he could do.

'He was fast, Eremon,' said Gorthyn, echoing his thoughts. 'But then all that family were. He was kin to Lleminawg the bounding one, Arthur's Companion, and there were few quicker in battle than Lleminawg the Irishman.' He hummed an old tune to himself.

'Yet for all his madness Eremon could command loyalty,' Gorthyn went on. 'Serach was a good man. In another time and place I could have made a comrade of him. I wonder what happened to them after they went back to Ierne. Can't have been easy. After all, they were born here.'

Cocking an eyebrow in invitation, Nai waved at the straight road ahead of them.

'A gallop? Why not. It will shake some life into these old nags. Too long in the stable, that is what you have had, my beauty,' said the big man, patting his pony's neck.

They heeled their horses and took off in a shower of gravelly soil, the big man whooping and shouting, frightening the water-fowl on the lake so they splashed into the air and did not settle until the riders were long passed.

'Not usual, to hear reports of Saesons this far west,' said Gorthyn as the ponies slowed to a trot and then a walk, puffing and blowing.

'Perhaps Gereint is wrong. Perhaps it is only a raiding party trying its luck.' He glanced around the barren landscape of gravel and reeds, laughed drily. 'Must be cursing themselves for fools.'

The big man sighed. 'I don't know, cousin. I had hoped we were safe for my lifetime.'

Nai shrugged.

Camlann haunts us, he thought. It shapes our lives. None of us are ever free of what might have been. If Arthur had lived, this present lawlessness would never have been loosed upon the world. Custennin would not have dared rule as he does, breaking the oaths he swears to his followers, taking and putting away wives in his efforts to breed an heir. He would have been answerable to the Amherawdyr.

Likewise Eremon would never have turned rogue, a sheepdog preying on its own flock. He might well have taken service with Arthur, as his kinsman Lleminawg did before him, and Dovnuall Frych with his love of inflicting pain on others would have gone with him. Both would have found a better use for their talents.

And I would not have become Nai the Silent, Nai Still Tongue, the man with the halting growling voice. I might have chattered as much as Gorthyn, and thus lost what little reputation I have for wisdom.

He smiled ruefully to himself, and urged his pony on to catch up with Gorthyn, who had already begun to climb the bluffs at the end of the long shingle beach.

3

With the fair wind and weather won by the sacrifice of a white horse to Wotan, the *Sea Stallion* made good time on her voyage to the west.

As they travelled the crew kept watch for some sign that the rumours were true, that the countryside was emptying, its inhabitants either fleeing over the sea to Armorica or dying from the succession of plagues which had swept through the land for the last hundred years, but always they saw the thin plumes of cooking fires – and once a great column of greasy black smoke that roused memories of burning villas and made the men laugh in anticipation of good times to come.

All the while, during the first two days of the voyage, the cliffs fell smooth and sheer to the water, and the gulls wailed around the mast, following them in the hope of food.

In after years Ceolric made the voyage many times, and his memories became confused. Perhaps it was not on this first passage but another that the blue cliffs made such an impression on him, perhaps it was not then but later that they pulled the ship up on a deserted part of the shore and spent the night beneath a headland shaped like a man's head, even fringed with grass in imitation of hair.

But certain things did remain fixed in his mind. Sailing along part of the red coast, he asked Garulf the name of the river mouth they passed in the morning, and the older man replied, 'Ux, or Isc.' Much later, long after noon, they passed a second river mouth and again Ceolric asked its name. The steersman replied, 'Isc, or Ux,' so that the youth wondered for a time whether they had moved at all, or whether some trick of wind and current had brought them back to where they were that morning, until Garulf, laughing, explained the two rivers bore the same name.

On the second night the crew were all much more tired than on the first. Lack of sleep had caught up with them, and there was a cold wind blowing in off the sea, so that they huddled close round the crackling fire, half dozing, the talk desultory. Only Wicga seemed as lively as ever.

'Tell us more about the Emperor and his cavalry,' he said to Garulf, nudging the Frisian awake. 'I have never fought the British. Are horsemen truly as dangerous as men say?'

Garulf roused himself, frowning at the stiffness in his joints. He grunted and looked round the company, measuring how wakeful they were, before answering.

'Dangerous? Yes, they are dangerous. They move fast, sending a blizzard of spears at you, and when you have been weakened enough they charge home with lance and sword.'

'And they can thrust home?' Wicga asked eagerly. 'I would have thought the impact would unseat them.'

'Not the skilled riders. The less skilled, yes, but the skilled ones are cunning. They cling to their horses with their calves – not their

113

knees as you will sometimes hear – and somehow manage to brace themselves against the shock.'

'And you have seen this?' Wicga leaned forward, eyes bright.

'I have.'

'Camlann,' prompted Ceolric, who had been hanging on every word and did not want the talk to end here.

'Camlann,' repeated Garulf. 'I had been in Frisia for a while, learning the art of guiding the prow across the yellow waves, for one can never know too much of the sea.

'Then I came back to the lands of the Gewisse. Bieda sought men for his mead hall, and it was good to be in the haunts of my youth again. Cerdic was silent then, licking his wounds, for Arthur and the Lords of Dumnonia had grown tired of his constant raiding and had burned his hall around his ears.

'Bieda wanted fame and glory, to surpass his rival Cerdic Elesing.

'He bestowed rings freely on his followers, and we knew there would be a price to pay, yet we were willing.

'Many of the British were restless under Arthur's rule – for twenty years he had kept them from each other's throats, a thankless task. Now they sought freedom from his curb, and to this end some of them made alliance with men like Bieda, who promised them land and riches in return for their aid.

'I do not believe they wanted Arthur's death. I think they wanted his wings clipped, his power pruned so that he was once again merely the leader of the Warband of Britain, a servant of the princes and not their master. But if they had thought on it more deeply, if they had not been blinded by their own greed, they would have seen that a man like Arthur could never be less than Emperor, whatever they chose to call him.'

'You sound sorry,' said Wicga.

'I am. This island was a better place when Arthur was alive. Yes, I know it sounds strange, coming from me who fought at Camlann. I fought against him because I was Bieda's man, and a warrior must follow his lord, not because I thought Arthur was my enemy.'

'But if Arthur were living, we would not be here now!' protested Wicga.

'True enough. In his day the boundaries were marked and kept, and none dared expand their territories or found new earldoms. To my mind that was no bad thing.'

'No bad thing!' repeated Wicga. 'If you believe that, then why are you with us now?'

Garulf smiled. 'Because I live in the world as it is, not as it was or might be. Arthur is gone, and more's the pity, to my mind.'

'Tell us about Camlann,' urged Ceolric.

'Camlann,' he said, closing his eyes and rocking back and forth. 'Bieda marched us there, to meet with his new allies, and had we known where we were going I think most of us would have turned back.'

He shuddered. 'I had never fought in a battle like that. I doubt if any of you have either. It was carnage, the slaughter of thousands, the death of a generation of fighting men. Rarely do more than a few hundred meet in the field these days, and though the old tales tell of mighty hostings, of thousands gathering to feed the ravens, as if such armies were once common, I think the gleemen exaggerate for the glory of their heroes.'

'Up to seven men, thieves; up to thirty-five men, a band; over thirty-five, an army,' muttered Wicga, quoting an old saying.

'Bieda and his neighbours had raised an army of nearly four hundred men, all battle hardened, besides their servants and followers. We marched because there were not enough ponies in all the lands of the Gewisse to carry such a force, and what horses the *ealdormen* could find were used for carrying our supplies.

'It was late in the year for such a venture. Months had gone into gathering the host, into arming the warriors, into preparing the food for them. Four hundred men and their retinues cannot live off the land. I remember that the leaves were turning as we crossed the Avon and moved into hostile country, skirting the edge of Sallow Wood.

'It had been an ill summer, and the trackways had never dried out from the previous winter. We slithered through mud, making slow headway.

'At last we came in sight of the tidal marshes which protected the northern flank of Dumnonia. Here some of our allies awaited us, and here too came word that Arthur was on the move, drawing together all those still loyal to him.

'Even then I wondered about the wisdom of what we were doing, but a man must follow his lord, and I had feasted in Bieda's hall, and drunk his mead, and taken the rings he bestowed.'

Garulf smiled wistfully. 'Arthur caught us by surprise, of course, which was ever his way. Nobody ever moved as fast as he did. We woke one morning to the sounds of the warhorns blowing, and knew – though it seemed beyond belief – that the Battle Emperor of Britain was upon us.

'You asked if horsemen are dangerous. These were Arthur's Companions, unmatched in the making of war, and they made our allies look like children mounted on donkeys. They cut through them, turned and cut again, moving like thunderbolts, the blue steel of their upraised blades gleaming in the sun.

'Then it was our turn. The only way to stand against good cavalry is to make the shield wall, the battle pen, to form in a square with all your spears bristling outwards like a hedgepig, and to *hold firm*. If the square breaks they are in among you, and then you are doomed.

'It was terrible work. We stood shoulder to shoulder, shield to shield, locked together, not daring to move. The sky clouded over and it began to drizzle: a fine penetrating rain that damped the bow strings and left them useless, that soaked you to the skin and made the grass greasy underfoot.

'They rode across our front in long lines like ribbons in a girl's hair, crossing and recrossing so it seemed the columns must crash into each other though they never did, showering us with javelins. All around me men went down, and we shuffled closer to fill the space and keep the shields locked. Though we did not know it we were shifting crabwise to the right all the time as each one tried to hide behind the shield of the man next to him. The Britons were herding us, slowly but surely, towards the edge of the marsh.

'Gradually our shields fell, either because they were so splintered and weighted with spearheads that they were worthless, or because their owners were dead or badly wounded.

'After a long while there came a moment of silence. The Britons stopped their war cries, the battle horns went quiet, and the horsemen withdrew. It was then that I realized how far we had shuffled from our original position, how near we were to the treacherous marsh.

'A man rode out before the British lines, sword in hand. He sat and surveyed us, trotted along our front like a farmer inspecting his flock. I knew him, even at a distance. It was Bedwyr, the first of Arthur's Companions, his oldest friend since Cei's death a few

116

years earlier: the most dangerous man in all Britain after Arthur himself.

'He studied us for a while, made up his mind in no great hurry – he was giving the horses a blow, of course – and then the end began.

'Did any of you ever hear the Companions when they decided to charge home? After they have softened you up with all that dancing back and forth, those little rushes when you think they're going to ride right down on you and then they swerve off at the last moment, there suddenly comes a time when the lances drop forward and you have perhaps ten heartbeats in which to say to yourself *this is it*!

'There's a noise they make, quite unlike all the whooping and shouting that goes on earlier. It's a droning, made from deep in the throat – I can't do it and anyway it doesn't sound the same coming from just one mouth. You have to imagine it rising from three hundred throats, a hideous racket that makes your bowels turn to water, an inhuman sound that begins as they ride in for the kill. It's the most terrifying sound I've ever heard.

'We broke, as Bedwyr had known we would break. It was like a rampart of sand trying to hold against the sea: first one part is breached, then another, the gaps widen and suddenly instead of a wall there are only a few scattered islands hanging on a moment longer before they too slip away.

'I do not remember much about it. I saw Bieda cut down by a sword stroke; I saw the axes of those nearest him rising and falling as they struggled to protect his body; I saw the shattering of spears and the splintering of shields. A pony barged me and I went sprawling in the mud; I heard the horns sounding the recall and the horsemen went back, leaving their infantry to finish us off.

'I was in the tall reeds at the edge of the marsh. As I staggered to my feet I could see that the cavalry were withdrawing to meet a new threat, and then I was forced to run and hide to escape those who were bent on hunting us down.

'Afterwards it was said that the whole thing had been planned from the beginning, that we and a part of our allies' army had met early in order to lure Arthur to the battle site, where a second force would fall upon him once he was so heavily engaged he could not regroup his men to meet the new enemy.

'I do not believe that. I was there, and it did not feel that way. I think the second part of our army was simply late to the field, by accident or through stupidity rather than by design. If anything, I would guess things were the other way about: as I said before, the Emperor had struck faster than anyone expected, catching our leaders unawares before our full host had gathered.

'I was luckier than most. I managed to slip away through the reeds in the confusion. Not many others returned alive from Camlann, on either side. I heard afterwards that the combat continued until scarcely a man remained upon his feet, until the ground was littered with the corpses of warriors and horses, until the waters of the marsh were dyed a deep red by the blood that had been spilt.'

He stopped talking, reached for a water bottle to wet his throat, sat shaking his head at the memory.

'So you did not see what happened to Arthur?' somebody said.

'No. I did not see him.' He shrugged. 'But then the only person I recognized all the long day was Bedwyr, and that only because he rode out alone between the hosts.'

'I heard that Arthur was the last to fall,' said Wicga.

Garulf laughed. 'So the gleemen sing. But it makes a better story that way, doesn't it? I have no idea what happened to him. I did hear that he was wounded in the first cavalry charge and played no further part in the battle, but the same person told me Bieda was killed by Bedwyr himself, and I don't think that was true.'

'Sa, sa,' said Wicga. He stared into the fire, thinking. 'They are gone now, the Companions of Arthur. There are none left alive, for the last of them fell at Camlann. I understand a little of your sorrow, Garulf, for it is always a sadness to see a thing of beauty end. But tell me this. Are the horsemen of Dumnonia whom we shall shortly face as deadly as the Companions of old?'

Garulf shrugged. 'Some are. It is only ten years since Camlann. Many men now living were trained by the Companions, especially here in the west. What they lack is a leader to match Arthur, but his like will not come again in our time.'

'So.' Wicga's gaze travelled around the ring of firelight, pausing as he weighed this man or that in the scales. 'If they come against us, and they will, we must choose the place we meet. And whatever else may happen, we must stand our ground.'

'Not hard,' said one of the crew.

'I trust not,' answered Wicga, and there was a cold menace in his voice which made even Ceolric his son shiver.

One by one the men rolled themselves in their cloaks and slept with the sound of the sea in their ears, while the moon rose high in the heavens and the cold stars glittered down on them.

4

Again Budoc woke from a nightmare, dragged himself panting from the depths of sleep, until his breathing calmed and the sweat dried on his body and he realized he was safe.

He had dreamed he was riding with the Hawk, riding down through the woods by the sea to the village.

'Scotti!' said the Hawk, pointing through the trees.

Three vessels of wood and hide, larger versions of the coracles used by the villagers, tugged at their anchors on the still waters of the creek.

Budoc heeled his pony to gallop down the slope, but the Hawk snatched at the reins and held him back.

'Not so fast, cousin. Will you ride at them alone and unarmed?'

Budoc looked down at himself, and to his horror found he was dressed in his hermit's robe, that he bore neither weapon nor shield.

The Hawk kept his hand on the reins. 'It was fighting against the Scotti on the river bank by Peryddon that I fell, old friend. I would not see you slain in the same fashion.'

'What of the villagers?' demanded Budoc.

'Too late for them. Your prayers have not kept them safe.' The Hawk laughed, a harsh and bitter laugh unlike anything the hermit remembered hearing from him in life, and turned so that Budoc saw him full face for the first time.

The other had been dead for a long while. The right side of his head was a ruin of blackened flesh and splintered white bone. The blow that dealt the damage must have killed him instantaneously, though now his eyes glittered with an unnatural life as he fixed the hermit with his gaze and said:

'The war did not end at Camlann, any more than it ended at Badon. You shame us, cousin, with your bleating and pleading to God. Did it never occur to you that the Lord your God might grow bored with your endless petitions?'

The ruined face was thrust into his. He could smell the other's fetid breath, the stench of the grave clinging to his clothing.

'They are coming for you, cousin. Take your things, the contents of the chest you carried with you to the monastery and home again, and hide them somewhere safe. Then hide yourself, and be ready, for I say again – they are coming for you.'

'Gwalchmei,' he muttered in the safe gloom of the hut. Gwalchmei, the hawk-faced falcon of the plains, the best of walkers and the best of riders; Gwalchmei who never returned empty-handed from any quest, the golden-tongued nephew of the Emperor.

Strange to dream of the Scotti. It had been thirty years or more since their curraghs raided these southern shores, though the northern and western coasts were still troubled by them; five years or more since Gereint mab Cadwy had destroyed the last of the Irish settlements along the River Oak.

The dream must be connected with his vision in the pool. If the Scotti were to come – it seemed unlikely, but he had learned over the years to trust his dreams, especially dreams as vivid as this one – what should he do?

Lying on the field of Camlann, helpless against the things that prowled the night, convinced that he was dying, he had sworn an oath. If he survived, he would go to Armorica, to Lesser Britain, study in one of the religious houses there, and spend the remainder of his life contemplating the infinite nature of God.

The Abbot had warned him of the dangers of too much fasting and meditation. Many monks had fallen into the temptation of seeking visions for their own sake. It was all too easy, once the fleshly prison had been mortified, to achieve a trance state, to quit the body and behold angelic choirs singing the praises of the Lord – or whatever else one wished.

He had tried to avoid such self-indulgence. Yet there was no denying that he had frequently lost all sense of time while praying or meditating on the Mystery. Of itself there was nothing wrong with that, provided it was God's will which was being done, and not his, a mere sinner.

Budoc paced up and down the hut. He had slept late – his illness had wrought havoc on his sleeping pattern. He could hear harsh cawing of the rooks in the trees outside. Everything sounded normal.

The most sensible thing was to go to the village. If the Scotti had already landed he could decide what to do next. If they had not, then he could tell the locals of his dream, try to persuade them to flee inland. They looked upon him as a holy man, one standing in a long tradition stretching back into a forgotten past, exactly the sort of person who might be sent prophetic dreams. There was a good chance they would heed his words.

Of course, if it all proved to be a false alarm, they would never listen to him again. But in his heart of hearts he did not think it was.

He left the hut, blinking in the bright sunshine, and walked towards the cliff path. After a few paces he stopped, recalling the Hawk's parting words: *Hide your things.*

He returned to the hut and pulled out the carved chest he had carried with him from Caer Cadwy to the monastery in Armorica, and thence back across the Narrow Sea to this quiet corner of Dumnonia. At times Budoc had wondered if he were not deluding himself, if he truly needed to lug this great box any further, but its contents were important to him.

Near the top were eight carefully wrapped goblets of finely blown green glass which had belonged to his grandfather; quite unlike the crude work one found nowadays, they were his last material link with his Roman ancestors. Under the glassware was a knee-length tunic of rich red cloth and matching breeches, which had formed the basis of his parade ground uniform in the days when he had been one of Arthur's Companions. And under them lay the sword he had carried at Camlann, still sharp though he had no intention of ever wielding it in anger again.

Not every object within the chest belonged to him. For one in particular he was no more than a temporary guardian, in fulfilment of the oath he had sworn long ago to Arthur and to Gwenhwyvar.

(Especially Gwenhwyvar . . .

Face like stone bleached of all colour, deep fissures running from nose to mouth, dripping hair plastered flat to her head, leaning over the pallet on which he waited helpless to discover whether he would live or die . . .

And her voice cold and merciless as the moon and stars commanding him to live that he might keep his oath . . .)

Budoc hoisted the carved box onto his shoulder and strode from the hollow where the hut stood, making for the headland at the mouth of the estuary.

He was panting through gritted teeth by the time he reached the cliffs. He lowered the chest, massaged his shoulder-blade where the sharp edges had cut into it, and looked around for a suitable hiding place.

Here the cliff tumbled sheer to the restless sea in a mass of splits and crevices. Birds nestled on the ledges below him, oblivious to his head peering cautiously out over the abyss. Far below the waves broke like thunder in clouds of spray and spume, frothing against the rocks.

Further out he could see patterns of blue and green and olive on the sea bed. The other side of the estuary was lower and gentler than the one on which he stood, and was covered with red kelp growing along the shoreline where the rocks slanted slightly inland in flat layers like beds worn smooth by the endless actions of the waves.

He found a cleft in the cliff face beneath him large enough to take the chest, and gently lowered it into position, arms trembling with the strain. It came to rest just out of his reach, and for a moment he wondered how he was ever going to recover it.

But at least it was safe for the present, and only visible if one leaned right out almost to the point of overbalancing, as he was doing now. Nobody would find it unless they already knew it was there.

Satisfied, he straightened and, moving quickly now, descended from the cliffs to the shoreline, following the route he had ridden in his dream. The sun was high in the sky, and the waters of the estuary glittered and danced in the strong light.

Nothing moved apart from a few seabirds preening and diving far out in the channel.

He knew something was wrong, knew it with a cold and sick certainty. At this time of day the main fishing run might be over, but there should still have been a few coracles scattered across the inlet. More to the point, he should have been able to see the smoke of the cooking fires hazing the air above the trees.

Cautiously he went forward, taking advantage of the cover afforded by the woodland, using skills he had not used for ten years or more.

What he saw when he reached a place from which he could look down upon the village without being seen came as no surprise. Three curraghs, war-boats of the Scotti, were drawn up on the strand.

He had come too late.

CHAPTER SEVEN

1

At last the voyage was over.

It had been a journey of wonder and splendour, fit to match any of the legendary voyages their forefathers had made. The wind Wotan had sent had never faltered, not even on this third day, not even when they reached the place where the smooth straight-falling cliffs beside which they had sailed for so long gave way to gnarled crags and deep indentations, to promontories folded over and over upon themselves, to islanded pinnacles battered by waves and surf, and Wicga had ordered them further out to sea.

He had been worried lest the *Sea Stallion* be caught in some current and flung against the jagged rocks. Ceolric, watching, had seen that Garulf had been equally worried that the wind which had blown fair and strong ever since they left Cerdicesora would fail them at last, leaving them becalmed far out on the deeps.

But it had not failed, and when they worked their way inshore again they were within sight of a long headland jutting out into the waves like a half-submerged monster, all neck and shoulders, which Garulf said meant that they were very close to their goal.

Hearing this Wicga began to encourage the crew, saying again what he had said before. Others in this land had built for themselves, in the space of a single generation, a kingdom able to withstand the attacks of its neighbours. They could do likewise, here in the west. Already they were entering the empty lands, occupied only by harmless peasants and fishermen; soon they would reach the sheltered place Garulf remembered, where they would put ashore and found the kingdom of the Sae-ware, the Sea Folk.

By the time he had finished the headland was well astern, a dark loom on the horizon.

Ceolric had been busy about his duties while his father was talking. Having heard the speech so often he had scarcely bothered to listen – though he had taken care to look eager in the proper places. Instead he had watched Garulf standing by the steering oar.

The Frisian's face, tanned and wrinkled by his years at sea, had been set in a distant expression whose meaning Ceolric could not read. Garulf was brooding, though whether on the captain's words or on something else Ceolric could not tell.

At length the older man seemed to wake from his trance. He beckoned to Ceolric, and started to tell him about the estuary towards which they were running.

To Ceolric's eyes all this stretch of coast looked much alike, a featureless mass of rounded humps, seeming harmless from a distance but disguising rocks, shoals, strange cross-currents and ever steepening waves as one came closer.

Once Garulf had pointed it out he could just see a shape like a snail with its head out of its shell nestling under the grey blur of the cliffs. Had he not been told he would never have guessed there was a channel to the west of the snail's head; he would have assumed the line of the cliffs continued unbroken.

As the sun began to sink towards the sea, and Garulf took the helm to bring them safe into the estuary, Ceolric offered up a prayer to his ancestors and to the founder of his line, Wotan the god of wind and war, the master of magic.

The *Sea Stallion* came heeling round, the great green sail belling and filling with the wind of evening, following the dancing track of red and gold the sinking sun had laid upon the waters.

Under Ceolric's bare feet the ship shivered like a living thing. Wicga turned and grinned at him, lips pink against the brown and grey of his beard, shouted above the noise of wind and sea:

'Watch this, boy, and learn how it's done!'

The headland loomed, seemingly a solid mass. The *Sea Stallion* was turning to run towards the shore, shaking under the strain as the crew fought to bring her round.

The following waves raced forward, still moving faster than the vessel, and the planks creaked as the swell overtook them, tightening and loosening on their bindings, so that it sounded as if a company of rats were scrabbling along the hull.

Suddenly the narrow mouth of the inlet was before them. The water boiled about the rock-strewn cliffs on either side, and the salt spray dashed across Ceolric's face, blinding him.

The stallion figurehead gave a little nod as the prow faltered in its rise. The quivering of the body and the toss of the head made the ship seem like a horse gathering itself for a jump, and she plunged towards the gap between the cliffs, outrunning the waves in her haste to reach journey's end.

Garulf the Frisian wrestled frantically with the steering oar (which even at the best of times had only a limited effect on their course), struggling to keep them near the western shore, for they knew that just inside the entrance much of the channel was blocked by a sandbar, and travelling at this speed they would tear the mast out of her if they ran aground.

Then they were through, before they had time to be afraid, through and into the calmer waters of the drowned valley. The sail went slack as the headland stole the wind, and they slid forward slowly, gradually losing way, till Wicga shouted for them to man the oars.

So they ended their voyage as they had begun, creeping towards the shelter of a small cove like a many-legged sea beast, the crew laughing as they rowed.

The men pulled on the oars with the steady rhythm they could maintain for hours, and the ship was filled with the music of the blades dipping in the water and the creak of the rope rowlocks, with the squeals of cleats and blocks and the muted thunder of the sail as it was furled and lowered with its yard.

From his seat on the oar bench Ceolric gazed at the shore. On the larboard side steep cliffs fell jagged to the sea. Gulls and gannets and kittiwakes clung to narrow ledges or circled above them, fussing and quarrelling, ignoring the passing ship. As he watched, a gannet hurled itself free of the cliff, stalled and dived, a white plume marking the spot where it had struck the surface of the estuary. After a few moments the dark head reappeared, gulping down a fish.

On the other side the slope was gentler. Wooded hills gave way to great shelves of rock, speckled with limpets and smothered in layers of red and brown weed.

'No signs of life,' muttered one of his fellows.

'The native villages are hidden away out of sight,' said Garulf from his post at the steering oar. 'Imagine a mutilated left hand laid palm down on a bench. We are travelling along the wrist. The thumb is a creek hidden from us by yonder headland, and has been split by an axe to the depth of its top joint, so that it divides at the low water limit.'

He waved his hand in the air to demonstrate what he was saying.

'The forefinger is a second, much longer inlet, opening some distance above the thumb. Then the fool's and leech fingers form the main channel, lying together for most of their length and forking at the top joint. That leaves the little finger, which is a stub cut off at the first knuckle. Its entrance is opposite the thumb.

'The natives live nicely tucked away from prying eyes along these various channels. There are more creeks off the western side, between the leech and little fingers. But it's years since I was here last, and I cannot remember exactly.'

They drew level with a small cove on the starboard shore. Ceolric could see the shimmer of a stream sluicing through the yellow sand.

'Do we beach her?' asked one of the crew, hopefully.

Wicga thought for a moment, while the oarsmen rested and the *Sea Stallion* slid forward under her own momentum, the wavelets gurgling sweetly against her hull.

'No, best not tonight. We will run no risks till we know the mettle of the natives. Tonight we keep water under our keel, and a normal watch. Garulf, Ceolric, take the skins and fill them from the stream, then, if it seems safe, scout inland a little.'

They brought the ship as far inshore as they could without grounding her. The two men slipped over the side and waded through the surf to the beach, then followed the shallow stream until they found a pool deep enough to fill the containers. 'I'll take the skins,' said Garulf. 'You keep watch.'

On two sides the cove ended in low, rocky cliffs, perhaps twice the height of a man and easily scaled. On the third, directly ahead, it merged gently into a wooded valley; peering along the line of the stream Ceolric glimpsed what he thought might be rough pasture, well screened by the trees.

Nervous, he laid a hand on the war-knife at his hip. Garulf stiffened, whispered:

'What is it?'

'Nothing. A bird in the undergrowth.' For the first time Ceolric realized the older man was as apprehensive as he.

'There. Finished.' Garulf straightened stiffly, joints popping, blinking wearily. 'I think we are safe enough. The people here are farmers and fishermen, not warriors. All the same, somebody is watching us from among the trees.'

Ceolric started, tightened his grip on the long knife. 'Where?'

The Frisian smiled. 'It will do no harm to let him know we have seen him. Behind the pine tree with the crooked top, on the right of the stream. Do you have him? Good.' He picked up the skins, heavy now with the weight of the sweet water, handed half of them to Ceolric. 'I think he is no more than a herdsman. They probably graze sheep or cattle on that pasture. Still, no doubt your father will keep a good look out tonight.'

'Should we scout inland as Wicga said?'

The older man shook his head. 'No. No, let them think us voyagers who have sought a safe harbour for the night. If we scout now, they will realize our interest is in the land, not the sea. At the moment we are no threat to them. They have nothing worth taking, except their livestock, and we are hardly likely to want to ship their cattle, are we? Let them be, and they will leave us in peace, in the hope that on the morrow we will go away.'

He turned his back on the half-seen watcher and strode confidently down to where the ship waited, lifting gently on the breath of the sea. Ceolric followed nervously with an uncomfortable itch between his shoulders.

Willing hands reached down to haul them aboard, and the oars plied the water once more, easing them clear of the shore, then spinning them around under the captain's direction to the place he had chosen for the night's anchorage.

Garulf repeated what he had said on the beach. Wicga nodded in agreement, glancing around at the crew for any signs of dissent. One or two grumbled, having hoped to stretch their legs, then fell to arguing over whose turn it was to stand the first watch.

Like most vessels of her kind, *Sea Stallion* had a crew divided into four watches. The most experienced were the bow men, whose duty it was to watch for rocks; the second group were responsible for the single trapezoid sail, and for baling at sea. These were the two watches before the mast. The two watches aft the mast were made up of the least experienced sailors, and were responsible for the anchor and mooring cables, and for baling in harbour. Ceolric, whose first voyage this was, was in the fourth group, the stern watch, and it was inevitable that Wicga would settle the argument by making them responsible for the first part of the night.

Slowly the day turned to dusk. The green hills of the valley became blue, their features merging into ill-defined patches of dark or light. Night birds began to flit across the estuary, feeding on the rising insects. On the far shore a dog howled, the sound echoing eerily over the water for a while, until it stopped as suddenly as it had begun. One by one the men wrapped themselves in their cloaks and slept.

Soon it was very dark. The moon would not rise for some time yet, and in any case the sky had clouded over at about sunset, so that even when it did rise it would cast little light. Ceolric found himself using his ears rather than his eyes, listening to the lap of the waves on the hull, counting the rhythm, waiting for the one which slapped harder than its fellows. He could hear the rasp of shingle being dragged down the beach by the hissing undertow. He could hear the rustle of the night breeze in the leaves. He could hear the groans and breathing of his sleeping companions, the occasional twitch of those who kept watch with him.

The attack, when it came, caught them all by surprise.

2

The warriors stood on the clifftop, the salt breeze ruffling their long hair, their faces grim as they stared out to sea, squinting against the light.

Long, slim and swift, the war-ship was running free before the wind, her square sail taut-curved, the wave thresh white at her throat.

Nai thought that she was beautiful.

'I had thought they would be further ahead of us than this. The wind was against them at the start, I suppose,' said Gorthyn, frowning.

They drew back from the edge lest they be seen.

'It looks as if they do intend to enter the estuary of Porthyle. Good farmland, but little in the way of pickings for pirates.' Gorthyn was thinking aloud.

Nai coughed.

'Sheltering overnight?' said the big man. 'Perhaps. But I fear Gereint was right when he told us that these pirates seek new lands to settle.'

He sighed, turned to check his pony's girth. Nai stayed staring at the ship, wondering what sights she had seen, what manner of men were aboard her, whether they were eager or fearful now that their voyage was nearly done. (He too was afraid Gereint had been right: these were not casual raiders pausing for a night's shelter, but settlers come to take and hold some of the rich red farmland.)

'What worries me, cousin,' Gorthyn called over his shoulder, 'is that the estuary is vulnerable. Sometimes these Saeson dogs kill for the sake of killing, like a fox in a hen coop.'

The ship was turning now, where the sun's slow dying made the water dance, swinging round so that he could see the uneven stripes of the sail.

'Did I ever tell you the tale of how Cei and my great-uncle fought the Saesons at Penhyle?' Gorthyn picked up his pony's reins and prepared to mount. 'Stand, Broad-Belly, stand,' he hissed through his teeth.

Nai nodded. *Often*, he thought, hiding a smile.

He could see figures on the deck, half hidden by the billow of the sail. From where he stood the ship seemed to be aiming directly at the land, but he knew the mouth of the estuary lay out of sight somewhere over the next hill.

'It was only a skirmish, really,' Gorthyn said regretfully as he swung himself into the saddle. 'But so far as I know they have not been this way since.'

They rode along the edge of the cliff, seabirds crying around them, letting the horses choose their own route through the tangled furze.

The ship was gone now, vanished behind a headland. Not a trace of her passage remained.

'Even Penhyle at the head of the estuary is only an overgrown village.' Gorthyn was still thinking aloud. 'I went there years ago, when Gereint made me help with the tax gathering. You were healing of your wound at the time.'

And mourning Seradwen, thought Nai, *who had left me to marry a farmer not long before we rode to make an end of Eremon and his Scotti pillagers.*

She was a fine woman, long-legged and full-breasted, with far too good a wit to be wasted on a man who spends his life grubbing in the dirt. But she was not one to be a warrior's wife either, though she was my mistress for a while, for she made mock of what she called our childish obsession with weapons, our endless arguments over which was better, the war-knife or the sword. She thought our cattle- and sheep-raiding absurd, said it was an overblown game for drunks, nothing but a lot of shouting and waving of spears. The only people who were killed were the ones who fell off their horses, which is a surprisingly easy thing to do when you are drunk.

'I do not know the far side of the creek very well, but from what I recall there is nothing there,' said Gorthyn, breaking into his thoughts.

Nai raised a quizzical eyebrow.

'Well, you know what I mean. The people live well enough and the soil is fertile, but they are not rich. They are simple folk. I doubt if they are even Christian. *Pagans*,' he added, using the old Latin word for a country dweller.

'Still,' he said after a moment's silence, 'we'll find out tomorrow.'

They did not travel much further that evening. As the long twilight settled across the land they came to a little valley with a stream tumbling to the sea, and here they halted for the night, still several miles from the estuary but seeing no purpose in pushing ahead over unfamiliar ground to arrive in the dark.

Besides, both of them were hungry, and at this distance they had no qualms about lighting a fire, which they would have hesitated to do had they been nearer to the Saxon ship.

Nai took care of the ponies while Gorthyn gathered kindling, dividing the tasks between them without the need for speech. Then they cooked a piece of bacon over the fire, and ate it hot and sizzling, washed down with water from the stream.

Afterwards they talked, two old friends and foster brothers who had known each other for so long they had no secrets. They spoke of girls they had loved and men they had hated, of horses and hounds and comrades long gone, of hunting stags or boars in the summer and wolves in the winter.

Not once did they touch upon the Saeson settlers and the long ship they had seen. They did not speak of Custennin their king or Gereint their overlord. Nor did they mention Eremon their onetime friend and his Scotti followers.

At last they drew straws for who should take the first watch, and it fell to Nai to stay wakeful while Gorthyn wrapped himself in his cloak beside the embers of the fire.

Nai moved away from the light. He found himself a convenient rock in the shadows where the side of the valley became so steep it formed a miniature precipice, and there he settled.

He did not expect to be disturbed. The flames of the fire would have been hidden from prying eyes by the hollow of the coombe, and the smoke had been quickly wafted away by the sea breeze. Not many people used the old track along the cliffs any more, and it was some distance to the nearest settlement.

This had probably been pasture land once upon a time, held in common by the local peasant farmers. When he had hobbled the ponies he had noticed a ring of stones half buried under the long grass, and he guessed that at some stage they had made the base of a herder's summer bothy, a small shelter of woven poles laid atop a stone foundation.

How long ago? A hundred years? Two hundred, three? There was no way of telling. All that mattered was that it was a long time, so long that those who had built the hut had withered into dust, and all their hopes and fears with them.

It was Gorthyn's father, Erfai, who had first taught him to notice these things. Everywhere in Dumnonia one came across traces of old workings: barrows and cairns, ditches and mounds, stone rows and circles. There was scarcely a defensible site which had not at some time been fortified, not a river which had not at some point along its course had its banks improved.

Erfai had also shown him that the land itself altered over the years. Most people thought of the country as unchanging, as being fixed for ever into arable or pasture or woods. When Nai and Gorthyn were boys Erfai had taken them to the place where *his* father had been born: a Roman farmhouse now fallen into ruin.

He had led them out into the fields and shown them how the

brush and saplings were slowly covering the land. 'The forest is coming back,' he had said, and it was true. Even as boys they could see that within another few years the old field walls would be buried under woodland, and that only somebody very observant would think it strange that all the trees were of much the same age. Most people would just assume this had always been a wood.

The rock was cold, even through the thickness of his cloak. Nai stood, keeping his movements smooth and even so as not to startle any watchers, and took a few paces to warm himself.

The moon had risen high enough for its light to reach the middle of the valley. The stream was a silver ribbon flowing endlessly to the sea, with the night mist curling above it to mark its course where the water was hidden by the lie of the land.

The fire had burned very low now, only the ghost of a glow showing where it had been. Gorthyn's black bulk lay beside it, snoring softly. Nai moved nearer the ponies, keeping to the shadows, seeing how close he could get before they sensed him.

His own horse, Coal, turned his head and pricked his ears before Nai had gone very far. Nai froze, and Coal went back to sleep, deciding he represented no threat.

A dog fox trotted from the trees fringing the far side of the hollow, halted with one paw raised to scent the air, glanced idly at the ponies and loped towards the stream. It drank without haste, then paused to wipe its mask before melting back into the darkness.

Convinced by this that there were no other people within miles, Nai allowed himself to relax. He returned to his rock and sat down, lost himself in contemplation of the stars. There were the seven stars of Arthur's Wain, the Great Bear, the revolving axle of the heavens, which wheels ever round the still centre of things, the only constellation which never bathes in the ocean. And above them was Caer Arianrhod, the Castle of the Silver Round, the Crown of the North Wind, where Arthur went with all his men on a quest from which but seven returned.

Staring at the stars tired his eyes. He let them close for a moment, and slipped into a trancelike state where he was aware of every breath of wind in the trees, every rustle in the long grass, every movement around him.

When Eurgain was a child her mother would sing her lullabies, silly little songs like:

Dinogad's coat is coloured bright
Mama made it from marten skins
Sewn together all snug and tight
To keep her baby warm at night

On a winter's evening, when the winds whistled around the hut the children would snuggle under their covers against the wall and squint shyly around the posts that divided them from the living area, watching the red glow of the fire burning on the central hearth.

They would listen to the slow rhythm of the adults' speech, hoping their mother would not see the fire reflected in their eyes. If she did, and if she thought it was past time they were asleep, she would come over and sing to them, her voice soft and sweet against the deeper burr of the men's conversation.

Eurgain stirred in her sleep, her mother's voice fading away though she could still hear the growl of the menfolk, talking about taking the coracles out across the estuary.

It was cold. Perhaps the fire had gone out. She half opened one eye, wondering why her mother had stopped singing before she was properly asleep. The fire seemed to be a very long way away, a tiny glow down in the valley, and her bedding seemed to have taken root, to be growing all around her.

The ground was damp. The bracken fronds glistened in the moonlight. She shook herself, not understanding what she was doing out in the open in the middle of the night.

She was lying on the edge of the wood, above the top field. How strange. What was even stranger was that the village seemed to be having a celebration of some kind, because there was a great fire burning in the space between the huts, and she could see shapes moving back and forth around it in a shuffling dance.

She could hear them talking, the words travelling far on the still night air. The accents sounded odd, almost foreign, and a lot of what they said seemed to be nonsense words.

One voice dominated the others. It belonged to an angry man who was arguing fiercely with his fellows. He seemed to have something wrong with his speech, so that he could not pronounce his Ps or Bs properly (sounds between which she made no great distinction herself), making a harsh cutting noise instead.

When he spoke of children he said '*clanna*' and not '*plant*', and when he said something about the horsemen of the British he called them '*Cruidni*' not '*Prydani*' or '*Britanni*'.

He was saying that they should not have killed the children, which sounded very reasonable to her. Personally she did not see why anybody had to be killed, child or adult.

Then the man went on to say that the lord would send his warband, his horsemen, and this was not a good place to fight them.

He was right there, she muttered to herself. Her kinfolk would be cross if these strangers started fighting in the fields before the crops were harvested. They would frighten all the game with their shouting and screaming, gallop their heavy-footed ponies through the countryside without so much as a by your leave, demand food and shelter at any time of the day or night . . .

She could see her father's face swelling at the very idea, the veins throbbing in his temples and throat, the colour rising in his cheeks. He was a frightening man when he was very, very angry.

Eurgain stopped suddenly with her mouth open.

For a moment she seemed to be teetering on the edge of an enormous chasm.

She looked down at her hands, pale against the darkness of the earth. They were not the hands of a small girl. The veins stood out on the back, which somebody had once told her was one of the signs that you were now a woman, in the sense of being a responsible member of the community as opposed to the more obvious senses such as being able to bear a child.

She brought herself up with a jerk. She was sweating, though not long ago she had been cold.

The people in the village were moving towards the shore. (Who were these people and what were they doing in her village? Why was she up here alone on the hillside?)

They were taking the fishing coracles, lifting them out onto the water. One man was standing with his arms outstretched, head flung so far back his neck must be on the point of dislocation, looking at the sky.

Thin wisps of cloud rolled across the stars, blotting them out momentarily. Larger shreds gathered near the moon, writhing and boiling as if a great wind blew, though not a breath of it reached Eurgain on her hillside.

She looked again at the man by the shore and knew that this was his doing. Somehow he was calling together the clouds, sending them to hide the moon.

At this distance she could not make out his features, especially now the moonlight had dimmed, but she already knew how he would look. He would be thin-faced, vicious as a stoat. His head would be shaved in a strip running from ear to ear, and behind the bare strip the hair would fall to his shoulders. His eyes would be black and hard, their gaze penetrating.

She knew this because . . . because . . . Because she had seen him before, and something terrible had happened not long after, something she did not want to remember.

The coracles were fairly launched now. Each cut a dark vee through the ripples, reflecting the fractured light of the moon as it fought against the clouds the shaven man had summoned; and in the half-light she could just make out a series of dark heads swimming behind or beside the little fleet.

Five or six huge shapes prowled along the shore, paddling into the water then darting back to safety. They might have been wolves, but they were too tall and too rangy. If they were dogs they were like no dog she had ever seen, and she did not understand where they had come from.

Eurgain had thought of slipping down into the village while the strangers were away and trying to find her parents, who must surely be very worried about her by now, but the creatures frightened her and she thought it best to lie still.

She must have dozed again, for suddenly she could hear shouting and splashing, followed by the clash of weapons. A bird roosting in the tree above her head croaked in protest, was answered by others deeper in the forest.

The hounds on the shore flung back their heads and howled, the sound echoing across the water. The shaven man walked among them, soothing them, then led them away along the beach.

As they vanished from sight Eurgain eased herself out from under the bracken. She was stiff, cramped from being in one position for too long. When she stood she felt dizzy, almost as if she might faint, and only kept her head by digging her nails hard into the palms of her hands.

The dew-laden fields glimmered in the moonglow. Shadows chased across the hillside, clustered along the lines of the hedges. The sheep and cattle had been wakened by the baying of the hounds, and huddled uneasily in the corners of the pastures. Great swathes had been trampled through the ripening corn.

She stared at the colourless landscape, struggling to remember what had happened, but her mind kept sliding away from the subject, insisting that she was cold and hungry and that the need for food came first.

She was hungry, hungrier than she had ever been.

She had eaten in the morning before leaving home. Fish and bread, washed down with a draught of sheep's milk.

Why was she so hungry now?

When she left to fetch the boys her mother had been about to start baking. There would be fresh bread waiting for her – well, not so fresh now, not warm from the oven, but fresh enough.

Bread and honey. That would be good. Her stomach was hollow, painfully hollow, pressing against her backbone so hard it hurt, ached with emptiness.

How long since she had last eaten?

She had shared some of the mussels poor Bran had found on the beach that morning. (Why *poor* Bran? It was Edar who was the poor one, the weak one, the clumsy one. There was nothing wrong with Bran.)

So she had eaten well today. (Yesterday – the moon was high now.) Not excessively well, not as much as the day before, but well enough. Living in a land of plenty, her people saw no great virtue in being fat – unlike others she had heard of, where it was taken as a sign of wealth – and it would not hurt her to go hungry for a short while. Once her sister Dyfyr had starved herself for three days to lose weight.

(*Dyfyr, red hair tangled with dirt and sweat, rolling in the filth of the yard, bare white legs kicking and twitching while a thin creature humped and thrust, urged on by the cheers of his mates . . .*)

Eurgain shuddered.

What was the matter with her? What a foul thing to think, and of her own sister too.

It was never wise to imagine horrible things, in case they came true.

(*Had been true. Were true.*)

136

She swayed on her feet. Her eyes were shut, and somebody close at hand was making a series of little gasping grunts, meaningless sounds that suddenly seemed more evocative than language. She could feel the world whirling about her, as if she were a child again playing the game of spinning round and round on one spot then suddenly stopping, falling down and hugging the ground which dipped and bucked like the sea itself.

The grunting was coming from her own throat. (*She had known that all along, really.*) Somehow she had slipped to her knees in the tangle of long grass and brambles bordering the forest. There was a thorn pricking her right shin and another jabbing the soft flesh under the kneecap.

Her family and friends were dead.

They had been dead for a long time now.

That was why she was so hungry. Somewhere she had lost a whole day, a day spent running and hiding, watching the strangers and avoiding the great hounds they had brought with them.

Her eyes were screwed so tightly shut they were beginning to hurt. She ground the palms of her hands against the sockets, trying to blot out what she could see there.

A group of men, ill-nourished, some wearing clothing she recognized, the rest still dressed in shabby rags, so patched and darned one could see nothing of the original cloth. Some carried spears and small shields hung over their backs, and marched along glancing uneasily about the forest. Others – and these walked in the middle so that the armed men formed a barricade between them and the trees – carried round objects dangling two or three from each hand, pale things that swung and jostled together, bloodless cheek rubbing against bloodless cheek, faces still hideously recognizable.

Leading the group was the man with the shaven head, chanting an invocation in a tongue so convoluted she could not understand it at all, though here and there the odd word seemed hauntingly familiar. As she watched she saw that his stride followed the rhythm of his chant and she knew she was in the presence of a great spell caster, one who could woo and win the spirits of the forest in a way which she, for all her ties of blood and bone and place, could never hope to do.

She had lost everything. Family, friends and home. Now even her god and goddess would be taken away from her. What use would they have for her, the least of their former worshippers, when these newcomers had a wise man who could speak with them on equal terms?

Eurgain ground her palms harder and harder into her eye sockets, struggling to stop the memories.

She had let the group pass, guessing that they were going to the Sanctuary and having no desire to follow and witness whatever ceremony the shaven man intended to perform. (Something dark and foul, she knew, if it involved the heads of her kin; some ancient rite that had nothing, nothing to do with the way they had lived their lives.) Instead she had crawled away, crept towards the shore where she had played with the children the previous day.

Then there was a gap. The next thing she remembered was hearing the baying of hounds, and a deer which came bounding through the undergrowth even as she watched, open-mouthed in horror at the way it was bringing the hounds down upon her, knowing that the goddess who had spoken to her on the beach had abandoned her, that this time she would be found, caught, flung to the ground and used as her sister and cousins had been used.

She fled blindly, knowing she was making far too much noise, brambles and branches snagging her clothes, her hair, hurling herself into a pile of rocks, scrabbling through the dirt (sharp grains of grit driving themselves under her nails), frantically squeezing through a gap too small to take her, turning round inside the wider cave and peering through the opening like a frightened animal gone to earth.

The hounds came first, running noses to the ground, darting back and forth as they followed the scent, all save one scarcely breaking stride as they passed the place where her own trail must begin. But that one, a rangy, long-legged creature with powerful jaws, hesitated a moment as it found the traces of a different prey, not deer but smelling as distressed as any deer, something which begged to be chased and pulled down, ripped and eaten, warm entrails torn from the body and devoured before life had left the carcase (she stifled a scream at the thought, so vivid), hesitated and stared towards her hiding place, its eyes alive with knowing and ropes of drool hanging from its mask.

Then it was gone, in pursuit of its fellows.

The huntsmen came next, three of them, tall men wearing dark leathers, long yellow hair bouncing as they ran sure-footed on the track of the hounds, and by their hair and their size she knew them to be the three mailed warriors of yesterday, and guessed that the one in the lead was the one who had cut down Beli and Jago.

They too paused where the dog had paused, breathing easily as if they had been doing nothing more strenuous than strolling for pleasure.

The one she took to be the leader, his speech slurred and heavily accented, said: 'Hounds will turn her.'

The tallest of the three pushed the point of his spear into the earth so it stood by itself and used his free hands to fiddle with his hair.

'I had thought we hunted the old man, not deer,' he said, adjusting the leather thong at the nape of his neck.

'Ach!' The leader hawked and spat. 'Today, tomorrow – what does it matter, Serach?'

The third man, the one whose face was pocked with old scars, laughed. 'The druid says he cannot leave.'

The tall man, Serach, said something she did not catch.

'He is as trustworthy as any magic man,' said the one with the pockmarks.

'Which is to say not very,' Serach growled, adding bitterly: 'If you had held your men better we would not need the druid so badly.'

'Enough!' said the leader, holding up a hand in warning. 'The massacre was unfortunate, but untrained men tend to become excited when the killing starts. What is done is done – though it is true you did not help matters, Dovnuall Brecc,' he finished, using the Irish version of the British 'Frych' – freckled.

Dovnuall grinned and rubbed his crotch. 'She squirmed so prettily, the red-haired girl. Forgive me, Eremon.'

The leader laughed, and even Serach managed a bleak smile. Watching, Eurgain felt sick.

'We will need workers to feed us,' said Eremon lazily. 'To-morrow or the next day we shall raid the town.'

'Penhyle?' questioned Serach. 'So soon?'

'We must keep the men busy. Once they have slaves to watch over, they will be easier to control.'

Serach looked doubtful, but Eremon ignored him.

'As for the old man . . .' Eremon looked around him, staring directly at Eurgain's hiding place. She squeezed her eyes tight shut, like a small child playing peek-a-boo (if she could not see him, then he could not see her), and held her breath.

'The druid claims his spells will prevent the old man from leaving,' said Eremon, and now that her eyes were closed he sounded like a kindly man, sweet-voiced for all the strangeness of his accent.

'The druid's magic is subtle. The old man will be trapped here unwittingly. He will not think of leaving, nor realize that he could. His sense of duty will hold him here. Since he has failed to help the villagers, he will believe that to redeem himself he must save the woodland sanctuary from desecration.'

'I do not understand,' said Dovnuall, pecking at the ground with the butt of his spear.

'It does not matter,' said Eremon. 'All you need to know is that the old man will not flee. The druid says that he can sense the power: not the wood alone, but something else, something mightier than the wood.' He grinned cruelly. 'The old man will stay, and sooner or later we shall find him – and with him we shall find what we seek.'

'But not I think by these hounds that Vortepor gave you,' muttered Serach. 'They seem better suited to hunting deer than men. Listen, they have turned their prey!'

'There is time yet,' said Eremon. 'Tomorrow. Tomorrow we raid Penhyle for slaves, able-bodied men and women. We shall not kill more than is needful, Serach, which will no doubt please you. Some of the inhabitants will escape. They will escape because I, Eremon of the Eoganacht Maigi Dergind i nAlbae, Eremon of the lands of the Children of Eogan in the Plain of the River Oak in Albion, have decided they may live. They will escape because I, Eremon heir to Cairbre of the Hundred Battles, have permitted them to escape, and for no other reason. Do you understand me?'

Serach nodded, subdued. 'I understand, my prince.'

'I do not want their homes burned,' Eremon continued, staring this time at the man with the scarred face. 'It is you I am talking to, Dovnuall Brecc. I know your love of flame. No firing of the thatch, however tempted you may be. This is a warning raid, a looting raid, a slaving raid. I want the survivors to have homes to which they can return after we are gone.'

'As you will, my prince,' Dovnuall said submissively.

'The druid will give us the heart of the land. I do not wish to rule over a desert.'

'And when the warriors come? Our peasants cannot stand against trained men,' said Serach.

'By the time Gereint or Custennin send their men against us we shall have the land bound to us in the old way, by blood and the great rite of bringing into being. It will be ours in a fashion these mongrel weaklings do not understand.'

'Now the hounds have the deer,' Serach said drily, and indeed the baying of the hounds far off in the woodland had changed.

Serach pulled his spear from the ground.

The three of them looked at one another and laughed, then sprinted away in the direction of the hounds, vying to be first to reach the deer.

When they had gone Eurgain eased herself from her hiding place. Most of what they had said had sounded like nonsense, though when Eremon recited his titles she remembered tales of a settlement of Scotti a day or more's journey to the east, a settlement which had grown so arrogant in its might that eventually the Lords of that region had banded together to destroy it. That had been when she was a child, when her mother (*her mother who was dead, murdered by these pirates*) was young and fair.

They intended to attack Penhyle, the town at the head of the estuary. They would find little loot there. It was not a rich place. She had visited it once, with her father and uncle. Her uncle's wife had been born there and still had kin among the people of the town. It had a market where they had traded wool for iron tools, and her father had given her a bronze pin which she still wore in her tunic.

Her father. Was it his head she saw, swinging from the hand of an Irishman as she cowered in the bushes, or was it her uncle's? She had not looked too closely.

Again the horror of it rose up and overwhelmed her.

All this she remembered as she stood swaying on the edge of the fields above the village.

Everybody she had ever loved was dead.

They had been dead for almost a day and a half.

It did not matter what she did now. If she chose to walk down to the houses and the raiders returned from wherever they had gone, or the magic man with the shaven head came strolling back along the beach with those hideously intelligent hounds, then she would die, and there was nobody to care, nobody at all.

She opened her eyes. The clouds had scattered, and the sounds of battle had stopped. The fields shone in the moonlight. At her feet was a cobweb glittering with silver dewdrops. If she moved forward she would break it.

The pirates were singing, out on the water, singing a song of death and destruction. She could tell what it was about by the rhythm, though she could not hear the words.

She was starving. She had never gone hungry in her life, not even in the depths of winter, not even when she was a child and the snow covered the earth for nearly a moon, a thing unheard of on this stretch of coast.

There would be food in the huts, but it was not worth the risk. Better to starve in the forest. And she knew that though she felt as if she were dying from lack of food it would be a long while yet before she came to any harm.

She turned and retreated into the cover of the trees.

4

Lulled by the sweet lapping of the wavelets against the timbers of the ship, Ceolric had slipped into sleep.

As the scream sounded he jerked awake, looking over his shoulder to see what had happened. There was a splash on the far side of the boat, followed by the noise of somebody thrashing in the water. He leaped to his feet, starting to draw his knife, and felt a hand on his shoulder.

He turned, completing the draw (everything was happening with a dreamlike slowness) and saw a white face grinning at him over the bulwark.

The moon had risen and was trying to fight free of the clouds. By its light Ceolric saw droplets of water fall sparkling to the deck as the man heaved himself aboard, a thin spear in his hands.

Without thinking, Ceolric swung the heavy knife from above his left shoulder in a backhanded stroke, all his weight behind it. The blow caught the man across the neck, and knocked him tumbling over the side of the vessel in a sprawl of arms and legs.

Something hit Ceolric hard in the back, sent him reeling into the bows of the ship, banging his head on one of the chests stowed there. Sick with pain, he lay still for a moment, and by the time he had recovered his wits the *Sea Stallion* seemed to be full of struggling men.

A half-naked figure flung itself upon Garulf. The Frisian calmly stabbed his attacker with a short spear, but the man wriggled on down the shaft, slashing wildly at his face with a dagger. Garulf dropped the spear and pushed the man into an oar bench.

The attackers were smaller and slighter than the Saesons, but as savage and careless of wounds as any company of bearsarkers.

Ceolric hauled himself to his feet. His hands were shaking and his head hurt. He looked round desperately for a place where his fellows were making a stand, and at first found none. Then he saw his father.

Wicga had set his back to the mast. Wielding his longsword in both hands, the captain had cleared a space around himself, bellowing all the while to rally his crew. Now Garulf joined him, seemingly unharmed and holding an axe, and for a time they held the heart of the ship, keeping the attackers at bay.

Ceolric tried to force a way through to reach them, and found himself wrestling with a wet body, the rim of a small shield cutting into his ribs, his free hand gripping a sweat-slicked wrist as he strove to keep the other's blade from his throat. He brought his knee up into the man's groin, hammering as hard as he could, convinced his ribs were cracking under the pressure of the shield edge. The man fell, and he flung him aside.

Clouds drifted across the moon, plunging them into darkness, but it was too late to stop the fighting. The attackers were everywhere, shouting in a half-familiar tongue, swarming over the crew as hounds swarm over a stag.

Ceolric saw his father die, taken by a long spear from behind the mast. The moon came out just before the blade went in, so that the point shone dull silver as it entered Wicga's back. The captain staggered, dropping his sword, blood gouting from his mouth as he was jerked against the mast by his killer's attempts to free the spear from his body.

The youth's mind could not accept what was happening. His friends were dying, some of them quickly and some slowly, and the deck was a mass of tumbled bodies.

Garulf reeled towards him, mouth working. 'Swim, boy, swim.

Over the side and swim for the far shore. These are demons, not men.'

He hesitated, and the older man, his hands trembling with fear or rage, pushed him to the bulwark and urged him over the side.

The water roared and bubbled about him. Lungs bursting, all sense of direction lost, he surfaced into darkness, the moon having vanished behind the clouds again.

Clumsily, he trod water, striving to find his bearings. Behind him he could hear the noise of battle, so he struck out towards what he hoped was the far shore, praying to his ancestral god that no tides or currents would sweep him out to sea.

Although he could swim after a fashion (paddling like a dog while his legs threshed the water) he had never needed to swim this far in his life. The water was cold, though not so cold as it had seemed in the early evening, and he swallowed several mouthfuls before he found his rhythm.

Eventually he heard the pounding of breakers on rocks. The moon came out while he trod water again, gasping for breath, his arms and legs leaden with exhaustion. Ahead of him he saw the white glow of spume against a black reef, so he altered course, aided now by the current, and let himself be swept away from the rocks and deposited in the calmer waters of a small cove.

So at the last he half staggered, half crawled ashore through the moonshadowed foam, and collapsed on the dry, bone-white sand above the fringe of twigs and seaweed which marked the limits of the high tide.

PART II

CHAPTER ONE

1

Once the first shock of seeing the Scotti curraghs was past, Budoc
had begun to notice other things about the scene before him.

There were guards standing in the shelter of the huts. He could
not make out much detail because they were hidden in the
shadows (deliberately?) but they were there. The grass in the
fields had been badly trampled, and in places it looked as if
something had been dragged across the pasture.

Now that he was quartering the village with his eyes, searching
for signs, he could see more and more. An arm, part of a torso, a
pair of feet jutting forlornly from behind one of the buildings. A
pyramid of round objects piled neatly against one wall. A crow
perched on a roof, looking sated.

What had happened to the villagers was all too clear.

Behind the huts was a green hill. From the summit, he knew,
one could keep watch not only on the estuary but also on the land
approach. If he were the leader of these Scotti, he would have set
a sentry or two on the top, concealed among those rather scrubby
pines . . .

Yes.

A glimpse of pale cloth, a dull flash of metal. At least two men,
possibly three.

Under ordinary circumstances this would have been a good
time to try slipping past unseen. The attack must have taken place

147

a while ago, judging by the amount of clearing up that had been done. The sentries would be bored and careless, with no reason to suspect there might be somebody behind them.

But the circumstances were not ordinary. He doubted if he had the strength to run very far or very fast: even the brisk pace at which he had descended the cliffs had badly sapped his stamina. And if he did run, where would he go? There were no warriors at Penhyle, at the head of the creek. The nearest force would be at Din Erbin, Gereint's stronghold on the River Oak, and that was a long way for an old man on foot.

Besides, he did not want to go. He wanted to stay here at the Wood. He was its Guardian, the latest in a long line stretching back into the distant past, and he did not want to betray his trust.

If he remained, what then?

Gwalchmei had told him to hide himself because 'they' were coming for him. He did not know who 'they' were, but he trusted his dreams enough to think the advice good. After all, Gwalchmei had been right about the village.

So he would hide and wait, hoping that what he should do would become clear in time.

Having reached a decision, Budoc moved away slowly and carefully in the direction of his hut. He did not think it likely that the leader of the Scotti would have put any sentries out on this side of the village – there was nothing to guard against – but he acted as if they existed.

He slipped from shadow to shadow, listening for sounds of warning from the birds and small creatures of the wood, placing his feet with care so as not to break the dead twigs littering the ground. He paused often, sniffing the air for the scent of men, hesitating in the sun-dappled shade like a wild thing fearful of hunters.

He passed within a few paces of a doe and fawn, keeping downwind so they suspected nothing, easing himself through the bushes without disturbing the foliage, silent as the ghost he sometimes felt himself to be.

He did not take the path along the cliffs. It was too exposed, too dangerous if he were seen. He stayed within the woods where there were plenty of places to run and hide, avoiding the clearings and the open space of the Sanctuary itself.

At length he came within sight of the hut. Again, he was almost certain none of the Scotti were nearby, but all the same he squatted on his haunches in the cover of a thicket and watched, while a spider used his thigh as an anchor for its web and a little green bird settled by his head and sang of summer.

The hut nestled in the shelter of a hollow. Behind it was a steep escarpment of rock which made it difficult if not impossible to approach from the rear. He could see no signs of disturbance on the path leading to the door, and the hut itself looked deserted.

He waited until the light changed from the harsh glare of midday to the long flood of late afternoon, and in all that time nothing moved except the birds and the insects.

When he was satisfied he circled through the bushes and approached the path at an angle, teasing aside the stems and fronds like a man wading very quietly in deep water, not breaking cover until he was beside the door.

The leather hinges creaked as he pushed it open. The only hiding place was behind the door itself. He was inside and ready to face an attacker with a speed he had not thought he still possessed, and not until it was too late did he remember that he carried no weapon.

Fortunately the hut was empty.

Now there was not a moment to waste. He gathered whatever he thought would be useful, and rolled it all up in a bundle of spare clothing. Water-skins, food, small knife, needle and thread . . .

Propped in one corner was a spear, a hunting weapon, crudely made and badly balanced in comparison with the spears he had handled in the past. He took it anyway.

Then he stood listening in the doorway, suddenly afraid the Scotti might have found the hut while he was inside. The birds were still singing, undisturbed. All seemed safe, so he moved, latching the door behind him and scuttling down the path until he was again under cover, his heart beating furiously.

He had of course brought far too much, more than he could possibly carry any distance. Already he was sweating. (It ran down into his eyes, making them sting; he tried it on his tongue, found it sharp and unpleasant.) He would have to divide the stuff and create caches around the wood and the cliffs. Then if – *when* – the Scotti did come hunting him he would have food and water to hand in a variety of safe places.

The rest of the afternoon and evening were spent in finding

suitable sites: a hollow tree in the forest, a chimney in the rocks above the cliffs, the heart of a gorse thicket. All of them were places with several escape routes, places he could reach or leave without being observed.

To his surprise he discovered he was enjoying himself.

That first night of exile he spent in the branches of an oak tree, wedged between two boughs with his back to the trunk. Although he was perfectly comfortable sleep refused to come.

In his heart he knew he should have spent the hours of darkness in prayer, or meditating on the state of his soul. He did try, briefly, but each time something conspired to distract him: the rustle of the leaves in the wind, the calling of the night birds, an itch between his shoulders.

Instead he found himself lost in his memories, memories so vivid the events could have been unfolding before him here and now.

The Long Man, tall Cei, the best and bravest of them all, his arm around sweet Celemon his daughter, peering near-sightedly at a new brooch . . .

Lleminawg, face alight with laughter, demonstrating the steps of a dance . . .

Gwalchmei, earnest in debate, leaning forward across the table to make some point . . .

Teleri alive with passion, fingers strumming her harp and head flung back as she proclaimed that strange and mysterious tale in the Great Hall at Caer Cadwy . . .

Arthur.

Arthur the Magister Militum.

If he closed his eyes he could see Arthur now, limping slightly as he strode across the Great Hall, the whole place coming alive around him as he moved from the door to the dais . . .

No.

That was not right.

The limp came later, *after* the first meeting with Teleri. Indeed, one might say that was the whole point: she had in a sense foretold it, though whether knowingly or not he had never been sure.

Try again.

Remember the brazier crackling and spitting with the poor-quality coal shipped across the Severn Sea. Remember Arthur holding out his hands to warm them – hands scarred by a dozen small nicks white against the brown, with big blunt fingers and thick sandy hairs.

Remember Cei standing in one corner, head slightly bowed, thinning fair hair loose around his face, frowning at the map on the table.

Remember Arthur saying in his deep and melodious voice, 'Somebody should go to meet them. They'll not get further than Lindinis by nightfall, not with the weather as it is,' and Cei looking up with a grimace at the thought of leaving the comfort of Caer Cadwy.

Remember, as if it were happening now, all over again – and what you would not give that it might be so – shrugging and offering to go yourself . . .

2

Once Vortepor and the Dyfed embassy were in the safe keeping of Glewlwyd the Gatekeeper, mab Petroc considered his duties as an escort to have been discharged.

Leaving Moried the task of ensuring that the wounded were taken to the surgeons and the dead to their rightful place, he went straight to Arthur.

The Warlord was alone, reading a scroll. He looked up with a brief frown of annoyance as mab Petroc knocked and entered, a frown which quickly vanished when he saw the other's state.

'You had to fight? In Lindinis?' He rose from his chair and eased the other into it. 'How much of that blood is yours?'

Mab Petroc glanced ruefully at his tunic. 'Not much.'

'What happened? Were there any casualties?' He poured a goblet of wine and thrust it into mab Petroc's hand.

'I am afraid so. Six dead, five wounded. Moried has taken them to the doctors.' A spasm of shaking seized him, and Arthur helped guide the cup to his mouth. He swallowed convulsively.

The Warlord pulled up another chair. 'Always worse when it is all over,' he said. 'Deep breaths, cousin, deep breaths.'

Mab Petroc tried to laugh and found he was close to tears.

'Picts,' he said when he had more control of himself. 'The Dyfed embassy have been hunted by Picts ever since they set out. Somebody did not want them to reach you.'

Arthur stared at him blankly. 'Strange. What would the North have against Vortepor of Dyfed?' He reached out and flicked the scroll. 'I was reading Tacitus when you came in. He gives a fascinating description of the North four hundred years ago. "The nights are short . . . If there is no cloud it is said you can see the glow of the sun all night."'

Knowing Arthur was talking to give him time to recover, mab Petroc sipped at the wine, letting its glow warm him. Then he relayed to Arthur all that Vortepor and his adviser Fingal had told him, and gave a detailed account of what had happened.

'Spiral tattoos,' Arthur mused. 'Very faintly it reminds me of something – a tale I might have heard years ago, spun around a campfire to pass an evening.' He tugged at his hair in frustration. 'No, I cannot remember.'

'I thought I could ask among the Companions. Talorcan is from beyond Bannog – it might mean something to him.' Mab Petroc hesitated, continued: 'Moried and I examined the bodies closely. We have both fought in the north, had dealings with the Pictish tribes, but we did not recognize anything about our attackers.'

'What are you suggesting?'

Mab Petroc poured himself another cup of wine from the flagon on the table. 'When we speak of Picts, we mean the Painted People of the old Caledonian Federation, yes?'

Arthur nodded. 'Go on.'

'Some have permanent tattoos, some wear war-paint. Some are tall and red-haired, some are broad and dark, with ruddy skins.' He sipped the wine, held it in his mouth a moment, swallowed thoughtfully. 'I know there has been much move-ment over the years, so that it is foolish to talk of tribal types – I mean, even in the west of Dumnonia, an area renowned for the broad shoulders and short legs of its inhabitants, there are big fair men like Cei.'

'There has been less change in the north,' said Arthur. 'Tacitus wrote of the red hair and huge limbs of the Caledonians all those years ago. He thought they were of German origin, which is interesting.'

'Really? I did not know that.' Mab Petroc paused, marshalling his thoughts. 'What I am trying to say is that these people last night were not like any northerners I have ever seen. They were broad-shouldered powerful men, which is common enough, but their skins were swarthy, not ruddy. And the weave of their clothing was like none Moried or I had ever seen before.'

'You mean you do not think they were Picts?'

Mab Petroc sucked in his breath, swallowed more wine. 'I do not know. I do not know what they were. Picts in the sense of being tattooed, Picts in the sense of their weapons being of northern make . . .' His voice trailed away as he realized how vague and uncertain he was sounding.

Arthur rose to his feet, paced restlessly about the room.

'Whoever they are, they must have some connection with the Iardomnan, with this Hueil and his band of Scotti raiders. Your idea is a good one. Speak with some of the northern Companions, see what they know. Spiral tattoos are not easy to forget.'

He wheeled abruptly. 'Vortepor and Fingal, what is your opinion of them?'

'Vortepor is even worse than his reputation. If he told me the sun will rise in the east tomorrow I would doubt him. His men are afraid of him, and I would guess he has a cruel streak. Having said that, what he wants is reasonable enough. Now the Saesons are no longer an immediate danger it is time we did something to protect the western shores of Britain, and striking against this Hueil would be a good way to start. It will mean giving your tacit approval to Vortepor's succession when his father dies, and that will be hard on Dyfed, but . . .' Mab Petroc shrugged.

'We are not yet in a position to interfere in the internal matters of the kingdoms,' Arthur said thoughtfully.

'Fingal is one of those who loves to be privy to the secrets of the great, a maker of mysteries, a spinner of plots.'

'You do not like him?' said Arthur, amused.

Mab Petroc grinned. 'At first he thought I might be of use to him. But after the attack, when he saw how I had fought, he decided I must therefore be stupid. In his world, the wise rule and the fools do the fighting.'

'What word of Agricola?'

'Harder to tell. They spoke of him as if he still ruled and Vortepor were merely his emissary. I am not certain. It could be this last winter has left him in ill health, and Vortepor is now the real master of Dyfed.'

'So.' Arthur paced for a few moments in silence, his long-legged stride swiftly carrying him from one side of the room to the other. 'They want me to mount an assault on the Western Isles at the back of the world. For some reason a band of distinctively marked northerners, who are Picts only in the literal sense of the word, think it worth travelling some five hundred miles and giving their lives at the end of it to prevent this request from reaching me.'

'It makes no sense.'

'No, none. These tattooed men sound like members of a cult. Goddess worshippers, snake worshippers.' Arthur spun on his heel, his hair a halo of red gold in the light from the brazier. 'Could Vortepor have offended some cult?'

'Easily, I should think. He is a very offensive youth.' Mab Petroc drained his wine, continued more seriously: 'But why attack him in Lindinis, so close to Caer Cadwy? Why risk your wrath? And why did the attacks not start until he left his home on his way here? It cannot be a coincidence.'

'No, it cannot. The first idea is more likely, though as you said it makes no sense.' Arthur flung himself into his chair, toyed with the dragon brooch that held his cloak. 'I must go to greet Vortepor in the hall. I told Glewlwyd to delay them a while.'

He sighed. 'It was easier, cousin, when all we did was fight. Three years since Badon, and three years of nothing but intrigue and plots. What we need is some symbol to bind the kingdoms together in peace as they were bound in war.'

He shook his head, returned to the matter in hand. 'Have those cuts cleaned and dressed. Then find Talorcan and the other northerners and see what they know of spiral tattoos. Join us in the hall when you are ready.'

After visiting the surgeons, mab Petroc stood shivering in the cold wind that swept around the hilltop. The sky and landscape alike were grey and featureless except for the distinctive shape of Ynis Witrin rising above the colourless marshes to the north-west.

Arthur had been kind. Mab Petroc had handled last night's affair like an ill-trained youngster given his first command, he who was a veteran of many years' service, he who had always prided himself on behaving like a Roman soldier and not a wild barbarian warrior. He should have set more sentries. Had it not been for the scream – *who did scream?* he wondered suddenly – they would have been caught inside the house with no hope of escape.

He looked around him in the hope of seeing someone who might know where to find Talorcan.

The third person he stopped suggested he try the stables, so he made his way down the hill, avoiding the guest house, still turning over in his mind the meaning of last night's assault and his own failure.

Talorcan was deep in conversation with a horse doctor when he found him, gloomily discussing the chances of the old bay stallion slumped in the stall beside them.

'He carried me at Badon, though he was past his prime,' said Talorcan. 'Five times, up and down that hill. You remember, cousin?' He turned to mab Petroc, a note of pleading in his voice, as if the latter's confirmation would miraculously cure the horse.

'I do,' he said, which was not strictly true. He remembered Talorcan talking about it afterwards, but he could recall very little of the actual battle.

'And he carried me at Bassas when he was a youngster, his hooves trampling the Saesons like corn.' Talorcan flung his arms around the stallion's neck and kissed the veined muzzle. 'Ach, Rudvrych of the noble heart!'

Mab Petroc and the horse doctor exchanged a look. 'It is old age, my lord,' explained the doctor. 'Against old age even the best of us are powerless.'

In the dull light of the winter day Talorcan's dark brown hair seemed almost black against the reddish coat of the stallion. His face, even in his grief, had a ruddy tinge to it, quite unlike the white skin of some Irishmen or the swarthiness of an Iberian. He was unmistakably a Pict, of a physical type common in the north. Looking at him, mab Petroc was in no doubt that the assailants of the previous night had been of a different people.

He explained what he wanted. Talorcan frowned, unwilling to be distracted from his sorrow, then reluctantly released Rudvrych's head.

'Spirals. I have heard of them . . .' Like Arthur, he chased an elusive memory. 'The Western Isles. Something obscure and forgotten. Some cult who claim to preserve a relic of great value.' He tugged at a forelock. 'I am sorry. Whatever it was, it made no great impression on me. A childhood tale, something of the sort, about a clan on one of the islands who called themselves *Plant Menestyr*, the Children of the Cupbearer. I cannot remember the significance.' He shrugged. 'They were bogeymen, I think – you know the sort of thing –' his voice rose a pitch in imitation of a nurse '– be good or the Sons of Menestyr will come and take you away to walk their spiral maze.'

'And what happened then?'

'Mmm? Oh, I think you died. Yes, that was it. Only the Sovereign Lord of all this land could walk the maze and live. It was death for anybody else.' He patted the stallion's neck, made soothing noises. The dull eyes blinked wearily in response.

'You could ask Degaw. Her father came from the West Coast, before he was driven out by the Scotti.'

Mab Petroc thanked him and left him in peace to comfort his dying horse.

Talorcan and Degaw lived on the western side of the town, in a soundly built house of wattle and daub, with a well-thatched roof. The walls needed whitewashing, but that was true of most houses at this end of the winter.

He knocked cautiously on the door, aware of his reluctance. From inside came the sound of children at play, and a woman softly singing a lullaby. He knocked again, louder, and the singing stopped.

The door opened. The smell of cooking drifted past his nose, and his stomach rumbled loudly.

'Hungry? You may share the children's food if you wish.'

She leaned against the door jamb, a small woman beginning to put on weight around the hips.

'If you want Talorcan, he is in the stable. Rudvrych his war horse is refusing to eat, but then he is very old now.'

'I know. It was you I wanted to see.'

She stared at him unblinking for a moment, then ushered him inside.

'Sit down,' she said, pushing him towards a stool by the hearth while her two small sons rocked back on their heels and goggled at him. 'Let me take your cloak. It is too good to trail in the ashes.'

It was warm in the house. A cauldron was bubbling over the fire, filling the room with the smell of stewed chicken. He closed his eyes and knew he could easily drop asleep here, sitting by the hearth while outside the wind howled round the thatch.

'Thank you.' He spoke loudly, hoping to cover the gurgling of his stomach.

'You are hungry,' she said. 'Do they not feed you in the hall any more?'

'Last night I slept in Lindinis.'

She produced four bowls and ladled out the stew, serving the children first. 'The bread is on the table. Eat, man. You have lost weight since . . . since Badon.'

'Talorcan suggested you might be able to help me,' he said after a long pause.

'What? A great warrior like yourself in need of help? You surprise me. I had thought you sufficient unto yourself.'

'Please,' he said, and raised his left hand helplessly.

'How is your son?' she asked brightly. 'Still with his mother's people? Do you see him at all these days?'

'He is well, and growing fast. In a few years he will be able to come here to Caer Cadwy.'

She ladled more stew into his bowl. The two boys sat open-mouthed, gazing from one to the other, understanding their mother was angry but not knowing why.

'Good. A shame his father will be a stranger to him, but I suppose it is no different from sending him to be fostered.'

'I brought back six dead men this morning,' he said to silence her.

She sat very still, the ladle poised above the pot.

'Anybody I know?'

'All of them, I would think.' He reeled off the names, and watched her face change.

'What happened?'

He told her, not sparing himself. When he had finished she laid her forearms on the table and smiled at him ruefully.

'I was born among the Creones.' Her face was wistful. 'We were a small and scattered people, living in the wild lands to the west of the Great Glen, a place of mountains and lochs and islands. Not long after I was born my father was driven from his home by the Scotti, and forced to take refuge among his kinsmen on the east coast. But despite our exile, when I reached a certain age he insisted I undergo the traditional ceremony of womanhood.'

She pulled back her sleeves and revealed her forearms, which she always kept covered. From the wrists to the elbows her skin was a riot of green and blue.

'Not many people wear these marks any longer,' she said with mingled pride and embarrassment. 'Even when I was a girl the custom was dying out.'

Mab Petroc stared in fascination. Now that he looked more closely, he could see the patterns in what he had at first taken to be a formless mass of colour. Against a blue background – and for a moment he forgot what that meant, forgot that every last piece of her skin had been pricked with needles to make raw wounds into which woad had then been rubbed – green leaves and stems twined and interwove. From among and behind the leaves peered foliate faces, large and small, friendly and malevolent.

She clenched her fists so the tattoos writhed in a semblance of life. 'They do not stop at the elbows,' she said softly.

'Did it . . . Did it hurt?' he asked, and wondered how many others had asked the same question.

'Yes. But the women of the Creones do not admit to feeling pain.'

'Does Talorcan have these?' He frowned, trying to remember if he had ever seen the other man uncovered.

'No. He is of the Decantae, and their customs are different. They paint their faces and bodies before going on a raid, though Talorcan has not done so since coming south to join the Warlord.'

She pulled down her sleeves, then collected the empty bowls, wiping them clean and piling them on a corner of the table. The children resumed their game on the floor, bored by the adult talk.

'These people who attacked us last night . . . Talorcan thought you might know something of them.'

'The Sons of Menestyr, with their spiral tattoos.' She sniffed contemptuously. 'Yes, I have heard of them. They live on the Isle of Shadows, where Cuchulain is supposed to have gone to learn the mastery of weapons from the warrior woman Scatha. It is said they are of the Attecotti, though I dare say to a southerner like yourself that means nothing.'

He shrugged lightly. 'I confess my ignorance.'

'The Attecotti are the Old People. They claim they were here first, before any of us.'

For a moment her words conjured the image of white-haired men and women hobbling on sticks, then he realized what she meant. 'They were here first?'

'In the Island. They feel about us much the way we feel about the Saesons and the Scotti, or the Romans before them. We are interlopers.'

158

His mind reeled. 'But it is our Island,' he protested. 'Prydein. The Isle of the Mighty. There were none here before our ancestors.'

'The Attecotti claim they were here first,' she repeated. 'They say their fathers raised the standing stones and circles, named the hills and plains, dwelt in the forests, long before Prydein son of Aed the Great conquered the Island.' She smiled wickedly, added: 'And if you think about it, he must have conquered it from *someone*.'

'But . . .' He stopped, confused.

Degaw waited a while, watching the boys moving pine cones around the floor in imitation of a battle. 'They have a secret language which is neither British nor Irish,' she said when she was certain he was not going to continue. 'They look much like the rest of us – though the red hair which is common among the Caledonians is unusual among them.'

He nodded. The Caledonians were the most powerful of the old northern tribes, the dominant force in the loose alliance of barbarians collectively known as Picts.

'Their ways are strange,' she said solemnly, which brought a smile to his face, for the Romanized southerners said precisely the same about the Picts, who were rumoured to copulate in public, like dogs, and trace descent through the female line.

'The Children of Menestyr are one of the larger clans. At home they are ruled by seers – what would you call them – ?' she wrinkled her brow '– priestesses, I suppose. The men spend much of their time away, raiding by land and sea, mainly for slaves that they sell in Ierne. The leader, the male head of the clan, is always called Pedrylaw Menestyr.'

'The Skilled Cupbearer?'

'Yes. That is his public name. I do not know what they call him in their own tongue.' She gazed thoughtfully at her sons, who had nearly completed their re-enactment of Mount Badon. 'Did Talorcan tell you about the labyrinth?'

'Be good or the Children of Menestyr will make you walk their maze?' he said with raised eyebrows.

'It does exist, you know,' she said evenly. 'And all accounts agree nobody except the Priestesses can tread its spiral path without dying.'

'Talorcan mentioned the Sovereign Lord of all this Isle?' he prompted.

She laughed. 'So they say. But the Attecotti have never acknowledged any lords at all, so it is akin to saying . . .' She paused, opened her eyes wide and pronounced with great emphasis: 'Nobody. Nobody in the world.'

There was a whine in the wind now which had not been there earlier. Little pellets of dry snow blew horizontally into mab Petroc's face, stinging his skin. The sky was black and menacing with only a faint lightening in the west to show the position of the sun. He shivered and hunched deeper into his cloak, almost bumping into a pair of figures who came scurrying out of the chapel.

'Cousin!' gasped a voice, and a strong hand clutched his arm, steadying him. 'What a day! Will this winter never end?'

The two men were so well muffled against the storm that he could not see their faces, but he recognized the faint Irish accent.

'Lleminawg? I thought you had gone home for the winter.'

'I did,' said the other, pulling the scarf free of his mouth to speak more clearly. 'But it was dull in my father's house, and like a fool I thought: spring on the way, and time to be up and doing.' White teeth flashed in the brown face. 'It sounds as if yourself has been having all the fun?'

Mab Petroc grunted.

'We were on our way, the Bishop and I, to hear this woman sing,' said Lleminawg.

'Woman? What woman?'

'Why cousin, the one you brought here this morning. The Dyfed woman.'

He shook his head, feeling slow and stupid. 'What Dyfed woman?'

Lleminawg laughed, not unkindly. 'Your wits are dull today. The bard, cousin, the bard.'

'She is to sing?'

'Indeed and she is.'

'She craved a boon of the Emperor,' said the second man. Mab Petroc squinted against the storm and confirmed with a sinking heart that this was Bishop Enoch. 'One of the deacons came to find me. She asked the Emperor's permission to tell a heathen tale before the assembled court.' Indignation rang in his voice.

'A heathen tale?' mab Petroc said mildly. 'We often hear the old stories on a winter's evening.'

'Not like this one,' snapped the Bishop over his shoulder. 'Not told by an unknown female who has spent the last few days travelling alone in a company of men.'

'The Bishop is concerned for our morals,' Lleminawg said delicately, so that mab Petroc found himself wondering what the Irishman, who was not renowned for his religious fervour, had been doing in the chapel.

'The way of the Lord is not an easy one,' said the Bishop, 'as you would do well to remember.' He paused in the shelter of a porch, scowling at the sky. 'And you, my lord. I hear you have blood on your hands again.'

'I am a warrior. The blood on my hands is what keeps you safe at your prayers.'

The Bishop snorted. 'A specious argument. If you and those like you would give yourselves truly to Christ, there would be no need for this violence. The disasters which have befallen our country are a direct consequence of our failure to obey God's laws, plagues sent to drive our feet back onto the paths of righteousness. Only by placing ourselves utterly in His hands can we hope to overcome our enemies.'

This was an old argument, and mab Petroc did not feel like rehearsing it in a draughty porch during a snowstorm on a freezing cold afternoon. He changed the subject.

'Tell me, have either of you ever heard of a cup, a holy relic of some kind? It might be heathen, or it could be Christian.'

'No,' said the Bishop at once. 'Never.'

Lleminawg tapped his teeth with a fingernail. 'The tales are full of them. Cups and cauldrons. The High King of Ierne, Cormac mac Art, had a golden cup which could distinguish between truth and falsehood, given him by Manannan mac Lir. Finn had a healing cup from the Giants. Tadg mac Nuada had a cup he got from the Land of Immortals which turned water into wine . . .'

The Bishop hissed impatiently. 'Blasphemy! A mere imitation of Our Lord's miracle at the wedding in Cana of Galilee.'

'But the cups themselves,' said mab Petroc. 'Do any still exist?'

'Are you mad, my lord?' spluttered the Bishop. 'Of course they do not "still" exist, because they never *have* existed. These are objects in fables invented by the Devil to ensnare the minds of fools.'

Lleminawg shrugged expressively. 'There is said to be a gold cup which once belonged to Cormac in the Royal Treasury at Tara of the Kings. But I have never been to Tara.'

'You have never heard of anything in the Western Isles?'

The Irishman shook his head. 'Why do you ask?'

Mab Petroc glanced at Bishop Enoch and smiled. 'Come,' he said. 'The storm is easing. We do not want to miss this woman singing.'

3

Budoc shifted in the boughs of the tree. The night was warm and he was sweating again, yet he could still recall the cold of that long winter thirty years ago.

There was an irony in sitting here all alone, hidden in a tree on a stifling hot summer night, thinking of the enforced companionship the freezing winter had brought.

He could remember how it had been, how those warriors not on duty had gathered in the Great Hall, even those with houses of their own, sleeping beside the warm hearths while the wind whistled in the eaves.

During the day and evening they had told each other stories (some true, most not) or refought old campaigns, building cloth mountains on the table tops and using fir cones for trees, tracing the course of rivers with skeins of wool, moving little pegs of wood hither and thither across this landscape to represent march and counter-march.

Or they had played dice and knucklebones, gambling away the jewellery they carried about them; or board games like gwythbull, in which one side seeks to break through a ring of hunters, and tawlboard, where the king-piece and its four supporters occupy the centre squares with eight opponents ranged against them.

Or the warriors had argued about the care of horses: how long they could be pastured on the same piece of ground before they turned it sour; the advantages of grain over other foodstuffs for making them strong of limb and sound of wind.

Or about the use and nature of weapons: the advantages and disadvantages of the war-knife as against the sword; whether spear shafts should be made from ash or holly; the decline of the sling as a weapon of war; the reliability of the bow in bad weather.

And of course they had talked about women: on the one hand the common girls they had known and tumbled or wanted to know and tumble, and on the other unattainable creatures such as Celemon daughter of Cei or the Lady Gwenhwyvar herself, women to whom they spoke but shyly if at all, with a courtesy and mildness that contrasted with their normal speech.

A wind sprang up and rustled the leaves above Budoc's head. It was a clear night, and through the gaps in the foliage he could see the stars treading their slow dance about the earth: fair Andromeda in her chains; the patient Bear-Keeper, driver of the Wain; the Swan in sideways flight.

His mind turned to Caer Cadwy.

On feast days – and there were many – the Warband ate till they were full: good meats like ham, beef, lamb and pork, or venison and wild boar if the hunting had been lucky, mopped up with wholesome vegetables and well-made bread. And they drank deep of sparkling yellow mead and strong red wine, or if they preferred there were ales and malts and bragget, which is made by fermenting honey and ale together, and can turn even the strongest head though it be warming on a winter's night.

(The thought of the food made Budoc in his tree salivate. It was years since he had eaten well.)

After the feasting, when the noise died down, the entertainers would appear, the jugglers and conjurors and acrobats, performing tricks to bemuse even the wisest of men.

But what the warriors liked best of all was to hear the tales of old, both spoken and sung, and the new tales concerning themselves and their Companions: tales of battles and quests and famous last stands, of those who suffered great misfortunes yet survived by their faith to win through at the end, of unyielding love triumphing against overwhelming odds.

A favourite story was that of Gwenhwyvar's wedding feast, and how Arthur had with her connivance stolen her away at the last possible moment, just as her father was about to pronounce her wed to Melwas the Young Prince of the Summer Country.

(And when that tale was being told there was not a man present in the body of the hall who did not wish he had been at the wedding feast to give Arthur and Gwenhwyvar his support, but only a handful who could truthfully say that they had been – and chief among them were Cei and Bedwyr, the first of his followers and now the greatest of his captains.)

Yet even the best of tales pall with repetition, and even the sweetest of companions develop annoying habits when one lives with them too long. People began to think the winter, the third since the battle of Badon Hill, would never end, for if one day held bright sunshine and the promise of spring, the next would bring snow or freezing showers of sleet from a grey sky. There were times when it seemed to the warriors that they had been cooped in Caer Cadwy for ever.

Restless, Budoc fidgeted in his tree. The rough bark cut into his legs, despite the pad he had made of his spare clothing. His limbs were stiff, and he wondered whether he would be able to climb down in the morning, or whether he was doomed to stay here caught halfway between heaven and earth until the Scotti found him.

He had been right not to trust Vortepor. The man's motives on that first occasion had been transparent – to link himself with the Warlord Arthur so thoroughly none would dare challenge his right to rule Dyfed. He had been as obvious about it as he had been about the sheep's eyes he had cast at Gwenhwyvar. A disgusting man. None of them had liked him, though they had treated him with the courtesy due the son of an old and faithful ally.

In later years Vortepor had become more devious. He had fomented unrest among the Saesons of the south and east, presenting himself as a fellow victim of a tyrant emperor. The man had been cunning: Arthur had never been able to find sufficient evidence to warrant a direct attack, and without such evidence, any move against Vortepor would have alienated the other Princes of Britain.

Someone like Bishop Enoch would have said that the disasters which had befallen Britain were a direct consequence of the inhabitants' departure from their proper obedience to God. The British were sinners, moral failures, like the Israelites of old. To chastise them, to make them turn again to the paths of righteousness, God had sent and was sending a series of plagues from overseas.

First had come the Picts and the Scotti, vomiting forth from the north and north-west in their coracles like insects drawn to honey. They had been driven back by godly men, fierce in the ways of the Lord. Then the British had lapsed again into sin, forgetting that it was by the will of God and not the force of arms that they were protected. This time the Lord had sent a far worse infliction in the shape of the Saesons.

Once more the Lord had relented a while, and thus the golden years of Arthur's rule. But the British were a nation of back-sliders, returning to their foul sins as a dog to its vomit. The lesson must be taught again, and again.

Budoc could see the logic of this point of view. While in the monastery in Armorica he had read part of the great History of Orosius, the Bishop of Tarragona in Spain and friend of St Augustine. Orosius believed that the history of the world was the story of the slow accomplishment of God's will. Men either helped or hindered, according to their natures.

'If the world and man are directed by a benign and just Divine Providence,' Orosius had said, 'and if man is both weak and stubborn, then he must be guided benignly when he has need of help; but when he abuses his free will he must be corrected with stern justice.'

Lying on the field of Camlann, and later when recovering from his wounds, the thought uppermost in his mind had been that Arthur had fallen because of the selfish stupidity of the Princes of Albion.

In a sense Medraut and Iddawg, traitors though they had been, were unimportant. It was the Lords of Prydein who had destroyed the one hope of peace in the island. Men like Vortepor – who should have been exposed at birth – and his rival Cadwallon of Gwynedd.

The history of Britain since the departure of the Romans and the collapse of central authority was the history of petty prince-lings vying with each other for some advantage. Their jealousies had prevented them from uniting against the Picts and the Scotti, had necessitated the use of Germanic mercenaries to defend the island. When those mercenary troops had rebelled, the princes had failed to unite behind either the High King Vitolinus, known as Gworthingern the Thin, or the House of Ambrosius. Governed by self-interest, they had supported first one side, then the other.

Arthur had dragged them to heel, but even then they had snapped at the hand which fed them, like the mangy curs they were. At the last they had brought him down, using Medraut and the Saesons to do the work they were too cowardly to attempt themselves.

Was this God's judgement? Or was it merely the usual foolishness of mankind? Budoc yawned, and tried to think of something else.

A pity he had not found an excuse to kill young Vortepor. It could have been managed, smoothed over as an accident. Agricola must have known what kind of man was his heir, and he had other sons to take his place. (Most of them dead now, slain on one excuse or another lest they challenge Vortepor's rule.)

But without Vortepor, he might never have known Teleri.

Even out of evil, good may come.

4

The three of them, mab Petroc, Lleminawg and Bishop Enoch, entered the hall with a handful of other latecomers brought by the promise of something new after this long winter of the same old songs. They found places on a bench near the door, and had no sooner settled themselves than Glewlwyd demanded silence.

Teleri stood forth, her back to the panelled wall which divided the women's quarter from the main hall, so that behind her carven images of the hero Cadwy strove with monsters and fought with armies. The harp was in her hand.

'It is an old tale I would tell you,' she said, 'and a dangerous tale.' Though she spoke without any apparent effort her voice could be heard throughout the building.

'A dangerous tale,' she repeated, and smiled.

'Our ancestors knew there is a power in the telling of tales, a power of incantation, a power of binding, a power of making.

'There is such a power in the story I would tell you this night. Such a power, that some say one who begins it must finish it, must tell it through to the end or die untimely. Others claim nobody has ever completed the story, not in its full and true version. They claim that by embarking upon it the teller has doomed himself, that he will die with the final words upon his lips.'

She riffled the strings of the harp.

Her audience seemed frozen in their places.

'I swore long ago I would tell this tale once and once only, and that in the hall of the greatest of the Lords of this island. Only at Arthur's court would I tell it, the Story of the Young Son, whom some call Mabon and some Pryderi or Peredur.

'And this is that story.'

Her fingers raced across the strings in a crash of discords. There was a moment's silence while all held their breath, then her voice began again, strong and mellifluous, while outside the hall the wind whistled and wailed.

In the beginning, before the coming of the conquerors and kings from across the sea, the only inhabitants of this land were the People, living in the body of the Goddess. The People had many names for the land, just as they had many names for the Lady. Sometimes they called the land 'Albion', for the whiteness of the chalk which was a sign of Her. Sometimes they spoke of 'the Sea-girt Green Space', which was a good description of how the land appeared to them. And sometimes they called the land 'the Honey Isle', for the richness and the sweetness which surrounded them.

It was a land, too, of great forests of mighty oaks, dangerous places full of bears, wild boars, lynx and wolves, and even worse things, demons and ghosts.

Under the guidance and protection of the Lady and the Lord Her Lover, the People cleared themselves small areas in which to build their houses and plant their corn, and gradually they began to drive back the Forest and the spirits which lived within it.

For a while all seemed well with them, though still they feared the Forest and the foul things that walked in it.

Then the Lady, who was old and wise as the stars, and more beautiful than the firmament of heaven with its clouds, decided it was time.

She lay with the Lord Her Lover for a day and a night and a day, and all the beasts of the field and the fowl of the air and the fishes of the waters gathered round, to watch and ward, for this was the time when she would beget a son. And the People were there also.

This son was to be the hope of the People. He would come not as a warrior (though he would fight when it was needful), nor as a hunter (though he would hunt at times), nor as a magician (though thrice in his life he would work great magics). He would come as a child of peace, as a healer, as a planter of corn and maker of gardens, as a raiser of horses and a tamer of pigs.

He would be all the good things to the People: the sun warming the crops, the gentle breeze and soft showers, the sweet dew falling from the heavens; the lambs frisking in the fields and the calves lowing; fish in the river and birds in the sky.

In his time there would be plenty, and for this reason his name – his first name, his true name, the name he bore before all others – was *Gwair*, which in the tongue of the People means the Awakener, the Quickener of Life. He would be the wellspring of all endeavour, the fountain of life, the cauldron of inspiration.

But there were Others living in the Forest in those days, Others who did not love the Lady and her People. These Others were the spirits and ghosts of time past, creatures of dark enchantment, fierce and dangerous beings. Chief among them was the Grey Man, Pwill, who had wanted the Lady for himself, had wanted to father his own child upon Her.

(That child would not have brought life and love and laughter to the People, as Gwair was to do. He would have brought death and hatred and sorrow.)

When the hour drew near the Lady retreated to a cave in the side of a hill with only six women for companions. There she laboured, hard and long. It was not an easy birthing, the birthing of Gwair.

He was born on May Eve, at the best time of year. In the fields the beasts knelt, in the air the birds sang, in the waters the fish leaped, for they knew that in him the world was made anew. All over the land the People kindled fires with their fire-drills to celebrate his coming, then climbed the hills to watch the sunrise, washing their faces in the morning dew and bedecking themselves in greenery.

On the third night after his birth, worn out by her struggles, the Lady fell into a deep and healing sleep. One by one the women who had accompanied her nodded and dozed, while the tapers they had set around the cave burned down to their sockets, guttered and went out, and the fire sank from its former glory to a dim bed of grey ash with only a faint glow at its heart.

They slept until dawn, and when they woke the child was gone.

Teleri's voice stopped, though the sound of the harp welled through the hall.

'You have heard this story before, all of you. I see by your faces that you recognize it. The divine child who comes at the dawn of summer to remake the world and who is stolen away at his birth – it is a familiar tale. All women know what it means to give birth to a child only to lose it, and all men know too, in their heart of hearts, what it is to father a child that dies untimely.'

The harp played on as she began to speak again.

When Gwair was stolen there came a great clap of thunder, and when the sun rose the land was swathed in mist. The leaves withered on the trees, the crops failed in the fields, the flocks and herds grew thin and died. The land became desolate and deserted.

In the place where he held court Teyrnon the Lover of the Lady saw the desolation fall, and knew that someone had stolen away his son. He gathered his war host, and called upon his brothers and his kinsmen, summoning them to his aid.

First came Nudd the Fisherman, Lord of the Borderlands by the Sea. He was a great healer, though the day would come when he could not heal himself. Next came Taliessin of the Golden Brow with Myrddin the Prophet, and these two were mighty magicians. Lastly came Taran, Beli and Bran, and these three were skilled in all arts, from harping and smithying to fighting and hunting. Each of these heroes brought with him a host of warriors, which added together made seven hosts, and these seven hosts were the first gathering of the army of Albion, which we call Prydein.

Teyrnon took counsel with his brother Nudd, and with Taliessin and Myrddin. They read the stars, and the waves of the sea, watched the flights of birds across the misty grey sky, consulted the bones of their ancestors.

Then they knew that Gwair had been stolen out of this world, into the land of shadows and darkness, into that country from which no one had ever returned – the Kingdom of the Grey Man. And they knew that they must journey beyond the borders of this world to fetch him back.

'Do you know what happened next, you of the court of Arthur the Soldier?' Teleri asked teasingly, her hands moving across the harp strings. 'Do you know how they sailed in three ships, these heroes and their followers, out across the edge of the world? Do you know of the battles they fought, and the marvels they saw, and the deaths they died, one by one, on their voyage? It would take a year to tell of their adventures, and even then much would be left unsaid.'

The music rang with the sound of waves beating upon unknown shores, with the clash of weapons and the thunder of great storms, with the roaring of monsters and the sighing of wind.

At last they came – those of them who were still alive – to a place that was neither land nor sea, where the water grew thick and viscous like liquid mud, and the waves moved slowly, lazily, quite unlike anything they had seen before. The breeze which had propelled them thus far faded then failed altogether.

For a timeless while they hung suspended between the flat surface of the sea (if it was the sea) and the empty grey vault of the sky. In that place there was no colour, and no life.

Afraid to break the dreadful silence the People conversed in whispers, flung ropes from ship to ship to draw them together, and finally broke out the oars.

Gradually the sweeps set them moving again, slowly at first, plying reluctantly through the strange liquid as if pulling against a great weight.

Taliessin and Myrddin painted their faces, one white and one red, and began to gather their powers to them. Nudd stood in the bow of the leading ship, directing their course with hand gestures, while the others prepared their weapons, softly singing spells of victory into the blades.

Taliessin and Myrddin moved to the front of their two boats, so each vessel now had a man in its bows, and no ordinary man at that, but a master of magic.

The ships sped on, deeper and deeper into the gathering mist.

'Up oars!' bellowed Nudd. The ships grated and groaned as they slithered across some solid obstruction, and then the crews were blinking in bright sunshine.

Teleri took up the harp again and sang:

> *Perfect was the prison*
> *Where they held the young prince,*
> *   Gwair was well guarded*
> *   By bondsmen of Pwill,*
> *And the lake bound him round*
> *Like a chain of blue steel.*

The ships came gliding slowly to rest amidst this new brightness. All around them lapped clean water, blue in the summer sun, while before them towered a great green tor with curiously terraced sides. At the foot of this hill, hard against the shoreline, was a stockade built from massive tree trunks.

The People dipped their oars into the lake, washing them clean, and started to row towards the shore. A flight of cranes flew directly overhead, and Teyrnon smiled, knowing this meant the Lady was with them even here, at the heart of the Grey Man's power.

Then they saw a line of white globes along the outside of the wooden wall: the skulls of their predecessors who had been unwise enough to attack this place. Then living faces appeared above the palisade, shouting and screaming, waving knives and spears that glittered in the sunlight.

The ships swept shorewards. Inside the fort drums beat and gongs clashed. Red-hot slingstones whizzed around the ears of the People, hissed and splashed in the waters of the lake; but still the ships came on.

Now Taran and Beli and Bran rose to their feet, and began to chant their name songs. As Taran sang, the oaks of the stockade burst asunder, spilling the defenders to the ground. As Beli sang, the willow wattles of the houses and hurdles unwove themselves. As Bran sang, the alder piles on which the settlement was built heaved themselves up out of the muddy shore.

Teyrnon let forth a great shout of triumph, and those few defenders still standing found their spears and knives shattered in their hands. The cooking fires overturned in the confusion, and flames began to lick at the wreckage.

They fought among the ruins, the warriors of the People and the survivors of the Others, while the fires raged around them, fought hand to hand, seizing whatever they could find to use as a weapon. The Others would not give up, fighting on with tooth and claw even after they had taken terrible wounds. The People fell, despite the advantage their magic had given them, until at the last only the Seven Lords were still standing.

Wearily they surveyed the dead, their faithful followers, lying tangled with the mis-shapen bodies of the Others.

'Now are we come to the end,' said Myrddin. 'Let us return to the lake and wash ourselves clean of the stench of war, that we may embark upon the final stage of the quest in a state befitting those of our blood.'

So they moved through the ashes and the smouldering fires,

through the mounded corpses of the host of Prydein and their enemies, down to where the waters lapped gently at the shore.

There they washed themselves and their clothing in preparation for what was to come. As they returned to the foot of the hill one among the dead suddenly rose from the place where he had been lying, and stabbed at Nudd with a long-bladed spear, piercing his thigh. The Fisherman screamed.

Before the echoes died away Teyrnon's sword had struck the head from the body of the Other. Then they gathered round while Taliessin eased the spear from the wound and staunched the blood.

'Not a death blow,' said he of the Golden Brow.

'But hard will be its healing,' said Myrddin, 'through all the ages of the world. A fool am I that I did not foresee it, the malice of Pwill.'

Teyrnon shaded his eyes and gazed up at the tor, his face grim.

'I must go on alone. In this time and place the deed is mine and mine only.'

His companions understood, for they too had been or would be Lovers of the Lady, even as they also had been or would be Her Father and Her Son. They knew this venture had been acted out many times before and would be many times again, and they knew that in this version it was their part to wait with the wounded Fisherman, while it was Teyrnon's to go forward and dance the spiral dance.

At the foot of the tor was a single standing stone, twice the height of a man, pitted and scarred with the passage of the years. Hanging from one side was a great horn, bound with bands of gold and silver. Teyrnon took this horn and blew upon it three mighty blasts, and with the third the horn split asunder. When the sounds had died away Teyrnon stepped past the standing stone.

So the Great Lord mounted the hollow hill while his kinsmen watched from below, treading out the sacred path. He danced three paces forward and once sunwise round the tor, one pace back and once withershins round the tor, then he paused and drew breath. Face stern, he started again: a single step back and one sunwise circuit, then three leaps forward and one withershins circuit.

The onlookers could see that he was panting now, and the sweat was dripping from his forehead. He wiped his brow and came forward again three paces to make a sunwise circling, then back one pace before a circling withershins. Finally he took a last step back and danced a sunwise round, which brought him to a dark patch on the hill a little below the summit.

He ducked and vanished from their view.

Thus he entered the high castle on the shelving hillside, where it was dark even at noon unless torches were set burning. He entered by the one door, which lay at the centre of the labyrinth, crawling on his hands and knees through the gloomy passage which ran straight and true to the depths of the tor.

At last he came out of the passage and into an open space as black as pitch. He waited, listening, and could hear soft breathing all around him, echoing from the walls and the corbelled vault of the roof.

He raised his sword over his head and swung, the blade whining as it cleaved through the dank air. Sparks showered as he brought it down on the stone floor, and the sword burst into incandescent light.

'I have come for my son!' he shouted.

By the fierce glow from the blade he saw faces: nine figures, each frozen in place.

'Where is my son?'

The figures moved forward, and he saw now that they were female under their heavy cloaks: three girls to his left, three matrons in the middle, three older women to his right. He brandished the sword, watching them flinch from the light, cried again:

'Where is he?'

'He is here.'

He could not tell which of them had spoken. While he hesitated, they edged a little closer, and as they moved so the light of his sword dimmed – not much, but enough to let the darkness press in upon him all the more heavily.

'Bring him forth,' he commanded.

Of a sudden the boy was there between the women and himself, nestling in a golden cup shaped like a water lily, broad and low. Under the rim was a band of dark blue enamel set with white pearls.

'A question, Lord, before you leave.'

The voice spoke out of the shadows which had gathered when the brightness of his sword faded.

He waited, his free hand poised to snatch his child and run. (Though he knew he would never make it through the tunnel with the women on his heels.)

'Whom does he serve, your son?'

'The voice hissed and sang through the chamber,' said Teleri, striking the strings of the harp.

Her audience heard it then, the question echoing around the enclosed dark space, and Teyrnon knowing that if he did not make the right answer all would have been for nothing.

Inspiration came to him. Now he understood, understood everything. Drawing himself up to his full height, he said:

'He serves all things in the Isle of Albion. I, Teyrnon, swear it in his Mother's name.'

The question came a second time.

'Whom does he serve, your son?'

'He serves all things in the Sea-girt Green Space,' Teyrnon said.

'Even the servants of Pwill, the Grey Man?' the voice spoke again, very close at hand.

'All things in the Honey Isle,' he said for the third and final time.

'Then go, and take your child with you!' The voice shrieked and cracked, whether in pleasure or in pain he could not say.

He went as quickly as he could, shaking and trembling for all his powers and for all he was Lover of the Lady, crawling along the tunnel with the boy in his arms while eerie whisperings followed in his wake.

A long journey it seemed, much longer than on the way in, and the child was heavy and grew heavier as he went. The darkness pressed down upon him, and the sword at his belt (from which not the faintest glimmer of light now shone) tangled between his legs, impeding him.

At last he saw a faint lessening of the dark, the blurry paleness of the opening through which he had come a lifetime ago.

For an age the opening grew no nearer, and it seemed to him that he had always been here, wearily crawling through the blackness with a great weight in his arms, and that all else was illusion, false memory, like a daydream of a better place.

His strength was failing fast, and his own panting was loud in his ears. 'For the Lady,' he sobbed with the last of his breath, making a final effort in the knowledge that if this failed he was finished.

He came bursting out into the noonday sunshine and the green of the world like one reborn from a dark and perilous womb.

And as he stood blinking in the light it was as if a veil had been lifted from his eyes, and he saw that the hillside upon which he stood was in the heart of his homeland, and that all around him was peace and plenty, and the birds of his Lady singing in his ears.

Teleri played a final piece upon the harp, conjuring the sounds of birds in midsummer, then laid her hand flat across the strings so all was quiet.

5

Like Teyrnon the Great Lord with his precious burden bursting forth from darkness into light, Budoc startled into wakefulness, unsure for a moment of when and where he was.

The sun was streaming through the branches, and the dew was sparkling on every twig and leaf. He squinted against the brightness, breathed in the warm air, shifted cautiously on his perch, testing limbs frozen by their long immobility.

> *Three shiploads of Prydein we went on the sea,*
> *Save seven none returned from the Castle of Death.*

That was the song on which Teleri had based her tale – though she would no doubt have argued it was the other way about, that the story came first and the song later.

He had never believed her talk of the tale being dangerous to the teller. Dangerous to the *listener*, but not the teller.

Certainly it had proved dangerous to them, the Companions of Arthur, the mightiest warband in all Britain. It had filled them with a kind of madness, like a vision of another world.

He hauled himself to his feet, balancing on the curving bough and leaning his weight against the trunk. Now the time had come to leave his safe perch he felt curiously reluctant, cast about for excuses to stay a while.

The bundle of spare clothing could remain here, wedged

between two branches. So could a full water-bottle and some of the food, well wrapped to protect it from the insects.

He ate a few mouthfuls of bread and cheese, sufficient to quiet the rumbling of his stomach, and took stock of his position. He needed to know what the Scotti were doing, what was their purpose in landing in the Porthyle estuary. From what he had seen in the pool, they had designs on the sacred wood itself. It was his duty to resist them, if that were possible.

Simple enough. But he had no idea how to set about it.

He felt helpless. He seemed to be in the grip of a mental lethargy. His mind was useless, unable to plan beyond the moment, fitted only to losing him in vivid recollections of the past. In many ways the events of thirty years ago were more real to him than what was happening in the present – if he closed his eyes and conjured Teleri's face, he could see every pore, every incipient wrinkle . . .

He snatched himself back before it was too late.

Peering down through the thick foliage at the sun-streaked shadows of the woodland floor, he wondered whether this feebleness was a legacy of his illness.

Whatever, it was time to move, or he would never manage it.

He slithered and scrambled down the trunk, the spear clutched awkwardly in his mis-shapen left hand, and landed with a thump that jarred his teeth.

He regarded the spear with distaste. Ten years it had been since he had used a weapon in anger. The old skills were still there, lying dormant under a thin skin like a freshly scabbed wound, all too ready to break out again at the slightest provocation.

It had always been his curse. Cei had relished the very act of fighting, had gloried in the sense of contest, in the clash of sword on shield. Arthur on the other hand had treated combat as a grim necessity, something to be endured for the sake of what came after.

Budoc had loved the killing.

This was his sin, the reason he survived to live on alone bereft of friends and kin.

He laid the spear against the trunk of the tree and walked deeper into the forest.

Much later he heard the hounds far off on the other side of the wood yelping with excitement. They sounded like a pack being mustered at the edge of the hunting ground, and with a sudden flash of horror he knew exactly what they were being brought to hunt.

They howled, their mournful and hungry music drifting through the trees, wailing and dying then rising again.

He began to run, pacing himself, flitting between the trunks like a ghost, following the contours of the land while he struggled to think of a way of escape. He had to stay in the forest: the open ground by the cliffs would be fatal. He needed water, something to break his scent . . .

The boughs of the trees? Could he fool them by taking to the air?

Not here. The trunks were too far apart, the branches too flimsy. He would fall and break a limb.

They were coming fast, giving tongue in the fury of the chase. He knew from their sound that they were war hounds, not like the great mastiffs the British were said to have once used in battle, but fierce beasts bred in Ierne for hunting wolves and deer: heavy and hairy, large-limbed and long-muzzled, fleet of foot for all their weight. He had faced them before, and knew how dangerous they could be even to a well-armed warrior standing shoulder to shoulder with his comrades. Alone and defenceless, he stood no chance at all.

He plunged down a slope through drifts of long-dead leaves, wound between the thin white saplings of birch, ducking branches and feeling twigs rake his hair.

There was a stream at the bottom of the valley, murky and clogged with debris. He left footprints in the mud along its banks, but there was no time to worry, no time to do anything save fight through the clinging silt to the safety of the gravel bed.

Upstream or down?

Downstream would also bring him downwind of the hounds as they followed the long curve of his trail. The risk was that it would take him closer to the huntsmen travelling in the wake of the pack.

All his instincts told him to move inwards, towards his enemies, rather than let them run him down in aimless flight.

He went with the current, sliding his feet through the brown water to make as little noise as possible. The soles of his sandals turned slimy as the water soaked the leather, and looking behind him he could see swirls of mud and grit marking his passage.

In a half crouch he came to the concealment of a stand of willow, which was no concealment at all to creatures who hunted by scent, and paused to catch his breath. Slots of sunlight darted across the dirty surface of the stream, turned the brown humus of the far bank to luminous gold.

The hounds were howling, howling, and in the distance he could hear voices laughing and calling.

'"Into Thy hands",' he muttered, and plucked a willow stem, stripped it of its leaves till he was left with nothing but the long bare shoot, flexible as a whip.

Into this he tied a knot, his fingers moving without haste though the hounds were drawing ever nearer, then a second knot below the first, using his teeth to pull it tight when his left hand betrayed him as it was wont to do.

Murmuring 'Forgive me,' he cast the wand down the stream and watched it drift gently away on the sluggish current, threatening to catch on the piles of dead leaves and twigs, yet somehow never quite stopping.

When it was out of sight he followed, less carefully now, for the pack was very close their baying loud enough to cover the sound of his splashes. As he went he scanned the steadily deepening bank, searching for a place to leave the stream.

A deer coughed above his head. He looked up, saw pricked reddish ears and pointed face, then a flash of white rump as the roe bounded away, crashing through the undergrowth.

'Forgive me,' he muttered again, and hauled himself from the stream by an overhanging branch.

Behind him he heard the hounds give tongue as they scented the deer, and a moment later they raced up the slope, ignoring him as he clung unmoving to his branch, running like great grey wolves with no thought for anything but their prey.

When they had gone he dropped to the ground, brushing the green powder and dust from his hands and clothes. The huntsmen were whooping with delight in the distance, shouting advice and instructions back and forth. With luck – and by God's will – the deer would keep them occupied for a while.

In the meantime he could find a hideaway – not in a tree this time, he had had enough of trees – on the far side of the wood, using every trick he knew to break the trail of his scent.

*   *   *

By mid-afternoon he was safely ensconced in the shelter of a rocky outcrop near the cliffs, as far from the village as he could manage without abandoning the peninsula altogether.

He owed his escape from the hounds, as he owed so much else, to Teleri. She had taught him the magic of *Dlui Fulla*, the fluttering wisp, after his encounter with the leader of the tattooed men, the Pict who had called himself Pedrylaw Menestyr.

(In all his years at the monastery this knowledge was a thing to which he had never admitted. He had heard matters were arranged differently in Ierne, that there a druid might become a Christian priest without renouncing his powers, but in what remained of Gaul the magical practices of ancient times were frowned upon, regarded as the work of those allied to Satan.)

Pedrylaw Menestyr. The Cunning Cupbearer. Budoc still thought of him as a Pict, one of the Painted People, but in truth he had belonged to a far older tradition than that of the Caledonian Federation.

Dlui Fulla, the art of the fluttering wisp, like the tradition of which Pedrylaw Menestyr was a part, was ancient, stretching back into the days when the first men named and described the land.

You took a straw, a wisp of hay, a piece of string – even, if you were desperate, a switch of willow – and made certain preparations so that it could be used as a focus. (This was the civilized Roman side of him trying to describe something which essentially could not be described because it was more a matter of instinct than intellect.) You could curse with it, and call friends or foes to your presence – which was what he had done that day, summoning the deer to act as decoy. Or you could send visions to draw the soul from your chosen victim's body and bend it to your will – which was what Pedrylaw Menestyr had come close to doing to him, nigh on thirty years ago.

He shivered at the memory.

If Arthur had not saved him he would have become the Pict's slave.

CHAPTER TWO

1

When the strains of the harp had dissolved away into the echoes of the hall, Teleri's listeners sat silent, blinking like the Great Lord Teyrnon when he escaped from Gwair's dark prison, their faces puzzled.

'Is that the end?' someone whispered, and bodies began to stir through the hall, coughing and rustling as they murmured to each other, still in the world of the story.

Mab Petroc shifted on the bench, aware of Lleminawg at his side staring at the woman in fascination. The glimmerings of understanding ran through his mind, and he remembered the last words Degaw of the Creones had said before he left her house.

'If you go in search of the Children of Menestyr, do not take Talorcan with you.'

He had taken her hands in his and held them gently. 'It will not be my decision, you know that. If we move north, Arthur will choose who goes and who remains behind.'

She had laughed mirthlessly, returning his grip. 'Will he not listen to you, you who are his trusted friend?'

'Why does it matter whether Talorcan goes or not – if we go at all?'

The children had stopped playing and listened, enthralled at the sight of their mother holding this man's hands.

'I fear the Attecotti.' She grimaced. 'Not for any good reason.

But in our childhood stories they were always sorcerers of great power, untrustworthy and of murderous intent. And you will go, cousin. I do not need to have the second sight to foretell that. Now the Saesons have been defeated once and for all, the Warlord must find some way of keeping his warriors busy, else they will fall to quarrelling among themselves.'

'*I will try to keep him out,*' he had promised. '*I will try.*'

Lleminawg stirred beside him. 'There is your cup,' he murmured from the corner of his mouth. 'Set round with pearls and a child floating in it. Would that be the one you were wanting?'

'I think so,' he whispered back. 'I am going to talk with her. Do you wish to come?'

The Irishman grinned at him. 'I would have you know, cousin, I intend to wed. Bishop Enoch has warned me this woman Teleri may be an imp of Satan, sent to imperil our mortal souls. So yes, I will accompany you, but let it be clearly understood between us that it is only to protect you from her wiles. I myself am currently in a state of grace where women are concerned, courtesy of our good bishop, and therefore immune to her charms.'

'I wondered why you were in the chapel. Who is the unfortunate lady?'

'Elen, daughter of Tudwal.'

Mab Petroc whistled softly. 'Kynfawr's sister? Well done, cousin. An alliance with the royal house of Dumnonia will strengthen your family's position.'

'Much as I would like to claim it was my beauty alone which won her heart,' Lleminawg said modestly, 'I must confess my father had some small part to play in the negotiations.'

'You mean he arranged the whole thing.' Seeing the Bishop starting to move, mab Petroc rose to his feet. 'We shall drink to it later. But first, I would speak with the Lady Teleri.'

The two of them pushed through the crowd to the partition wall where the woman stood, packing her harp into its travelling case.

'Lady, forgive me,' said mab Petroc in his most courtly tones. 'Had I known you were with the embassy, I would have made better provision for your comfort last night.'

She straightened, her face slightly flushed. Their eyes were on a level, for she was his height or more, and he saw her pupils contract slightly, and something passed through him like the shock of a sudden pain, so he almost moaned aloud.

'Do the lords of Arthur's court hunt in pairs?' she asked, a faint smile playing about the corners of her lips.

He found himself studying the texture of her face, scrutinizing the thin lines that appeared with her smile, noting the pale freckles floating on the brown skin. The intensity of his desire shocked him, and from far away he heard Lleminawg's voice:

'Indeed no, Lady. But my cousin here, having met you after a fashion, agreed to perform the introductions.'

There was a silence, and he knew he must speak.

'My Lady Teleri, may I present Lleminawg mab –' for a moment he went blank and could not remember the name of Lleminawg's father, then dropped into the Irish form '– mac Niall.'

She did not seem to have noticed his hesitation. 'You are Irish then?' she said to Lleminawg. Her voice was sweet as honey, strong and husky in its depths.

'Yes and no,' said his friend.

'Ah, a man of mystery, like all the Irish. Never a straight answer to be had from any one of you.'

'That is because we recognize the futility of boundaries, of dividing the world into categories,' laughed Lleminawg. 'My ancestors were from Ierne, but we settled in this island several generations ago at the invitation of the then High King, Gworthigern the Thin.'

'And you yourself, Lady, where are you from?' asked mab Petroc.

Her face clouded. 'Once I was from the Iardomnan, but now . . .' She dipped her shoulders. 'I am a homeless wanderer.'

Lleminawg swept her a bow. 'A skilled bard is never homeless.'

'And a bard is a traveller by nature,' said mab Petroc. 'Is it not so, that no true bard ever stayed in one place for long?'

'It is as you say, but still my heart yearns after the land of my youth.' She turned to him, her thick black hair swirling after, the bronze clasps and silver buckles which adorned her dress signalling wildly as they caught the light.

'It was an . . . interesting tale you told us,' he said, his gaze falling to the pendant which nestled at the base of her neck.

'I am glad you found it so,' she said coolly.

'Come, cousin,' reproached Lleminawg. 'Interesting is far too weak a word for such a marvel. Say rather, *fascinating*.'

The pendant was made of jet, the colour of her hair, and

scribed on its surface were slim white lines that coiled around and around upon each other.

'Fascinating? Blasphemous was the term I would have chosen.' Bishop Enoch thrust his way between them, his thin features stiff with anger. 'Truly is it said the only thing lighter than a spark is the mind of a woman between two men. And it might have been added that the minds of the two men in conversation with her are no weightier.'

Mab Petroc felt the rage flood through him. Had Lleminawg not caught his arm he would have struck the Bishop down there and then, in the middle of Arthur's court. The Irishman's nails bit deep into his flesh, the pain calming him.

Oblivious to his danger, the Bishop confronted Teleri. 'Blasphemous too is the gown you wear, blue in imitation of the gown of the Virgin Mary, Mother of Our Lord.'

'Bishop,' warned mab Petroc, his temper under control now, but Enoch ignored him.

'"The songs of the poets are the food of demons," St Jerome tells us,' he quoted sententiously. 'How true, how very true, that is. Your story was a mishmash of lies, cunningly woven . . .'

'Bishop!' repeated mab Petroc, louder this time.

'And you, my lords,' snapped Enoch, 'you lapped up her lies like cats drinking cream, and now you sniff around her like hounds round a bitch . . .'

'That will do!' thundered mab Petroc.

The shout rang in all their ears. The Bishop's face had gone very pale, and he flinched when mab Petroc moved.

'You insult the Magister Militum's guest,' mab Petroc said quietly, aware of the heads turned in his direction.

Enoch's mouth was hanging open in a circle of surprise. He snapped it shut as he collected his dignity, then glared at the three of them before spinning on his heel to force a way through the silent crowd to the dais.

Gradually the hum of conversation began again.

Lleminawg glanced embarrassedly from mab Petroc to Teleri. 'I had best go after him. I want him to perform my wedding.'

He too thrust a path through the press in the Bishop's wake. Left alone, they stared at each other.

'I . . .'

'I . . .'

They stopped.

183

Teleri laughed. 'You first.'

'It was nothing,' he said. 'I was going to apologize. He is not the man Arthur would have chosen as bishop of this region. In his way he is not so bad, but he lives in difficult times. The Church has always been urban, and now the towns are dying he sees everything which does not conform to his ideas as a threat.'

'He is an important man?'

Mab Petroc thought for a moment. 'The Church is still wealthy, despite its decline. Yes, he has influence, and more so now the land is at peace.'

'Yet you do not fear him? You would have hit him if your friend had not stopped you.'

'Fear him? No, Lady. I am glad Lleminawg restrained me, for though I do not like Enoch, I respect his office. But I care nothing for his enmity . . .'

On the side of her neck was a small brown birthmark in the shape of a butterfly. Her skin was still glowing with the heat of the hall, and this butterfly stood out with great clarity. He found himself contemplating running his tongue across its wings, and lost the thread of what he was saying.

'Perhaps I should,' she said quietly.

'No,' he said dismissively. 'You are Arthur's guest. What the Bishop thinks does not matter.'

'What people like that think always matters, in the end,' she murmured so softly he had to strain to hear.

'It is noisy in here, and hot. Will you walk a little way with me?'

'Outside?' Amusement flashed across her face. 'It was cold and stormy when we came from the guest hall.'

'My house is not far, and I should change my clothing.' He plucked ruefully at his tunic, dark stained with the marks of last night's fighting.

'So you should.' She scanned the gathering. 'Do you know, my lord, you are the only one present who is not dressed in finery?'

'You disapprove?'

'It has a certain effectiveness. You stand out among the rest like an old crow amid a flock of brightly plumed birds.'

He laughed. 'It was not deliberate. I did not have time to change before I came to the hall.'

'Busy about the Warlord's business?' she said mockingly.

He bowed his head. 'Six of my men were killed last night, and others wounded. I would like to know why.'

Suddenly she was sober, the merriment gone. 'I will walk with you.'

They slipped from the light and warmth of the Great Hall, well wrapped in their cloaks, Teleri carrying her harp slung over her back.

It was snowing hard, the fat white flakes driven by the biting wind, settling on the rooftops and on the ground, blowing into drifts and piles against the walls.

Before they had gone more than a few paces their shoulders were wet and white. The storm increased with a sudden intensity, the wind shrieking across the hilltop like a demented being, and a whirling curtain of whiteness blotted out everything except the tiny space in which they stood. Mab Petroc staggered as a vicious gust caught him, clutched at the woman to save his balance, heard her deep and melodious chuckle in his ear.

'Is this wise?' she shouted. Her bony face was a mass of dark hollows, alive with excitement.

His vision blurred as snow caked his eyelashes. He blinked, reached out to take her hand and led her down the hill, steering by instinct, leaning into the wind, ignoring the dizzying dance of the white flakes.

The door of his house had frozen shut, the ice clinging to the jamb and edges. It needed both of them to force it open then drag it shut again, and as they did so a great cloud of smoke billowed out from the small fire in the hearth to greet them.

She coughed, waving a hand in front of her face, and slipped the harp from her shoulder to the floor, brushing off the snow that had gathered on its case.

'You live alone?' she said, glancing around the bare room.

'Moried sleeps here sometimes if the Hall is crowded.' He knelt beside the hearth and coaxed the fire into life. 'But yes, since my wife died I have lived alone.'

She shook out her cloak, spraying drops of meltwater across the floor.

'This is not what I expected. I had imagined somewhere grander.'

He smiled without humour. 'I have no need of more. Most of my time is spent in the Hall or in Arthur's private quarters. I have few personal possessions.'

'Other than your swords and shields.' She nodded at the blades and boards that formed the only decoration in the room.

'It is what I am,' he said. 'They are the tools of my trade.'

'And these are special?' Her long fingers brushed the wire-bound hilt of the nearest sword.

'No. They are better made than most, but they have no particular significance.'

She turned to him in mock surprise. 'They are not the spoils of war, taken from some vanquished foe? You did not win them in single combat one moonlit night on a hilltop in a forest? They were not forged for you and you alone by a lame smith in a bothy under a rowan tree on a high moor where the winds whistle and wail and no man ever goes?'

Despite himself he laughed. 'No. I have never owned a magical sword, and if I did I would probably either break it or lose it.'

'You disappoint me. After young Vortepor's description of your prowess last night I had expected a man with a sorcerer's blade.' She stared at him, the small pink tip of her tongue playing around her slightly parted lips. 'Is it true you killed most of the attackers yourself?'

Disillusionment flooded through him. Her expression was horribly familiar, one he had seen all too often on the faces of other women asking similar questions. He had thought she was different. Foolishly, he had judged her by the performance she had given in the Hall, and had decided on the strength of it that she must be a person of intelligence and experience, not another empty-headed seeker after vicarious thrills.

'Yes,' he said shortly. 'What do you know of them?'

She seated herself carefully on a stool beside the fire, smoothing the fabric of her blue gown, letting her hair fall so it framed her features.

'What do I know of them?' she echoed. 'That they have hunted me across the face of this land, driving me from place to place as hounds drive a stag. That they have killed without compunction those who have helped me or sought to hinder them. That they are many, and not all are marked by spiral tattoos. That they have friends and allies where one might least expect it, so that even here in Caer Cadwy I do not feel safe.'

'Why?' His voice was flat and harsh.

She moved, and the shadows shifted across the planes and hollows of her face.

'Because I carry a secret.'

'What secret?'

'One they would protect.'

He sighed heavily. 'Six men are dead, because I did not set adequate guards last night. Will you tell me why?'

'More are living because I screamed a warning.'

'Yes,' he said, pouncing on a question she might answer. 'How did you know they were coming?'

'I felt them. Even in my sleep I felt them, as the creatures of the fields feel the hawk hovering overhead.'

'Who are they?'

'They are the Sons of Menestyr, and they guard a treasure so ancient its origins are lost to all but a few.'

'And you are one of those few?'

'You heard the tale I told.'

He slumped onto a stool, trailing his damp cloak in the ash of the hearth. With a grimace he unbuckled his baldric and laid his sword aside.

'Let me start again. Lady, who are you and where are you from?'

'You know my name. And I have already told you I am from the Iardomnan.'

'So why do you travel in the entourage of a Dyfed prince?'

'I am a bard. I take service where I may find it.'

'Yet you are here by your own design, not that of your patron.'

She frowned. 'Say rather by our mutual desire. Caer Cadwy is famed throughout Prydein. Naturally I wished to visit it, and to sing in the Great Hall before Arthur himself.'

'Why do you avoid my questions?'

'Avoid them? I have answered all of them truthfully.'

He unfastened his cloak and tossed it aside.

'Who is your patron?'

Her lips twitched. 'If I must have a patron, then Vortepor of Dyfed.'

'Not Agricola?'

'Not Agricola,' she agreed.

'But Agricola approves of your accompanying his embassy? You have already admitted that your presence is a danger to those around you.'

'Agricola is old and weary. For years he has kept the faith, first with Ambrosius and then with Arthur. Now he would have some return, and he believes I may help.'

He studied her by the flickering light of the fire, and realized he had been wrong. Whatever else this woman sought, it was not vicarious thrills.

'What happened to your hand?' she said softly, leaning across the hearth to take it in hers.

'An old wound, from when I was young and careless.'

'And now you are old and careful?'

She drew his hand towards her and placed it on her breast. He could feel the warmth of her through the fabric.

'You are like a man frozen in winter,' she said.

He tried to think of a clever response, and failed.

'You did not like it when you thought I was interested in you only for your prowess with a sword,' she said, her eyes fixed on his. 'What comes next? Do I ask if you are equally adept with other weapons?'

He could not help smiling.

'And how do you answer, when they ask you that? Do you make your excuses and leave?' She nodded to herself. 'Yes, I think you do.'

She moved his damaged hand towards the brooch which held the shoulder of her gown.

'But supposing I told you it was not your skill with a blade or any other weapon that attracted me. Suppose I told you that it was your closeness to Arthur which interested me. Would you believe me?'

His thumb and little finger met on the clasp of the brooch.

'No, Lady, I would not believe you. I have my share of vanity.'

He squeezed and the pin popped from its fastening. The brooch slid free of the cloth.

'Besides,' he added, 'you would be wasting your time. What we do here will not influence Arthur one way or the other.'

She smiled enigmatically and released the gown. It fell in long slow ripples of blue that seemed to last for ever.

Afterwards they lay sated on the couch, watching the flames of the fire.

'Will you not tell me the truth now?' he asked. 'Who are you, and what is your desire?'

'My desire (other than for you) is simple. It is for Arthur to sail north and west with a company of warriors and destroy the pirates of the Iardomnan.'

188

'What are they to you?'

'I am a bard. It is a Primary Law of both Prydein and Ierne that a bard may travel as he or she wishes, without fear or hindrance. These pirates have made movement along the western seaboard of Britain perilous in the extreme. They have killed and burned and enslaved whole villages. An end must be made to them.'

'Yet you yourself are from the Iardomnan,' he said, frowning.

'That is another reason why they should be destroyed. They dishonour my homeland. They have a leader, Hueil mab Caw, who has bound them together as they have not been bound since the days of Drust mab Erp, when our grandsires were young.'

'And the Children of Menestyr?'

'They pursue me because I was once one of them. They have no connection with Hueil and his alliance of raiders.'

'They must want you badly.'

She hesitated, continued: 'They are the reason I left the Iardomnan. I had enquired too closely into their secrets.' She smiled lazily, traced the line of his shoulder with a finger. 'Even as a child I was curious. What of you? How did your wife die?'

He turned away. 'She died of the yellow plague.'

'I am sorry.' She frowned. 'Many people die of the plague. Why do you feel guilt?'

'I was not there.' His voice was low, so she had to strain to hear. 'I was with Arthur. It was the campaign that culminated in Badon Hill. She wanted me to go to her – she knew she was dying – but what I was doing seemed more important.'

'You were necessary to Arthur's plans?' she said softly.

'I believed so,' he said wearily. 'I pretended to believe so. Who knows?' He sighed, sat up. 'All my life we had fought the Saesons. Now the end seemed near. The last victory. I wanted to take part.'

He stared sightlessly into the fire. 'It was at Badon the battle madness fell upon me for the first time. Until then, there was a coldness that came upon me in combat, as if a part of me were watching everything that happened, assessing risks, weighing chances.'

'I understand,' she said.

'At Badon all that changed. The battle fury swept me up in its grasp. Since then I have not cared whether I lived or died.'

'And your wife?'

'Garwen?' He looked up, eyes full and glinting. 'They brought me word of her passing the night before the battle.'

She put her arm around his shoulders and held him while the tears fell.

After a moment she said gently:

'You warriors, there are times when you remind me of the strings on my harp. If the strings are too loose, the harp will not play. Too tight, and they break. Yet even when they are wound to the perfect tension so they produce notes of ideal beauty, they are still prone to snapping suddenly without warning. Even so with you.'

Through his tears he managed a sound which might have been agreement.

'She must have loved you very much. And obviously, you loved her. I do not think you need reproach yourself for putting the public need before the private. Many would see it as no more than your duty.'

He gathered his composure and looked her straight in the face. 'A fine tale, is it not, with all the makings of a great tragedy?'

She met his challenge and held it without flinching. 'I shall not sing of it. But you must know people do speak of it: how you loved your wife so much you have never recovered from your grief at her death.'

'Yes,' he said sadly. 'They do. And they are wrong.'

She drew in her breath with a hiss. 'I was not certain,' she murmured.

'Yet you guessed, Lady, you guessed.' He stood and replenished the fire. 'Oh, I loved her once. But we grew apart as we grew older – or at least, I grew away from her. She I think remained the same, while I was the one who changed.'

'Not to be wondered at. You followed Arthur.'

'And do still. And always shall, until the day I die,' he said without emotion, as if the bout of weeping had emptied him of all feeling. 'But my sorrow is for my failure to love her, and my guilt is for that betrayal. She deserved better than I gave her.'

'If she had not died, what then?'

'Yes,' he said flatly. 'What then? I never wished her ill, but her death freed me from a loveless marriage. And for that too, that unvoiced sense of relief, I feel guilt.'

She regarded him in the firelight, held out her arms to him.

'Come to me,' she said.

*   *   *

He woke to the sound of tapping at the door. The couch beside him was chill and empty, though he could smell her scent on the pillow and see the impress of her body on the wrinkled blanket.

'Who is it?'

'Moried. May I come in? It is cold out here on your doorstep.'

'Yes, come,' he said, pulling his cloak around him to hide his nakedness and bending to the fire, which was nearly out.

'I brought you some water,' Moried said cheerfully. 'Did you sleep well, my lord?'

He glanced up, alert for signs of sarcasm, but Moried showed nothing except his normal good humour.

'Acting as my body servant now?' he grumbled as he took the pitcher from Moried.

The younger man grinned. 'It was a good feast last night. The servants joined in with the rest, once the Lady Teleri had done with her tale. They are still sleeping it off.'

He waited until mab Petroc had finished dousing his head in water. 'There is a man asking for you at the main gate. A tattooed man like those we fought in Lindinis.'

'A tattooed man?' said mab Petroc in surprise. 'Here? And asking for me, not Arthur?'

He towelled himself dry and flung on some clothes, shivering in the cold air.

'Cei was there, talking to Glewlwyd of the Mighty Grasp,' volunteered Moried.

Mab Petroc froze, one boot on, one off. 'Anybody else?'

'Some of the youngsters.' Moried hesitated, added inconsequentially: 'He is a powerfully built man, this Pict.'

'Did he come alone?'

'No. He brought a small escort.'

Mab Petroc finished dressing and buckled on his swordbelt. 'Come on,' he said, and made for the door, vaguely aware of Moried following after him.

Once outside he was dazzled by the white glare from the snow on the rooftops. Some effort had been made to clear the lane running between the houses: valleys had been carved through the worst of the drifts, and the discarded snow lay in dirty pitted lumps in the lee of the buildings. Patches of black ice had formed on the cobbles, but he hastened as best he could until he reached the main road leading down to the gate.

Here the snow had been trampled flat and grey. Somebody had

spread grit in an attempt to combat the ice, which rendered the going a little easier, and he was able to make better speed.

He heard Lleminawg calling his name, and he turned precariously on the treacherous surface (his feet threatening to slip away from under him) to see the Irishman close behind, well wrapped in the distinctive plaids he wore as proudly as if they were a badge of office.

'Bishop Enoch complained of you to the Warlord last night,' Lleminawg panted by way of greeting.

Mab Petroc yawned. 'And what did Arthur say?' He pretended not to be interested in the answer.

'That you had spilled more blood in the defence of the Church than most men now living.' Lleminawg skidded on a patch of ice, waved his arms to keep his balance. 'To which the Bishop replied that you had been ensorcelled by a witch woman, and were so deeply under her spell you had almost laid hands upon him last night.'

'And?'

'And Arthur told him not to be a fool.'

Mab Petroc stopped, taken aback. 'So bluntly?'

Lleminawg shrugged. 'He spoke courteously but his meaning was clear.'

They proceeded in silence for a time, the Irishman shooting glances at his friend until he could contain himself no longer.

'Is it true?'

'Is what true?'

'Are you bewitched?'

Mab Petroc opened his mouth to make an angry retort, but instead found himself laughing aloud. 'Do you know, cousin, I think I might be?'

For a moment he forgot what he was doing, where he was going, and remembered only the way the firelight had lit her face and chest and long strong legs, leaving pools of darkness under her breasts and below her navel. A sense of joy filled him, a joy he had not known since he was a young man wooing Garwen, its intensity catching him unawares for he had not expected to feel it again in this life.

Moried was staring at him as if he had gone suddenly mad, and the expression on the younger man's face made him laugh all the louder. He wanted to sing, to dance, to caper on the ice, to carve her name in large letters in the snow so that all the fortress might know he loved her.

Lleminawg shook his head despairingly. 'You of all people,' he said. 'To fall for the fascinations of an unknown woman . . . Now had it been me, I could understand it, but not you, cousin.'

'Had it been you, you could understand it?' mab Petroc said mockingly. 'What nonsense you do talk.'

'You who are renowned for your coldness, your distance, your detachment, so that men wonder whether you have feelings like the rest of us . . .'

He stopped listening to Lleminawg and looked at Moried, who had guarded his back for the five years since Cynon fell at Agned, and wondered if he, who during those five years had become the closest to him of all the Companions, felt the same way.

'We had best hurry,' he said.

A crowd had formed between the guard house and the wall, a ring of bodies which expanded and contracted with its own slow rhythm. From inside came what might have been the sound of birdsong, an irregular, tuneless whistling. Puzzled, mab Petroc led the others forward, and the crowd parted to allow them through.

At the heart of the ring was a dark figure sitting cross-legged on his heels with his back to the ramparts, playing softly on a bone flute. Behind him were four others, men identical to those mab Petroc had fought in Lindinis, standing bolt upright in a line with spears pointing to the sky and shields slung from one shoulder like an honour guard. Their faces beneath the strange markings were impassive, but their eyes betrayed their unease, darting nervously around.

Cei stood on one side of the flute player, glaring at the escort. On the other side was the massive bulk of Glewlwyd the Gatekeeper. Most people would have been intimidated by this pair, but not the Pict, who sat huddled in his dark plaid with his head bent over the instrument.

He blew a final discordant blast and laid the flute aside.

'The Long Man wishes to wrestle me, but I told him we are both too old for such foolishness,' he said without looking up. 'It would prove nothing. Let him wrestle yonder barrel if he needs exercise.' He jerked his head at Glewlwyd.

Cei frowned and made to speak, then changed his mind.

The Pict tugged at one of the thin braids dangling down the side of his face. He seemed to be lost in thought, careless of the frozen ground or the bitter wind.

Mab Petroc waited, aware of Moried shifting from foot to foot behind him and of Lleminawg blowing on his hands to warm them.

The Pict tapped the flute to free it of spittle. 'There is a thing I have lost, warrior. They tell me it is in your keeping now. It is not a thing of any value, save to me. I have come to ask if you will return it.'

'What is this thing?' said mab Petroc.

'A slave woman.'

Mab Petroc shrugged. 'I have no slave of yours.'

The Pict raised his eyes, black and implacable as flint. 'Betimes she pretends to be a bard. A tall woman, of dark hair and countenance. She uses the name Teleri.'

The crowd murmured softly to itself.

Very gently, mab Petroc said: 'The Lady Teleri is not in my keeping. I cannot help you.'

There was a frown of annoyance, as if mab Petroc were being singularly obtuse.

'All I want is the woman. She is mine, a slave who fled long ago. They tell me she is under your protection. Give her to me.'

'She is not mine to give. And though as you say she is under my protection, it is not to me you must appeal, but to one far greater than I. For she is also under the protection of the Magister Militum, Arthur himself.'

Cei rumbled with approval, and the Pict looked at him as one might look at a dog which growls out of turn.

'The Long Man has wind.' He drew a straw from inside his clothing and pushed it through the mouthpiece of the flute, running it back and forth to clean out the tube.

'Who asks for the Lady Teleri?' mab Petroc said courteously. 'Where are your lands, and what is your lineage?'

The Pict rocked back on his heels and chanted:

'Not from Albion am I, but from Albany; not from Prydein am I, but from Pritdyn. From Manaw I come; from Arran I come. Across the bitter water I rode in my chariot of silver. Pedrylaw Menestyr am I, and I have come for what is mine!'

His voice became a shout and he rose to his feet in a single easy movement, the straw held in one hand, the bone flute in the other.

'I deny your claim,' mab Petroc said coolly, 'and stand here ready to prove its falseness with my body.'

The Pict thrust the wisp of straw towards him, weaving it back and forth through the air like a snake seeking the best place to strike, all the while muttering to himself:

'Evil, death and short life fall upon the warrior who rejects my demands. May the spears of battle slay the warrior who denies me what is mine. May the land refuse him as he refuses me, and may the rocks be piled high above his grave.'

Mab Petroc could not move. His feet seemed frozen to the ground, and his body caught as if in the thrall of a nightmare. The Pict's face loomed larger and larger, distorted with hate, the slim plaits bouncing as the frenzy grew greater.

He could not take his eyes from the spirals on the man's cheeks. The green lines stood out in hard ridges against the dark flesh, swelling harder and darker as the Pict allowed his rage to engulf him. Mab Petroc found himself trying to trace their pattern, the way they coiled one inside the other, sevenfold to the centre, not several lines at all but a single curling path that led inwards, then twined outwards and outwards again, then inwards and inwards, then outwards and outwards, circling, circling, till at last it led in, in to the heart, pulling him with it, sucking him down . . .

He was lost, and worst of all he knew it.

Then the voice came, deep and rich, strong and calm as the sea in summer.

'Enough. Get you gone, Pedrylaw Menestyr. Get you gone from this my land and these my people.'

Of a sudden mab Petroc was free, staggering on the hard ground of Caer Cadwy, his senses reeling, not sure where he was or what was happening. Immediately in front of him was a green mound with a track winding about it in a series of terraces. On the summit of the mound stood a giant, wild and shaggy haired, pointing a spear straight at him, and the head of the spear gleamed like fire.

Mab Petroc blinked and the vision vanished.

The Pict lowered the straw, and whatever it might have been a moment earlier it was now nothing more than a wisp of dried corn.

The Pict's expression changed as he stared over mab Petroc's shoulder. The anger and hostility faded, became something like surprise, and then a third emotion which mab Petroc could not at first read through the green weals of the tattoos.

Slowly, almost clumsily, the Pict sank to his knees and bowed his head. 'Arthur,' he said. 'Arthur Amherawdyr.'

He held the pose while the wind ruffled his hair and the crowd waited unmoving, then rose quickly to his feet and without a word of protest or a backward glance was gone, swallowed into the darkness of the tunnel through the ramparts, with his men hastening after him.

2

Budoc roused himself from his long dream of the past. The sun was near setting, which meant he had once more lost himself for several hours.

He scanned the expanse of grass visible from the cleft into which he had tucked himself, letting his gaze travel in a slow arc from left to right, then returning to his starting point and beginning again slightly lower. In this way he could examine everything twice from the same angle, and if there had been any movement between his first pass and his second the slight change in what he was seeing would register.

So far as he could tell there was nothing apart from the small random scurryings of mice and birds. It all seemed perfectly normal. The birds were singing undisturbed in the pines at the edge of the wood, and the gulls were wailing overhead.

Reverence, that was what it had been, the third emotion on the face of the Pict, the emotion he had been unable to read.

Thirty years ago. He had been young then, though he had not believed it, had thought himself middle-aged.

He was young no longer. He had failed to protect the people of the village – sweet Eurgain and Dyfyr, who had cared for him when he was sick and helpless, their mother who had sent them. If he were to protect the woodland sanctuary he needed help, strong arms and trained warriors.

Budoc eased himself from between the rocks, knowing it was possible he was being watched from among the shadows of the pine trees.

He moved in a crouch through the grass, disguising the shape of his body as best he could. If anybody were watching – and he had not forgotten the enigmatic bird mask he had glimpsed in the pool – they would not be fooled for an instant, but it helped quiet the prickling between his shoulders.

The wind blew across the headland, fanning the salt-burned

grass into long slow undulations like the waves of the sea. He dropped to his hands and knees and crawled the last few yards, keeping low against the edge of the cliff, blending his movements with the wind-stirred sway of the grasses, making for the haven of the tangled gorse which clung precariously to the thin soil.

He was almost swimming, holding his weight on toes, knees and fingers, throwing his knees wide to avoid lifting his buttocks. It was a technique he had not practised for years, and it put an unaccustomed strain on his chest muscles and the back of his neck.

The pale stems of gorse were a welcome sight. He drew himself up inside the cover of the spiky bushes with a sigh of relief, ruefully massaged his neck and chest. He was too old for this: too old and too unfit.

He looked back the way he had come. There was no sign of his passage through the grass – though no doubt a truly determined tracker could have found the odd crushed stem. More importantly, there was no movement from the fringe of pine trees.

Yet in one corner of his mind something did not feel right. It was nothing tangible, nothing he could have explained, just a faint sense of a brooding presence hovering out of sight.

He let his eyes slip over the landscape again and again, first rapidly, then so slowly he became familiar with every nuance of light and shadow. Gradually he became more and more certain that there was nothing human watching him. Whatever troubled him was something less tangible, and under different circumstances he might have attributed it to his imagination.

(White speckled bird with long trailing wings and blind eyes behind which a darkness moves.)

Budoc shivered and turned the other way, towards the estuary and the open sea.

He squinted against the brightness of the sea with its myriad points of sparkling light. The sun was red and gold, and the sea a mass of greens and blues and greys.

And there was the ship, running for the mouth of the estuary like a vision, her sail belling to the wind, heeling as she came, the spray bursting across her bows.

Budoc felt a stirring inside him. This was a true ship, not a wave-wallowing barrel like the clumsy hulk on which he had returned from Lesser Britain. This was a creature of the open sea, a far traveller on the Whales' Road, the kind of keel in which Hengist had crossed the grey northern water-wastes in answer to the call of Gworthigern the High King in the days when Rome was falling.

The pilot must know these waters, because he was bringing her in under sail alone, avoiding the sand bar by keeping close to the western shore. Budoc could see the dark heads of the oarsmen waiting on their benches, and suddenly, at the very moment the headland stole the wind from the sail, the oars sprouted like legs from her sides and levered her onward into the lee of the cliffs, where she vanished from his view.

He had scryed a Saeson longship in the surface of the basin when he sought to know what might aid him against the machinations of Vortepor and the Scotti warrior. At the time he had dismissed the ship as a phantom, an irrelevance.

Scrying was rarely reliable. He remembered Teleri drumming that obvious truth into him even as she taught him the knack of it, during those few days while the warband of Britain, the *teulu* of Prydein, prepared to sail into the unknown North.

3

All through the remains of that long winter and the frozen spring which followed Arthur drew to him anyone with some knowledge, however small, of the Iardomnan. A handful of sailors, the heirs to those who in Roman times had plied the seas carrying the luxuries of civilization north to be traded for the thick fleeces and woollen plaids for which the isles had once been famed. A couple of priests, who had sought to woo the natives from their idol worship, and had been lucky to escape with their lives. A few Picts, like Talorcan and Degaw, who had made the long journey south, moths drawn to the flame of Arthur's reputation.

It was Teleri who reminded them all of the ambiguity in the name. Iardomnan was an Irish word, and like many Irish words it held more than one meaning. Literally it meant 'the West Lands', the Western Isles and the adjacent coasts; figuratively it meant the Back Lands, or the Lands Behind the Known World.

The Iardomnan was rumoured to be an inhospitable land, swept by mist and rain. The natives were supposedly a mingling of British and Irish, the result of centuries of constant migration back and forth, east and west across the seas. They eked out a hard existence with a little raiding and piracy, their lives shortened by famine, disease or violence, and by the sea itself.

No two informants told the same story, and even Teleri, for all her claim to have been born there, was forced to admit she did not know every island or patch of coastline. It was a place of contrasts. Some islands were well wooded, others were barren. Some were large, others small. Some were inhabited by British speakers, others by Irish speakers. Some of the natives were peaceful farmers with homesteads like those found elsewhere in Prydein; others were warriors, masters of the hollow towers unique to the north, or of round forts of wood and stone akin to those in the south.

It was easier to lump all the natives together under the vague term of *Scotti* – reivers – for even apparently peaceful farmers and fishermen had been known to go raiding when times grew hard.

On one matter all accounts did agree: this was a region where land and sea merged so closely together in a jagged coastline that it was impossible to be sure what was a promontory and what an island, what a channel of the sea and what a landlocked inlet. Here the tides did extraordinary things, gushing through the narrow sounds in a whirl of current and cross-current, eddy and counter-eddy, while squalls and storms could appear without warning from a clear sky. These were dangerous waters, with rocky shores waiting on every side. Many a wooden ship had been lost, vanishing without trace, and not even the leather curraghs of the natives which could survive batterings that would sink a more solid vessel were safe.

If an attack on the Iardomnan were to succeed it would need careful planning.

Vortepor left Caer Cadwy as soon as the weather improved, taking with him Arthur's assurances of support. Teleri did not accompany him.

Nothing more had been seen of Pedrylaw Menestyr since he walked away through the tunnel under the ramparts. Although Cei led several patrols through the icy countryside, scouring the frozen land for some trace of the Picts, they seemed to have vanished as easily as they had appeared.

Teleri had been amused by Menestyr's claim that she had once been his property.

'A slave?' she said to mab Petroc. 'A bard may not be enslaved. It is a Primary Law of Prydein that a bard, like a child or an elder, must be treated hospitably wherever he or she goes, and making a slave of a bard is a crime unheard of among the people of Prydein, whatever the savage Saesons may do.'

They were sitting in the Great Hall playing tawlboard. Mab Petroc moved his king-piece towards the centre square, frowning as he did so.

Teleri laughed, and slipped one of her men forward to block his next move.

'That I am a bard is beyond doubt,' she said more seriously. 'It is easily proved, for none but a bard could know all the tales that I know.'

Listening, he glanced up, and was at once distracted by her face, whose planes and hollows were a matter of continual fascination and delight to him.

'What did Menestyr mean when he called Arthur "Amherawdyr"?' he asked, shifting a carved retainer across two places.

She countered at once, and he saw that he had lost unless she made some foolish mistake within the next few moves.

'Perhaps he was recognizing Arthur's innate majesty,' she said. 'Or flattering him, so he might escape with a whole skin from the dangerous position into which his anger had led him.'

'No more than that?' He brought another retainer across, too late.

'Perhaps,' she said, her whole attention on the game. She moved another man into the attack.

'He was in no danger.' He pulled the king back behind the cover of its supporters. 'He had Glewlwyd's promise of safe conduct.'

'Does Cei challenge all visitors to wrestle?' Now her assault was truly launched.

'Only if they seem capable of giving him a reasonable match.' Again he retreated. 'Because Cei is a large man, people think he must be foolish. He likes to foster that impression by doing foolish things.'

She raised a piece and held it poised between her fingers. There was only one square she need occupy, and they both knew it.

'The significance of this game,' she said irrelevantly, 'is that the world is a hostile place, that the still forces of the centre need to be constantly on their guard against attacks from the outside.'

She put the piece down in the exact middle of the square.

'If the king fails, the kingdom fails. A realm without a ruler is no realm at all, but a place of primal chaos.'

He tipped his king onto its side in a gesture of defeat. 'And if the ruler has left no heir?'

'Then a new lord must declare himself.'

Teleri spent hours describing what she knew of the coasts and currents to the men Arthur had chosen to act as his shipmasters.

'Would it not be easier if the Lady came with us?' asked one of the sailors.

Arthur glanced from Teleri to mab Petroc and back again.

'It would, and I hope that she will.' There was a sadness in his voice. 'But it is best to be prepared for any eventuality.'

Startled, mab Petroc looked at Teleri. She was intent upon the waxed tablet on which she had sketched the appearance of some of the islands as an aid to navigation.

'More of a hump; so. And this one, this one is rounded seen from the sea, but tree clad, with a notch where a gully runs down to the water, like this.'

Mab Petroc wondered how old she was. He guessed she must be a little younger than himself, but this was only a guess, for she rarely spoke of her past, changing the subject whenever the matter was raised.

The butterfly birthmark on the side of her neck flexed its wings as she turned, then was hidden by the swirl of her long black hair.

'Why so worried?'

He forced a smile. 'I was thinking I could not bear to lose you.'

'You will not if I can help it.' She spoke as if they were alone, her brown eyes intense. 'I shall cling to you as the ivy clings to the tree.'

Mab Petroc's smile spread and became genuine. He leaned forward and kissed her, oblivious of the watching mariners and of Arthur lowering his head to hide the sorrow in his eyes.

When the spring gales ended the court moved, travelling west from Caer Cadwy to Kelliwig in Kernow. That the court should move in the spring was not unusual. Caer Cadwy was still primarily a military base despite the town which had sprung up within its walls, dependent for its supplies on the surrounding countryside. The long winter had severely depleted the stores, so it was time for the court to shift elsewhere.

What was unusual was that Cei and the shipmasters went on ahead. Kelliwig lay on the north-western coast of Dumnonia, and though it was not and never had been a great port, the harbour was large enough to hold the kind of fleet Arthur had gathered for his assault on the Iardomnan. He hoped that by moving the entire court he would mask the movement of the warband, and thus be able to load them into the waiting ships and be away before his plans became common knowledge.

The journey was slow, along roads which worsened every year. The Fosse Way petered out beyond Isca, became a rough track running along the central ridge dividing the great forest of the north from the high moors of the south. The cavalcade stretched back for nearly a mile in an uneven column of families with their household goods piled on carts drawn by plodding oxen and mules; as the road deteriorated, the wagons broke down more and more often.

Whenever possible they camped for the night near villas or homesteads, not always to the pleasure of the inhabitants. But this did at least mean that the older or weaker members of the court were sure of shelter from the endless drizzle which dogged them westwards.

To escape the mud the wagons churned in their wake, many of the court took to riding ahead of the column. Even Arthur and Gwenhwyvar sometimes deserted the struggling cavalcade, ranging with a few chosen comrades along the spine of Dumnonia, searching out good sites for the evening halt.

On one of the few dry afternoons a group of them reined in their horses in the hills above the Fastwater, and sat for a while watching the play of light and cloud on the trees to the north and the brown wastes to the south.

'Look at the smoke,' said Gwenhwyvar. 'There are more people out there than one would think.'

From this distance the trees seemed to form an impenetrable canopy of green tinged with the freshness of spring, a canopy so thick and so solid it seemed impossible that anybody could live underneath. Yet when one started looking closely one saw that everywhere there were thin plumes of smoke drifting up into the sky, grey and white and sometimes so faint they were almost invisible against the blue of the heavens.

'Before the coming of the Saesons the east must have been like this,' Teleri said dreamily. 'Peaceful, full of people . . .'

'. . . living out lives undisturbed by the outside world,' added mab Petroc in the same tone of voice.

Gwenhwyvar laughed, not unkindly. 'Thus speak the lovers,' she said. 'It may seem idyllic from a distance, but I do not doubt that if you rode through the forest you would find the makers of those fires as racked by petty hatreds and jealousies as anybody else.'

'Besides,' said Arthur, 'the east is hardly a desert. And I have often thought that a Saeson master is probably no worse than any other.'

'The Saesons are heathen!' objected mab Petroc.

Arthur looked at him with a twinkle in his eye. 'So they are,' he said. He turned to Teleri. 'Tell me, for you have seen more of him than we have, how would you like to live in a land ruled by Vortepor?'

She shuddered. 'I would not.'

'Oesc of Kent is a good lord, from what I hear. Better than Vortepor will be.' Arthur patted his horse's neck. 'If the choice were mine, I had sooner live under the heathen Oesc than the Christian Vortepor.'

They moved on, swinging southwards behind the shelter of a small wood. Before them stretched the moors: lines of rolling, folded hills in a long vista of brown, yellow and green, touched with purple or blue in the far distance.

'Does anybody live there?' asked Teleri.

'Not many, not any more,' said mab Petroc. 'They did once, because you can still see the ruins of their houses and their sacred places.'

'Even their dykes,' said Arthur, staring into the distance. 'Judging by the remains they must have been a numerous people.'

'Of course,' said Teleri. 'I had forgotten. You were both born here.'

Mab Petroc laughed. 'Not here exactly. Further south, in the rich lands between the moors and the sea.'

'Then you are not far from home?'

He glanced at Arthur and at Gwenhwyvar. 'Home? Home is where your kin are, and these two are closer kin to me than any others except my son.'

She nodded, and for a time they followed the road in silence, dropping down into the valley of the Fastwater between stands of birch and hazel mingled with oak and ash.

'I do not think we shall be able to do this many more times,' Arthur called over his shoulder as he led the way down the slope, leaning back in the saddle with his legs well forward. 'I feel as if we are playing truant.'

'We are,' said Gwenhwyvar, tossing back her hair. 'It is strange, but I had always half imagined that once the Saesons were defeated we would be able to live out the rest of our lives in peace.' She gestured vaguely. 'It never occurred to me there would be so much to organize, so many decisions to make.'

'What does the Warlord do when the war is ended?' Teleri said softly.

'The war does not end,' Arthur said grimly. 'Now there are the Scotti. Next will be the matter of rulers like Vortepor of Dyfed, or the Sons of Cunedda. And we will never stop the Saesons altogether. More will keep coming, keep pressing for land.'

'And what is your authority?' Teleri asked gently.

Arthur shrugged ruefully. 'I am the Magister Militum, appointed by the will of my predecessor and the will of the Princes and Elders of Britain. Into my hand they put the defence of the island.'

'And you have defended the island with a genius unmatched in our day. But the country now is not the same as the one in which you grew up. With every passing year more is lost. The cities, which were at the heart of Roman rule and culture, fall into ruin. Wild beasts make their dens where wise men once pondered the affairs of state. Each landowner thinks himself worthy to rule his neighbours. The hill tribes of the west create for themselves elaborate dynasties to prove they are the heirs of Rome. In another generation there will be no Britain, only a mass of squabbling barbarians distinguished from the Saesons only by their language.'

Arthur gave her a quizzical look before pulling his horse to a halt and slipping lightly from the saddle. 'This is far enough, I think. Best it is not I myself who announce our coming to the villa in the valley. They will be flustered enough without having the Magister Militum arrive unheralded in their yard.'

The others also dismounted and stood gazing down at the farm in the valley, at the neat fields and the oxen pulling the plough while birds wheeled in their wake.

'What are you suggesting?' said Arthur to Teleri. 'We have done what we can to stave off the darkness. There will be no help from Rome, or from the remnants of the Empire. Romulus and Julius Nepos were the last emperors in the west, and it is fifteen years since Odovacer ended their rule.'

'Rome has failed, yes. Like Britain, the Empire has collapsed into a mass of struggling tribes. But Britain, Albion, could yet be saved, if one man were to claim the sovereignty of the island.'

Arthur made to speak, but she rode over his protest.

'Something new could be made. If there were a man respected as much by the Saesons in the east and the Picts of the north as by the hill tribes of the west and the magistrates of the lowlands – *if* there were such a man, Arthur, then he might be able to bind them all together under his rule.'

'Gworthigern claimed to be High King. Ambrosius the Elder wore the purple. Both in their way were great men, yet neither ever made a lasting peace.'

'They were not Arthur. There is in you a power and majesty they did not possess.'

She waited, and the others waited with her. History was full of men who had risen from being the leaders of armies to the rulers of empires: Theodosius, Maximus, Constantine III – even great Julius Caesar himself. And they were aware, Gwenhwyvar and mab Petroc, that this was not a new idea, that Arthur had often thought it over and discussed it with those he most trusted.

'This is not a chance meeting,' said Arthur. 'Everything you have done, attaching yourself to Vortepor and accompanying him to Caer Cadwy, telling the tale of Gwair's imprisonment before my court, has all been leading to this moment.'

She bowed her head in acknowledgement. 'Almost everything,' she said, with a glance at mab Petroc.

'You tempt me with the Sovereignty of Albion. Is it yours to offer?'

'It is mine to offer you the trial of it. And you are the first to be offered the trial since the symbol of sovereignty was hidden in the north after the fall of Caradoc mab Bran to the Legions of Rome.'

He regarded her steadily with a slight frown. 'Why do I need this symbol? Gworthigern did not have it, nor Ambrosius.'

'They failed.'

'And if I have it I will succeed?'

She shrugged. 'Who can say? But you will not succeed without it.'

'I have never heard of such a symbol,' mab Petroc said slowly. 'And if I were a landowner in Elmet or Loidis, the fact that the Magister Militum possessed some pagan symbol of sovereignty would add nothing to the lustre of his claim on the High Kingship. I would dismiss it as yet another fantasy of the wild tribesmen. What would weigh more with me would be Arthur's control of the army.'

'The Warband of Britain.' Teleri nodded understandingly. 'Of course. But it is not those people you need to convince. The ones who live within what was once the settled province of Britain, the ones whose grandfathers were loyal subjects of Rome – they will follow you anyway.'

She strode across the turf, swung to face Arthur, who was a few paces lower down the hill, so that their eyes were at a level.

'It is the others,' she said passionately, 'the people of the borders, the ones who live where Roman law and custom never ran so deep – they are the people you will need to convince. And among them the old tales are still current, still carry meaning, have not yet become stories fitted only for the very young or the very old. Indeed, if anything the old tales are gathering in strength.'

Arthur studied her for a heartbeat, his expression showing nothing of his thoughts. Then he hauled himself up into the saddle where he sat looking down at the three of them.

'My lady? How do you say?'

Gwenhwyvar ran her fingers through her hair, mounted with a single swift movement.

'Since you in any case intend to raid the islands, why not?' The pony fretted beneath her and she stilled it with practised hands. 'As to the rest, now we have won the war we have the harder task of winning the peace. If this will help, so be it.'

'Cousin?'

Mab Petroc boosted Teleri into the saddle, turned to answer the man he had served since boyhood.

'Yes, Amherawdyr, let us try,' he said, bestowing the title with an affectionate mockery. 'You said earlier there would not be many more times we would all be able to ride out together as we have today. I think you were right, and I think this will be the last time we take the field as a company. Hereafter you will be too important to risk, while Cei, Gwalchmei and the rest of us will become your lieutenants and will not fight as a warband.'

He mounted his own pony, sat grinning at his friend, in love with Teleri and thus all the world. 'If this is to be our last adventure, let us give it some greater purpose than the quelling of yet another reiver.'

Arthur nodded slowly. 'Some will say I aspire to the purple through ambition. Many will dislike what we seek to do, and not the least of them will be those very magnates of the lowlands you seem to think will support me without question.' He sighed wearily while the others watched intently.

'Gworthigern, Ambrosius – they failed because the Princes and magnates of Britain would not in the end support them.'

'And because of the rivalry between them,' reminded Gwenhwyvar. 'You have no rival. There is nobody in Britain of your reputation and stature.'

'Not yet,' said Arthur. 'Not while all goes well. But one will come before the end.' He stared unseeing at the distant hills, then roused and shook himself.

'What we have done at Caer Cadwy is no small thing. For all it is an armed camp we have built a place of peace and safety where the different peoples of Prydein can meet and work together.' He turned to mab Petroc.

'One last adventure, you called it. I think that after all these years of making war, making peace might be an adventure in itself. Certainly it may prove to be a harder thing. But it will be easier if I am more than simply the commander of the armies of Britain.'

'It is time for an emperor,' mab Petroc said quietly, his earlier flippancy gone. 'It is time, and past time. The island needs to be healed, and only an emperor can heal her.'

Every evening when the camp had been set up a group would gather together for weapon practice and training. Night after night Cei, Lleminawg, Gwalchmei, Talorcan, Moried, mab Petroc – without fail they would find an open space and exercise their skills.

All of Arthur's men fought in pairs, taking it in turns to watch each other's backs, but in the practice sessions they would often change partners, trying to recreate the confusion of battle. Most habitually favoured a particular weapon – sword, war-knife or short spear – and they would try to spend part of the time using something less familiar.

Above all else they accustomed themselves to fighting on foot, for it would not be possible to take horses to the Iardomnan. They relearned the art of making the shield wall, each man's shield protecting not only himself but his neighbour as well, and mastered the art of advancing in step like the legendary legions of Rome, keeping the line dressed and level.

At the end of the session they would sometimes stage single combats, trying out new moves against a live opponent. This was the part which attracted the most spectators, and often these duels would be fought against a background of shouted wagers. Mab Petroc gained a fine new pair of fleece-lined boots from Gwalchmei by betting on Moried to beat Talorcan using war-knife alone against spear and shield, and promptly lost them again when Talorcan won the rematch.

After these sessions mab Petroc would return to his tent, where Teleri would teach him a different form of attack and defence.

He was determined that never again would he be rendered helpless by the likes of Pedrylaw Menestyr. She taught him how to protect himself, and how to launch his own counter-attack. In the process she taught him much else, for just as one needs to know how to ride before one can fight from horseback, so too one needs to acquire many skills before one can oppose a druid.

She taught him how to scry, using water or crystal to see what has been and what is to come, and how to distinguish true vision from false. She taught him about herbs and fungi, about the speech of birds, about wood and stone, about the land itself.

One thing she did not need to teach him, and that was discipline. He found that his years of endless training as a warrior stood him in good stead, especially his ability to concentrate his mind on one thing to the exclusion of all else, and its corollary and converse, the knack of opening his awareness to the greater universe.

'I knew about Arthur,' she said on the last night before the cavalcade was due to arrive at Kelliwig. 'But you I did not expect. Like Cei, you are deceptive. On the outside you seem to be a fighting man, all brawn and scars –' she ran a hand down his torso, checking each of the old wounds '– but on the inside you are very different.'

She smiled languorously. 'So much deeper than I had expected. You are a man who does everything well, or not at all. I suppose I should have guessed. An exceptional leader will attract exceptional followers.'

He laughed. 'How does the old saw go? Judge a ruler by the quality of those with whom he surrounds himself?'

'Yes,' she said thoughtfully. 'And yet there is more to it than that. You are here because it is your fate to be here, just as it is Cei's fate, and Gwenhwyvar's, and Lleminawg's.'

She rolled over onto her side (the candlelight catching the sheen of perspiration along her spine) and spoke no more, so that afterwards when he remembered her words he wondered what she had meant by them.

'My turn to do the rounds of the sentries,' he said a while later, and dressed and went out into the night.

It was not cold, but it was damp, a light mist rising from the valleys and deepening the darkness. The sentries had wrapped themselves in their long hooded cloaks and taken whatever shelter they could find, merging into the trees and bushes with only the occasional cough or sniff to betray their positions.

He left the forward picket along the road until last. It was the furthest from the camp, and by then his eyes would have adjusted to the night. He knew that Talorcan, with whom he had not exchanged more than a few words since that day in the stables, was in command, and he wanted to see how the Pict felt about the expedition to the Iardomnan.

Once the torches of the camp were behind him the mist seemed to thicken. In places the bushes grew to the very verges of the track, looming black beside the paler streak of the road, and despite his night vision he walked with arms outstretched, like a blind man.

'Ware pothole!' whispered a cheerful voice from out of the darkness, making him jump.

He stopped and waited, peering into the gloom. 'Who is it? Where are you?'

'Snug under this tree, cousin,' said the voice. 'Three paces to your left, and mind the boulder.'

'Talorcan?'

'Aye. The others are spread in an arc across our front. There's nothing doing, apart from some odd noises earlier on. We think it was a boar woken from its sleep, but as to what woke it . . . Well, the Trinity and the Heavenly Hosts could no doubt tell you the answer, but not us poor mortals down below, and that is the truth, cousin.'

Mab Petroc groped towards the tree. A shadow detached itself from the trunk and guided him over the broken ground, pulling him into the shadows.

Beyond the tree the land fell away in a steep-sided valley that was almost a ravine. The slopes were clear of undergrowth, so that despite the mist and darkness he had a reasonable view of the ground any strangers would have to cross to reach the camp. Only the bottom of the valley was choked with a black mass of vegetation growing along the line of a stream that he could hear chuckling and groaning to itself as it threaded its way through the rocks.

'Good place,' he said.

'Pretty good. Not that I think anybody would be daft enough to try anything, but you never know your luck.' Talorcan nudged him in the ribs. 'Here. Have a nip. Put some wet in to keep the wet out.'

The Pict seemed to have recovered from the death of his horse.

'How is Degaw?' Mab Petroc returned the bottle, feeling the glow reaching right to his toes. (A pity about those boots with their warm fleece lining, but they had been cut to the shape of the Hawk's feet.)

'Oh, well enough, I thank you, cousin.' Talorcan looked away, studied the far side of the ravine as it drifted in and out of the mist.

'Is she worried about us going north?'

The Pict shuffled closer to the tree trunk. 'Well, by the Good God, yes she is.' He tucked the bottle away beneath his cloak. 'You know what women are like. She thinks she foresees disaster. "Save seven, none came home," as the poem says.'

He turned to mab Petroc, hesitated, screwed up his courage. 'Forgive me, but she does not care for Teleri. Thinks Arthur is foolish to place any trust in her.'

Mab Petròc felt his body stiffen before he could prevent it. Talorcan raised a hand to ward off his anger, and kept talking, almost babbling in his nervousness.

'Of course, she approves the change in you. You had become so distant, so unapproachable. You had not laughed or cracked a joke except when you were ready to fight someone ever since Garwen died. Now you are much more like your old self, save only that you cannot bear to hear any criticism of your woman. But what do we truly know of her? Nothing. And yet she asks us to sail off into the unknown, all the defenders of Prydein, in search of some mysterious object and in fulfilment of some old story.' He swallowed, licked his lips. 'That is what Degaw thinks.'

Breathing deep and slow, mab Petroc mastered his rage, forced himself to speak evenly. 'And you? What do you think?'

'Me?' Talorcan shook his head. 'I do not bother myself with thinking. I am Arthur's man, and that is enough. I go where he tells me, and fight where he tells me. The who and the when and the why of it are up to him.'

'But the Iardomnan?'

He grinned, teeth white in the darkness. 'I *want* to go, cousin. We have not fought as an army since Badon Hill, nor does it seem likely we will again. The Saesons are defeated. The Scotti, nuisance though they are, do not usually come in large numbers. As for the lesser lords of Prydein, though they may grumble not even the most hot-headed of them will defy us openly. This is our last chance for glory, and I would be there.'

Mab Petroc was no longer listening. On the far side of the valley a shape was flitting through the mist like a deeper patch of night, moving parallel with the slope, and behind it came others, four or five of them, smaller and slower.

The leading shape stopped and its followers stopped also. The mist parted, and he saw it was a stag, its coat grey and shadowy in the starlight, standing scenting the air, head turning restlessly from side to side.

'Not us,' breathed Talorcan in his ear. 'The wind is wrong.'

The stag coughed. The sound echoed across the valley, cutting gruffly through the stillness. It barked again, and the herd fled, bounding away over the crest with a flash of white rumps.

'What comes?' Talorcan murmured to himself. 'Men or . . .'

They trotted in single file along the rim: first a group of three, then four or five widely spaced, then a string of five or six travelling nose to tail, black and silver under the stars.

'Not after the deer,' said the Pict. 'Scavenging, probably.'

The wolves faded silently away into the night and the mist, and the hillside was empty again.

'Did you see the leader?' Talorcan fumbled under his cloak and produced the bottle. 'Here, cousin, have a nip. He was near the end, in the last group, the only one with a raised tail. The one in front of him will have been the chief female.' He tipped back the bottle and swallowed. 'There is a ranking among wolves as among men. The second male breaks the trail and leads the hunt, while the chieftain saves his strength till it is needed. They are wise creatures.'

'How do you know this?'

'I used to watch the wolf packs on the hills as a boy. Part of my early training it was. You see, sometimes my people would dress in wolfskins to go raiding. They would creep towards the enemy posts, scratching and stamping and snuffling like a wolf on the scrounge, drawing steadily nearer, then at the last moment they would leap to their feet and be in among them.'

Mab Petroc grunted, thought about what Talorcan had said, then chuckled. 'You are as bad as Lleminawg with his wild tales.' He yawned and stretched. 'I am away to my bed. I shall see you on the morrow.'

Still laughing quietly to himself at Talorcan's absurd story, he set off along the road.

Everybody was asleep apart from the sentries. He roused Gwalchmei, who was his replacement for second watch, reported all was well, and made his way to his own tent.

It was black and stuffy within. In his younger days, and when they were on campaign, he would have slept outside, wrapped in his cloak, careless of the damp. Now he was older and a privileged member of the court, he was expected to maintain a position in keeping with his rank, but there were times, like tonight, when he longed for the simplicity of the old days.

On the other hand a tent did give one a certain privacy – illusory no doubt, since hide walls did nothing to quell sound – but at least one was not on view. That had been useful over the past few days, and a lack of air was a small price to pay.

He stopped, head bent, half in and half out of the flap. There was a strange smell, one he did not recognize, or rather one he did not associate with the interior of his tent. Rank male sweat, not his own . . .

'Teleri?' he whispered, as if he feared to wake her.

He knew without needing to see that the tent was empty.

All the same he kindled a light from the flint and tinder beside the lamp – it would have been quicker to fetch a flame from one of the night torches outside, but he did not think of it until too late – and by its glow saw that he was right.

Teleri was gone.

4

The sense of loss filled Budoc afresh as he crouched in the tiny clearing at the heart of a gorse thicket on the top of the cliffs, a sense of desolation so powerful it might have been yesterday he had entered the tent and found her gone.

She had never lied to him, or to Arthur. She had allowed them to mistake her meaning, had permitted them to retain certain misconceptions, but she had never lied.

He had loved her.

He loved her still, would love her till the day he died.

If it were possible he would love her even beyond the grave.

Night had fallen while he dreamed of the past.

Careless of watchers he rose to his feet in sudden panic. This was more than the aftermath of his illness. He had been a fool. This was a sending, a dark magic of the kind Teleri had warned him about: a leeching of the will to bind the victim in an endless round of daydreams.

He had indeed been a fool. The means of his salvation was neatly wrapped in rags inside his wooden chest, now safely hidden in a crevice somewhere on the cliff face, a crevice he could only find by daylight. (And even if he did find it, he would need help to recover the chest.)

Clouds were gathering fast, thin wraiths passing before the stars. The moon seemed to be sailing through a storm, riding it out like a ship whose bow is sometimes buried under a weight of water, but always comes rising into the open air again. The clouds were thickening, the wind singing through the bushes, cutting through his well-darned robe, blowing from sea to sky like no natural wind he had ever known.

The wind whine rose to a howl. The gorse swayed madly all about him, yet the black pines at the edge of the wood seemed untouched. Shadows raced across the grass through which he had so laboriously crawled a while earlier, travelling with some arcane purpose of their own, while the moonlight dulled and brightened like a lamp caught in a strong draught.

He pushed a path between the prickles of the gorse, feeling them snag and tug at his robe. Then he was free, and running across the swathe of grass for the safety of the pines, the shadows lapping at his heels, the wind sucking at his breath, and the fear squeezing at his heart.

PART III

CHAPTER ONE

1

Eurgain crouched behind the tangled deadfall, watching the man with the shaven head.

He was alone in the centre of the grove. The rest of the Scotti stood waiting on the far side, the three leaders towering above the others, leaning on their spears, not talking.

She knew now what had happened during the night. A ship of the Saesons must have entered the estuary and anchored to wait out the darkness. The Scotti had paddled or swum across the water and attacked it, killing all aboard. This morning they had brought the severed heads to add to their other trophies.

The grove, the ancient and holy place of her people, was a rough circle of oak trees half as old as time enclosing a green lawn. In the middle of the lawn was a stone basin, fed by a spring so that even in the driest summer it was constantly filled with fresh running water.

The druid crouched beside it now with a ladle in his hands. All around him, scattered across the lawn like young saplings, were tall stakes driven firmly into the ground. Impaled on the top of each stake was a head, some of them large and some small, the blind eyes of each turned towards the basin.

As she watched the druid took a scoopful of water and moved from one stake to the next, splashing each trophy full in the face, so the water mingled with the dried blood and dripped pinkly to the grass.

She bit her lip to stop herself screaming.

When he had completed the circuit the druid took a stone mallet from his belt and struck the basin three times, swinging with all his force. The basin cracked, and the water ran out onto the ground.

For a time there was silence apart from the rustle of the wind in the leaves. Even the crows who had gathered to feast when the men were gone did not make a sound.

At a nod from the druid, Eremon the leader of the Scotti came forward carrying a bundle in his arms. The druid slipped out of his dark gown, his body pale and hairless in the sunlight, his arms thin and his ribs prominent. Eremon helped him into a robe fashioned from the flayed hide of a bull; he staggered under its weight, his legs bowing with the strain. Then Eremon placed a mask on the druid's head: a mask in the shape of a white speckled bird, with wings that hung down over his shoulders.

The warrior retreated to the edge of the clearing. The druid waited, the bird wings fluttering in the breeze.

Suddenly he leaped into the air with a great shout, and began to run from tree to tree, embracing each like a long lost lover, sobbing and moaning all the while.

Eurgain sank deeper into the cover of the fallen branches, scarcely daring to breathe.

With high kicking strides and many a leap the druid travelled from oak to oak, whistling and shouting, laughing stridently, crying like a bird of prey, mewing and barking, grunting like a boar, coughing like a deer.

When he had touched every tree he danced to the broken basin, swaying from side to side, shouting and wailing in a voice that cracked and broke:

'The land is empty; unknown the land. No name does it have; no people upon it. Empty land; unformed its contours.'

The wind riffled the wing feathers hanging down his back.

Then he stood on one foot in the muddy spillage from the basin and chanted:

'Land of the many stags, enfolded by the sea, shy deer in the woods, purple moss on the rocks, blackberries on the bushes, cold water in the streams, acorns on the oaks, sloes on the thorns, pigs in the forests, nuts on the hazels, whortles on the slopes.

'Stags in the oak groves, boars in the mast, honeycombs on the trees, trout in the streams.

'Fruitful the sea, fruitful the land, many branched the creeks, fast flowing the rivers, sweet the pools, deep the wells.

'Dew on the grass, gentle the rainfall, fine grazing on the lawns, corn in the fields, level the clearings, well made the houses, cared for the graves.

'Blue spears for reddening, strong the men's arms; fair the women, straight-limbed the children.

'In this land by the sea, this land of delight, the land of Eremon, mac Cairbre the King.'

All about her Eurgain could feel a rising wind blowing through the forest, carrying with it the sounds of scurrying and chattering. The crows took flight with a great cawing and calling, circled the grove once and flapped away towards the sea.

It was as if the whole world had shifted around her. She had been born in the village, had lived all her life there apart from the one trip to the town at the head of the estuary. She and her family had worshiped in this grove, had hunted and gathered in this forest. She had played in these woods as a child, had wandered through the coombes and hollows until she knew every tree. The spirits were her spirits, sometimes benevolent and sometimes angry, but always present, to be talked with, asked for advice, thanked for help, placated with offerings, loved and feared and reverenced but above all else familiar.

Now the very trees looked different, alien and hostile. Even this tangle of dead branches, this windfall which had lain here slowly rotting, the moss and the fungi steadily taking more of a hold with each passing season, ever since she was a child and had used it as a hiding place when playing with her sister and cousins, even this seemed different, strange and unfamiliar.

It had been *her* land, her people's land, for generation upon generation. Kings and conquerors and overlords came and went, demanding their share of the bounty while her people tilled the soil and fished the waters, living quiet lives where their only enemies were their sometimes friends, the elements themselves, wind, rain, drought and the everlasting sea.

The bones of her ancestors lay under the ground in barrows or in shallow graves, or were washed clean by the currents of the never-resting sea, their flesh fertilizing the soil which grew the crops or feeding the fish which were caught in the nets.

In the beginning, in the dawn of days, her forebears had come into a country that was empty and without form, a featureless wasteland. Little by little they had given shape to the wilderness, describing the woods, the clearings, the streams, defining the ridges, the hills, the creeks. They had created the land from the nothing which the first-comers had found through the long process of giving it meaning by their births, deeds and deaths.

Now the druid had undone all their work. He had driven out the spirits, returned the land to its primal chaos. Then he had laid claim to it in the name of Eremon, first chanting of its emptiness, then telling of its riches and the fruitfulness to come.

He had made her a stranger in the only home she had ever known. He had made her an outcast, lost in an alien forest.

It would be better that she were dead.

Budoc felt it too. One moment he was replenishing his waterskins in a stream, his mind blank, watching the play of sunlight on the ripples. The next he was standing upright, the skins forgotten, reaching for a non-existent weapon at his belt, listening to the screaming of the crows.

He turned, scanning the undergrowth, half expecting to see one of the Scotti coming at him with a spear. The stench of burning flesh was strong in his nostrils, as if he were back in his dream of the aftermath of Camlann.

All around him he could feel movement, could feel the birds and small creatures fleeing through the undergrowth, running from some unknown disturbance at the heart of the wood.

He gasped, reeled, almost fell into the stream. A great weight pressed down upon him, crushing him to the ground. He rolled over onto his back, struggling for breath, lips fluttering sound-lessly, gazed up at the sky and the faint white tendrils of cloud.

This must be what it was like to die. He had seen others struck down without warning while going about their business, seen them suddenly twist and clutch at themselves, collapse and lie panting, their mouths turning blue. The fortunate ones were those who died outright: the less lucky survived, stricken wrecks of their former selves.

Budoc struggled against the increasing pressure. His ears were popping. The air was being sucked from his lungs. His chest heaved like a smith's bellows as he strained to breathe.

The trees were calling to him, singing of their fear and pain, of axes and wedges and saws cutting at their flesh, of living roots torn forth from the earth, of basins shattered and water flowing out across the ground. The ghosts of those who when alive had nurtured the wood with their hands and their offerings, and who when dead had given the nourishment of their very bodies to the soil, moaned and gibbered around him; for they, the ancestral spirits of the land, were being driven wailing from their refuge.

He tried to sketch the sign of the cross with his broken hand – the other arm was trapped under his body – but his muscles would not obey him. All he could do was stare uselessly into the sky.

A black dot soared on the currents of the air, wheeled in a great circle above him, folded its wings and fell and fell, then opened them and looped away, tumbling through the air like an acrobat.

His eyes followed the pattern it drew while a voice deep inside told him this might be his last sight upon the earth. The rooks and crows were still shrieking raucously from within the wood, the noise deafening, even against the ringing in his ears.

Suddenly he realized he could breathe again.

He groaned and hauled himself to his feet, dazed and nauseous, shaking his head to clear his ears, staggered clear of the stream and sat down heavily on the grass.

All around him was silence. Even the crows were quiet.

He put his head between his knees, decided he was not going to be sick, raised it and took a few breaths, drawing the air far into his lungs and expelling it as slowly as he could.

His awareness of the wood and the ghosts, whether real or imaginary, had gone, departed as abruptly as his sense of oppression, but the feelings of danger and desolation remained.

He knew the cause. The Scotti had desecrated the sanctuary. What he could not undrstand was why.

2

Ceolric awoke to the taste of salt and sand.

It was not long after dawn. Around him the birds sang, gulls wheeled and dived across the estuary. In the woods behind him a cow lowed plaintively. The morning held the promise of another fine, hot day.

The tide was out. He walked down the beach towards the

water, his bare feet revelling in the wet, firm sand, and stared at the opposite shore. He had been swept further than he had thought, almost level with the bar blocking the entrance to the estuary. *Sea Stallion*'s final anchorage was invisible from here, hidden by a ragged outcropping of rock, its base covered with weed and barnacles.

He looked around uncertainly. He was hungry, but had nothing to eat, and nothing with which to catch anything, except the knife sheathed at his hip. (*Don't think about the knife. Don't think about last night. Think about today.*)

For lack of anything better to do Ceolric started walking up the beach, passing from the solid golden sand to the white powder that lay in drifts and stuck to his damp toes, on into the trees which fringed the cove, wandering aimlessly through them until he struck a path – whether made by men or animals he could not tell – which seemed to run parallel with the estuary.

He moved as silently as he could, from shadow to shadow, avoiding the broken twigs that littered the ground, ready to leave the path at the slightest hint of another human being.

After a while he realized that something had changed. He had been thinking so hard about not making any noise, about stepping over or round the dead sticks on the path, that he had paid no mind to his surroundings.

At some point the path had veered away from the sea. He had been aware for some time of passing between thick trunks, white or grey where they were not green with moss, but he had no memory of what kind of trees they had been, only that they had been large.

Now he had reached a place where the trees were smaller, thinner, where there was hardly any undergrowth. It was much brighter here, and he could hear cattle lowing in the near distance.

He stopped and looked about him. This part of the path seemed better trodden, broader and clearly the work of human feet. The trees had been cut close to the ground and the stumps left to grow new shoots, several from each trunk.

There had to be a settlement nearby. These shoots were one of its crops, providing poles for fences and hurdles, fuel easily gathered for the cooking fires, and bark for tanning.

He moved between the thin branches towards the edge of the wood, and found himself on a hillside looking out across a system of small fields divided by big earthen banks topped with thick thorny hedges. For a moment he was puzzled by the banks, then he saw how they would shelter the livestock from the wind and the rain, and how they would provide protection for both stock and crops from the animals in the surrounding woods.

Beyond the fields was a little creek, fed by a tiny stream. Along the line of the stream were five or six wattle and daub huts, their roofs thatched with a mixture of reed and bracken, the rough timber frames that gave them their shape poking awkwardly through the walls, so that they had an unfinished look. Drawn up on the grass beside them were some small coracles.

Out on the deep water of the creek were three much larger ships, spinning back and forth at anchor as if restless to be gone; not ships of wood, like the *Sea Stallion*, but of leather hides stretched across a frame. Ships of the Scotti.

Nothing moved except the sheep and cattle in the fields and the ships on the water. The huts might have been deserted, for all he could tell.

He stood there, on the edge of the wood, for a long time. He was both hungry and thirsty: there might be food in the huts, and the water of the stream was tempting. But somehow he could not summon the courage to cross the fields.

At last, licking his lips and cursing himself for a coward, he withdrew into the cover of the trees. Had he been a year or two younger he would probably have lain down and wept; as it was his determination that he was a man, not a boy, kept him on his feet, and if his eyes sometimes misted over, damping his face, there was nobody to see.

Not caring where he went, he wandered inland, away from the estuary, deeper into the wood, fighting his way through the brambles and the brash, following the lie of the land without bothering where it led him.

The trees here were older, taller and heavier. Little rustlings and chirpings came from the undergrowth as he disturbed the creatures of the forest, and once he put up a deer, seeing the white flash of its tail as it bounded away through the thickets.

Fallen trees lay like sea-wracked monsters, bare branches clutching for the sky, trunks buried in brambles and long grass. A few bore axe marks, but most rotted untouched where they had fallen.

He climbed over a bank of rocks and earth interwoven with

roots, and jumped down the other side, fording the muddy stream at the bottom. Looking back, he saw the bank had once been a dry-stone wall, the stones now overgrown with grass and moss. He could trace its line by the holly bushes growing up the steep hillside.

A sense of the age of the land came over him. The wall must have been built to channel the stream, to prevent it from flooding the ground on the far side. He could not imagine who would have wanted to do such a thing, who would have cared where the water flowed in woodland. His mind grappled with the idea that perhaps this had not always been part of the forest.

It seemed impossible. He had seen the kind of scrub growth that formed on abandoned fields, the way birch seedlings would sprout everywhere, followed by other species like oak and ash. He knew, because old people had told him, that if left uncleared the former fields would soon become a tangled jungle, quite impenetrable and not worth the effort of reclaiming. He also knew that after the equivalent of a man's lifetime had passed (assuming the man died peacefully in bed, which did not happen often), the matted undergrowth would wither away and the land could then be taken back under cultivation, if anyone wanted it.

This forest did not look like that. These trees were old. Some of the wreckage was of oaks which had fallen because they were dead, and everybody knew that oaks lived for hundreds of years.

So who had built the wall, a wall so ancient it had almost been swallowed by the land?

He looked around him uneasily. The birds had stopped singing. Sunlight dappled the forest floor, the mulch on which he stood, and all around him were the shadows cast by the great canopy over his head. Of a sudden the air was filled with the stir of nameless things. The wood felt charged with a feverish restlessness.

He swallowed, his throat dry, but did not dare drink from the muddy water. There were too many tales in his head, tales of young men or women who had wandered away from their fellows in the forest and drunk too deeply of the springs they found hidden in its depths, then waked to find whole centuries passed and all they ever knew crumbled into dust.

He had lost all sense of direction, except he knew by the light he must be travelling vaguely southwards, towards the cliffs at the mouth of the estuary. If he continued along the stream (the wall had vanished altogether) he would probably come out somewhere near the little beach where he had wakened.

Whatever spirits guarded this place – and he had no doubts they were many and powerful – would know him for an intruder. The bones of his ancestors did not lie beneath the humus, the ashes of his forefathers had not been scattered to the winds. He was not a part of this land, not bred to its rhythms; had not eaten of its summer bounty or suffered the hunger of its winters.

Any moment now he would feel a hand on his shoulder, be forced to turn and see the Hooded Ones, dressed in long leaf-coloured robes, their faces hidden within deep cowls, creatures from a child's nightmare. He would turn, impelled by those bony fingers, and they would brush back their hoods and make him look upon their faces.

He fled.

Ceolric ran until he could run no more. At some point he crossed a ridge, and slipping and sliding descended into the valley on the far side.

Gradually his terror came to seem foolish. Nothing had chased him, nothing had harmed him. He had not even seen anything. This part of the forest seemed friendlier, more like the woods near his father's hall when he had been a boy. There were birds here, birds of all kinds, singing and cooing as birds do, and somewhere not far away a woodpecker was drumming.

He found another stream in the valley bottom, flowing clean and clear over gravel. Squatting on the bank, he drank deeply, and could not help but remember filling the waterskins with Garulf. Was the Frisian still alive? He doubted it. There had been blood streaming down the steersman's face at the end, as if his scalp had been laid bare to the bone . . .

(*The fight in the ship was something he did not wish to recall. He had seen terrible things, impossible things. He would not think about it.*)

He set off again, climbing towards the headlands above the open sea, in the vague hope that a friendly ship might sail past and he might somehow be able to attract its attention.

The woodland became sparser, gradually died away: not all at once as it had above the fields, but little by little, the trees spreading thinner, the gaps growing larger, until almost without noticing it he was walking through long grass laden with wild flowers, and the ground had stopped rising and begun to drop to the cliffs above the sea.

He did not notice the stone hut until he was almost upon it. It lay in the lee of a hollow, protected from the worst of the sea storms by the lie of the land. It was smaller than the wattle and daub buildings he had seen earlier, and much better built. The stones from which it was made were of a kind he had never seen before: little, flat, and with a distinct green tinge.

The door hung awry on its hinges, the planks splintered and broken. The ferns beside the path had been trampled into the ground: not very long ago, judging by the breaks in the stems.

If the Scotti had been here once, they might not come again, and there was always the chance of something to eat or drink within.

Ceolric glanced nervously around him, then ran for it. Inside the hut was a stinking mess. Part of the roof had been torn down, as if the Scotti had been searching for something, and the floor was strewn with thatch. Mixed with the straw were fragments of wood and leather, the remains of a bed frame. The walls were daubed with strange signs and symbols he could not read but whose meaning he could guess. In one corner was a mound of man droppings, and in another a smaller pile of dog droppings. Both were crawling with flies. The straw where he kicked it was damp and foul.

There was nothing for him here. Shuddering, he backed away into the warmth of the sun, the hopelessness of his situation striking him afresh.

He was in hostile country, several days' journey from the nearest of his people, and he was alone. He would never see his crewmates again, never sit in company round a driftwood fire listening to Garulf's tales. He would never now know the true name of the man whose life Garulf had saved in the dying city of Lindinis, the man who had called himself mab Petroc. Wicga had guessed the answer, and had promised to tell him after they were settled in their new home, but Wicga would never tell him anything again.

Ceolric stumbled blindly away from the hut, chest heaving, seeking the safety of the forest, all thought of standing on a headland waiting for a passing ship forgotten. There would be no passing ships, and even if there were and they saw him, which was unlikely, they would not put into shore for a stranger.

'Who are you?'

He spun, hand falling to the hilt of his knife.

An old man stood beside a gorse bush, a sinewy arm out-stretched to the gossamer which glinted against the harsh green spikes, as if he had just this moment finished spinning it and now was checking his work.

'Who are you?' he repeated, speaking the tongue of Ceolric's father with a marked accent.

Ceolric stared at him, not knowing how to reply.

'No answer? Let me guess then.' The man moved forward, smiling a little, seemingly unmoved by the implied threat of the knife.

'You came from the ship I saw yesterday evening, yes? I would guess you beached somewhere up the estuary, and then were attacked last night. I heard the cries and sounds of battle. The raiders caught you, did they? You came a few days too late for easy pickings.' Now he spoke almost to himself, though he continued to use the German dialect. 'Still, the Scotti have saved Custennin the trouble of dealing with you, I suppose.'

Seeing the blank look on Ceolric's face, he added: 'Custennin. I suppose you would call him, what's the word –' he clicked his fingers in exasperation '– the kin-leader . . . No, that's not right. The *king*. That's the word I want. He is the king hereabouts. You might know him as Constantinus.'

Ceolric decided the old man was not hostile. Certainly he did not seem dangerous. He was of about average height for a native of these western lands, which meant he was considerably shorter than Ceolric himself. His hair, receding slightly from a high forehead, fell long and white to his shoulders, tangling on the way with his full beard. His clothing was blotched with stains of grass and bark, as if he had lately been living wild. The knee-length tunic was much darned and nearly colourless with age. It was his manner, though, which made him seem harmless; the way he peered at the youth from under bushy eyebrows, the way he waved his left arm in the air to emphasize what he was saying.

'We did not beach the ship. We moored on open water, under the shelter of the hills.'

'Ah,' said the old man triumphantly. 'Yes, much wiser. So how did the Scotti take you unawares? Are you the only survivor?'

Ceolric stared at him suspiciously, but the last question seemed to have no ulterior motive. 'Yes, I am alone. So far as I know none of the others escaped.'

'And?'

'And . . . I do not know. They were all round us. The watch must have slept.' He shuddered, clutched his knife to him like a talisman.

The old man frowned. His accent suddenly became much thicker, and the words came more awkwardly. 'How do you mean? I am sorry, it is a long time since I spoke this tongue.'

Ceolric switched into his mother's speech. Wicga had made him practise it on a regular basis, saying that an ability to talk with the natives was far too useful to risk losing.

'I was asleep. When I woke, they were climbing aboard from all sides. They took us by surprise. Garulf pushed me overboard and told me to swim after Wicga my father was killed.'

He stopped and glared defiantly at the old man.

'How curious,' muttered the other. 'You have the accent of the corner people.' (Ceolric decided he must have misheard that part.) 'Are you hungry?'

'Yes. Yes, I am.'

Without another word the old man turned and walked away into the trees. Ceolric hesitated, then realized he was meant to follow.

The old man led him far into the wood, through thick undergrowth high as their heads and under low boughs laden with leaves, till the youth had no idea where they were or how far they had come.

Finally he stopped and indicated a stump on which the boy might sit. Again Ceolric paused, then remembering his manners he squatted on his haunches, leaving the seat for his host, who had vanished behind the bole of a great oak.

After a moment the old man reappeared, carrying a platter of bread and cheese. 'There was some fish,' he said apologetically, 'but I am afraid it has gone off in this warm weather.'

Ceolric began to relax. The very ordinariness of the old man's conversation seemed to prove he meant him no harm.

As if he had heard his thoughts, the old man smiled. He seated himself on the stump, watched Ceolric eat for a while, then said very gently:

'My name is Budoc. It is not the name I was given at my birth, but one I adopted, in honour of the Abbot of Laure, when I resolved upon a contemplative life. What is your name?'

228

Not having understood a word except the last sentence, he said: 'Ceolric.'

'You were born in this island?'

'Oh yes. My mother was a lady, a princess, of the Cantii.'

The old man grinned. 'That explains your accent. And I never yet heard of a Saeson taking to wife a British woman who was not a princess.'

Ceolric frowned. Was Budoc mocking him?

'Your father – Wicga, I believe you called him – he was one of Oesc's men?'

'For a time, long ago. Then he wanted a kingdom of his own.'

'Ah, I see. So he led you here?'

'Yes. He thought that if Cerdic could found a kingdom in the lands opposite Wectis, he could manage it here.'

Budoc raised an eyebrow in surprise. 'That old renegade. Is he still alive?'

'Cerdic? Yes, though he is an old man.'

'He must be. So he calls himself a king these days, does he? What about Oesc? I heard that he was dead.'

'Oesc? Oesc died not long after I was born.'

Budoc laughed. 'Woe, for the mighty are fallen. Ah well, all things pass except the mercy of God.' He shook his head. 'Your father hoped to found a kingdom with a single shipload? Even Cerdic had five keels.'

'He intended to form a camp, to explore the territory, then send for more people,' replied Ceolric defensively.

Budoc nodded. 'That makes sense of a sort. But I still do not understand how his dream came to so sudden an end.'

Something about his tone of voice made Ceolric look up from the remnants of his food. The old man was studying him dispassionately, obviously weighing what the youth had told him.

'You think I ran away?'

'I don't know what to think. Still less do I know what to do with you.'

CHAPTER TWO

'Not a good night's rest,' complained Gorthyn. 'My sleep was troubled with dreams of forest trees tossing back and forth in a high wind, and even when I relieved you on watch it was no better. All night long they haunted me: images of boughs bending to breaking point, leaves torn loose and swirling in the gale . . .'

'A *nemeton*,' said Nai, slouching in the saddle.

Gorthyn looked at his friend curiously. 'Why, yes, there is a *nemeton* on the other side of the estuary. I had forgotten. The place must have been important once.' He shook his head. 'I doubt anyone remembers its existence now apart from the locals.'

'Pagans.'

The big man nodded, guided his pony between the honey blooms of the furze. 'They will worship there, in the clearing in the wood. Silvanus, I suppose they would call the god, if they call him anything at all.'

It was a glorious morning. The sun was bright on the dew, and a fresh breeze was blowing in from the sea. Gorthyn stretched, took a deep breath, let his legs dangle, his body flowing with the motion of the pony.

'Ha!' he said. 'It is good to be alive, even on so little sleep.' He glanced back at Nai, following a horse's length behind.

His friend seemed withdrawn today, wrapped deep within himself. Most warriors were noisy and boisterous, men who lived strictly for the moment, but not Nai. In part it was because of his old throat wound, which made talking painful, but in part it was because he was by nature a thinker.

Nor did this make him any less a fighting man. There was nobody Gorthyn would rather have guarding his back, nobody in the world. Gorthyn knew that his own failing was a tendency to rashness, to plunging ahead without care for the consequences. If Nai had a fault, it was that he underestimated his own abilities.

Gorthyn sighed to himself. Not far from here his kinsman Bedwyr – whom he privately considered to have been far and away the greatest of all Arthur's Companions – had destroyed a force of Saesons intent on raiding the small township of Penhyle. Now it would not be worth raiding, but in those days the land had still been prosperous. A lifetime ago.

Like Arthur himself, Bedwyr had died at Camlann, and the age of heroes had died with them. All that remained were lesser mortals, living in the ruins of Prydein.

'If we turn here,' Gorthyn called over his shoulder, 'we can cut across country to the hamlet I remember.'

Nai grunted and waved in agreement, so he wheeled his pony away from the coastal path they had followed for so long.

He steered by memory, seeing none of the signs of life he had expected, not even faint trails of smoke from the cooking fires. The countryside seemed deserted, and he began to twist and turn uneasily in the saddle, noticing from the corner of one eye that Nai was doing the same.

By the time they reached the hanger of pine trees Gorthyn remembered as clinging to the steep side of the valley above the hamlet, they were riding as if in enemy country, keeping several lengths between them.

It was dark beneath the pines, the ground lumpy and uneven, a mass of rotting windfalls buried under the brown needles and moss, so that they had to concentrate on guiding their horses' steps. There was no undergrowth, but the thin trunks grew so close together that the riders lost sight of each other as they halted and moved by turns, passing and repassing, cautiously advancing through the gloom.

When they came out into the light they halted. The hamlet lay before them at the foot of the slope, shabby buildings of crumbling stone and rotting wood. A roofless ruin, open to the sky, was all that survived of what had once been a respectable farmhouse at the heart of the settlement. The lesser houses and the wooden barns were badly weathered, and the paved court which stretched from the farmhouse to the creek was cracked and broken.

A knot of men and women were standing by the water's edge, near the remnants of the small boatyard, arguing loudly, waving their hands in the air. At the sound of hooves on stone they quietened and turned to watch the newcomers.

'Are you from the High Lord Custennin?' shouted one of the older men.

'Yes,' said Gorthyn, urging his pony on across the scarred paving stones. It was an easier answer than the full truth, and might help calm these people, who seemed near to panic.

He knew without needing to look that Nai would wait in the open space between the buildings and the creek, keeping a wary eye on the woods around them. He did not trust these peasants, and he did not like this feeling of being surrounded on three sides by water.

'Has he heard already then?'

'Where are the rest of you?'

'Are you his scouts?'

The questions came thick and fast. Gorthyn glanced back uncertainly at Nai, who shrugged.

'The Saeson ship is here then? In the estuary?' he asked.

'The Saeson ship?' repeated the man who had spoken first. 'The Saeson ship?' He laughed wildly. 'The Saesons are no threat to us, not now.'

Gorthyn frowned, not understanding. 'You mean it has gone?'

They all began to babble at once. He cast another despairing glance over his shoulder at Nai, then shouted:

'Enough! You!' He pointed at the one who seemed to be the head of the clan. 'You speak. The rest of you keep quiet.' He waited until he had silence, then explained very slowly, as if talking to a child:

'Gereint, who is Custennin's lieutenant in the east, sent us to follow the pirates' ship along the coast. Now, where is it?'

'Floating full of dead men off Small Cove.' The man licked his lips nervously. 'The demons from the other side came across last night and devoured its crew.'

'The demons?' Gorthyn repeated blankly.

'The Scotti. They have killed all of Rhodri's people, or made them their slaves. Last night the Scotti came across the water in the fishing coracles they stole from Rhodri's people and killed the Saesons. We must leave, before they kill us as well.'

The man had a wild look in his eyes. Gorthyn heard the creak of leather behind him as Nai shifted in the saddle, reaching for a throwing spear.

His head whirled. Clinging to the one fact in the man's recital he had actually understood – and ignoring for the moment the matter of the Scotti – he said: 'Will one of you lead us to this cove that we may see the ship for ourselves?'

They exchanged glances and muttered among themselves.

'Perhaps if they see the Saesons they will believe us,' somebody said, and after more muttering they pushed forward a young man, not much more than a boy, who without speaking walked past Gorthyn and his pony, leading the way along a track of beaten earth.

The two men set off after him, relieved to be away from the decaying hamlet and its unpleasant inhabitants.

The boy did not speak until they were well out of sight of his family. 'They thought you were outriders for a warband coming to deliver them from the Scotti.'

His voice was soft, so that for a moment the two warriors did not realize the remark was aimed at them.

Gorthyn narrowed his eyes. 'No Scotti have raided these shores for a generation,' he protested, ducking beneath a low branch.

'Tell that to Rhodri's clan,' the boy said contemptuously. 'We saw them come, two days ago, in three boats of hide. Then we heard the screams. We have not dared go near the water since.'

'How big were the boats?'

The boy shrugged. 'Seven oars to a side.'

'At least forty men then,' Gorthyn muttered to himself. 'More likely fifty.' He gave up trying to duck under the trees and dismounted. Nai followed his example.

'My Uncle Cian – he was the one you spoke with – says we should leave now, before the Scotti come looking for us.'

Gorthyn nodded. 'Your uncle is a wise man. Gereint will send his warband, but it will be a while before they arrive. You would be best gone.'

'We saw the Saeson ship come in yesterday evening, and thought perhaps the raiders were working together – I have heard of such things.' He looked questioningly at the big man, who nodded. 'Last night we heard them fighting. This morning we crept along this path and saw the wreckage the Scotti had left behind them.'

While he spoke they came through a final screen of pine trees, the needles soft underfoot, and found themselves standing on a sunlit beach.

They left the ponies grazing on the bitter grass beneath the trees. The boy marched purposefully towards the water, threw out an arm, and said: 'There!'

Grinding listlessly on the rocks was the ship they had been sent to find. Her deck was crawling with life: they could see the grey and white of gulls' feathers, the yellow of their beaks, the flash of wings outstretched for balance.

Nai grinned crookedly, gestured invitingly to Gorthyn. The bigger man glanced back longingly at the ponies, shrugged, and started wading.

The water struck cold even through his leather riding breeches. A freezing ringlet encompassed either leg, moving higher with each pace, till they reached his crotch where they merged and became one. Deliberately he kept his eyes off the boat, only registering the position of the hull.

Gasping he gripped the bulwark and heaved himself aboard, a clumsy blond bear of a man fumbling for balance. Collapsing head first onto the deck, he gave a moan of revulsion as his hand touched something soft.

With a thunder of wings the gulls took off, squawking and wailing at being driven from their meal. Gorthyn took one quick look around him then jumped over the side, no longer caring about the cold, only wanting to be away from the ship.

'The gulls have been busy,' he called. 'And the flies.'

He was shivering by the time he reached the shore and risked a rapid glimpse over his shoulder. The gulls had already returned to their meal.

'All Saesons, so far as one could tell. The heads have gone.'

The boy stared at the ship in horrified fascination. Behind his back Nai raised an eyebrow, nodded.

Gorthyn continued briskly: 'The Scotti must have taken their dead with them. They've stripped everything of value, and then just let her drift.'

'The tide will take her later,' said the boy.

'We have a choice, cousin,' Gorthyn said. 'We can ride for Gereint, and hope to return before the Scotti do too much damage. Or we can divide, one riding for Din Erbin, the other remaining here to do what he can.'

Nai frowned, hitched his belt uneasily. He indicated the boy with a twitch of his head.

'What about one of his people? They were planning to leave anyway.' His voice was a hoarse and breathless growl. The boy jumped.

Gorthyn thought about this. Nai's suggestion made sense, and the more he considered it the more sensible it seemed.

'Will your people do that?' he asked the boy. 'Carry a message to the east? They need not travel much more than a day's full journey,' he added, remembering none of these countrymen would have ever been more than half a day's walk from their home.

'I will go, if Uncle Cian will let me,' said the boy.

'Good. Follow the coastal path until you come to a broad estuary like this. Cross over by the ferry – I will give you a ring to show the ferryman – and climb the hill to the hall. Do not be afraid of the doorman, but show my ring again and deliver the messages we will give you. They will feed you and let you sleep before you need come home – wherever home is by then.'

Nai leaned forward and growled in his ruined voice: 'What is your name, boy?'

'Pedrawg.'

Gorthyn laughed. 'That was the name of my father's grand-father A good omen!'

On the way back to the hamlet they allowed Pedrawg to draw ahead of them so that they could speak without being heard.

'Best if we do not mention Eremon,' whispered Gorthyn. 'They barely trust us as it is, and if they discover the leader of the Scotti is known to us, we shall receive no help from them.'

'If it is Eremon,' said Nai.

'Do you doubt it?'

'No.' Nai shook his head regretfully. 'No, I do not.'

'Three ships. One for Eremon, one for Dovnuall, and one for Serach.'

Nai watched him thoughtfully. Gorthyn's face was set and grim. The thin scar on his left cheek which was usually masked by his natural high colour stood out in red relief against the taut skin. That was why Nai had suggested sending one of the locals to fetch aid: he knew Gorthyn would have insisted on staying behind, and he did not trust him not to cross the estuary alone and challenge Dovnuall Frych to single combat.

'We must cross,' said Gorthyn, echoing his thoughts.

'Sentries,' Nai protested mildly.

'They are pirates, reivers, not true warriors. We can slip past them if we cross high enough.'

'And then?'

Gorthyn swung towards him, his face distorted with passion. 'I want them, cousin. I want them dead. Dovnuall first, then Eremon. They tortured Erfai my father then killed him like a dog.'

Nai rubbed at his throat. Erfai had been his foster-father too. The two of them were Erfai's closest male kindred, and on them fell the duty, the honour and necessity, of avenging his murder.

What exactly the two of them could do against the Scotti, he did not know. If one guessed there had originally been fifty of the raiders, how many were left? The Saesons were doughty fighters, not the kind to be overwhelmed easily even if taken by surprise, and there had been a full shipload of them. Supposing ten of the Scotti had been killed or disabled in last night's fighting (and he did not think he was being over generous: it was likely to be more) that meant about forty were still active.

Forty men against two.

Not good.

And yet what choice did they have? They could not skulk on this side of the water while Eremon did as he wished on the far shore. It would be three days at least before Gereint reached them with the warband; three days in which Eremon could consolidate his hold on the peninsula. Whatever purpose Vortepor of Dyfed had in sending him here (and Nai did not doubt there *was* some purpose), three days was a long time.

Penhyle was vulnerable, of course, but Cian's people could see that the little town was warned of the danger. There was no need for the pair of them to go as well.

Which meant they were honour-bound to essay the crossing, however dangerous. If they did not, then their lives would have been a lie.

No warrior expected to die in his bed. Few lived long enough to grow grey hairs. The recompense for a short life was undying fame, and fame could only be won through the doing of great deeds. In the meantime the warriors lived well, feasting on fine food and drink, listening to good poetry, accepting gifts of fair clothing or rich jewellery, grants of weapons or lands.

When the war horns sounded they paid for these favours with their courage and their loyalty: loyalty to their leader, to the people he ruled, to their kin and comrades. They had made brave promises when they drank their lord's mead and took the gifts he gave them: only a coward and a liar failed to honour these boasts.

Nai and Gorthyn had sworn to protect the Portion of Erbin under its lord, Gereint. The far shore of the estuary was debatable, the borderland between the Portion of Erbin and the Portion of Tamaris, part of neither one nor the other.

(And that, Nai realized with a start, never having thought about it before, was because it contained a sanctuary within a wood, which like all sacred sites traditionally belonged to the boundaries between territories, to the line of division between one place and another.)

Debatable ground or not, their oaths bound them to a greater loyalty, to the defence of the realm of Dumnonia under Custennin and his heirs. It was their duty to oppose the Scotti in any manner possible while they waited for reinforcements.

Nai knew this, knew he had no option but to cross the water and face whatever lay upon the far side. Gorthyn, driven not only by his oaths but also by his need for vengeance, was eager to go, was even now planning the crossing.

But Nai was afraid. He did not fear death in battle or even the pain of being wounded – or rather, like any sensible person, he did fear them, but was able to put them from his mind. What he feared was Eremon mab Cairbre. He had feared him since childhood.

When they were boys together Eremon had always been his superior: a faster runner, a better horseman, more accurate with a javelin, quicker with sword or knife, blessed with a golden tongue. In all their practice fights Eremon had been the victor, and there had been an inevitability about that dull afternoon five years earlier, when the spear point had tracked his every move and finally flung him from the saddle in a flash of agony.

Eremon would kill him if they met again.

That was what he feared, to die at the hands of a man as worthless as Eremon mab Cairbre.

*   *   *

It was late afternoon by the time they succeeded in persuading Cian to carry them over the estuary. Even then he only agreed on condition they cross at a point well out of sight of the village on the opposite shore.

Pedrawg memorized the message for Gereint, and began his journey, saying he could spend the night at a village along the way where he had kin. The remainder of the clan loaded their few possessions into coracles and small boats and paddled off up one of the creeks; they intended to camp the night at its tail, then set off inland when Cian rejoined them. Pedrawg would cut across country on his return, steering by the sun, and catch them as best he could.

The tide was coming in rapidly. They loaded the two reluctant ponies into the wooden ferry – both horses had done this before, often, across the mouth of the River Oak, but the ferry there was in a much better state of repair than this one. Cian's boat was rotting apart; it looked old and well used, and more than half its timbers needed replacing.

'Don't you people ever mend anything?' Gorthyn mumbled crossly, not expecting a reply.

'Why bother?' returned Cian, driving the ferry out into the open water. 'The world is coming to an end. What we have will see us out.'

Grunting with the effort, Cian rowed them against the current, explaining in gasps that if he could just bring them to the other side of the main flow the tide would drift them down to where they wanted to be.

Nai, who was holding the ponies, legs balanced against the chop and sway of the boat, looked at the grey-green water and shuddered. From where he stood, near the rotten stern which would probably have fallen off had he given it one good kick, the western shore seemed utterly deserted. It was pretty enough – plenty of small beaches divided by rugged grey outcrops, backed by well-formed trees – probably good grazing and planting land, rich land, like the red regions to the east. On his left, near the open sea, was a line of impressive cliffs, falling steeply to the water at their feet. It might be the sort of place to find a hill fort, a promontory fort, protected on three sides by cliffs and water.

Perhaps they could have a look, if they had time and were able. Both Gereint and Custennin were always eager to find defensible sites, and if the pirates were to make a habit of visiting this estuary, it would be a good idea to have a small garrison some-where near the mouth.

The grating of sand and mud under the keel roused him from his thoughts.

'Over the side!' shouted Cian. 'Quick, over and hold her. Get the horses off as fast as you can.'

Nai had never understood why people in boats always became so excitable the moment they reached shore. With deceptively quick, dignified movements he eased the ponies over the side into the mud, laughing at Gorthyn who was buried thigh deep in the stuff (it was green and foul smelling), clinging to the side of the boat as if she were likely to float away at any instant.

'Give me a push!' said Cian, the boat bobbing lightly on the surface now the weight was out of it.

Gorthyn shoved the ferry so hard he almost fell flat on his face. Nai laughed till the tears ran down his face.

'He landed us here deliberately!' he managed to splutter after a while. 'Just to see you muddy your breeches, my hero.'

Gorthyn watched the receding ferry with a scowl. 'At least we did not pay him anything.'

'Only because nothing we have would be of any use to him. What would a peasant like that do with a copper token?'

The big man dragged himself out of the mud and moved along the bank until he found a place where he could wade out into the water without having to pass through mud first. As he washed himself he said:

'He was right though. The world is coming to an end. What is it now, eighty, ninety years since the Empire abandoned us? Every year the savages drive us back a little further.'

His voice was bitter. Nai smiled coolly, the scar on his throat very white against the brown of his neck.

'Every year we lose a little more of what we once had,' Gorthyn complained. 'We still call ourselves Romans, you and I, but our forefathers would have called us tribesmen. To people like Cian it probably makes less difference than he thinks, though even they have withdrawn into themselves, into tight-knit communities which have hardly any contact with the outside world. I remem-ber my father telling me that it used to be a proper boatyard, that place back there, supplying half the fishing folk hereabouts with their needs. Nowadays everybody thinks he can lash a skin coracle together, so none of them dare risk the open sea except on days so calm the water is like glass.'

Nai shrugged. 'It has been the same since Arthur fell in our fathers' day,' he growled. 'Neither Custennin nor his cousin Gereint can match the men of old. We are dwindling, friend, dwindling into night. Soon even our songs will be forgotten.'

It was a conversation they had shared often.

When Gorthyn felt himself clean again they mounted their ponies and rode along the shore. After a while Gorthyn turned inland. Nai frowned, but followed without comment, keeping his eyes on the trees. A light breeze rustled the leaves, so that time and again he thought he saw movement behind the foliage, and the beginnings of an old fear stirred deep within him.

'Cian dropped us well above the village,' Gorthyn said softly. 'If we follow this coombe it should bring us out on the hillside above their fields. Keep your weapons ready, cousin.'

Nai unslung his whitewashed wooden shield and slipped his arm through the strap. At once he felt more confident. In a quiver bound to the saddle were his javelins; he untied it and slid it across his back, so that he could reach over his shoulder and withdraw the spears when he needed them. He took one now, and kept it in his right hand, and the ash shaft was a comfort.

The further they went from the estuary, the narrower grew the valley. At length they struck a path, perhaps no more than a deer trail, which led in the right direction, and they followed it cautiously, looking and listening.

Riding now several horse's lengths behind Gorthyn, Nai found he was relying on his ears rather than his vision. Small animals rustled in the undergrowth, and birds gave cries of warning, but each time the warning seemed to be for them, and not for an ambusher lurking under cover.

The path climbed as the valley shrank, until at last the coombe vanished and they were clear of the woods. They allowed the ponies to rest while they took their bearings.

Below them fields sloped back down to an arm of the estuary, and there beside the water was the group of huts they had come to find.

'No signs of people. Animals in the fields though,' muttered Gorthyn.

'Do we go down? It will be dark soon.'

'I don't know. What do you think?'

Nai shrugged. 'Two of us, together? There's a track, see, skirting the fields. If we take that we can turn and ride for it if anything goes wrong.'

Pushing the ponies onto the track they rode slowly down the slope, side by side. Behind them the sun had sunk below the level of the hills, flushing the sky with the first hints of pink. It still shone far out on the estuary, so that the waters around the eastern shore danced with the golden glow of early evening, while they rode through shadow.

They had not gone very far before a voice cried: 'Stop! Wait!'

Gorthyn wheeled his pony to face the way they had come. Nai raised his shield to cover himself and held the javelin ready to throw, scanning the ground ahead and to the sides in case this was a trap.

'It's a girl,' reported the big man. 'She seems to be alone. She's out on the track now, running towards us. I think it's safe.'

Nai relaxed a little, though his eyes did not stop moving.

'Don't go down there,' panted the girl as she came closer. 'Everybody is dead except me.'

She stopped at a distance from Gorthyn, trembling from head to foot. 'They fell upon us the day before yesterday. I was in the woods, up there, and I saw what happened. It was like a nightmare come to life. They killed and killed . . . I fled through the night, hid, fled again . . .'

She shuddered.

Gorthyn dismounted and put an arm about her, dwarfing her. 'Softly, then, softly,' he hissed between his teeth, as he might to a nervous horse.

'They were all killed, all my kinfolk.' Her voice rose.

'What happened to the Scotti?' he asked gently.

She shuddered. He felt rather than saw the movement against his chest.

'Last night they took the coracles and paddled out to the other ship. I heard them fighting. Not many returned.'

'Where are they now?'

'They went inland. To the wood. But they may come back to sleep.' Her voice was desperate.

'Then ride behind me. Guide us to somewhere we can defend through the night.' He boosted her onto the horse, scrambled up himself. 'Come, Nai, my friend. This may be such a night as songs are made from!'

241

'If anybody lives to sing of it,' muttered Nai, kicking his pony into action.

Eurgain brought them to the summit of the ridge above the estuary. In the light of the setting sun her hair, which the two men had thought a dark brown, shone like burnished copper. Suddenly Nai saw that beneath the dirt she was beautiful.

Gorthyn looked about them, flared his nostrils. 'Open ground. Should give us some warning. What do you think, cousin? Among those rocks?'

Nai followed his gaze to the tumble of boulders. 'Tether the ponies in the angle behind us,' he growled. 'No fire. One of us on watch till dawn.' His speech was more for the girl's benefit than his companion's.

She watched the two of them curiously as they dismounted and made their preparations for the night. 'Who are you?' she asked, staring at their weapons with wide eyes.

'We are of Gereint's household. We were sent to see where the pirates' ship was going.' Gorthyn shrugged ruefully. 'It seems we have found more than we sought.'

'They killed the pirates last night,' said Eurgain.

'I know. I saw their handiwork.'

'I crept down to the fields,' she said as if she had not heard him. 'I did not know what to do, where to go, and I was hungry. I thought . . .' She drew a breath, continued: 'I thought it would be better to be dead, even such a death, than be alone and starving . . .'

'And then?' prompted Gorthyn, his voice still soft.

'Then shouts. The sounds of fighting, screams of fear and pain.' She shivered. 'I was going to steal some food, but they had left the hounds on the shore, and the wizard was with them.'

Her voice cracked and she began to shake.

They digested this for a while, Gorthyn wordlessly stroking the girl's shoulder, once again soothing her as he might an animal.

'Where do you think they have gone?' he asked when she seemed calmer.

Eurgain twisted around to look at him in surprise. 'The wood, of course!'

He glanced at Nai, almost invisible now against the darkness of the rocks.

'Which wood?'

'Sanctuary Wood!' she exclaimed impatiently.

'Hush!' murmured Nai. 'Something bothers the horses.' He spoke quietly rather than whispering because he knew that the sibilants of a whisper carry far on the night air.

They listened intently. An owl hooted somewhere in the trees down the slope. A small animal squealed and thrashed frantically in the undergrowth. The ponies snorted uneasily.

Nai squeezed past Eurgain, pushed her deeper into the cleft, bidding her try to keep the ponies still. Moving beside Gorthyn he muttered: 'See anything?'

The larger man pointed to the grass in front of them.

Although it was a windless evening the grass was moving, swaying in the gathering dusk, swaying in a long slow sinuous pattern coming ever closer to their refuge.

Nai drew out a javelin and cocked his arm.

Gorthyn laid a warning finger against the other's left wrist, waited, suddenly tapped twice.

Nai threw with all his force. The spear hissed as it ploughed the gloom, travelling twenty paces to its target.

Something reared up from the grass, twisted and crashed back to the ground. To Gorthyn it seemed like a wolf; Nai thought it more like a large dog. Even as they watched it surfaced again, but this time it was unmistakably a man, a man with a spear in his shoulder.

He staggered a few steps, trying to run but lacking any control over his legs, and fell forwards onto his face, driving the spear further into his body before the shaft snapped.

Everything went very quiet.

Neither warrior moved a muscle, though all the world seemed to be waiting for them to act.

The owl hooted, closer now, came floating towards them through the air, a white blur of wings that swooped across the grass and over their heads to vanish behind the boulders.

'Mount and ride?' queried Gorthyn.

'I think not yet.' Nai glanced behind him at the girl holding the ponies. 'This is as secure a place as any we are likely to find. Let us wait to see what happens next.'

'The moon will not be up until well after true dark. If we wait, we must wait till then, or break our necks in the woods.'

Nai smiled.

Gorthyn snorted affectionately. 'Nai the Silent,' he mocked.

243

'Well, I suppose you are right. We had better remain and take what God sends us.'

For a long time nothing happened. Gradually they relaxed; Gorthyn went back to talk with the girl while Nai remained on guard, watching the night come welling up from among the trees of the valley. Slowly the stars came out, and by their pale light he could see the dark outline lying still amidst the long black grass.

'Where is this Sanctuary Wood?' asked Gorthyn.

Eurgain's face was invisible, but the astonishment was obvious in her voice. 'In the valley beyond this ridge, of course. Everybody knows that.'

'I do not,' he said sweetly. 'You must remember I do not come from your village. I know the other side of the estuary fairly well, but I have only been here once before in my life, and then I was travelling west in a hurry to the stronghold of my lord's lord, Custennin.'

'The High Lord Custennin?' she said, curious. 'What is he like?'

'Tall, brown-haired, and ruthless. What is your Sanctuary Wood like?'

She still seemed puzzled by his ignorance. 'The sanctuary itself is a round clearing in the trees. In the middle is a spring in a basin. They say that once there was a hut over the spring, in the old days, but it is gone now. We used to take offerings from our fields and lay them around the basin after every harvest.'

Her voice acquired a cadence as she spoke. He guessed she was half remembering a tale told by firelight during long winter evenings, and for a moment he grasped some sense of what the Scotti had taken from her – the warmth and security of home, the companionship of a close-knit community where everybody is related, several times.

'Gorthyn,' called Nai. 'The body has gone.'

He left the girl and eased forward, keeping to the shadows. The moon was up, and the grass on the hillside shone crisp and clear in its light. Of the dark form there was no sign, though they could see by the trampling where it had lain.

'I saw something move on the edge of the trees,' explained Nai. 'When I looked again, the body had gone. The spear is still there.'

'Look!' said the big man. 'They have come for us.'

*   *   *

244

One by one the Scotti stepped out from the shelter of the trees. Whether it was because the uncertain light made them all the more menacing, or because of what he thought he had seen in the long grass, Nai found himself quivering with fear.

'Steady, cousin, steady,' whispered Gorthyn. 'Whatever they are, cold iron hurts them. We have proved that already.'

They were on foot, all of them, bareheaded in the moonlight that turned their brown locks to silver and washed the flesh from the bones of their faces. By their garb the two Britons knew them for Scotti, but they did not move as the pirates usually moved, in an ill-disciplined huddle with their captain at the fore. Rather they spread like a pack of hunting dogs, fanning out in a rough line that bowed into a curve, so the flanks approached the cluster of rocks first while the middle held back.

'Do you think they can use their weapons?' murmured Nai, his fear gone now the danger was close.

'Not so well as we,' said Gorthyn in his normal speaking voice. 'You throw better than I; try them with a javelin.'

The raiders carried small round white shields, and were armed with spears and knives. Only the man in the centre of the line bore a sword. They advanced at a steady pace, confident and un-hurried, walking with their eyes fixed upon the rocks, not looking at each other to find courage in the presence of comrades, as Britons or Saesons might have done.

Nai threw, aiming for the figure on the right. Even as the javelin struck he had whipped a second into the air, this time casting at the man on the left of the line.

Gorthyn, watching the right wing, saw the man reel, javelin in chest, hands coming up to wrestle with the shaft. Then a cloud passed over the moon, and by the time it had cleared there was a gap in the line, and a dark shape lying in the grass.

The second cast did not land so cleanly. The spear took its victim in the arm, spinning him around to his knees. He wrenched out the javelin and hurled it back at Nai, but he threw awkwardly so the spear tumbled harmlessly through the air and bounced off the rocks.

'Clumsy,' scoffed Nai. 'They are clumsy, cousin. Shall we venture forth and scatter them?'

Gorthyn drew his sword. The distinctive rasp of metal on the wood of the sheath echoed through the night.

'Why not? Let us teach them the members of Gereint's house-hold are neither fishermen nor pirates, but warriors.'

In that moment the battle madness was upon them both, and had Eurgain not made some inarticulate sound of protest they would have left the shelter of the rocks and charged down the hill at the enemy.

Instead they stayed in the mouth of the cleft, waiting for the attack. It came with an unexpected savagery. The Scotti hurled themselves forward, snarling and slavering like animals, shouting in their almost incomprehensible dialect, shoving and jostling in their need to get at the Britons.

It was now that Gorthyn's great strength came into play. Bracing his legs like tree trunks, using his shield to batter aside any foe foolish enough to come within its range, hewing with his sword at his attackers, he could have held the gap alone. But he had Nai behind him, Nai who did not crowd him but ensured none slipped past his guard.

Suddenly it was over, and somehow, though they could not be certain how it happened, there were no bodies lying at their feet.

'You were right,' gasped Gorthyn, cleaning his blade on the grass. 'They are clumsy.'

Nai looked thoughtful. 'Did we kill any?'

Gorthyn dabbed at a scratch on his wrist. 'I would like to think so. But if we did, where did they go?'

Eurgain came forward, having quieted the ponies, and wrapped a piece of cloth around the big man's wrist. 'Some fell,' she said. 'Their friends dragged them away, I think.' She shrugged apologetically. 'It is hard to tell in the moonlight.'

'Ware!' bellowed Nai, leaping between her and the entrance like a man demented, shield held out before him.

A javelin glanced from Nai's shield, the sound loud and menacing in the confines of the cleft. Another clattered off the rocks and skidded across Gorthyn's feet. He stared down at it.

'Would you say they are improving with practice?' he said drily. 'I see no reason why they should practise on me.'

A stone bounced off Nai's shield rim, sending him staggering against the girl.

'I think we must leave,' he said when he had recovered his balance.

Gorthyn crouched behind his own shield to pick up the javelin at his feet and hand it to Nai. 'If you see anything . . .' he said, his voice trailing away as he moved back to the ponies, slinging the shield across his shoulders to free his hands while he checked their girths.

'Nai, will you take Eurgain?' he asked.

Nai nodded without turning round, his eyes watching the hillside for any sign of the Scotti. It crossed his mind that perhaps they were making a mistake, perhaps they would do better to remain under cover, but then another javelin came from nowhere to land firmly in the middle of his shield, just above the iron boss, dragging his arm down with its weight. Had another followed he would have been defenceless; fortunately he had time to wrench it free, tearing the shield's hide cover and splintering the wood in his haste, before the next skittered along the rock at his side in a shower of angry sparks.

'Which way shall we ride?' said Gorthyn. Behind him the ponies stood ready, trembling almost as much as the girl who held their reins.

'Keep to the open, I think,' said Nai. 'We cannot sensibly ride under the trees in this light, and in any case, I think that is where they are strongest.' He scratched his head, an unwittingly comic gesture neither of the others found amusing. 'If we keep to the ridge, parallel with the estuary, aiming northwards, how far does the land remain clear?' he asked Eurgain.

'Not far,' she replied, her voice quavering slightly for all her efforts to control it. 'But if we go the other way we must cross a deep valley if we are to avoid the trees, and I should not think the horses would find it easy.'

'And if we take that direction we shall be driven against the sea cliffs,' muttered Gorthyn. 'Let us risk the northern road.'

They mounted fast, Gorthyn heaving the girl up behind Nai, the pony stamping and sidling awkwardly, jostling the big man into the rock wall until he lost his temper and clouted it across the nose.

'Go!' he shouted when the girl was safely aboard, and whacked the pony across its hindquarters.

Despite its double load the pony burst out of the cleft so fast Nai almost lost his seat, and as they rounded the cluster of boulders it broke into a gallop, running sure-footed across the grey grass.

Gorthyn heeled his own horse out of the shelter, wrestling furiously with the reins, for the beast had panicked (he himself was not far from panicking) and wanted to run blindly into the trees where he believed the enemy waited. More by luck than judgement he turned it to follow Nai, wishing, as a spear shattered on the boulders, that he had worn mail to come on this scouting trip rather than a light leather jerkin.

Something howled in the undergrowth behind him. Trusting the pony to pick its own footing, he glanced back and saw grey shapes flitting wraithlike beneath the trees, pacing them. His skin crawled.

The spine of the ridge swung to the north-west, and Nai stayed with it, reckoning the slope on either side far too dangerous for a midnight gallop. Gorthyn's pony, having worked off its initial panic, had steadied now to staying close behind the other, which was battling bravely with the added weight of the girl.

The howling came again from among the trees below them. Nai, his eyes watering with the wind of their passage, blinked and searched the black mass of foliage for some hint of its cause. The girl screamed. He wrenched his attention back, and heaved the pony round in a circle.

Rising from a mass of brambles was a figure in white, its arms flapping like a living scarecrow, its head lolling at an unnatural angle. By the time Nai had fought the pony to a standstill he was near enough to see the figure's eyes were shut.

Eurgain was sobbing and screaming incoherently into his shoulder. Suddenly he realized that the sound she kept repeating was 'Father, Father'.

Gorthyn leaned across and swung with his sword. Only the very tip connected, scraping a long weal in the thing's cheek, and as the blade touched the eyelids flicked open. Nai was so close now, his pony fretting and snorting, that he could see the moon-light reflected in the liquid sheen of the eyes though he knew no man could live long with a neck at that angle.

'Ride!' shouted Gorthyn, but although they both tried with all their skill they could not coax either horse past the figure in the brambles. The ponies bucked and reared, twisted and shied, ran in tight circles, did everything except go forward.

'They will be on us in a moment!' Gorthyn cried out in desperation.

The grey shapes he had seen earlier came bounding out from under the trees. There were far more of them than either man had expected. Nai threw a javelin, then used the haft of another to beat his pony, mad now with terror, back the way they had come, where the things seemed fewest. Gorthyn forced his own horse to keep pace with Nai's on the right-hand side so that the girl was covered by both shields.

Together they rode at the shadowy line of their pursuers. Gorthyn wielded his sword, once, twice, though he could not be certain if he had struck anything.

Nai couched the javelin like a lance and, gripping with his calves for all he was worth, stabbed down at a wolflike shape. Despite his precautions the impact almost unseated him; only by dropping the spear could he save himself.

Then they were clear, and running once more along the spine of the ridge beneath the moon's cold light, following their own track through the silver grass, neither with any idea of what to do next.

'We cannot return to the rocks!' shouted Nai, his damaged voice hoarser than ever.

'Do you think they drive us?' bellowed Gorthyn. 'Try to trap us against the cliffs?'

The ponies were blowing hard when they came again to the pile of boulders which had given them shelter. The Britons did not hesitate, but kept going, pushing the poor beasts on along the ridge, snatching quick glimpses over their shoulders at the things loping gently in their tracks.

'They seek to run us ragged!' Nai yelled.

Gorthyn nodded, only half hearing but able to guess what his companion had said.

Having prevented them from breaking inland the creatures now had them trapped in a comparatively small area. On two sides they were bounded by water, the estuary and the sea itself; on the third side the deep valleys would be virtually impassable in the darkness. The fourth side, of course, was barred by the raiders themselves.

Gorthyn let the others draw slightly ahead then looked behind him again. The pack had spread, some running faster than others, though none seemed to be running at full pelt. He still could not make up his mind exactly what they were, but they seemed closer to wolves than any other creature, although he had always been told wolves did not really hunt men in packs outside old wives' tales.

A great whoop burst from Nai, and a moment later he, Eurgain and his pony had vanished from sight. They had reached the valley the girl had warned them about. Gorthyn's horse faltered, then, driven by the howling behind, scrambled down the slope, slipping and sliding, he trying to keep his weight back and failing more often than not, the pony stumbling, falling to its knees, pushing up again, carried as much by the slope and its momentum as any effort it was making now, skidding to avoid the trees and bushes, its rider scraped and scratched by the brambles and hanging branches, until suddenly they were on the flat beside a stream and he slid slowly and inevitably over its neck and the ground was hard indeed.

Winded, he staggered to his feet, watching the rim of the ravine – lit with shadowless clarity by the moon – for any sign of their pursuers.

'Are you all right?' said Nai, who had dismounted and was checking his horse's legs.

Gorthyn grinned, his teeth white in the dark. 'They're not following!' he said, not yet believing it.

'Called them off, I expect. Why risk coming after us in the dark when they have us trapped till daybreak?' Nai straightened, and, seeing the big man was still breathless, began to inspect his pony for him. 'There is something the matter with the girl. She won't speak or move.'

'Shock,' said Gorthyn. 'What she's been through these last few days would have killed most people. We'd best keep her warm, if we can, till morning. How are the ponies?'

'Finished. But they will be all right after a rest. They don't seem cut or bruised, though God alone knows why not. None of us is fit to go far.' He scanned the hillside. 'You don't think there is a way round?' he said uneasily.

'Bound to be,' said Gorthyn cheerfully. 'But I think you were right the first time. They will bide until dawn to move against us again.' He looked about him uncertainly. 'Let us find a place to wait out the remainder of the night.'

'This way then,' said Nai, turning upstream. 'The other leads to the sea.'

They spent a restless night, worrying about the girl, worrying about the enemy. Although they took it in turns to stay on watch, the one who was supposedly sleeping never did more than drowse, coming awake with a violent start at every rustling leaf.

When the dawn began to lighten the sky they were glad to drop all pretence of resting, to rise stiffly to their feet, splash water from the stream over their faces, and try to rouse the girl.

250

'This is more than just shock,' said Gorthyn. 'She has withdrawn deep within herself. Look at the way she lies huddled in a ball. When did it happen? She was frightened yesterday, but not like this.'

Nai moved to his side and stared down at Eurgain. 'I think it was when that thing forced us to turn back on the ridge last night.' He rubbed at the shadows beneath his eyes. 'She muttered something about "father". I thought at first she was praying, but afterwards I wondered whether she meant it *was* her father.'

Gorthyn shivered, gazed blindly at the stream, the morning mist rising grey from its surface, the narrow channel clogged with sticks and leaves and needles, seeing and not seeing it.

'Why do you think they stopped last night? Had they followed us down we would be dead.'

Nai coughed, clearing his throat, scratched at the scar. 'I think they are more afraid of us than we of them. Last night they probably took us for scouts from a larger force and wanted no more than to prevent us from leaving the peninsula.'

Gorthyn frowned. 'How many of them do you think there are?'

Nai shrugged. 'Not so many as there were. Perhaps twenty left unwounded. And those hounds.'

He began saddling the ponies. Gorthyn bent over the girl, gently shaking her shoulder. She did not move, so after a moment he strode to the stream, cupping his hands to gather water, and returning splashed it across her face.

She awoke with a shriek, sat up wild-eyed, glaring at him.

The big man grinned. 'I should have been a leech. I missed my calling.'

Her eyes suddenly went very round, showing the whites.

'No!' he said sharply. 'Stay with us. We need you.'

She gasped, panted heavily, gradually brought herself under control, though her body was still racked by fits of shivering.

'It was all real then,' she said, her voice shrill. 'I hoped it was a nightmare.'

Nai freed the ponies from their tethers and led them to the stream. 'Which is the easiest route out of this valley?' he rasped without looking at her.

'Upstream,' she said. 'Where are you going?'

Surprised, he swung round and stared at her. 'You mean where are we going. You don't want to remain here alone, do you?'

Hope dawned on her face. 'You mean you would take me with you?' She glanced uncertainly from one to the other.

'Of course we will,' Nai said impatiently. 'We cannot leave you here with those savages about. What do you take us for?'

She shook her head. 'I don't know. I don't know anything about you. I don't even know which of you is the leader. Sometimes it seems to be him –' she pointed at Gorthyn '– and sometimes you.'

'I'll tell you,' Nai laughed. 'It's a secret, so don't tell Gorthyn. I am the one in charge, but because he is so big and his feelings are easily hurt, I allow him to think that he is the one who makes the decisions. Anyway, he likes talking, and I do not, because it hurts my throat.'

Her eyes went to Gorthyn, who twitched his brows, solemn-faced. She giggled, pushed aside the blanket with which they had covered her during the night, and stood.

'Thank you,' she said gravely, half bowing to each in turn. 'I am all right now.'

'Good,' said Gorthyn, with heartfelt relief. 'Now,' he added briskly, and though he did not rub his hands together Eurgain felt he should have done, 'tell us what you know about these raiders.'

She drew a deep breath, and the words came gushing out of her. 'I hid and overheard them talking. They were going to attack Penhyle, and the leader was telling his two chieftains – most of them looked half starved, but these three were big men with shirts of ring mail – not to kill all the people but to let some get away. He said that the druid would win the land for them, and I hid and watched the druid chanting and dancing, and he made the wood I had known all my life seem like a bad place, so I ran, but earlier I had seen them taking the heads to the sanctuary and that's when I saw the leader, Eremon he was called, talking with the others . . .'

Gorthyn held up a hand. 'Whoa, whoa. Eremon, you said?'

'One of the others, Dovnuall I think his name was, Dovnuall Brecc – he had a pockmarked skin, you know?'

She looked at Nai, who nodded encouragingly.

'But no, it was the tall one he was talking to then, Serach, and he said his full name . . .'

'Eremon of the Eoganacht Maigi Dergind i nAlbae,' Nai said quietly in his ruined voice. 'Eremon mac Cairbre.'

'With Serach and Dovnuall Brecc,' Gorthyn frowned. 'It is true then. Dovnuall Frych,' he mused, giving the name its British form. 'Freckled Dovnuall. I have a score to settle with that one.'

'Who are they?' demanded Eurgain. 'You know them?'

'Since childhood,' said Gorthyn. 'Cairbre was lord of the lands around the River Oak. His great-grandfather settled there in the days of the High King, Gworthigern the Thin, and for many years lived peacefully with his neighbours. Cairbre's brother was Lleminawg the Fated, who fought beside Arthur, but after Arthur fell at Camlann his descendants grew too proud. Eremon is mad, and always has been. He dreamed of ruling eastern Dumnonia – and probably the west as well, in time – and his rule would not have been a pleasant one. So we put him down.'

'Not easily,' said Nai, rubbing the scar on his throat. 'He gave me this.'

'And Dovnuall killed my father.' Gorthyn's face was grim.

'He . . .' Eurgain faltered. 'He raped my sister. They all did, but he began it.'

'It is in my mind that Dovnuall Frych has lived too long.' Gorthyn shook his head like one waking from a dream. 'So, Eremon has indeed returned to Prydein. And with a druid, you say?'

'I didn't know what he was until I heard them talking. His head is shaved like this –' she ran her fingers through her hair '– and he has a face like a weasel.'

'Like a priest,' growled Nai.

Gorthyn grinned. 'Not all priests look like weasels.'

'I meant the hair.'

'All holy men shave their heads the same way. Druid, priest,' the big man shrugged. 'What's the difference.'

'This one is evil,' said Eurgain.

'So are some priests,' muttered Gorthyn. 'And he performed some kind of ceremony in the sanctuary?'

'First he brought the heads of my people there and set them up on stakes. Later he added the Saeson heads. Then he chanted about the fruitfulness of the land.' Tears started behind her eyes. 'He took it away from us. It was as if we had never been.'

Nai put an arm around her. At first she stiffened, tried to pull away, but when she realized he was offering no more than comfort she leaned into him and let the tears run freely.

'What do you think?' said Gorthyn.

'I think we should look at this sanctuary.' Nai checked the

bundle of javelins in the quiver on his saddle. 'Either we do that, or else we make a run for it. But Gereint should arrive before long and Penhyle will have been warned of the danger by the people from the ferry. There is no need for us to do anything, and I tell you, cousin, the prospect of another skirmish with these filth fills me with delight.'

To his surprise, he found it was true. His fear of Eremon had left him.

Gorthyn flung back his head and laughed. 'You are right. From the sound of it, there are only the three trained men among them. The rest are peasants given arms. Let us investigate this wood.'

CHAPTER THREE

1

Ceolric woke to light and the sound of birds singing. He rolled over, felt rather than saw somebody leaning across him.

'Who's there?' he said in his father's tongue, sitting up quickly, one hand reaching for his war-knife.

'Be easy,' said a voice in the same language. 'You are safe.'

He grunted ruefully. 'Your pardon,' he said in British. 'I could not remember where I was.'

'Come, break your fast with me,' said the hermit, also switching to his native tongue. 'Bread and honey. The bread is a little stale, but one cannot have everything. There should be some dried figs somewhere as well; I had them from a pedlar in return for treating his foot-rot. I wonder where I put them.'

He rummaged through the depths of a sack.

Ceolric watched him for a moment then rolled to his feet, a more urgent need than food pressing upon him.

They had spent the night within the wood, hidden from prying eyes in a clearing at the heart of a thicket of gorse and brambles. The hermit had shown Ceolric the passage through the briers, leading the way on his hands and knees, then had returned to lace the brambles closed behind them.

The clearing reminded Ceolric of the secret places he had played in as a tiny child. He had inherited a den very like it from his older brothers: a place where he could hide from the household slaves and play his games undisturbed.

His siblings were his only kin, now his father was dead. One brother and the two girls were settled in Cantware, but his eldest brother was somewhere in the wild lands near Sallow Wood, on the western frontier of the Gewisse.

He had forgotten that in yesterday's panic. Alone and with nothing except his war-knife and clothing, he stood small chance of reaching Cantware in the far south-east. But Sallow Wood was a different matter, a third or even a fourth part of the distance.

Feeling happier at this thought he returned to the middle of the clearing, where the hermit had laid two platters of food on the ground. The old man was still wrestling with the sack, which Ceolric now saw was a faded brown cloak tied in a bundle.

'I found the figs,' the hermit said triumphantly, waving at the plates.

Ceolric squatted down and started to eat. 'You live well, much better than I would have expected.'

Budoc put the sack aside and sat awkwardly. His movements seemed stiffer today, less free, as if he had aged overnight.

'The villagers provided for me. You see, we Britons are accustomed to the idea of individuals adopting a contemplative life in old age. Even before we began to follow the way of the Nazarene it was not unusual for people to withdraw from the society of their fellows and live in comparative seclusion. The wise men of old did it, and for much the same purpose, though the Truth had not been revealed to them.'

He snorted. 'No, I am unjust. Let me say rather that they followed a truth, a way, of their own, and I do not think God would condemn them for that.'

Ceolric had grown used to these passages after half a day spent in the old man's company. He understood the hermit was a Christian, a worshipper of the Trinity, and since the man seemed both harmless and amiable he had stopped worrying about it.

'Did you withdraw from life because of your hand?' he asked around a mouthful of bread.

Budoc looked startled. 'My hand? No.' He held his left hand up before him and examined it dispassionately. At some time it had been badly slashed; a thick ridge of white scar tissue ran across the back from the base of the little finger to the base of the thumb. Although the fingers moved, they moved as one, and not very far at that. Ceolric had noticed he rarely used the scarred hand, favouring the other.

'No, no. That happened years ago, when I was a very young man. I was fighting Irish raiders, Scotti, at a place on the northern shores of Dumnonia, and I was careless.'

'You were a warrior?'

The old man smiled at him. 'Yes, I was a warrior. It seems hard to believe now, doesn't it?' He got up from the log, his joints popping and cracking, stretched his sinewy limbs. 'I was a warrior throughout my youth and prime. I was an ageing man when I became a monk, and I would guess that was not long after you learned how to throw a spear.' He smiled again, sadly now. 'So you see, I am a very old man indeed, which is why the presence of these raiders in the village disturbs me so.'

Ceolric stared at him blankly.

The hermit shrugged. 'For many years I have done nothing except watch the changing seasons and contemplate the nature of God. Yesterday I felt something happen.' He studied the youth with serious eyes.

'Not far from here is a holy place, a grove in the forest sacred to the Mother and Son. Do you know who I mean by that?'

'The Mother of all, and her Son who dies and comes again. Baldur the Beautiful.'

'In parts of this island he was sometimes known as Mabon, the young son. Elsewhere they called him Lleu, the Bright One. It does not matter what we call him, so long as we recognize him. I know him as Christ, the Anointed One. Yesterday the grove, his holy place, was desecrated. Somebody is trying to use its powers for their own ends. I must put a stop to it.'

'Why you?' asked Ceolric. The old man did not strike him as a likely figure to put a stop to anything, even if he had been a warrior in his youth.

'There is nobody else. Will you help me?'

Although the words were phrased as a question he was not really asking.

Ceolric considered for a moment. ' "Hapless is he who must needs live alone",' he said aloud in his father's tongue.

' "Courage shall be in a man",' returned the hermit in the same language.

' "By glorious deeds a man prospers among any people",' finished Ceolric. He nodded. 'They killed my father and my friends. There is a blood feud between us. Tell me what you wish me to do.'

'First we must see what faces us. We must visit the sanctuary.'

They crawled through the tunnel between the briers. Budoc paused to remove all traces of their passage, saying that they might want to use the hiding place again. Then he led the way under the trees.

Although Ceolric had always believed himself capable of moving quietly, the hermit seemed to make no noise at all, never to put a foot wrong and break a dead stick or rustle the leaf mould. It was as if he were gliding just above the ground.

'I doubt if we will meet anything,' he said over his shoulder. 'There is nothing up here to attract the raiders except the sanctuary itself, and I would not think they will have set a guard over it. But there is no harm in being prepared.'

He stopped and reached behind a tree trunk, produced a spear and handed it to Ceolric, who stared at him in astonishment.

'Close your mouth, lad. You'll catch flies.' He took a few paces, looked back when Ceolric did not follow. 'I left it there earlier,' he said impatiently. 'Come!'

It grew gloomier as they penetrated further beneath the trees, and the youth found himself glancing around uneasily, starting at the red flash of a squirrel, jumping at the screech of a bird.

Suddenly Budoc held up a hand (the maimed one) and gestured towards a thicket of fern and bramble. Beyond the thicket was an oak tree, and there lay one hind chewing cud and another beside her reaching for the lower branches and plucking the acorns, both so stippled by the sunshine and the shadows of the leaves that they were hard to see.

Even as Ceolric saw them the hinds sensed some danger. They leaped to their feet, coughed twice in warning, and crashed away through the undergrowth.

Budoc put his hands to his head in mimicry of despair and frustration, then motioned Ceolric aside behind the trees.

Long before they could see anything they could hear the jangle of harness coming closer, and voices softly muttering, and then there rode into the clearing around the oak tree where the deer had lain, two men, one carrying a girl pillion, mounted on shaggy brown ponies.

'. . . could have had venison,' the man who rode alone was saying.

Had Ceolric been by himself he would have faded back into the wood until he was well clear and run for his life. Though he had never seen native horsemen before he could tell that these were warriors, and dangerous. The speaker was a large, brawny fair-haired man, bigger and more powerful than most Saxons; the other was smaller and thinner, dark-haired and dark-skinned, but he rode with an air of watchful intensity that frightened the youth. Both were well armed, carried shields – the dark man's somewhat battered, as if he had been in a fight recently – and wore cuirasses of leather polished a deep and supple brown.

'Stay here,' whispered Budoc, slipping silently from his side.

The youth did as he was told, holding his breath while he watched the hermit work his way between the trees till he was ahead of the horsemen. Only when he was sufficiently far away for his sudden appearance not to be seen as a threat did the old man step out from the cover of the trees.

'My greetings to you,' he called, his arms raised to show he bore no weapon.

Ceolric was expecting a reaction of some kind, but the speed of the dark man still took him by surprise. A throwing spear was in his hand before Budoc had finished speaking, and his eyes, having dismissed the old man as a threat, were raking the woods in search of an ambush.

'Come forward,' said the big man, reining in his pony. 'Let us see you clearly.'

He waited until Budoc was within a few paces, then said: 'Are you alone? You look harmless enough, I must say.'

The girl leaned forward from her place behind the dark man – though she was careful not to obstruct his throwing arm – and stared at the newcomer.

'Why, it's the hermit!' she exclaimed.

'It is indeed,' said Budoc. 'And no, I am not alone. I have a friend with me. And we are glad to see you.'

'Nai?' queried the big man.

'One behind the ash fifteen paces away in the direction of winter sunset,' rasped the dark man. 'I see no others.'

Ceolric was startled both at the sound of the raw and ruined voice and at the ease with which the man had spotted him. He came out, carrying the spear sloped across his shoulder so it did not look menacing.

'A pirate!' snarled the big man. He glowered at the youth, at the hermit, at the youth again.

'You did from the boat come, boy?' he asked in heavily accented Saxon when it became obvious nobody was going to offer any explanation.

It took Ceolric several moments to work out what he had said. 'Yes,' he replied in British. 'The raiders slew my friends, but I escaped.'

'Ran away like a rat,' growled the fair man. 'What are you doing now? Looking for something to steal?'

'Seeking vengeance.' Ceolric kept his answer brief to avoid betraying his fear by a tremor in his voice.

The big man flung back his head and roared with exaggerated laughter. Then he leaned forward in the saddle and said: 'Let me tell you, boy, these are our woods and our valleys. What walks in them is ours, and it is for *us* to decide whether it lives or dies, not some dirty little thief.' He held Ceolric's eyes with an unblinking gaze.

'Now, because I am a merciful man I shall give you a chance. Walk westwards along the cliffs until you come to a place you can steal a coracle, then paddle away to your gallows-bait friends. If I see you again I shall kill you as I would kill any other vermin I found infesting good land – but for the moment you may live. Now go!' he barked.

Ceolric glanced uncertainly from one to the other of the horsemen. Only in the eyes of the girl did he see any signs of sympathy. Shouldering the spear (which had somehow finished up pointing at the fair man, though he seemed singularly unmoved by the implied threat) the youth turned aside to push a path through the undergrowth.

'Wait,' said Budoc, so softly the word barely reached his ears. He waited.

'Gorthyn mab Erfai mab Amren mab Petroc,' said the hermit slowly, making every name in the lineage bite the air so it seemed they hung between them. 'You are a fool. You are a fool if you turn away an armed man prepared to assist you.'

Gorthyn went pale, crossed himself, made the sign to avert the evil eye. Then he gathered himself and sneered:

'No doubt the very argument Gworthigern the Thin used when he invited the Saesons to his aid in the first place.'

The hermit laughed. 'Well spoken! Perhaps you are not such a fool after all.'

'Who are you?' demanded the big man rudely. 'How do you know my name and family?'

'I am Budoc, and as Eurgain has told you, I am a hermit. I know you by your resemblance to your father, and because I have heard that the son of the man I once knew rides with a companion called Nai.' He raised his hands, amusement on his face. 'You see? There is nothing magical about it.'

Gorthyn peered at the old man suspiciously, then turned to the girl. 'You are sure you know him? Is he to be trusted?'

Eurgain looked startled. 'Of course I know him. As to trusting him . . . My father did. I do.'

'And where is your father now?' muttered the big man, staring from Budoc to Ceolric in a manner the latter did not care for at all.

'They are not Scotti,' Nai said wearily in his ravaged voice. 'And the old man is not a Saeson. We can trust them well enough for the present.'

Gorthyn frowned, shrugged. 'On your head be it,' he said.

Nai showed his teeth in a mirthless grin.

The two groups quickly exchanged stories, Ceolric and the hermit giving their own versions of what had befallen them, Gorthyn doing all the talking for his party while Nai kept watch on the trees.

'Hounds?' said Ceolric when the big man had finished. 'I have heard of dogs trained to battle, though I have never seen them.'

Gorthyn ignored him, spoke directly to the hermit. 'They must have called them off last night once they had us trapped in the woods. It's curious that they have not arrived to finish us.'

'Perhaps they have gone,' Ceolric suggested eagerly.

Gorthyn turned on him a look of such contempt that he blushed and slipped behind the hermit.

'The lad has a point,' Budoc said mildly. 'They seem to have lost a large number of men in a short space of time. I doubt if they are keen to face more warriors.' He looked to Eurgain. 'You think they killed everybody in the village?'

She nodded awkwardly, the muscles of her face tightening.

The hermit reached out a hand – the damaged one, the stiffened fingers at variance with the warmth of the gesture – and squeezed her shoulder.

'I am sorry,' he said. 'They were good people.'

He released her and stared up at Gorthyn, frowning slightly. 'Sounds like blood lust. I have seen such things before, and not confined to the Scotti either. Once they start killing, they cannot stop.'

The big man met his gaze, returned the frown. 'Eurgain says they came here, into the wood.'

'I know. I felt the magic worked by their druid. Ceolric and I were on our way to the grove to see if we could undo it.'

'And how were you going to do that?' There was a note of contempt in Gorthyn's voice, faint, but clear enough to the listeners.

Budoc smiled. 'Follow me and you will find out.'

The big man glanced across at Nai, grimaced angrily, and allowed the hermit to lead the way.

They went on in silence for a while, Budoc deep in thought. Leaves flashed blue and silver as the breeze lifted them, and the air was heavy with the scents of pollens. It seemed impossible that anything could be wrong in such an idyllic place.

Even Ceolric, who had a superstitious dread of the island's forests, felt tempted to sit down with his back to a convenient trunk and while away the morning watching sunbeams dance.

Budoc alone seemed completely unaffected.

'We are almost there,' he whispered to Gorthyn. 'Do we enter the sanctuary as a group, or should we scatter?'

The big man reined in his pony. 'What do you think, Nai?'

'Leave the ponies here. We cannot all escape on them, and they may panic if we do find something. You and I first, you with sword and me with javelins. Then Eurgain and the hermit, then the Saeson with his spear.'

Ceolric watched the Britons dismount and leave the ponies to browse. Ahead were clear signs of a path, descending into a hollow. He trailed sulkily in the rear, giving the horses a wide berth, lest they lash out with a hoof.

The girl peeped over her shoulder at him and half smiled. He straightened and strode after her, watching the way the sun caught her hair and filled it with the glow of molten copper, trying over her name in his mind. *Eurgain*. In his mother's tongue that would mean something like 'golden fair' or 'fair excellence', an apt name for so beautiful a creature.

'What is this sanctuary for?' he muttered to Budoc, asking the question so he would have an excuse to edge closer to the girl.

'It is a place where our ancestors talked to the land. Some say it answered them.'

Gorthyn was not at ease. The girl had vouched for the hermit, which might mean he was what he appeared to be – but that naming had been disconcerting. As for the Saeson . . . Vermin was vermin, whether Saeson or Scotti.

Nai held up a hand for silence. Before them was the daylight of a large clearing. Gorthyn eased himself around the gnarled trunk of an oak and peered out across the open space.

A double ring of posts met his eye, arranged according to some strange design he could not fathom, though the pattern of them nagged at his mind. Each post bore a blind burden, part pecked by the rooks and crows that sat calling harshly back and forth in the surrounding trees.

Gorthyn considered himself a strong-stomached man, but the sight was almost too much for him. Some of the heads were very small, and many of those nearest him had belonged to women.

Nai tapped his arm. 'Is it clear?'

'Clear?' he mumbled. 'Oh yes, it is clear all right.' He swallowed hard. 'Keep the girl well back. Don't let her see this.'

'What about the boy?' whispered Nai. 'Some of them were his friends.'

Gorthyn nodded. 'Him too,' he muttered, surprised at his own magnanimity.

Between him and the open ground were the remnants of a bank which must once have divided the grove from the forest, its soil bound together by the roots of the trees which poked and twisted through it like serpents.

His eyes returned to the posts. Nothing moved except the flies floating lazily around the heads.

'Wait for me,' he breathed in Nai's ear. He scrambled down the bank, the earth sliding beneath his feet, the roots reaching to trip him, and stood on the edge of the clearing, watching and listening.

Even the birds were still.

He began to walk across the open space, very slowly, gingerly, all his nerves and instincts screaming that there was something unnatural, something wrong about this so-called sanctuary, something over and above the posts and their hideous fruit.

A flicker of movement made him jump, shield raised, to face the danger. Nai bellowed a warning at his back.

263

A white stag bounded across the clearing, leaping with an effortless grace, travelling at speed but not pushing itself to the limit, and Gorthyn, recognizing this as a sign from some god (which god he had no idea), remained perfectly motionless, waiting to see what the creature would reveal to him.

It jinked between the posts with their foul burdens, and he raced after it, all thoughts of caution abandoned, his feet slipping in the grass, desperate to follow where it led.

The ground grew wetter and soggier, until he was squelching through mud. The stag leaped over something that lay at the heart of the circle, twisted through the maze of stakes, and vanished on the far side of the grove, but by then what it had shown him was enough to make him forget about magical beasts for the moment.

He knelt in the centre of the lawn, careless of the seeping damp, his battle-scarred hands digging at the broken shards of stone, trying to free the water so it could run in its proper channel.

Waiting under the cover of the trees while the big man walked out into the open, Ceolric found himself wondering whether he would not have done better to remain by himself. The hermit was friendly enough, but he had the feeling he had been only a heartbeat from dying when Gorthyn first clapped eyes on him.

He was not at ease in the company of these strangers. Nor did he care for this sanctuary of theirs. It made him feel uncomfortable. The girl was pretty, though . . .

She was staring at the edge of the clearing, at the old man and the dark warrior crouching among the branches. He followed the direction of her gaze. The dark one, Nai, was standing absolutely motionless, so still he seemed a part of the tree, all his senses concentrated on his friend in the open grove. In that moment he seemed to Ceolric the most dangerous man he had ever met, even more dangerous than big blustering Gorthyn.

He turned to Eurgain, thinking he should try to distract her from the horror of what lay beyond the fringe of trees.

'I am sorry about your family,' he said awkwardly.

'So am I.'

Her voice was cold and dry.

'You – ah – you know these two warriors?' he went on, struggling to start a conversation.

At first he feared she had not heard, and was about to repeat the question when he realized she was studying him, scrutinizing him as she might have scrutinized a strange fish in her father's catch.

'No. Gorthyn told you. We met for the first time yesterday evening.'

'Oh. Yes, of course he did.' Ceolric was holding his breath in a desperate attempt to check the burning of his cheeks. The words came out half strangled. 'It is just that I wondered. Why does Gorthyn keep calling the dark one, the one with the damaged voice, nephew?'

'He doesn't. That is his name: Nai. I believe it is not uncommon. Most names mean something. Is it not so among your people?'

Ceolric shrugged. 'I suppose it is. I do not think of them that way in my own tongue. A name is a name, until you start speaking another language.'

'You have a funny accent. Not like I thought a Saeson would talk, all growls and barks like a dog.'

'My mother was of the Cantii, in the east of this island, I learned your tongue from her, but she died when I was still quite young.'

'And now you are old?' she asked with a flash of mischief.

'Older than I was.'

'We are all that,' she said, and her face was sad again as she turned back to watch the clearing.

A shadow fell across Gorthyn where he knelt beside the shattered basin. He glanced up and saw the hermit.

'Nai is pulling down the stakes,' Budoc said grimly. 'I made the children stay behind the trees.'

'Look what they have done,' said Gorthyn. 'Look!'

Even to his own ears his voice sounded strained.

'The stag showed me. Did you see it?'

The hermit squatted beside him. 'Yes, I saw it.' He helped Gorthyn sort the broken pieces of the basin into which the spring had bubbled.

'What shall we do?' the big man asked plaintively. 'We cannot mend it.'

'No,' said the hermit wearily. 'No, we cannot mend it.'

Together they scooped aside the mud and dirt blocking the channel, letting the little brook flow as it should.

'You said you knew my father,' said Gorthyn.

Budoc nodded.

'It was one of the Scotti who face us now that killed him.'

'Dovnuall Brecc,' said the hermit.

Gorthyn stared at him. 'How did you know that? Who are you?'

'I rode with your father and your grandfather once upon a time.' The old man grimaced. 'My son is dead. With no close kin of my own, I started to follow the doings of my former comrades and their children. As I said before, there is nothing very surprising about it.'

Gorthyn straightened, looked around him. Nai had pulled all the posts from the ground and gathered them together in a great pile.

'What are we going to do with them?' said the big man. 'We cannot just leave them.'

Budoc pointed. 'See where that tree has fallen?'

On the far side of the lawn was the broken trunk of a great oak tree, brought down in one of the winter gales. When it fell the roots had ripped up the boulders and rocks through which they had grown, tearing them from the earth.

Gorthyn strode across the lawn, beckoning to Nai as he went, more decisive now that Budoc had suggested a solution to the problem. He made his way to the roots of the fallen oak (still encrusted with dirt and lumps of rock three men could not have lifted), and peered into the deep pit.

'We could bury the heads here,' he said to Nai.

Together they ferried the posts to the hole (watched all the while by carrion birds in the boughs) and pushed them in, then kicked down enough dirt to hide them.

Gorthyn rubbed his hands in the clean earth. 'If we roll some rocks on top, then fill it with soil . . . Call up the Saeson. He can do the digging.'

The hermit murmured a prayer while the others waited at a respectful distance.

Then Gorthyn bent at the knees, put his arms around a boulder, and straightened. Breathing heavily but evenly the big man staggered a few paces and let go. The boulder thumped to the ground, half bounced, and slid into the pit.

Gorthyn turned to the youth with an air of challenge.

Ceolric frowned, searched about him for a suitable rock, found one on the far side of the hole. It was larger than Gorthyn's, and differently shaped: the Briton had chosen a solid lump not much longer than it was broad; the Saxon chose something shaped more like a pillar.

He clamped his hands around one end and began to wrestle the stone up out of its bed of earth. It came slowly. When the end was high enough he slipped his shoulders underneath and pushed with all his strength, straightening his legs. The slab tipped end over end, collided with Gorthyn's rock, driving it deeper into the cavity, and came to rest in an upright position, like a menhir, with most of its length buried in the hole.

Gorthyn laughed, clapped the youth on the back, then stepped forward and peered into the pit.

'Well, that should prevent anything digging them up again.' He glanced at Eurgain, who sent a stream of dirt down into the hole, muttering the old prayers to the powers of the place, though she knew they were lost to her, lost by the druid's magic. At the same time Nai started throwing in some smaller rocks, and Ceolric followed suit. Soon the pit was half full.

Gorthyn dropped another great boulder beside Ceolric's pillar.

'One more,' he puffed, swaying slightly.

Nai looked up, saw the expression on the big man's face, and contented himself with a nod, though his eyes followed Gorthyn as he sweated over a third boulder.

At length they had finished. They stood in a ring to admire their handiwork.

'That should keep them safe,' said Ceolric.

Nai laughed sardonically. 'I should hope so. All that remains now is to stop the Scotti adding a fresh pile.'

'And to do that,' Budoc said quietly, 'we must break their druid's hold upon the land.'

They turned to stare at him.

'Can you not feel it?' he said. 'A sense of wrong?'

The others nodded: Eurgain first, for she felt it most strongly, then Ceolric and Gorthyn, both still puffing from their exertions, and lastly Nai, who was watching the hermit with the intensity with which he would have watched an opponent in battle.

Budoc strode to the centre of the grove, to the broken remnants of the basin where the spring welled up from the earth.

'Not the first time such a thing has happened. They use their magics to change the world around them.'

His voice was resonant, and there was an air of command about him which had earlier been lacking except in that brief moment of their first meeting when he had called Gorthyn to account.

Who is he? thought Nai.

'Pray with me,' said the hermit, bowing his head and crying out in a great voice that sent the carrion birds leaping from the boughs of the trees and scattering into the air, croaking dismally.

> 'Aid us, oneness of Trinity; pity us, threeness of
>   Unity
> Help us who are placed in peril as of a mighty sea
> So that the machinations of our foes may not suck
>   us under
> Protect us, Lord, with your unconquerable power.'

This is no ordinary man, thought Nai. *That is a war shout, like the one they say Cei raised before the hosts of the Saesons at Badon Hill: a shout that slew three score champions of that nation before ever a weapon was bared.*

> 'Here I stand:
> Might of Heaven
> Bright of Sun
> White of Snow
> Light of Fire
> Power of God protect me
> Wisdom of God defend me
> Eye of God oversee me
> Ear of God overhear me . . .'

Ceolric shivered. Although he knew little of the god Budoc was calling upon, he recognized the form of words, and he could feel the powers the hermit was summoning to the grove, could sense the air rippling and bending around him even as the waters of the deep ripple and bend before the passage of the Leviathan.

> 'Invoking these powers
> against those dark forces that oppose me
> against the incantations of false prophets
> against the black laws of paganism

268

against the deceit of idolatry
against the spells of druids
against all knowledge forbidden the human soul
against the bloody rites of the Crooked Lord of the
     Mound . . .'

Now Gorthyn shuddered, for he had heard tales of the Crooked Lord, the Bowed One of the Mound, the eater of children who dwelt on the Plain of Adoration in Ierne.

'The Son with me, the Son before me
the Son behind me, the Son in me
the Son under me, the Son over me . . .'

Eurgain held her breath as the hermit completed his prayer of protection, muttering her own appeal to the Mother and Son whose shrine this was, begging for an end to the slaughter and a return to the eventful eventlessness of her life before the coming of the Scotti, when nothing changed save the passing of the seasons and the timeless turning of the stars about the axis of the world.

Budoc knelt and plunged his maimed left hand into the spring. He flung back his head (white hair fluttering as if in a gale, though there was no wind) and shouted to the sky, where the black birds flocked and wheeled:

'Cursed be those who have wrought these harms
Cursed be those who slay the farmer and the fisher
Cursed be those who kill the little ones.
Cursed be those who seek the Isle of the Mighty
Cursed be those who desecrate her shrines
Cursed be those who bloody her shores.
Cursed be those who break their oaths
Cursed be those who betray their ancestors
Cursed be those who forget their honour.
Nine times I curse them
By three and by three and by three
In the name of the Father and the Son and the
     Holy Spirit
In the name of the Matron and the Mother and
     the Maid

In the name of the Crow and the Rook and the
Raven.'

As he finished he flung up his arms to the heavens, and the birds
descended upon him, mobbing his lean form so that he was
hidden from sight beneath their blue-black mass.

Ceolric would have darted forward to rescue him, but Nai held
him back.

'No,' he said in his voice which was itself like a raven's croak.
'This is part of it.'

The youth watched aghast as the birds seemed to crawl all over
the old man, shouting and crying, fluttering away to make room
for another then returning, screaming raucously, demanding to
be allowed space.

'What has he done?' demanded Gorthyn. 'What has he done?'

'Wakened something,' said Nai. 'Something that was sleeping.'

'Who is he?' The big man had moved closer to his friend so he
could not be overheard by the youngsters above the noise of the
birds.

'I am not sure.' Nai frowned. 'But I am beginning to guess.'

He was about to say more when the birds rose in a thunder of
wings, spiralled around the hermit's head and funnelled away
into the sky.

Suddenly there was silence.

2

For a long while nobody spoke. Budoc staggered to his feet, his
face lined and drawn, his robe more ragged than ever, but
otherwise miraculously unharmed.

After a time Gorthyn shuffled his feet, realized what he was doing
and stopped at once. 'What is the quickest route to the village?'

'Straight up the hill to where we were last night,' said Eurgain.
'And then down the far slope by the path we took yesterday
evening.'

Gorthyn grunted, glanced at the sky. 'Not yet midday,' he
muttered to himself. 'Well enough, we have time to spare before
sunset.' He turned briskly to the others, who stood looking at him
– all except Nai, who had returned to watching the woods around
them with his customary vigilance.

'Come, let us find somewhere we can take counsel.'

By tacit agreement nobody mentioned what they had just seen, and nobody made the obvious suggestion that they should stay where they were in the open space of the lawn. Instead they trailed after the big man, Budoc needing a helping hand from Eurgain to climb the bank.

'I think,' Gorthyn said when they reached a fallen log marking a fork in the path, 'that we must visit the village. We need to know how many Scotti are left and what they are doing.'

He glanced at Nai, who was inspecting the canopy of leaves around them, then continued: 'What we do depends on their numbers. Help should arrive soon.' He sighed, scratched his head. 'It might be best if you three returned to one of Budoc's hiding places and waited for us there. Ceolric . . .'

Ceolric looked up at the mention of his name. He could not understand the purpose of the discussion; to him it seemed obvious they should move as fast as possible now Budoc had broken the druid's magic.

'We are wasting time,' he said. 'We must go to the village and see what befalls us there. We should all go; we should stay together.'

Gorthyn scowled. He had begun to develop some tolerance, if not liking, for the youth. Now, at the criticism of his leadership, that tolerance evaporated. About to make a savage reply, he saw both the girl and the hermit watching him.

'Very well,' he growled. 'Let us go to the village.' He swung sharply on his heel 'You three start walking; Nai and I will fetch the ponies and catch you up.'

Still seething he stormed away along the path in the direction of the horses, Nai following with a wry grin.

'We had better make a start,' Budoc said quietly. 'I do not think he is in any mood to wait for us.'

Aided by the girl, he scrambled up from the log, pushed aside a low branch and started along the other fork, at once blending so completely into his surroundings that when Gorthyn looked back, regretting his anger, he could see only the two youngsters slipping like shadows between the trees.

'The hermit,' Nai said thoughtfully, hauling himself up into the saddle.

The big man grunted.

'Who do you think he is?'

Gorthyn shook his head. 'I do not know.' He looked curiously at his companion. 'What was it you were going to tell me?'

Nai eased his pony into a walk. 'Did you notice his hand?'

'Not specially. There was something wrong with it.'

'A sword cut severed the sinews, a long time ago.'

They rode in silence for a while, Gorthyn waiting for his friend to reveal his train of thought.

'He said he knew your father,' Nai said, his voice so harsh it startled an answer from a crow in the treetops.

'Many people did.'

Nai shifted in the saddle, stared at his companion. 'A one-handed man who knew your father and is now . . . what? Old enough to have fought at Camlann.'

Gorthyn reined in his pony. 'No,' he said, disbelieving. He ran blunt fingers across his close-cut beard. 'No,' he repeated, amused. 'No, it cannot be. My father's uncle died fifteen or more years ago. Do you not remember the song? *After many a slaughter, the grave of Bedwyr on the side of Tryfan.*'

Nai quirked an eyebrow. 'And I have heard the same poets sing concerning the grief of Cei at Bedwyr's death, yet I have also heard Cei was killed long before Camlann. Did not Arthur and Bedwyr take vengeance on the sons of Menestyr after Gwydawg their brother slew Cei? How then can Cei have mourned a man who long outlived him?'

'You mean that poets do not see the truth as we do? You are right. But I find it hard to believe that old man was once the mightiest warrior in all Britain. Many a fighting man turns to religion when he grows older, and there must be plenty of people with scarred hands.'

Nai laughed. 'You say that after what we have just seen? What we witnessed was not the work of some old man turned monk or hermit. That was High Magic.' He rubbed at the scar on his throat. 'Budoc was calling on the powers of Albion herself, on the powers of the holy isle which transcends our earthly kingdoms, on the realm of Bran the Blessed and of Caw the Sleeping Giant, on the Raven and the Crow.'

'Hold hard!' spluttered Gorthyn, but Nai leaned forward in the saddle, talking him down, ignoring the interruption.

'Do you not know that some say the soul of the Emperor

Arthur wanders the island even now, in the shape of a great black bird?'

'Oh come, cousin,' protested Gorthyn. 'I enjoy a good tale as much as the next man – more than the next man – but . . .'

'But what?' Nai stared at him until he was forced to drop his gaze. 'Who was the Emperor's wife, the mother of his sons?'

Gorthyn flung his hands into the air. 'What, cousin? Must I be catechized?'

'Who?' There was something relentless about Nai. Gorthyn had seen him look like this in battle.

'Gwenhwyvar,' he said with resignation, realizing he would get no peace until he had played out his friend's game.

'And who was her father?'

'Her father?' repeated the big man, puzzled. 'Let me see. Gwenhwyvar verch Ogrvran Gawr,' he muttered to himself. 'Gwenhwyvar daughter of Ogrvran the Giant.'

'Ogrvran. And what do you think that might mean?'

'Mean?' said Gorthyn. 'It was his name. It does not have to mean anything, any more than your name means nephew.'

'But if it did?'

'Sweet Jesu!' The big man raised his eyes to heaven in despair. 'Then it would mean . . . Vran, Bran: raven, crow, any big black bird. Ogr, ogr . . . Keen, I suppose.'

'So, the Giant Keen-Raven was the father of Arthur's wife. And have you never heard of the giant Bran, the Crow Lord, the great Guardian of this isle, whose head continued to protect the realm from invasion long after his death?'

'Yes, but . . .' Gorthyn began feebly.

'You know all this, with your love of ancient tales, but you do not understand it. Do you not see that Bran sleeps, and in his sleep he sometimes stirs, casting shadows in the world of men? If you like he dreams, dreams of heroes saving his island from danger, and when he dreams strange things happen. Do you not see that the hero comes again and again, in many different guises, sent by the Guardian to aid his people, but whatever his guise his sign remains the same, is always the raven and the crow? It was on the Guardian that Budoc was calling, on the great powers of Prydein. He was fighting the druid's magic with a magic of his own.'

The big man wriggled uncomfortably. 'Even if what you say is true – which I do not believe – it does not make Budoc the same person as Bedwyr.'

He tugged at his beard, shot a weak grin at his friend.

'It is a story, that is all. It has nothing to do with the way things are. It's . . . it's like what they say of Cei, that his breath would last nine days and nine nights under water, or that he could go nine days and nine nights without sleep.'

He gestured expansively as he warmed to his theme. 'Or the stories about horses that can gallop all day and all night carrying seven people, or warriors who can single-handedly defend fords against the entire hosting of their enemies . . .'

'But you saw, Gorthyn!' snarled Nai. 'You saw what I saw. He called the birds to him, and they came.'

'I did not see him call them,' the big man said obstinately. 'They mobbed him, I will grant you, but there may be many reasons why they did that. Have you never heard the priests in church talking of the trickery of the druids of old? He probably feeds them so they know him . . .'

Nai grunted scornfully. 'I do not doubt that he did feed them once, fed them with the corpses of the men he had slain. I say he is Bedwyr.'

Gorthyn frowned, thought about it for a moment. 'I do not believe it,' he said flatly.

Nai shrugged.

They rode in silence for a while, the big man scowling as he considered the implications of what his friend was suggesting.

'No!' he said. 'He cannot be. Bedwyr must be long dead, else we would have heard of his doings.'

'Not necessarily, not if he had retired from life. As you yourself said, many people do. What of the Empress Gwenhwyvar herself? The bards say she rode away from Caer Cadwy when word came of Arthur's fall, and no man knows where she went or what befell her. But that I think is no more than a tale, like Cei being able to stay for nine days under water. I have heard rumours that she took the veil and now rules a house of nuns where once she ruled the household of the Amherawdyr. If she still lives, why not Bedwyr of the Perfect Sinews?'

It was years since Gorthyn had seen his friend so animated, or heard him deliver so long a speech.

'Bedwyr Bedrydant,' he repeated. He shook himself violently, trying to drive out the host of fancies that buzzed within his head. 'No, cousin, no! I do not believe it!'

Nai grinned, knowing he had almost convinced his friend.

'Perhaps I am wrong,' he said in tones which meant the opposite. 'But at the very least grant me this, that friend Budoc was once upon a time a person of some importance.'

'Oh, I'll give you that, certainly. But Bedwyr? No!'

They caught the others at the edge of the wood, where the land rose steeply to the ridge on which they had made their stand the previous night. The hermit was moving slowly, laboriously, and Gorthyn, though he could not quite believe Budoc was his kinsman, out of common courtesy dismounted and offered him his horse.

'You can ride?' he asked doubtfully as he prepared to boost the old man up into the saddle.

'I expect I can manage,' said Budoc. From the corner of his eye Gorthyn saw Nai conceal a grin.

Safely mounted, the old man looked down at Gorthyn and said: 'It might be a good idea if Nai were to scout ahead. I do not like this feeling of being in the bottom of a valley and not knowing what lies on the heights.'

Gorthyn nodded slowly. Although phrased as a suggestion it had sounded more like an order. But it did make sense, and the big man shared the hermit's sense of unease. Besides, now Budoc was mounted he made an altogether more imposing figure, and Gorthyn, whatever else he might have doubted, shared Nai's opinion that the hermit had once been accustomed to command.

In the meantime Nai had urged his pony up the slope to the skyline, the iron-shod hooves cutting turf sods and sending them flying like birds before a thunderstorm. Three hinds broke cover where they had been browsing along the edge of the wood. A skein of wild geese flew overhead, breaking and remaking their V-shaped formation. A wind rose and rocked the trees, tearing loose the older leaves, flinging them skywards in green and yellow spirals. Of a sudden the air seemed filled with omens.

Gorthyn opened his mouth to shout, to call Nai back to the safety of the valley. Then he stopped, told himself not to be so foolish, for in any case it was far too late. Nai was briefly silhouetted on the skyline, and then he was gone.

'It is good to be in the open again,' said Ceolric, oblivious to the big man's apprehension. 'I do not like the forest.'

'I do not like valleys near the sea,' snapped Gorthyn. 'You never know when pirates are going to sneak up on you.'

'This is a very pleasant valley,' Ceolric said, ignoring the second part of the other's speech. 'If one cleared some of those trees, one could grow good crops here. And the hillside looks like good grazing.'

Gorthyn snorted.

As Nai approached the top of the ridge he found false crest after false crest, luring him higher and higher. When he glanced back his companions were hidden by the folds of the hill, but the skyline drew him onwards, though he was aware a good scout should not lose contact with his main force.

The pony was blowing and its stomach rumbling when at last he reached the summit. He let it recover while he took stock of his position. Before him lay the long, wind-patterned grass, over which they had galloped last night; beyond were the tops of the trees marking the slope leading down to the village. Through the greenery he could see the twinkling of the estuary, deep blue beneath the summer sky, and beyond even that were the purple outlines of the hills he and Gorthyn had crossed before they found the ferry.

The freshening breeze brought the taste of salt and the mewing of gulls. Nai, like Ceolric, was glad to be clear of the trees; he preferred a wide field of vision and the wind in his face.

Riding slowly along the line of the ridge, he searched for the pile of boulders in which they had taken refuge. It was smaller than he had thought, so that at first he doubted whether he had found the right place, but the trampling and the signs of horses were unmistakable.

Nai dismounted, throwing the reins over Coal's head. Quartering the grass, he examined the area where they had fought, seeking some sign of where the bodies had gone. Had they been dragged away by the hounds, or had he imagined that, confused by the darkness? But the grass was too crushed for him to be able to tell what had happened.

He tried casting back along the tracks to where the Scotti had emerged from the trees. He had no difficulty following their trail from the rocks to the beginnings of the wood, but once under the trees the signs vanished, as if the Scotti had sprung out of thin air.

'They probably did,' he muttered to himself.

Remounting, he kicked the pony into a trot and retraced his steps through the rustling grass. The others had almost reached the summit, and when Gorthyn saw him the big man blew out his cheeks in an extravagant sigh of relief.

'I had a bad feeling,' he said.

Nai smiled. 'There is nothing here. It looks as if the Scotti appeared from nowhere when they left the trees. I can see no sign of their passage through the woods.'

Gorthyn shivered. 'I do not like this,' he muttered, staring about him uneasily. 'I do not like this at all.'

The party halted to draw breath on the last of the false ridges. The men, except Budoc who remained upright in the saddle, squatted in a semicircle, and Nai produced a blanket for Eurgain to sit upon. He also produced some dried meat for them to chew while they held a council of war.

Gorthyn spoke first, his eyes fixed on the hermit's face. 'Does it need all of us to go into the village? Would it not be easier, and safer, if Nai and I went alone while the three of you returned to the wood?'

The old man shook his head. 'No, I had rather we remained together. I think it unwise to divide our meagre forces until we have the measure of the enemy. Besides, I must confess to my share of curiosity – I would see these Scotti, perhaps learn something of what drives them to commit such acts as the massacre of Eurgain's kin. And if I come with you, then surely it is simpler if the youngsters come as well.'

Gorthyn glanced at Nai, who showed no reaction. 'Very well. We will scout the village first. If it is empty – and since we have seen no sign of the raiders all day it now seems likely is Ceolric was right – I think it best if the Saeson and I explore inside the huts, while Nai stays outside with you and Eurgain. If they are still there in strength, then we must think again.'

Everybody turned to Ceolric. He flushed, pulled his long knife partway from its sheath, thrust it home again. 'I am willing.' The girl shot him a small smile of encouragement.

Budoc quieted a pony which was fretting slightly, and gazed at Nai, who was chewing stoically on a lump of meat.

'Are you satisfied?'

Nai looked up at him in surprise, squinting against the sunlight. He swallowed, shrugged, swallowed again.

'Then let that be our plan.'

*   *   *

The first thing they noticed was the silence.

The previous day there had been sheep grazing in some of the fields. Now those same fields looked like a battleground. Blood-stained bodies lay everywhere, some frozen in death with black legs sticking pathetically into the air above dirty grey fleeces, others (and this was worse) still writhing painfully in a weird silence. The scavengers had been at work, and even as the group's stunned gazes swung from corpse to corpse a crow took flight with something glistening in its beak.

Over it all hung a stench of death and mutton, so strong that Gorthyn looked up, expecting to see a grey cloud hovering.

'It smells like autumn, like the Bloodmonth,' murmured Ceolric.

'The Bloodmonth?' said Nai.

'When the livestock we cannot feed through winter are slaughtered and devoted to the gods.'

'They loosed the hounds on them,' Budoc said quietly.

Gorthyn stared, his face a mask of distaste. Close at hand was a dead ewe, her belly eaten away and her flesh torn into shreds. He could see teeth marks on the remaining skin.

'Why?' he asked of nobody in particular. 'What pleasure was there in this?'

Eurgain shuddered as they passed a huddle of grey wool atop the bank. 'This one's still alive.'

Gorthyn steeled himself to look. The intestines had been ripped from the living body, but somehow the creature refused to die, lay there writhing in agony. He drew his sword and struck once, hard, so the blade bit into the earth beneath the body.

'It seems . . .' Eurgain swallowed, tried again. 'We were never a rich people, not like Cian's clan over the water. But the waste! All that slaughter of people, and now even the beasts!'

Ceolric put his hand on her shoulder. 'We will stop them,' he promised. 'It will not happen again.'

She laid her hand over his. 'I know you mean well, but that is little comfort to my kin.'

Gorthyn had been about to point out that if the Scotti had not arrived on the scene first, the Saesons would have wrought something remarkably similar, when the hermit caught his eye and winked sardonically. The big man closed his mouth without speaking.

'Two of the curraghs have gone,' growled Nai.

The stream broadened and slowed as it neared the cluster of huts and the creek. The companions found that they too were moving more slowly as the settlement came closer.

There were no signs of life. The huts looked dilapidated: the clay daub had fallen off in several places, baring the woven wattle walls. Even at a distance the timber of the main frames appeared worm-eaten and rotten. The thatch had started to sag, and the reeds and bracken had turned a dull grey brown. The hamlet seemed unattractive and unwelcoming, despite the brilliant sunshine playing on the arm of the estuary beyond.

Gorthyn drew a deep breath.

'Will you wait here?' he asked Budoc.

The old man wrinkled his forehead and peered at the huts. 'If I must.'

Turning to Ceolric, Gorthyn said: 'We will take the ones on the left first. We go in together, in silence, and we take them fast. Understand?'

The youth nodded.

'Nai, will you keep a javelin ready for anything other than us that comes out of any of the doors?'

'Have no fears,' rasped the dark man, adjusting the quiver on his back.

Budoc stretched down an arm to the girl. 'Come, up behind me on the pony. Then we shall be less worry to this warrior.' He grinned at Nai.

They watched the Saeson boy and the big man walk away from them along the path: both fair (if anything Gorthyn's hair was a shade the lighter), both almost of a height, but one nearly half as heavy again. Both held weapons, Gorthyn a yard-long sword which seemed puny in his great fist; Ceolric his war-knife, almost the length of his forearm, the grey blade wickedly sharp.

'He will be safe with him,' Nai whispered to Eurgain. 'Despite his bluster and his sulks, he would never desert a comrade in arms.'

She smiled shyly, not yet willing to admit she cared. 'I know,' she said. 'I know.'

For all his size Gorthyn could move like a cat. He frowned when Ceolric made some slight sound, eased his way towards the leather hanging that covered the doorway of the first hut, and waved the youth into position on the far side of it.

Gorthyn's lips fluttered as he counted silently, readying himself

279

for what must be done. He nodded to Ceolric and raised the hanging far enough for him to slide his considerable bulk around the door jamb without creating a disturbance.

It was hot and stuffy inside, and the stale air reeked with the unmistakable sickly scent of wounds going rotten. He waited for his eyes to adapt to the gloom, aware of the boy slipping in behind him, and while he waited the hut seemed to fill with the uneven rasp of heavy breathing coming from somewhere by the far wall.

He moved forward, skirting around the central hearth, ducking his head between the roof posts, the long sword ready in his hand.

The snoring stopped. Gorthyn froze, holding his breath, eyes straining to make out the shape huddled deep into the couch of skins and ferns.

The man snuffled, grunted, rolled over, moaning softly to himself. Gorthyn struck, hard, and the man made a small choking sound.

Again he waited, listening, sniffing the foul air.

'Pull back the door curtain.'

Ceolric did as he was told and the light came streaming in.

There were more bodies lying against the walls, wrapped in animal pelts so that they merged into the couches. The one closest to Gorthyn had been dead for some time, eyes bulging blankly from under a flop of hair, the bedding around him dark stained with blood where his wounds had burst open in his final throes.

'They are all dead,' whispered Ceolric. 'Why have they just been left like this?'

'Eremon,' growled Gorthyn. 'He has no time for weakness. His followers must keep up with him or else be abandoned.'

He ripped aside the skins and examined the body of the man he had killed.

'See? He would have died anyway in a few days. The weapon rot was deep into his wounds.'

'He looks half starved,' said the youth, staring at the bony ribs and distended belly.

'He is. I would guess that is why they chose to come with Eremon. Much of Ierne is barren, poor land like our own high moors. Anything is better than endless hunger.'

'Even this?'

Gorthyn laughed. 'Perhaps you are right. But what did they

expect? I spent years learning how to use spear and sword and knife and shield, and no doubt you did the same. Carrying a weapon does not make you a warrior, as they discovered.'

He straightened, frowning, wiped his blade on the dead man's blanket. 'Come. We must make sure of the rest of the village.'

Most of the other huts showed signs of recent occupancy – one was filled with sides of beef, all that remained of the butchered herd – but it was not until they entered the last that they found any signs of life.

'Is it a wolf?' Ceolric breathed into Gorthyn's ear as their eyes adjusted and they saw the long grey form stretched beside the cold hearth.

'Too big,' Gorthyn murmured. 'It must be one of Eremon's hounds.'

The creature lay on its side, barely breathing, ignoring their presence. There was a deep wound in its flank which Gorthyn guessed had been caused by one of Nai's spears the previous night. The hound had received better care than the men they had seen: its coat had been shaved and an attempt made to dress the gaping hole. He put out a hand and the great head rose from the floor. Yellow fangs snapped at his wrist. He straightened and stood clear.

'Kinder to make an end,' he said his sword arcing down.

The hound twisted away. The sword bit harmlessly into the earth floor. Off balance, the big man was momentarily helpless as the creature leaped for his throat, lips pulled back in a yellow-toothed snarl.

Ceolric hurled himself forward, using his weight to drive the beast aside, so its jaws closed harmlessly above Gorthyn's shoulder. Half stunned by the collision, the youth tripped over the ring of stones around the hearth and fell among the cold ashes.

Gorthyn dropped his sword and caught the hound by the throat, lifting it into the air, his hands grappling and squeezing, striving to meet through the thick coat. The thing's breath was hot and fetid in his face.

Its paws scraped ineffectually at his chest. He heaved, pushing his thumbs deep into its windpipe. Suddenly the hound began to hurl itself from side to side, wriggling uncontrollably despite its wound. Gorthyn felt his balance going and flung the creature from him, desperately searching for his sword.

'Wotan!' screamed Ceolric as he leaped forward, knife sweeping towards the grey hound's belly.

The hound danced aside and the youth crashed into the wall of the hut, dislodging great chunks of mud daub.

Seizing his sword, Gorthyn swung awkwardly at the beast across the hearth. Again the creature sidestepped, snapping viciously at the Briton's exposed wrist. Gorthyn's ankle turned on something underfoot, and he stumbled, giving the hound time to dart for the doorway.

'Nai!' bellowed Gorthyn at the top of his voice. He glanced down to see what had tripped him, and fought back the vomit that rose in his gorge. It was a human shin, the flesh hanging in ragged strips, red and white around the bone which protruded at either end.

He heard the clatter of a javelin ricocheting off the wattle walls of the hut. Something was growling outside, growling and scrabbling at the leather hanging. Hooves thundered in the confined space between the huts.

Gorthyn hurled himself at the opening, tearing aside the curtain. Blinking in the daylight, he saw the grim figure of Nai galloping down at him, spear poised for use as a lance. He leaped into the shelter of the doorway as the horse reared and Nai pushed home his lance, transfixing the hound, pinning it to the wall of the hut. Still it snarled, biting at the shaft in its side, refusing to die.

Nai sprang from the saddle and struck off the thing's head.

The big man leaned against the door jamb, the tension flowing out of him. 'Well done,' he said weakly. 'Well done, cousin.'

Nai pulled his spear free of the hut wall and wiped the blade till it shone blue in the bright sunshine. 'Where is the Saeson? I promised the girl he would be all right.'

'Here,' said Ceolric, screwing up his eyes against the dazzling light. 'My head hurts.'

Gorthyn put an arm around his shoulders. 'We have done it, my friend. We have done it.'

'I am sorry I was not more help,' said Ceolric, subsiding slowly to the ground.

'You did well.' The big man patted him on the back, and turned to seek Budoc and Eurgain.

CHAPTER FOUR

1

It was Gorthyn, of course, who waded out through the muddy water to examine the curragh, while Nai stayed ashore laughing at the expression on his face.

'I think they have abandoned her,' called the big man. 'No oars, and the sail has gone.'

'If it were not for one thing, I would believe that they have gone for good,' said Nai to the hermit.

'And that is?'

'I can understand Eremon leaving his mortally wounded men. It does not surprise me in the least. But I cannot imagine him deserting one of his precious hounds. He would have slain the brute himself rather than leave it to suffer alone.'

'So you think they will return?'

Nai massaged his throat, taking his time over answering. 'It does not feel as if they will, but . . .'

'Surely they would have taken all that meat from the cattle they killed,' said Ceolric. 'They would not have left it behind.'

'There should be a lot more of it.' Eurgain looked close to tears. 'At least as much again. Ours was a good-sized herd.'

Ceolric put his arm around her and drew her into his shoulder.

'What do you think, Gorthyn?' said the hermit as the big man floundered onto dry land, muttering and cursing. 'Have the Scotti left, or merely gone to raid somewhere like Penhyle?'

'They have gone. They will not be back. Yonder curragh is stripped of everything useful.'

'What should we do?' asked Ceolric, voicing the question that was in everybody's mind.

'We must find a place we can defend,' said Nai. He rubbed again at the scar on his throat. 'How safe is the Sanctuary?'

'The five of us could never hold it against an attack,' objected Ceolric.

'We will not be attacked!' snarled Gorthyn.

'That is not what I meant.' Nai studied the hermit, who was looking more and more exhausted as the day wore on. 'Is the Sanctuary safe?'

'It will not easily be taken again, and certainly not by the same man.' Budoc's face was pale and drawn in the bright sunlight. 'In any case, the druid will have felt what I did at the Sanctuary. He will be suffering from the aftermath, even more so than I. He will not be active for a while.'

'Good.' Nai nodded thoughtfully, glanced round at the others: Ceolric and Eurgain serious, but content to let another decide what should be done; Gorthyn intent upon his every word and move; the hermit slumped in the saddle of the big man's pony, head bowed and eyes closed now he had said his piece.

Nai cursed the wound which had made speech so hard for him, for now if ever in his life he needed to be eloquent. It was Gorthyn he had to convince: the other three would fall in with whatever course of action was proposed. Somehow he had to persuade Gorthyn that Eremon would not so easily abandon his plans, and though he did not know how or why, he knew those plans centred upon the Sanctuary.

'Cousin, you told me you dreamed the night before last of forest trees tossing in a gale.'

'Yes,' Gorthyn frowned. 'What of it?'

'I too, whether waking or sleeping, dreamed of trees.'

'You said nothing.' The big man was puzzled.

'Because I knew nothing. I did not understand what it meant.' Nai shrugged helplessly. 'I am not sure I understand now, but the wood is a place of power – we all felt it today. I believe the wood was calling to us, calling for aid.'

Gorthyn stared at him, let out a yelp of laughter. 'Then we have done it small service. Budoc did all that was needful.'

He felt a glow of triumph. 'Quite so. This has been too easy for

284

us. I think we have yet to play our part.' He indicated the hermit, who seemed to be asleep in the saddle. 'For him it has not been easy at all, and it may well be that our turn is to come.'

'What do you mean?'

'Eremon will be back. He has gone to much trouble and has so far gained nothing. I think we should conduct ourselves accordingly, as men – and women,' he added with a bow to Eurgain, '– who find themselves in the country of their enemies.'

Gorthyn scowled, ran a rasping hand across his short golden beard. 'You may be right,' he said reluctantly. 'And if you are wrong, then no harm will be done by being cautious.' He too glanced at the hermit dozing on the pony. 'The wood is a place of power, yes, but why should Eremon be looking for such a thing? And Vortepor of Dyfed, what has he to do with this?'

'Vortepor?' said the hermit without opening his eyes or raising his head.

'We know Eremon met with the Protector of Dyfed not long ago,' said Nai, concealing his surprise that the hermit had been awake and listening all the while.

'And you assume some connection between that meeting and his arrival here?'

There could be no doubt about the old man's present wakefulness. His head was cocked to one side, and his eyes were bright and sharp.

'It seems likely.'

'So it does, so it does,' muttered Budoc.

'We should leave,' Gorthyn said suddenly. 'If Nai is right, we are not safe here. We have much to discuss, much to think over, and we should find a place we can defend where we can talk these matters out at our ease.'

'My hut,' suggested the hermit. 'It will need cleaning, since the Scotti have befouled it with their presence, but if they do return it is so obvious a place to seek us they may dismiss it as too obvious and pass us by.'

Nai laughed, seeing the sense in this. 'Your hut? Why not!'

Despite his fears there seemed no great urgency to be gone, and before leaving the village they filled the saddlebags with food and drink.

Nai and Gorthyn rode while the others walked. The hermit had insisted on dismounting, saying he would fall asleep again if he remained in the saddle.

285

They travelled along the shore, thus avoiding the fields and their carcasses. Nai looked out at the bright waters of the estuary, waters which he guessed should at this time of day have been dotted with fishing coracles, and saw only emptiness.

He glanced back at Eurgain, who was walking behind him with Ceolric. She was crying to herself, very quietly, and the boy was striding along beside her, stiff and awkward, unsure whether to notice her distress or ignore it. Nai frowned at him. The youngster started guiltily, glared defiantly. Nai shook his head in exasperation, and mimed putting an arm around the girl's shoulders.

Ceolric opened his mouth, closed it again. His eyes stared in mute appeal at Nai, who repeated the mime. Ceolric swallowed, his Adam's apple bobbing visibly, and gingerly eased his arm around Eurgain. They stopped, and Nai let Coal's sway-backed motion carry him on, leaving them behind.

'That was kind,' said the hermit at his side.

He looked down at the white head, grinned, glanced behind him. Gorthyn was ostentatiously ignoring the couple, guiding his pony around them as if they did not exist.

'Even Gorthyn is capable of tact,' he murmured.

The hermit laughed, raising his face to the sun.

Nai studied him. It was a strong face under its hair and beard, but then in his experience, most hermits were strong-willed. The weak were quickly driven mad by solitude. He could imagine this man leading warbands in his youth; despite his sometime vagueness, Budoc was a man accustomed to being obeyed. But what had happened in the Sanctuary was something else again, and every time he tried to think about it he found his mind sliding away to another subject, like the way the needles of the pines along the foreshore were a much paler colour on the underside, so that as the breeze ruffled them one caught glimpses of light green mingled with the dark . . .

What Budoc had wrought in the wood – and Nai was not at all sure what it was the old man had done – had somehow created the world afresh.

As they left the shoreline and began to climb up out of the drowned valley, Nai found himself studying every leaf, every play of light and shadow, as if he had never seen them before, listening to the rustle of small creatures about their business in the long grass, to the trilling and babbling of the birds.

Even the coarse black hairs of Coal's mane were not truly black at all, but a multitude of browns, and the sticky burrs caught in the trailing coat were of a green so vivid it made him want to weep.

Behind him Gorthyn also seemed to have succumbed. The big man had reined in to let the youngsters catch up and was staring at the estuary. Nai knew he was not looking for boats or signs of Eremon's return, but simply studying its beauty.

For it was beautiful, this corner of Dumnonia, beautiful in its trees and its streams and the lines of its hills. Nai felt a sudden surge of love for his land, for Dumnonia of the steep valleys and deep delvings, a surge so powerful he had to bow his head to hide the tears in his eyes.

'What do the Scotti want?' he asked the hermit.

'The Scotti?' Budoc considered the question. 'The land. The druid tried to make it theirs. First the druid broke the centuries of tradition which tethered Eurgain's people to the land and the land to Eurgain's people. He made it virgin, without form and void, as it was in the beginning before the coming of men. Then he began the long process of naming, of defining, of reshaping.'

'But you stopped him.'

The hermit nodded, and Nai did not pursue the matter.

'What will they do now?'

Budoc gave a crooked smile. 'Leave, I trust.'

Nai frowned. 'Vortepor. What of Vortepor?'

'I think Vortepor outfitted this expedition in the hope your friend Eremon might do him a service.' The hermit paused for breath as the slope steepened. 'Eremon had his own plans, and Vortepor's desires have been forgotten.'

'This is what I do not understand. Why Vortepor?'

Budoc made no move to answer. They climbed the hill in silence and passed beneath the trees on its heights.

This was the fringe of the wood in which the sanctuary lay, Nai realized. A thin path wound before them, skirting between thickets of thorn and stands of bracken. He ducked beneath the hanging boughs, wondering whether he should dismount, feeling the twigs scraping through his hair.

'I knew Vortepor once,' said the hermit, shooting Nai a look from under shaggy brows.

'That does not surprise me.'

He halted the pony beside a hazel bush and disentangled a

branch from his shield strap. The birds had stopped singing, and the sudden quiet seemed unnatural.

Coal's head came up with the ears pricked.

Nai pulled the shield onto his arm and reached for a javelin, a small voice inside him shouting, '*Fool, fool, fool!*'

They came from all directions at once, shrieking their war cries. The rush bore Budoc down and away before Nai had time to react. Hands were reaching for Coal's reins, pulling them from his grasp. Fingers were clutching his shield rim, dragging it down; somebody else had hold of his right leg and was trying to push him out of the saddle. He could feel himself slipping as Coal bucked and plunged with teeth snapping and eyes rolling. The spear was long gone from his hand, and he was falling into a forest of arms and legs . . .

Gorthyn waited where the trees began for the youngsters to catch up again. Nai and the hermit were ahead of him, already lost to sight among the dappled shadows. The pony fretted impatiently under him, and he gestured at the youngsters to hurry, feeling a twinge of jealousy at the way the Saeson's arm was draped protectively around the girl – she was really very beautiful.

He wheeled the pony and entered the wood, lying almost flat along the horse's neck to dodge the raking branches. Bits of broken twig and leaf showered around him, and he brushed them away as he straightened in a small clearing, eyes straining through the sun-streaked gloom for some sign of Nai and the hermit.

They were about ten full paces ahead of him, only their movement making them visible among the shadows.

He looked back, making sure the children had closed the gap, and in that brief moment of inattention it happened.

The screaming seemed to fill the wood. Broad-Belly quivered beneath him, danced sideways, frothing at the mouth, head tossing. He tightened the reins with his left hand, reached for a spear with his right, knowing it would make no difference.

They were swarming all over Nai, dragging him from his horse, a rush of men like pale ghosts, waving knives and spears, ululating like forest demons as Nai tumbled into their midst.

Gorthyn threw – not an easy cast among the trees – and saw a man on the outskirts of the mob fall clutching his stomach. Then Nai's pony was rearing, yellow teeth snapping, surging through the crowd as they clung to him like dogs on a stag; Gorthyn whistled, and Coal ran towards him.

'Run!' he shouted over his shoulder to the youngsters. 'Deep!' he added, by which he meant further into the cover of the wood, though he had no time to explain, for Eremon had unleashed his war hounds and the grey shapes were racing after Coal.

He threw a second spear at the nearest hound and missed. Broad-Belly was near as panicked as Coal: he locked his calf muscles tight against the pony's flanks and urged it forward a step, crooning wordlessly, soothingly, while he fumbled for another spear.

Coal caught one hound with a kick to the ribs that sent it flying into a tree stump. At the same moment Nai surfaced from the mob and shouted, 'Go, go!'

Gorthyn hurled the javelin, saw it take a hound full in the chest and bring it down in a confusion of teeth and legs. Nai was gone, buried under a mass of bodies.

Loath to abandon his comrade Gorthyn waited while Coal barged past him, holding Broad-Belly by his own brute strength rather than any skill. The youngsters were away, vanished into the undergrowth, and a third hound was bounding at him, teeth bared. How many more? he thought as he struck down with the sword he did not remember drawing, catching it in mid-leap with a shock that nearly jarred him from the saddle.

Broad-Belly had wheeled in a full circle and was backing towards a tree. Something poked him in the side. Sheer horror shivered down his spine and he knew that he was dead in the brief instant before he realized it was only a branch.

Now some of the Scotti were coming at him. Sweat stung his eyes. He sheathed the sword and seized a javelin, cast and hit his man. If they closed with him they would swarm over him as they had swarmed over Nai. He bellowed, saw the foremost runners flinch, and put his heels to the pony's flanks.

He let Broad-Belly have his head, clung blindly to his back as they careered out into the heat and light of the hillside. He thought – he hoped – the last of the hounds was down, for he feared their ability to follow a trail even in deep woods.

The Scotti he did not rate so highly, and he brought the pony under control part-way down the slope, pulled the now sweating beast round to his left, along the line of the hill. At the same time he unslung his shield and slipped his arm through the straps.

He could hear them crashing through the undergrowth.

Marking the spot where they should appear over the brow of the hill, he chose two javelins from the quiver, quieted the horse and tucked the shield against his body – this was why he had turned to the left along the hill, so they would come against his shielded side.

Though he did not know it his lips were drawn back in a snarl.

They came streaming down the hill, yelling and shrieking in the excitement of the chase. He threw high, arcing the spears above them one after the other, the second in the air before the first had landed, letting the javelins plummet behind the full weight of the iron heads.

Then Broad-Belly was galloping away, hooves churning the soft ground, and behind him a man was screaming his death throes.

He had to find the children. Having drawn the pursuit to himself, he had given them time to escape, but now he *had* to find them again. His mind whirled, close to panic. Horses were useless among trees – they were youngsters, not children – the Saeson was probably capable enough with spear and knife – but men afoot can run down a horse and rider over a distance – make the hunters the hunted.

Was Nai still alive?

Slowing Broad-Belly to a trot, he glanced back the way he had come. The Scotti had abandoned the chase for the present, but he did not doubt that they would come again when they had regrouped.

He whistled for Coal, knowing the pony would not have gone far, and turned for the trees.

Winded and bruised in every part of his body, Nai stopped struggling.

'After him!' a voice shouted.

The weight on his chest lessened as many of the Scotti obeyed. His arms and legs were pinned, and he could see nothing because someone was sitting on his head with the coarse cloth of their tunic swamping his breath, but at least he was no longer in danger of being crushed to death.

'Let him up!' the same voice commanded.

Rough hands with sharp nails seized him, spun him through the air. He blinked.

'It *is* you,' said the voice triumphantly. 'I thought it was, but it is not easy to be certain when one is lying on a hilltop peering at a small boat on bright water.'

A finger wearing a ring with a red stone flicked at his scarred throat.

'I did think I had finished you that day. Tiredness slowed my hand.'

He squinted reluctantly past the trumpery ring and saw the face that had haunted his nightmares for so long.

'Nai.' The name was a caress. 'You were never a talkative man. Have you nothing to say, no greeting for your old comrade?'

A dozen possible replies passed through his head.

'Nai the Silent they call you now,' Eremon laughed. 'Nai Still-Tongue.'

He closed his eyes and allowed himself to sag in the grasp of his captors. Gorthyn and the others must have escaped, else Eremon would have been crowing his victory.

The blow cracked across his cheek.

'Once you were renowned for your courtesy, cousin.' Eremon seized a handful of his hair, pulled it painfully tight. 'Do not shut your eyes while I am speaking to you.'

He could feel the hot breath of the man holding his right arm on the back of his neck – smell it too, fetid with rotting teeth.

Eremon smiled. 'My druid, Nai, my magic man. Do you know what happened to my druid? He fell down, fell down foaming at the mouth, blood bursting from his nose, prattling of crows and ravens eating his flesh, of a sorcerer with four companions undoing his work in the sacred grove.'

The smile disappeared. 'Five of you,' he said. 'Two were old friends and old foes of mine. One was a Saeson whelp, one a bitch from the village, and one a holy man. *The* holy man.'

Nai looked where Eremon pointed. The hermit lay curled on the ground, apparently unconscious, his tunic rucked around his waist so that his bare legs made him seem singularly weak and defenceless.

'I have a patron, Nai. A great patron, in both mind and body.' Eremon laughed, and his men laughed with him. 'My patron believes this old man –' he kicked the frail body, grinned eagerly when Nai winced in sympathy '– knows the whereabouts of a certain object. It seems unlikely, eh?'

Nai lifted an eyebrow.

'This of course is beyond you. Even if Gereint knew, he would not confide in you. Why should he? You are not a man of family.

None of your kin are famed for their deeds, none of them ever held great estates. You are nothing, Nai mab Nwython.'

'Better to be nothing than Vortepor of Dyfed's lapdog,' said Nai, and at once regretted rising to the bait.

'So you do still have the power of speech. I was beginning to wonder. Excellent. I shall enjoy your death the more.'

Eremon gestured to his men. Two raised the hermit and slung him between them. Others came into view carrying a wooden chest in rope slings, and behind them a tall man with a body dangling over his shoulder. Nai recognized him as Serach, another childhood familiar. The body shifted as Serach adjusted his balance, and Nai caught a glimpse of oddly shaven hair above a thin face smeared with dried blood.

Nai himself was allowed to walk free, though his hands were bound behind his back and he was hedged by men with spears at the ready. They had not reached the edge of the wood before they heard the sounds of people approaching, and there, looking disgusted, came the heavy figure of Dovnuall with the rest of those who had set off in pursuit of Gorthyn.

'No?' said Eremon.

Dovnuall spat, shook his head.

Nai laughed aloud. 'Two men, a Saeson boy, a peasant girl and an aged hermit. How many have you lost?'

Dovnuall thrust his face into Nai's. The pocked skin was unhealthily flushed, the breath sour.

'A whole shipload of Saesons we slew,' he growled.

'In memory of the time when we too were protectors of this land,' Eremon added smoothly.

'And better we were at that protection than the likes of you and Gereint.' Dovnuall's eyes were wild, not far from madness.

'Oh come!' said Nai, hoping to goad Dovnuall into giving him a quick release. 'Let us have a little honesty between old comrades. You kill because you love killing, not for any noble purpose.'

'Ask your friend the holy man about killing for the pleasure of killing,' Eremon said slyly.

Dovnuall stepped back, giving the prisoner and his guards room to pass, then leaned forward and hissed in Nai's ear:

'The hot knives will sear your flesh. You will writhe like Erfai your foster-father ere I am done with you. You will see the smoke rising from your skin, smell your own burning.'

Nai snorted and allowed himself to be herded away.

They returned to the village, which seemed smaller and oddly soulless in the afternoon sun. All the way Nai scoured his surroundings for some sign of Gorthyn and the others, but apart from the dead man lying forgotten on the bare hillside there was no hint that his companions existed.

When they arrived Eremon despatched some of his followers to fetch the curraghs, which had apparently been hidden in one of the creeks. Then he squatted in the clear space between the huts with the wooden chest before him, while the rest of his men gathered round in a circle.

'Come, Nai. Join us.'

Accepting the inevitable, Nai lowered himself awkwardly to his knees and rocked back onto his heels. Dovnuall and Serach took up positions behind him. The hermit and the man with the bloody face, whom Nai assumed to be the druid, were dropped on the edge of the ring. Neither had yet shown any sign of regaining their senses, and Nai was beginning to worry about Budoc, even though he was aware it would make small difference in the long term.

'Vortepor wished me to find something for him,' Eremon said in friendly fashion. 'You knew about Vortepor?'

Nai nodded.

'But not, I take it, what he wanted?'

'No.'

Eremon slapped the chest with his hand. The sound was muffled, as if the box was full.

'He sent a man with me, a Pict from the far North. This Pict was supposed to recognize the thing we sought.' He fell silent, ruminated for a moment. 'A strange people, the Picts. Have you ever had aught to do with them? No? This one was most curiously tattooed with strange designs borne up in great weals of flesh. Later I will show you how they looked.'

He paused and snapped his fingers. One of the crew placed a leather bottle in the outstretched hand; the Irishman drank then held it to Nai's lips. It was mead, country made (probably by the late inhabitants of the village), stronger than he preferred but welcome for all that.

'Unfortunately this Pict fell overboard when we were no more than a half-day's sail from the coast of Dyfed.'

Behind him Dovnuall sniggered.

'A tragedy.' Eremon shot a glare of reproof over Nai's shoulder. 'However, I was able to find a man of even greater ability to fill his place. Was that not lucky – or rather, did the gods not smile upon my venture?'

'It would seem so,' Nai said drily.

'Such high hopes I had! Vortepor's gold and silver to bring the loyalty of a warband, two faithful companions to captain my vessels, a magic man to ward off ill, a treasure to be sought and a reward to be claimed – who could want more?'

The wind scuffed the summer dust, sent it swirling round the circle.

'I could. In my vanity I decided such an opportunity was too good to be missed. And I must confess, I had taken a dislike to Vortepor, a gross and overbearing prince whom I suspect of past cowardice. He told me a long and many-stranded tale, in which at one point he stood watching at a window while others fought on his behalf. You or I, cousin, would have joined the battle, but he did not.'

Eremon shook his head in sadness at the frailty of others.

'So. You know my love of this land, of my forefather's holdings along the River Oak. Those I cannot have, not now, but it was in my mind that this side of the Porthyle estuary, which is part of neither the Portion of Erbin nor the Portion of Tamaris, was like a slave girl ripe for her master.'

He shuddered suddenly at some memory Nai did not share.

'Vortepor's tale was long and dull. The only interesting section concerned my father Cairbre's older brother, Lleminawg.'

'The Leaping One, the Fated One,' muttered Nai.

'Ach, Nai, I have missed your quick wits and long memory. I do not suppose . . .'

He peered hopefully at his captive. Nai stared back without blinking.

'No,' Eremon said regretfully. 'I did not think so. You are like Serach, a man of strong loyalties.' He cleared his throat.

'Alone my uncle walked into the place of shadows to fetch out what Arthur desired. To Vortepor there seemed a certain – what is the word – *symmetry* in sending me to rescue the same object from its exile.

'Of course, whatever power or honour it may convey belonged rightfully to Lleminawg, since he was the one who completed the quest. And if any man living is his heir, it is I, Eremon mac Cairbre of the Eoganacht Maigi Dergind i nAlbae.'

'Ah,' said Nai. 'I understand. You thought to steal it for yourself.'

He slumped to the ground as Dovnuall struck him a great buffet on the side of the head, and lay there with his ears ringing, watching Eremon's mouth move. It was a while before any sound reached him.

'. . . saw you cross the water, knowing you could not leave again until the druid lifted his enchantment. You have been my prisoners all along, which is why I saw no urgency in taking you captive.'

Nai swallowed, shook his head to rid it of the ringing, considered making a reply, felt Dovnuall shift behind and above him and thought better of it.

'Yet it seems Vortepor was not as trusting as he appeared. For my magic man, whom I thought loyal to me alone, bears upon his shoulder a smaller version of the very design with which our non-swimming Pict was so profusely tattooed.'

He paused for effect.

Nai shrugged. 'What of it?'

'Do you not see? The druid must have been in league with Vortepor all along!'

Nai started to laugh, and once begun could not stop. He ducked the swipe Dovnuall aimed at him, and rolled on his back in the dust, helpless with his hands behind him, his bruised ribs hurting.

'Let him have his merriment out,' he heard Eremon say. 'After all, he has not long to live.'

That sobered him as more blows could not have done.

'Eremon, you are a fool,' he said when he had tossed the tears from his eyes. 'Surely not even you could think Vortepor would allow you to walk away with this treasure? No doubt he has suborned Dovnuall – or even the incorruptible Serach,' he added hastily as Dovnuall bellowed and reached for him with hands that looked capable of strangling an ox.

'Enough!' barked Eremon.

The Irishman waited until they were all seated again before he continued, still speaking directly to Nai as if the two of them were alone.

'A fool, you called me. Well, you may be right. I like you, Nai, and it is a sorrow to me that I did not kill you cleanly, that day five years ago.'

The true horror of this remark, Nai thought, lay in the fact that Eremon intended it kindly, as a sort of compliment.

'Has the druid returned to the land of the living?' Eremon demanded.

'No, lord,' said a man on the edge of the circle.

'Bring him here.'

From the way in which they carried him, like reluctant men forced to shift a rotting carcase trying to keep the contact to a minimum, Nai guessed that they were mortally afraid of the druid. They dropped him unceremoniously in front of Eremon and hastily returned to their places.

'See!' said Eremon, and ripped aside the dark robe.

There on the bony shoulder was a spiral design drawn in faded green on ridges of flesh.

Nai leaned forward to look more closely. 'They use needles to draw thread under the skin,' explained Eremon. 'That is what pushes it up in those hard lumps of scar tissue.'

Their eyes met over the druid, and for an instant they might have been boys again, sharing their wonder over something new and strange.

'You are certain this makes him Vortepor's man?' Nai said without thinking, and at once cursed himself for not reinforcing Eremon's doubts of his followers.

'Vortepor, or some other power. A man wearing this is not loyal to me alone.'

Nai pursed his lips and nodded wisely. He was aware he was near to breaking point, to making some facetious remark which would send Eremon into one of his furies. Dealing with the Irishman was like dealing with a wild animal: one never knew what he would do next.

And Eremon terrified him, in a way that Dovnuall or Serach did not. Even being close to the man made his skin crawl, and he was not sure that he had not wet himself in the wood when he first heard the still-melodious voice. It was not that he was afraid of dying – everybody dies: some sooner, some later. It was not that he could not master his fear of pain – Dovnuall would hurt him very badly (he had seen Erfai's body five years ago, and knew what the pockmarked man could do) but it would pass, as all things pass. It was Eremon himself, the man's very presence, that turned his bowels to water.

'A pity he is not awake to help us,' Eremon was saying. 'Your friend tried to conceal this chest, but we sniffed it out, we sniffed it out.' He turned pale eyes on Nai. 'Which reminds me. Vortepor gave me a gift of a fine pack of hounds. You have treated them badly.'

Nai held his tongue.

'This box.' Eremon patted it. 'Within lies what I seek, what Vortepor seeks, what the tattooed men seek. Once I hold it in my grasp, as Lleminawg's heir, the nations of Prydein will bow the knee!'

The chest seemed ordinary enough. It was about a full pace in length, which was to say a little shorter than the smallest of the Scotti present, and perhaps half that in width and depth. The dark panels were crudely carved with borders of leaves, the sort of work an untalented apprentice might churn out. The clumsy hinges and latch were of rusty iron. To Nai it seemed the kind of chest to be found in any household, part of the furniture handed down through the generations, unremarked until the worm ate through the base and forced one to find a replacement.

'You frown, cousin. Perhaps you do not understand. Dovnuall and Serach do not understand either. Their counsel is that we should flee before the coming of Gereint or Custennin himself – no doubt you sent messages ere you crossed the water?' He read the answer in Nai's expression. 'I thought as much.'

He rose to his feet, towering above Nai and the circle of eager faces. 'But though my druid has betrayed me, though the power of the *nemeton* is lost to us – *this remains*!'

He kicked the chest, then bent and heaved back the lid.

The inside seemed to be full of clothes, old blankets or something similar. Eremon lifted out the first bundle and placed it on the ground. Slowly he unwrapped the contents, and placed them in a line before him.

Eight goblets of green glass sparkled proudly in the sun.

'Pretty!' said Dovnuall.

Eremon grunted.

Next he drew out a swathe of red cloth. His audience gasped at the richness of the colour, and gasped again as he shook it into the shape of a tunic, embroidered with veins of gold.

'They say Arthur's Companions dressed in such splendour,' muttered Serach.

'Indeed and they do,' said Eremon, pulling a matching pair of breeches from the chest.

297

'A king's ransom on their backs,' said Dovnuall.

'For this alone our time has not been ill spent,' said Serach.

'We are not yet done.' Eremon fumbled within the box, paused and grinned at Nai.

'Tell me, cousin. Do you believe Arthur is dead? I mean . . . Dead and gone for ever, as you will be by this time tomorrow, as friend Gorthyn will be once I set Dovnuall and Serach on his trail.'

'Ten years is a long while to be silent if he is not,' Nai said carefully.

The Irishman nodded, eyes brimming with unshed tears. 'Aye, there is that. Yet somehow I always hoped . . . I would have offered him my sword, you know, had he come again.'

He raised it slowly from the chest, playing on the drama of the moment. The sheath was of fine tooled leather over wood, the chape of polished bronze. The hilt was unadorned, with a simple wooden guard rounded to the fist, balanced by a plain iron pommel. The grip was shagreen, untanned leather roughened to prevent the slip of a sweat-slicked hand.

Eremon drew. The rasp of iron on wood echoed round the village. The blade was blue-grey, the double edges and the point streaks of silver in the afternoon sun.

'Now that is a glaive,' breathed Eremon, yet so quiet was the ring of men that all present heard him clearly. 'A killing blade.'

He sheathed the sword and laid it on the ground beside the tunic and the glasses.

In quick succession he produced a series of bronze or silver brooches and cloak pins, and a leather belt with an ornate silver buckle. Then came a pair of golden arm rings, and a collection of small tokens that Eremon tested both with his teeth and the tip of his knife, and pronounced to be mainly silver or, less commonly, gold.

'The rest seems to be rubbish. A copper amulet, a wooden cup, a handful of beads. Ah, these are amber, I think.' He held them to the light and nodded happily before setting them aside.

'And now,' he said excitedly, 'my thumbs are pricking, my fingers are tingling. Nothing remains save one last object, neatly wrapped in woollen cloth. The shape is right – I can feel the outline through the coverings.'

He undid the bundle inside the chest, so that none but he could see what he had found. They could tell from his face, however, that it was everything he had sought.

Glee, pure and unalloyed, was writ in every line of his countenance.

'Behold! The Sovereignty of Albion!'

He shouted, and as he shouted he raised the vessel high above his head in a blaze of sun-fired glory.

Nai blinked despairingly against the light. It was a chalice of red copper, a large bowl with finger-ring handles on either side and a cunningly curved stand for a base. The bowl was inlaid with enamel of a dark blue like the deeps of the sky at dusk, and to complete the illusion a line of pearls glowed along the rim like the stars at twilight.

Eremon held the chalice in the air for longer than was necessary, long after the sharp intake of breath from his followers had died away. He licked his lips nervously, his arms beginning to tremble.

Watching, Nai stifled the urge to laugh as he realized that the Irishman had expected something to happen, had expected some tangible sign of the chalice's power, like a bolt of lightning or a rumble of thunder.

Gulls mewed overhead as they swept from the estuary to the feast in the fields. Eremon's face darkened with fury. A vein throbbed at his temple, and Nai suddenly saw how the Irishman would look if he lived to be old.

'How?' screamed Eremon. He pushed the chalice higher into the air. 'How?'

The only sound was the gulls, wailing in mockery.

Slowly Eremon lowered the chalice. 'I do not understand,' he said softly. 'I do not understand.' He stood at the centre of the circle, head bowed, thinking. For a long time there was silence.

At last he roused himself. 'You, repack the treasure in the chest. You and you, take the prisoners and put them in one of the huts. Dovnuall, Serach: six men apiece and find Gorthyn. Alive if you can, but it matters not.'

The men he had indicated moved about their tasks. One seized the druid's ankles and dragged him through the dirt to the nearest hut. Budoc was better treated (they were not so afraid of him, not having seen what he wrought in the Sanctuary), and lastly Nai was hustled after the others into the darkness of the hut, where he was tethered by one leg to a roof post.

Outside he could hear the sounds of Dovnuall and Serach

organizing their parties amidst much shouting and cursing. He did not envy them. Gorthyn would be very angry by now, and hunting a trained warrior in a wood with plenty of hiding places was not a game for peasants.

Through the doorway he could see Eremon sitting in the dust staring at the chalice. From time to time the Irishman took a swig from the bottle of mead and looked truculently about him before resuming his study.

'Set guards around the hut and close the curtain!' he roared suddenly, glowering in Nai's direction.

Even though Nai knew he was invisible in the gloom he shrank back against the wooden pillar, trying to make himself as small as possible. Eremon's failure to rouse the power of the chalice had driven the Irishman beyond the brink of madness. (He had always been mad, but before there had been some kind of control and a great deal of charm.) Now, looking at his face, contorted with hatred and anger, Nai was aware this was a man who could and would do anything at any time.

Somebody loosed the door curtain and he was plunged into the illusory safety of darkness. He heard feet moving around outside the hut; a man coughed from the far side of the wall. Any vague hope of somehow freeing himself and digging a hole through the wattle and daub barrier vanished.

He lay there for a while, too dispirited even to struggle against his bonds, listening to the breathing of the druid and the hermit, readying himself for the slow and painful death which would be his when Dovnuall returned.

'You were right,' Budoc said softly. 'Your childhood playmate is a fool.'

'You are awake!'

'Obviously. Can you reach the druid?'

He tried, wriggling on his belly with his hands bound behind him until he reached the end of the tether.

'No.'

'A shame. If we could wake him as well, we might be able to make common cause.'

'Are you all right?'

The hermit considered for a moment. 'I have been better. Hold a while and I shall have my hands free.'

Nai closed his eyes and waited in the dark. He was tired, and his bruises ached, but at least he was not alone.

'Ah!' exclaimed the hermit. A moment later Nai felt hands fumbling at the bindings on his wrists.

'Be thankful I have not trimmed my nails recently,' whispered the old man, his beard tickling Nai's neck. 'There!'

Once Nai had released himself from the tether round his ankle they went together to the druid, who lay sprawled like a dead man where he had been dropped. Only the steady burr of his breathing betrayed that he was still alive.

'What happened to him?'

Budoc laughed humourlessly. 'When you were a child, did you ever dam a stream to make a pool, then let it all go in one great rush of water? Remember what happened to the things downstream of the dam? It was like that for him when I took back the Sanctuary.'

'Who is he? Eremon seemed to think his tattoo made him Vortepor's man.'

'By birth or by affiliation he is an Attecotti. And he is not Vortepor's man.'

'Attecotti? The Very Ancient People? Who are they?'

Budoc turned to him. Nai's sight had adapted to the dark, so that he could dimly discern the outlines of the old man's face: the high forehead, the tangle of hair and beard.

'A hundred, two hundred years ago they were a power in this land, much feared by the Romans. Together with the Picts of the North and the Scotti of Ierne they swept across Prydein in a series of devastating raids. St Jerome tells us they were cannibals, which may or may not be true, but such rumours made their name a byword for terror. Their power has dwindled since those days, but they still claim to be the oldest inhabitants of these islands.'

Nai shook his head in bemusement. 'And Vortepor of Dyfed? And the chalice which so entrances Eremon? Did you see how he looked when he first held it in his hands? He was waiting for something to happen.'

The hermit sighed. 'It is a long tale. But since I do not think we can escape until nightfall, and since we seem likely to be undisturbed till your friend Eremon has recovered from the shock of his disappointment, we may as well pass the time in that fashion as any other.'

He seated himself on one of the beds of bracken and animal skins, grinned at Nai, seeming quite unworried by their situation.

'The winter when the embassy from Agricola of Dyfed came to

Caer Cadwy was one of the worst in living memory. At times it seemed to us we had been trapped within Caer Cadwy for ever, so when word of the strangers was sent on ahead their coming was eagerly awaited . . .'

Gorthyn would have been enjoying himself, had it not been for his uncertainty about the fate of Nai and the hermit.

Had they been killed in the ambush he would have expected to find the bodies lying where they had fallen. But although they had left their own dead behind the Scotti had taken Nai and Budoc with them, which probably meant they were still alive.

Probably.

Nai's pony, Coal, had come trotting up to him once he had outdistanced the Scotti. Then he had ridden around the perimeter of the wood, hoping the youngsters would have the sense to come to its edge when they realized they were safe from pursuit.

He had not gone far when a low whistle attracted his attention, and there was Ceolric's tousled head poking through the undergrowth.

Gorthyn kept explanations brief. A strong sense of urgency nagged at him, made him eager to be moving.

'Eurgain, can you ride?' he asked when he had finished describing what had happened.

'A little,' she said doubtfully. 'I have sat on mules or asses.'

'You will do.' Gorthyn slid from the saddle. 'These are war ponies, well trained, very different from the stubborn beasts you know. They will obey you, and it takes real danger to spook them.'

He fondled Broad-Belly's veined muzzle, and the horse nudged him, sending him staggering a pace.

'They are friends, partners in battle.' He slapped the sweat-streaked shoulder. 'But for what I would do now, they will be of little help. Thick woodland is no place for horse and rider.'

'What do you want me to do?'

He smiled at her. 'The Scotti will be out and after us before long. Ceolric and I will set a trap or two for them. The ponies would be in the way, and I would see them safe. I want you to take them to the far side of the wood. Can you do that?'

She nodded. 'How . . . How will I find you, afterwards?'

'What about the hermit's hut?' said Ceolric. 'I know where it is.'

302

'Good,' said Gorthyn. 'Go to the hut and wait there till we come for you.'

He unhooked his quiver of javelins from the saddle and slung it over his shoulder, replaced the quiver with his shield, which would only hamper him in the woods. Then he searched through Nai's saddlebags until he found a length of twine, and shoved it inside his tunic.

'Go well, Eurgain.' He heaved her up onto Broad-Belly's back. The pony nickered and stamped a hoof. He gave her Coal's reins and slapped the pony's rump.

Ceolric stared after her until she was lost to view among the trees.

'Now,' said Gorthyn, rubbing his hands together. 'Let us build our killing ground. There is a certain gully I saw earlier which I think would lend itself to our purpose.'

He started striding through the wood, eager to begin his counter-attack, then halted after a few paces when he discovered Ceolric was not coming.

'She will be all right,' he said. 'It is Nai and the hermit that worry me.'

Ceolric shook himself, grunted, and followed Gorthyn into the wood.

'This time they will pursue us in strength,' the big man explained. 'Between us we have thwarted Eremon in all his endeavours. Your shipload of Saesons bloodied him before he was ready, took the edge off his men. Nai and I slaughtered several the night we found Eurgain.' He shook an arm in the air to emphasize what he was saying. 'And though I do not pretend to understand the business in the Sanctuary, the hermit seems to have destroyed his magic. If I were one of Eremon's men, I would be wanting to be done with this ill-fated venture.'

'So they will come after us?' Ceolric panted in his wake.

'Yes. Eremon will send them one last time in search of you and me. That is the way his mind works. We have made a fool of him and he will have vengeance.' Gorthyn halted to let the youth catch up. 'So we must discourage them. A few dead – or better, a few with nasty wounds to make them scream and shout. I tell you, boy, there are not many things more terrifying than listening to your friends sobbing out their lifeblood in the knowledge that you may be next, especially in a strange place like this.'

Ceolric shuddered.

It did not take them long to build the trap. Gorthyn had chosen a place where a deer trail passed along a narrow gully perhaps twice the depth of a man's height. The entrance and sides were buried under thick bushes, leaving the path itself the only possible route.

'The bushes will act like a funnel, do you see? In the heat of the chase it will not occur to them to find a way round.'

He bared his teeth at the youth. 'Now we need a nice boulder, like those we moved this morning.'

Ceolric frowned. To his mind this all seemed over-elaborate, but he sensed there was no point in arguing with Gorthyn. The two of them scoured the neighbourhood until they found what he wanted: a huge stone of layered green and black, spattered with moss, half buried in the soil.

The big man bent and wrestled with the boulder as if it were a living thing, rocking it back and forth, all the while crooning under his breath, 'Come to me, come to me.' Suddenly he heaved and straightened; the great mass burst from the earth and hung in his arms, the loose soil trickling from countless crevices.

'Can I . . .' began Ceolric, tentatively stepping forward.

Gorthyn's face was puce. The muscles and veins of his forearms and neck stood out like cords.

'Give me room,' he said hoarsely.

Ceolric scuttled aside. He had seen feats of strength before, but never one like this.

The big man edged one foot before the other. His breathing was ragged with strain. He slid the other foot forward. The blood was pounding in his ears.

This was *his* trial, *his* sacrifice. He had no magic like the hermit, no wealth of knowledge like Nai. He was Gorthyn mab Erfai, and he had nothing to offer for the safety of his friend except the strength of his body.

Step by step he brought the boulder to the brink of the gully. Seeing what he intended, Ceolric raced ahead to make a bed of small stones and pebbles atop the dry gravel bank.

With a final exhalation of breath Gorthyn lowered the boulder gently into the cradle the Saeson had built. He stood swaying like a tree in a gale, fire nagging through his back, the muscles of his arms and shoulders feeling as if they had been wrenched out of shape.

When he had recovered a little he adjusted the boulder's

balance, so it was on the very verge of falling into the gully, and wedged it in place with a chock stone. Then he took the line he had found in Nai's saddlebag and stretched it across the path at the height of a man's foot, holding it in place with a series of forked twigs. One end he tied to the sturdy base of a bush; the other he fixed around the chock stone.

'Can you throw a javelin?' His voice was almost as harsh as Nai's.

Ceolric nodded.

'Then up into the bushes with you.' He pointed to the far side of the gully, opposite the precariously balanced boulder. 'Take four. I doubt you will have time for more. Put three upright in the ground, and the fourth ready in your hand. I will lead them here. When the rock falls, cast your spears, then run like the wind for the dead ash tree we passed earlier. I shall meet you there.'

'And . . .' The youth glanced doubtfully from the line to the boulder. 'And if it does not work?'

Gorthyn glared. 'If it does not work, do as the god guides you.'

He turned away and set about laying a trail along the path leading to the gully. He snapped a spray from a bush, leaving the broken branch hanging in mid-air, the fresh sap a splash of unmissable colour. Behind him he could hear the youth working his way into position.

Then he went hunting the Scotti.

This was the part he would have enjoyed, had he not been worried about Nai. They had always ridden together: without Nai he had nobody to tell him whether his plan was too complicated. (The boy obviously thought it was.) They were a team, he and Nai. When the dark man was with him he did not need to guard his back, to keep checking behind him. The Saeson was well enough (for a Saeson), but he was not his comrade, tried and tested and never found wanting.

Finding the Scotti was not hard. They were in two groups. One was thrashing about to the north, between him and the village. The other, more dangerous, was sweeping quietly round from the south. The idea was doubtless that he and the youngsters should hear the beaters in the north, and fleeing from them run directly into the hands of the southern band.

Gorthyn grinned to himself, wiped the palms of his hands on his breeches, and glided south through the trees towards where he had glimpsed the grey figures.

He showed himself around the bole of an oak. From their cries he knew they had seen him. Feigning dismay, he stumbled a few paces then halted like man striving to give his companions time to win clear.

A slingshot whizzed past his ear. With a bellow of rage he flung a spear: it caught on a bough and crashed to the earth in a cascade of leaves. They were coming fast, too fast. His second javelin he whipped low, sending it skimming across the bushes to bury itself in the chest of the lead runner.

He fled, shouting his triumph, and they followed, their feet pattering on the dead leaves.

It was a wild run he made, weaving and ducking the occasional missile (fortunately they were too eager in the chase to halt and aim very often), hurdling the undergrowth and fallen trunks, pulling them along in his wake as if they were attached by a rope.

He had a small lead, barely enough, when he entered the mouth of the gully. He jumped the twine and raced to the far end, hurled himself behind the shelter of a holly, careless of the sharp leaves, struggled to control his breathing. Years of sitting astride a horse had left him unfitted for sprinting.

If this did not work he would be in trouble . . .

The Scotti came to the gully and saw the obvious signs of his passage. The first missed the line, stepped over it without noticing its presence. The second tripped and the third collided with him, knocked them both sprawling. The fourth hesitated, unable to pass, and while he dithered the boulder bounced down the slope and caught him on the thigh.

The crack of shattered bone carried to Gorthyn where he waited. Sword in hand he plunged out from the holly. The first of the Scotti had stopped and turned to see what was happening behind him. Gorthyn swung the long blade deep into the man's side, jerked it free and swung again.

Ceolric sent a javelin into the tangled mass of limbs which was the pair on the ground, and hurled another at the fifth man, who was trying to lift the boulder from his fellow with the broken thigh. It struck him in the shoulder, sent him reeling against the sixth and final hunter.

The air was full of screaming. The man trapped under the rock was sobbing; Gorthyn's victim was writhing on the ground, his cries weakening as his life blood left him; the pair who had tripped were squealing while they wriggled in a futile attempt to avoid the Briton's avenging sword. Even the fifth man was gasping as he sought to pull the shaft from his shoulder.

Only the lastcomer was silent.

Looking down at him from his vantage point among the bushes, Ceolric saw that he was a man as large and fierce as Gorthyn himself, clad in a mailshirt, his sweat-streaked hair shining gold even in the shadows of the ravine.

He lifted his head to stare at the Saeson. The face above the brown beard was a mass of red craters, the eyes hard and piercing.

Ceolric flung a spear. It missed.

The warrior laughed. Ignoring the youth, he lifted the boulder from the injured man and tossed it casually aside.

'Gorthyn,' he said, the name dropping like a stone into the spreading pool of silence as the Scotti one by one lapsed into unconsciousness. 'Gorthyn mab Erfai.'

2

'Teleri was gone,' said the hermit. His voice cracked on the syllables of her name.

The hut reeked of sweat and damp. The bedding, piles of straw and bracken covered with animal skins, was stale and needed changing. The druid's breathing filled the fetid space, rasping and uneven, a sound become so familiar they no longer noticed, would have been aware of it only if it ceased.

Nai peered through the gloom at the outline of the hermit couched on one of the beds.

'You loved her very much.'

'I did.' The old man rubbed his temples with steepled fingers. 'I gave her my heart, and she returned it to me unbroken.'

'What did you do when you found her gone?'

'Roused the camp, waked Arthur himself.' Budoc shook his head. 'Nobody had seen her. She had vanished without trace, like a creature of the Hollow Hills in the old tales.'

He fell silent. Nai waited awhile, then prompted:

'The smell in the tent. Somebody else had been there?'

'Yes. One of the tattooed men. That part was not hard to answer. But that they had slipped unseen through all our guards and pickets – that was not so easy.'

Budoc rolled onto his side, sat up, his head brushing the sloping roof. 'Arthur alone did not seem surprised, or even worried. We expected him to be angry – and why not? None of us were new to the business of war. We had all fought in his campaigns against the Saesons and the Scotti, and we knew full well the dangers of a lax watch. The fact that we were in friendly territory was no excuse. Yet he was curiously unmoved. His only comment was that we must travel with all speed to strike against Hueil and his band of reivers . . .'

Leaving a small escort to accompany the court at its own pace, the rest of us rode fast for Kelliwig.

We came down through the wooded hills to find the horseshoe bay a forest of masts and the town filled with sea-tanned strangers eagerly awaiting our arrival.

Arthur wasted no time. He had us aboard the ships before dusk, and we sailed with the tide under cover of darkness.

I am not and never have been a sailor, though I was born and raised within sight and sound of the sea, and it is my hope that when I die it will be with the rush of waves as they break upon a beach or headland echoing in my ears. Sea-sickness has never bothered me, and I can understand the urge which sends men across the water-wastes in search of new shores, can even feel it myself at times, a deep restlessness which comes each spring when the skies lighten and the trees begin to bud.

But of the arts of navigation and shiphandling I know nothing.

So I can tell you very little concerning the voyage, except that we sailed northwards, past the promontories of firstly Dyfed and then Gwynedd, keeping the coast of Prydein firmly on our right and the shadow-blur of Ierne ever to our left. As Gwynedd fell behind us the weather worsened, day after day of soaking drizzle and low cloud, till we moved in a world of our own, a grey murk where none could distinguish between sea and sky.

The damp clung everywhere. The sails, the ropes, the oars: all glistened with droplets of moisture. The leather of our arms and armour turned mildewed if not kept mercilessly clean. Hair, beards and clothing were coated with myriad shining pearls. The taste of salt was constantly on our tongues, and everything below decks stank of mould.

Most of us – myself included – had only the vaguest picture of where we were going. The Iardomnan was an unknown region at the ends of the earth, neither of Prydein nor of Ierne yet betimes claimed by both. That we should voyage through fog and cloud to reach the islands was entirely apposite, merely added to their aura of mystery.

We passed through the North Channel which divides Prydein from Ierne. Although I had always known that those straits are narrow, I had never realized precisely how narrow they are until I heard the surf booming on both sides of us at once.

At this point our charts failed us, which was no more than we expected. Land – whether islands or part of the mainland it was impossible to tell – loomed continually through the mist where our charts showed nothing save open sea. The captains relied upon Teleri's drawings to steer our course, kept leadsmen in the bows sounding the depths beneath our hulls, and sent nimble lookouts shinning up the masts whenever the fogs lifted, which was not often.

We saw no other vessels, which was not surprising. So large a fleet had not sailed in these waters for a hundred years or more, and nobody except a fool would have dared challenge us. When we put into land to replenish our provisions we found fires still burning on the hearths of empty houses, the inhabitants fled to the forests of the interior. They had learned the hard way to be wary of men from the sea.

For most of us it was an uneventful voyage. The novelty was soon a thing of the past, and though we took turns at the oars when we were needed, there was little we could do to help with the daily running of the ships.

I do not know how long the journey lasted. Just as it was difficult to distinguish between air and water, so too it was hard to tell day from night, in the perpetual fog which shrouded our passage. One waking period blurred into another, and at times it seemed there were only the vast sky and the rolling grey-green sea, and nothing else in all the world.

Talorcan was aboard the same ship as I, an old vessel built in the Roman style, and we spent long watches strolling on the deck, keeping out of the way of the seamen, talking of the Northlands.

'Degaw's people, the Creones,' he said one day. 'Do you know what their name means?'

I thought about it for a while. 'Broken edges? The People who live along the craggy coast?'

'Something like that.' He shivered as the spray dashed our

faces. 'The People of the Rugged Bounds. These are the lands where all divisions become strange. Here the laws of nature by which we live our lives are suspended.'

I had never seen him so serious.

He wiped the water from his hair and beard. 'The tribes hereabouts have always formed alliances and counter-alliances.'

'In that they are no different from the other parts of Prydein,' I said.

'The Caledonians, the Hard Men, combined to fight Rome,' he continued as if he had not heard me. 'Later came the Picts, the Peht, the Painted People.'

'One federation grew from the other.'

He frowned, not caring for the interruption. This was not the man with whom I had shared a bottle a few nights earlier, the man who had been worried lest he offend me.

'My ancestors, the Decantae, called themselves the Noblemen, the High Born. We thought of ourselves as conquerors.'

The deck pitched alarmingly. A wave broke over the bow, drenched us in freezing water. The crew scurried to adjust the sail.

'And whom did they conquer, your ancestors?' I asked when the ship seemed once again on an even keel.

He smiled uncertainly, tugged a lock of salt-stained hair. 'I am not sure. But when I was young and my nurse was telling me tales of horror she mentioned two tribes who had once been our neighbours.' His gaze appeared fixed upon the rolling whitecaps, but I knew he was not seeing them.

'One tribe were called the Smertae.'

'The Smertae? The Smeared People? Smeared with what?' Even as I asked the question I guessed the answer.

'They used to daub themselves with blood before going to war.' His normally ruddy skin looked pale and pinched with cold, almost blue around the mouth and nose.

'You southerners, you lump us all together as Picts, all of us from beyond Bannog. But we were and are many different peoples, and we never knew the heavy hand of Rome. Old customs survived longer among us.'

He spat over the rail. 'As a youngster I painted my face and body with the ancient symbols of the Decantae before going on cattle raids. When I went south to serve Arthur I stopped, not wishing to be thought a barbarian.'

'Who were the second tribe?'

'The Lugi. The Black Ravens.' Talorcan frowned. 'I have been thinking about what you asked me in the stable that day when Rudvrych was dying, you see. Degaw and I talked about the Attecotti and the Children of Menestyr, and then I asked around among the other Companions from the North. The Black Ravens were so named because they were dark of skin and hair.'

'Like the tattooed men in Lindinis.'

'Yet in my youth,' he continued, again ignoring my interpolation, 'the Lugi and the Smertae were forgotten peoples, remembered only in stories. They were bogeymen with which to frighten naughty children.'

'As were the Children of Menestyr,' I said, beginning to see the light.

He leaned against the rail, feet braced against the rocking of the vessel. 'Let us suppose it was these tribes my ancestors conquered, or branches of them.' He gestured vaguely, fumbling for words. 'Perhaps groups of them had always lived in the Western Isles, or perhaps they fled the coming of the Decantae, fled to the marginal lands of the Iardomnan. There they mixed with peoples from Ierne, part of the constant ebb and flow across the seas. But all the while they retained their language, the old tongue, and the memory of a time when they or their kinfolk ruled the whole of Prydein and raised great monuments of earth and stone to proclaim their mastery of the land.'

'And the Attecotti?'

'They *are* the Attecotti. The descendants of the old tribes, the forgotten tribes – the Lugi, the Smertae and the gods alone know how many others whose names are lost. Our people, yours and mine, crossed the Narrow Seas from Gaul and conquered the old tribes in the dawn of time, took their women and taught them our common tongue. But suppose some remained free – where more likely than here, beyond the bounds of the lands we know?'

I nodded slowly. 'But this Sovereignty they protect, or claim to hold . . .'

'Yes, cousin, yes.' He gripped my arm excitedly. 'Who more likely than they to hold such a thing? And think, what do we know about these Children of Menestyr?'

I shrugged. 'They attacked me in Lindinis.'

'But did they? Did they, cousin? Surely not.'

Frowning I shook my head, seeing again the wild figures charging across the snowy court. 'What do you mean?'

'We have assumed all along that the Children of Menestyr are our enemies. But are they?' He beat upon the rail with his fist, more impassioned than I had ever seen him. 'They wanted to prevent Teleri from telling her tale in Arthur's Hall, so they attacked Vortepor. (And to my mind, no great loss if they had slain him on the road.) Failing, they tried again in Lindinis, and found you.'

He grinned. 'No doubt a nasty shock for them, a man madder than themselves. But it was not *you* they were attacking. What they wanted was to find Teleri, and you stood between them and their objective.'

'And then she told her tale,' I said.

'And the urgency was gone. Pedrylaw Menestyr himself – and if there is any truth in the old stories I heard as a child then he is the leader of them all – came to the gates of Caer Cadwy to demand her return. And told you he was not from Albion but from – how did it go?'

'Not from Albion, but from Albany; not from Prydein, but from Pritdyn.'

'The old name for the whole island, used now only for the North. And why? Because only in the far north do the original inhabitants survive.'

Holding up a hand to stem his enthusiasm, I said: 'He still wanted Teleri returned. He claimed she was an escaped slave.'

'True,' said Talorcan. 'And he nearly ensorcelled you. Had it not been for Arthur he would have stolen your mind.'

I shuddered.

'But when he saw Arthur he changed. Did you not see?' he pressed, insistent, forcing me to examine my memory though I had tried hard to forget the events of that morning. 'Whatever else he had expected, it was not Arthur. And he knelt to him, and named him Emperor.'

'What are you saying?'

He looked at me with caution in his eyes, as if he had suddenly remembered to whom he spoke. Ever since the death of Garwen my wife I had had a reputation among the Companions for being a man of uncertain temper, and Talorcan knew that what he was about to say might offend me.

'Speak freely,' I said.

'Teleri and Pedrylaw Menestyr are of the same clan. They are guardians of some secret they believe confers the Sovereignty of all Prydein on its rightful holder. Teleri heard rumour of Arthur and came to lure him North for whatever ceremony is necessary. She used Vortepor of Dyfed to make her approach, knowing that if she arrived from nowhere she would be but one among many seeking audience with the Warlord. Arthur would not have sailed to the Iardomnan for a tale of a magic cup – he would have laughed in her face – but the depredations of Hueil provided her with a convenient and quite genuine reason.'

'And Menestyr?' I demanded coldly.

'He opposed Teleri's plan, not believing a southern Warlord worthy of the Sovereignty. He sought to prevent her from reaching Caer Cadwy, and failed.' Talorcan glanced sideways to see how I was reacting to this. 'Then he entered the fortress – and think how much courage that must have taken – and encountered Arthur.'

Grimly I stared at him while he gathered breath to continue.

'Menestyr recognized him, cousin. You heard and saw for yourself.'

'You are guessing,' I growled.

'Aye,' he admitted honestly. 'I am. But nothing else fits what we know. Once Menestyr had seen Arthur, he withdrew his opposition to Teleri's plan.'

The pain and loss rose within my breast till it seemed they must burst forth. I struck the rail with my good hand, felt it splinter beneath the force of the blow. I spun on my heel, half blind with rage and anguish, surveyed the deck and the white faces of the crew, searching for a sign of mockery in their frightened gazes.

'Where is she?' Even to myself the words were an incoherent jumble, yet Talorcan seemed to understand.

'I believe she left of her own free will,' he said gently. 'Like you, I thought at first she had been stolen away. But . . .' He spread his arms wide.

'Where is she?' I repeated.

'Waiting for us, cousin. Waiting for us on the Isle of Shadows.'

After a time I left him and went below to the small cabin I had been allotted, in search of my copies of the sea-charts by which we sailed.

The Isle of Shadows was where Cuchulain, the great hero of northern Ierne, went to learn the mastery of weapons from a woman. Another place of mystery, of legend.

The chart – and I was aware of how unreliable it was in these waters – showed a large land mass lying to the north of the lesser isles where Hueil had his lair. The Romans, upon whose maps the chart was based, had named it *Scitis*, which could have been – *could* have been – the way they had heard the natives say the word for shadow: Scatha.

And Scatha was the name of the woman who had taught the warrior Cuchulain.

I studied the map, wishing I could talk with Arthur, but he of course had sailed aboard a different ship.

We had agreed, Arthur and his closest advisers, that after we had dealt with Hueil, the Magister Militum would attempt the trial for the Sovereignty of Albion. But we knew nothing of the where or the how of it, nothing except what little we could glean from the old tales. Without Teleri we were lost.

(And yet, and yet . . . Arthur had suspected she might not sail with us.)

Talorcan – and for a man who claimed never to bother himself with thinking he had obviously been doing a lot of it lately – believed we had been manipulated into venturing north.

I felt sick and shaky, much the way I had felt years before when a Scotti sword had nigh hacked my left hand in twain. All that sustained me was the memory of Teleri herself, and the manner in which she had spoken the day the four of us had ridden ahead of the column, when she had persuaded Arthur and Gwenhwyvar and me that the Sovereignty of Prydein was a prize worth seeking.

That I might have been deceived by her was one thing. That Arthur might have been deceived was possible, though less likely. But that Gwenhwyvar the wise could have been deceived by a fellow woman – that I could not credit.

And there lay the only comfort I could find, the only hope that the Teleri I had known and loved was not a lie, with Gwenhwyvar the Thrice Royal, whose judgement of another had never been known to fail.

On the last night of the voyage the seas ran steep and fast, and we could find no safe anchorage to wait out the hours of darkness. We went on of necessity, sailing into unknown night, through a gloom fit to match the gloom within me, until suddenly and miraculously the sky cleared.

Above us hung the Pole Star, marking the still spot in the heavens about which all else revolves. Beyond were other familiar stars, and in the north was Caer Arianrhod, the Crown of the North Wind, where we must go before we were finished.

I remembered a sunlit wintry day when Teleri had looked at the lines of my hand – my right hand, those of my left being mutilated by the glassy slick of scar tissue – and predicted I would far outlive my friends. I had laughed, being yet young enough to think this no great matter.

Now, as the stars glittered cold and dead as ice and the bitter black water rolled unceasingly around us, it did not seem so small a matter after all. Now it seemed we had moved beyond the world I knew to a place where anything might happen. At dawn we would make landfall: Arthur and Cei at the main anchorage under Hueil's stronghold, Gwalchmei and I at a lesser bay in the east, whence we might take the enemy in the flank.

You must have felt it, Nai. The fear of action. All warriors know them, the slow watches of the night before a battle when there is nothing to do save dwell upon the morrow, when sleep eludes and the imagination runs wild.

Being on board ship made it worse: one was powerless, unable even to stroll around the guard pickets.

I was afraid, more afraid than I have been before or since, and a part of me recognized the absurdity. Just as for Teyrnon in Teleri's story the capture of the village proved no more than the prelude to the recovery of the child, so too tomorrow's skirmish was merely a task to be completed before we moved on to our true purpose in sailing north.

Gradually the sky paled and we saw the land before us: long low-lying woods with white-capped mountains towering in the blue distance; a weather-worn land, brooding and ancient, the rugged edges of the mountains smoothed by eons of wind and water. An old land for an old people.

Talorcan stood beside me on the deck as the old ship nuzzled her way into the deserted bay. I remember there was an otter playing in the waves along the beach, but otherwise there were no signs of life. Hueil had called his warriors in to the supposed stronghold of his fort, and the rest had wisely fled.

'Peaceful,' said Talorcan.

I turned to look at him and recoiled in surprise.

His face was painted with blue patterns: crescents and serpents mixed with streaks of jagged lightning. He was wearing a cloak, tight wrapped against the breeze of morning. Seeing my expression he flung it wide.

Save for a short kilt he was naked, and his whole body was daubed with blue designs, geometric shapes woven into an intricate working which both baffled and entranced the eye.

'A good day to die,' he said softly, and covered himself again.

'To die?' I started to remonstrate. 'You will not die, cousin.'

He looked at me with faraway eyes. 'We are on the verge of a great mystery,' he said, and spun on his heel, strode to another part of the rail to watch our approach to the shore.

Busy with the preparations for our landing, I paid him no further attention. He was not the first and would not be the last to go into action with a head full of odd notions, and as the commander of our party I had no time to spare.

We disembarked through the surf, unloading our supplies onto the beach and forming into a column. Then we marched through the woods, thin pines bearded with lichen and hanging moss, green and dripping with moisture, the ground soft and treacherous underfoot. I remember it was very dark, and quiet save for the sound of our passage.

Finally we came out into the hard crystal light of a hillside above the sea, where the wind whipped cloud shadows across the glistening grass.

The fortress lay to our right at the head of an inlet, just as it had been described. It was a single ring, an earthen bank steep and slippery as any wall, topped with a wooden palisade. The main gate was protected by two out-thrust wings that created a funnel, so any attackers would find themselves squeezed closer and closer together until they were crammed shoulder to shoulder in the confined space.

It was child's play to us to capture such a place. We were the Companions, and we could have done it in our sleep.

By the time we were ready it was raining, a steady mizzle. The bowmen were useless, as they nearly always are, but we had a plentiful supply of slingers, who are not so affected by the weather.

The slingers prevented the defenders from concentrating their forces at any given spot. We made a rush across the ditch, carrying the simple tree-ladders we had brought with us, and began to scale the bank. At the same moment Cei launched his assault on the main gate, bursting it open with a battering ram. (Afterwards the praise singers said he had kicked it down, alone and unaided, but that is typical of their nonsense.)

Then it was merely a matter of hunting down any defenders who still showed signs of resistance. Hueil their leader was killed by the gate, and once he was dead the heart went out of them.

I have made it sound easy, and it was easy. The fighting did not last long – we probably spent more time on the hillside making our preparations and waiting for the signal from Arthur than in the actual attack. The clearing-up was a slow business, but then it always is. The fort had been used as a holding place for the slaves Heuil had captured, and of course some of the defenders tried to hide among them. Sorting one from the other took time, involved much shouting and arguing, for the slaves were at first as afraid of us as they were of their original captors.

So it was a while before I realized I had not seen Talorcan since we began our wild charge.

He was not among the wounded, now being cared for in Hueil's Hall. Nor was he within the compound itself.

I found him curled by the ditch, naked except for the kilt. He was oddly diminished, seeming smaller and younger than in life. A slingshot had struck him in the forehead, shattering his brow. He must have been killed instantaneously.

There was one last incident. The dead were thickest around the main gate, where the fighting had been fiercest. Somebody told us that Hueil had fallen here, so Arthur and Cei went out of curiosity to view his body. As they walked among the dead one came alive and stabbed Arthur in the thigh with a broad-bladed spear. Cei crushed the life from the man with his bare hands, but the damage was done.

It was a deep and messy wound, not fatal of itself, but dangerous. By the time the surgeons had cleaned it out Arthur had fainted with the pain and loss of blood.

'This alters everything,' said Cei. 'We must take him home with all speed.'

'If we can.' Lleminawg looked doubtfully at the sky.

The heavens were darkening rapidly. Black clouds were sweeping inland from the sea, covering the face of the sun. Shafts of golden light lanced fleetingly across the mountains. A storm was rising, and quickly.

'We are too many for this anchorage,' said one of the captains. 'We must sail, and soon.'

Cei and I exchanged a glance. We could not hold this fort against the natives if they chose to come against us, nor would there be any advantage in doing so. The expedition had been intended as a punitive raid, not a mission of conquest.

Gwalchmei had already begun the process of loading the freed captives aboard the fleet. Now he hastened them along, telling them we would leave behind any who were not aboard when we were ready to depart.

We did what damage we could to the stronghold, fired the hall and the huts, smashed down the timber palisade. The earth banks were too solid to destroy, and we knew that within a few years another chieftain would arise and refortify the site; but perhaps he would be more circumspect in his dealings with the South.

Our dead and wounded – of whom there were not many – we carried to the ships. One by one the war galleys and the lumbering transports upped anchor and clawed free of the inlet, standing out for open water, oars threshing the steepening seas.

Lleminawg and I brought Arthur aboard the sturdiest vessel, while Cei and the Hawk scrambled into a galley which would act as our close escort. The storm was almost on us, and the forerunners of the fleet had already been swallowed by its darkness. I think all of us, by which I mean all of the Companions, were close to panic: we had never seen Arthur so badly injured, and we were in a strange element, one over which we had no control.

Not until we were ourselves clear of the inlet did I have space to stop and reflect.

'We are on the verge of a great mystery,' Talorcan had said. They were his last words to me, and I had dismissed them as the usual flutterings of nervousness before a battle.

Talorcan had behaved oddly on the ship, not in his usual fashion, more like a man possessed. Now he was dead, while Arthur had been wounded in exactly the place and manner of Nudd in Teleri's story, wounded under identical circumstances. And it was because of Teleri's tale that we were here, running before a rising storm: being driven, I realized with a start of horror, away from the main fleet and further to the north.

'What happened?' demanded Nai.

The old man frowned. 'I do not know.' He raised a hand to forestall Nai's protest. 'Oh, I know in the broadest sense, because the others told me later, though none of us ever discussed it in detail. We did not want to.'

Nai rose to his feet from where he had been squatting beside the hermit and peered through a chink in the door-hanging.

Eremon was sprawled in the dust beside the chest, the leather bottle clutched in one hand, the base of the chalice gripped in the other. He was either asleep or unconscious, and the presence of the obviously empty bottle made Nai suspect the latter.

His ragged followers moved uneasily about the village, giving his long form a wide berth, shooting frightened glances in the direction of the wooded hills behind them. Their faces were pinched and wizened; watching them, Nai felt a twinge of pity for their situation, trapped in a strange land with an erratic leader.

'I cannot remember what happened for myself,' said Budoc. He gritted his teeth and pummelled the straw bedding. 'Not in the way I can remember something like the black head of the otter sporting in the water as we approached the land before the attack on Llacil's stronghold. If I close my eyes I can see the gleam of morning light on the sleek head, can recreate the moment in my mind.'

The druid was still snoring steadily. Nai pinched the man's cheek, but there was no reaction.

'All that remain to me are fleeting images.' Budoc's voice was choked with frustration. 'Towering black seas and a creaking ship awash with cataracts of bitter water. The crack of the breaking mast audible even above the storm. The deck canted to the waves, and the frantic rise and fall of the axes trying to free us from the drag. Lleminawg and I scrambling down the hatchway to find Arthur before it was too late . . .'

3

Watching from his vantage point, the last of the javelins clutched firmly in one hand (the wood warm and comforting to the touch), Ceolric saw Gorthyn take a step back.

'Dovnuall Frych,' the Briton said softly.

The newcomer swung his sword through the air so it hissed like a living thing.

'Will you give fair fight?' he demanded. 'No spears in the back from your tame Saeson?' He jerked his head at Ceolric on the rim above him.

Gorthyn regarded him proudly, fiercely. 'Aye. You and me alone,' he said. 'Hurry. My blade thirsts for your blood. A source of great grief has it been to me these many years that you are still alive.'

'Then a fair fight it shall be, a fair fight and a short one!'

Dovnuall came striding jauntily down the gully: a big man, as large as Gorthyn, wearing a mail-ring shirt and a dark cloak pinned by a brooch of red bronze, his face a mass of pocks and hollows above a wild beard.

There was a small round shield set in the crook of his left arm, and a short knife in that hand; in the other he carried a sword, its blade neither so long nor so broad as the one Gorthyn held.

He came to a halt beside the tangled bodies and grinned, showing a mouthful of broken teeth. 'A pity you lack a mail shirt. Yon leather will not stop much.' He gestured at the dead. 'Take a shield, old friend. You will need it.'

Gorthyn smiled, a hard and cruel smile, his eyes never leaving the other while he bent and freed a targe from the arm of the first man to die.

It was very quiet now the screaming had stopped. As Ceolric slithered down the slope into the gully his ears were pricked for sounds of another party of Scotti, for he did not believe that Dovnuall's idea of fair combat would extend to Gorthyn.

The two big men moved away from the ravine, giving themselves space to fight, walking stiff-legged into the clear hollow at its end. Meanwhile Ceolric gathered the spears he had thrown earlier, and, having made sure neither of the others were looking in his direction, cut the throats of the wounded. To his mind these were enemies, the slayers of his father and the crew of the *Sea Stallion*, the ravagers of Eurgain's village, the rapers of her sister. The only safe enemy was a dead one, whatever Gorthyn might say about inflicting painful wounds to frighten their fellows.

The warriors faced each other, Gorthyn tired and dirty in his worn and scratched leathers, Dovnuall resplendent in his mail and cloak.

'You seem weary,' Dovnuall said solicitously. 'Soon you will be at rest, like Erfai your father.'

The tiredness visibly fell from Gorthyn's limbs. He straightened, standing tall and proud for the first time since he had shifted the boulders in the Sanctuary.

'The crows will feed on your corpse!' he shouted, and sprang forward, sword whistling as he slashed and sliced at the Irishman with furious energy.

At first Dovnuall gave ground, but Gorthyn was not to be lured into the gully – even in his battle madness he retained a healthy distrust of the Scotti, and feared a stab in the back from one of the wounded.

'Stand and fight, damn you!' he growled.

Dovnuall chuckled. 'Now, now. Your father went without all this fuss, going quietly on his way with no more than a rattle in his throat, though it took him a long time to die. Are you a lesser man than he?'

Gorthyn lashed out, and they met again, shoving like bulls, thrusting like stags, sending splinters flying from each other's shields: two big men accustomed to winning their battles by overpowering their opponents.

At last they fell apart, both gasping for breath.

'You are stronger than I thought,' panted Dovnuall.

Gorthyn grinned mirthlessly. 'Stronger than old men and helpless women?'

A third time they met, their blades singing and their war-boards thudding as they showered blows upon each other.

Ceolric watching felt a surge of excitement. Gorthyn was the more powerful man, and little by little his greater strength was starting to tell. Dovnuall was reeling under the succession of impacts on his shield, and his counters lacked the vigour they had possessed at the beginning.

But the fight was not yet finished.

The Irishman had slipped his targe down from his elbow to his wrist, disguising the short blade in his left hand. Now, when he thought Gorthyn might have forgotten about it, he feinted with his sword and struck low and fast with the knife.

'Ware left hand!' screamed Ceolric, seeing what was coming and fearing he was too late.

Either Gorthyn had not forgotten, or else he heard the warning. He brought his shield down on the knife, so that it caught in the wood, then jerked sideways. Dovnuall yelped as the knife was wrenched from his grasp and sent spinning across the clearing.

Gorthyn let out a great shout of triumph, a bellow that froze the Irishman where he stood, and smashed his sword into the other's ribs. Mail rings and bone gave alike under the force of the blow.

Taking the hilt in both hands, Gorthyn swung again at his reeling opponent. Dovnuall groaned and fell. The Briton was on him at once, bringing the sword down so hard the sound of it was audible clear across the hollow.

Screeching wildly, Gorthyn bent to pick up the severed head, held it dangling by the hair, displayed it to Ceolric in triumph.

'A gift for Eremon!' he said. 'Cut me a post like those the Scotti used!'

Ceolric gaped at him.

'A post, boy. Quickly!'

Taking a heavy knife from the outstretched hand of a dead man (he was not going to risk the edge of his own blade) the Saeson hacked at a sapling, cutting through the trunk in a shower of green splinters and trimming the shoots until he was left with a pole.

'They are coming,' said Gorthyn. His head was cocked to one side and he was listening intently. 'Hold this.'

He gave the trophy to Ceolric, who took it gingerly, keeping it well clear of his body.

'They are barbarians,' Gorthyn said through his teeth. 'Savages. I too can be savage.'

Ceolric watched while he propped Dovnuall's headless corpse against a tree so the neck was in shadow and one arm was entwined with a gently waving branch. From a distance it looked as if Dovnuall was beckoning him closer.

'That should frighten them,' the big man said with satisfaction. 'You killed the others?'

The question came so suddenly it caught Ceolric by surprise. He felt his face flush.

'Yes.'

'Good,' Gorthyn clapped him on the shoulder. 'Do not look so guilty, boy. They deserved to die, like that filth.' He nodded in the direction of Dovnuall. 'Now, tell me how to find the hermit's hut, then go there yourself and stay with the girl and the horses until I come.'

'Why? What are you going to do?'

Gorthyn relieved him of the pole and the trophy.

'Leave Eremon a gift on his doorstep,' he said, and winked.

CHAPTER FIVE

1

'It maddens me,' said the hermit, 'maddens me that I cannot remember.' He pounded the bedding in frustration. 'For years it has gnawed at my head, disturbed my dreams. For a time I found peace in the Sanctuary, but now . . . Now it all comes together, Nai, and I cannot remember why.'

'Lleminawg. It has something to do with Lleminawg,' Nai whispered over his shoulder from his place by the door. Outside the sentry shuffled from foot to foot.

'The Dancing One, the Fated One,' muttered Budoc. 'He was doomed, and I seem to recall that like Talorcan he knew he was doomed, doomed by the name he had been given at birth. There is a power in names, Nai.' He managed a half smile. 'Nephew, sister's son: champion. Will you be my champion if the need arises?'

Nai turned, raised his eyebrows, spoke lightly to cheer his fellow prisoner. 'The man who did that –' he nodded at the sleeping druid '– has no great need of my aid. But what I have is yours, if you wish it.'

'The seeds of our downfall lay in what we did upon that isle,' Budoc muttered to himself. 'Had we acted differently, Camlann might have been averted.'

'Hueil's isle?' said Nai.

'No. The second island – though perhaps it was part of

the first. Who knows? The isle on which we were ship-wrecked.'

It was a mighty storm. The seas became mountains, tremendous walls of water thundering across our bows, spinning us helpless as driftwood. What began as rain soon became sleet and hail: the men turned blue with cold, their numb hands failing on the ropes. Not long after the mast fell and was hacked free the steering oar was also carried away, and then we were indeed at the mercy of the waves.

Somehow we survived. By now we were taking water faster than we could bail. Many of the crew had gone, snatched away by the storm, and those remaining made much play of launching a boat. Lleminawg and I took one look at the flimsy shell and decided to stay with the ship, preferring to trust her old timbers to float a while longer.

The boat dropped over the side, heavily laden with men. She was half swamped almost immediately, and fell sluggishly behind to be swallowed by the waves and darkness. Until then I had not realized how fast we were moving, how rapidly we were racing through the gloom in the grip of the wind and current.

I never saw any of the boat's passengers again.

Only a handful of us had stayed aboard. We had no means of working the ship with neither mast nor steering oar, so we could only wait, shivering in the wet and cold; wait while the storm tossed us from black ravine to grey mountain, praying that we would not slip sideways to the force of the gale.

Although we could barely see through the murk, it was worse if you closed your eyes. Then you felt every lurch and slip, every pounding impact. The ship would fall into each trough, struggle slowly to climb the face of the next wave, hang suspended half in air half in water at its crest, then slip and slide down its back before again dropping to the depths.

This seemed to go on for ever, though I doubt if it really lasted very long. We could feel the ship being shaken apart beneath us, the timbers creaking and cracking under the strain. Lleminawg, who having grown up near the mouth of the River Oak knew more about boats than me, was white with fear – not for himself, but for Arthur.

'All I can think is that we should lash him to a plank,' he bellowed in my ear. 'This hulk will sink soon.'

'What about an empty barrel?' I shouted, some half-remembered fabulous tale of shipwreck echoing through my mind.

He scowled, shrugged – and in that instant we struck.

I went flying through the freezing air, the grey waves curling to meet me, white where they threshed wildly against some obstruction hidden beneath the surface, and I had time to see this and hope I would avoid the reef or bank or whatever it was, and then I was deep in the dark water, having somehow missed the moment of transition, deep in the silence of the ocean, my ears popping and lungs bursting.

Lleminawg told me afterwards that he thought I was dead. It seems my flight was not the smooth continuous passage I remember, that I hit my head with horrifying force on the broken stump of the mast before being catapulted over the side.

Convinced my neck must be broken, he hauled Arthur onto his back, binding him in place with his belt. The Warlord was awake, but dazed and weakened with loss of blood. The ship had struck a sandbank and was being pounded to pieces by the surf: knowing it would be a matter of moments before she fell apart around them, Lleminawg climbed the rail and hurled himself and Arthur into the maelstrom.

A Saeson would tell you it was not my Weird to drown, not then, any more than it was Arthur's Weird or Lleminawg's Weird to perish in the surf.

Lleminawg fought his way ashore and collapsed exhausted on the beach. Others followed, among them Moried, who saw my body swirling in the white water, seized it and dragged it to land though like Lleminawg he was certain I must be dead.

After a time the storm abated and the survivors took stock. None was unhurt, and most had suffered internal injuries in the battering of the waves, injuries which were not at once obvious. I myself apparently answered every question put to me in a cheerful and resolute fashion, and it was a long while before they realized I was with them only in body, my spirit having fled to some happier place.

For the place in which we found ourselves was not pleasant. It was bleak and desolate, swept by a bitter wind. Further inland was no better, though the dunes and grass were gradually succeeded by sandy soil and patches of heather. Stagnant, marshy water lay in the hollows, making the going difficult, and it was hard to steer a course in such a featureless landscape.

(I recall nothing of this at first hand. They told me later that I took my turn at carrying Arthur, who had lapsed into deep sleep, and otherwise encouraged the weakest among us on our night march in search of shelter, but I recollect none of it.)

Come first light we paused for a rest. Two of our number died as we crouched in the buckthorn, huddled together for warmth. We scraped shallow graves in the sandy soil and left them.

Lleminawg was the first to see the distant figures bent against the wind. We stopped and waited for them, believing (because we wanted to believe) that this was rescue, refusing to accept what was quickly obvious, that this was a party of men in no better shape than ourselves.

The Hawk was in the lead, his fierce face haggard and flenched by the gale. His first question was for Arthur, and he was not content until he had looked upon the Warlord for himself.

'Where are we?' was his second, but none of us could answer.

Lleminawg looked over the newcomers in the vain hope that he had somehow been mistaken, had missed the man he sought.

'Cei?' he asked quietly.

Gwalchmei did not need to speak. His wind-raw features said all that needed saying.

It was now they realized my mind was not with them, for I gave no indication of understanding, though Cei, after Arthur himself, was my oldest and dearest friend among the Companions.

The slim warship had weathered the storm better than our full-bodied transport, yet like us she had struck the banks, ploughing deep into the sands to be pounded apart by the waves. Gwalchmei and a handful of others had struggled ashore through the surf, but of Cei there had been no sign.

Cei was gone, Arthur was maimed and unconscious, and I was lacking my wits. The Hawk took charge, with Lleminawg and Moried to aid him, but the heart had gone out of the Companions. One by one they stumbled and fell, succumbing to their wounds, and did not rise again.

At the end there were seven of us, the significance of which was not lost on Lleminawg, though he kept a wary eye on me, expecting me to collapse at any moment.

Lleminawg, Gwalchmei, Moried, Atlendor, Menw and Arthur and I. We seven came to the Old Ones.

Not all of us were to return.

*   *   *

'Something is happening,' said Nai. He lifted an edge of the door curtain and saw that the guard had moved into the space between the huts, and was peering at the path through the fields.

'Listen,' said Budoc.

They heard the footsteps of the second sentry as he moved around the hut to join his comrade. One of the Scotti waved uncertainly at somebody outside Nai's range of vision.

'What is it?' demanded Budoc.

Nai shook his head. 'I am not sure. Serach and Dovnuall returning, I would guess, but something is wrong.'

'Gorthyn,' Budoc hissed triumphantly.

'Let us hope they do not feel vengeful,' Nai said drily.

A sorry procession wound into sight, the tall figure of Serach unmistakable at its head.

'No sign of Dovnuall,' reported Nai. Budoc joined him in the doorway.

'Not many left. Six, seven.'

'Half their number dead,' said Nai. They exchanged a glance.

'What is the matter with Eremon?' the hermit asked suddenly.

The leader of the Scotti still lay sprawled beside the wooden chest, the splendid chalice clutched in one hand. Despite the movement around him he showed no sign of waking.

Nai shrugged. 'Drunk.'

'Good. With luck they will not dare finish us until he is awake.'

Nai grunted dubiously as the tall Irishman knelt beside Eremon and tried to rouse him. Eventually Serach abandoned the task, straightened and dusted off his leggings.

One of the Scotti spoke and pointed at the hut where the captives were being held. Nai felt his heart flutter. Serach stared at the doorway, almost as if he knew Nai was watching, then looked down at Eremon with an expression of disgust.

'Leave them,' he said very clearly. 'Nai was once my friend.'

He pulled his cloak around him and stalked towards another hut. 'Keep guard!' he ordered, and disappeared within.

The Scotti murmured among themselves, cast nervous glances at the wooded hills. One or two looked longingly at the boats.

'If they dared they would slip away this night,' said Budoc.

'In their own lands they would have gone long since.' Nai rubbed at the skin under his eyes. 'What of us?'

'Us?' Budoc let the leather curtain fall as the guards returned to their posts. 'Come darkness we shall leave.' He spoke absently, as if the matter were of no great importance. 'I must have the chest, you see.'

'And the chalice, I presume.'

'Ah, the chalice!' Budoc crossed to the bed he had chosen earlier, stretched out upon it, hands behind his head, and once again took up his tale.

Seven of us, I said.

Moried had guarded my back ever since the battle of Agned. He was a good man, loyal to the Magister Militum and steadfast in adversity. It was Moried who kept me moving when I would have given up like the rest, cursing and cajoling my witless form to take one step after another.

Lleminawg the Dancer and Gwalchmei the Hawk were two of the deadliest warriors of Arthur's court. Lleminawg was famed for the speed and grace of his reactions, while Gwalchmei was renowned for his golden tongue and for never failing on any quest however hard its execution.

Atlendor was from Calchwinyth of the limestone hills, where Caswallon and Caradoc the Mighty once ruled the far-reaching tribe of the Catuwallon. Though he was a prince of high lineage in his own land, a member of a family which had prospered under Roman rule yet retained its ancient ties with the people, Atlendor preferred to serve Arthur.

Menw was a strange man from the mountains of Dunoding. Some said he had trained to be a druid before becoming a warrior, and certainly he knew much lore concerning herbs and potions, and was gifted at the art of going unseen, both of which were – or are – druid traits.

Neither Arthur nor I could be anything other than a burden on our comrades. Arthur still slept – Menw pronounced it a healing sleep, though Lleminawg guessed he said this to quiet their worries. I stumbled along, supported by Moried, with no idea of where we were, babbling of highly scented blossoms and trees laden with fruit.

To me, and this part I do remember, we were not staggering through a drear wasteland of sand and buckthorn. In my head we were marching proud and strong through a fair country where fine flocks and herds grazed on the rich grass, a country where sweet flowers bloomed and there was fruit ripe for the plucking on every tree, a country where the streams and pools were filled with fat fish and the game beasts were waiting for the chase. To my eyes it was a land of plenty where a man might live like a king at his ease.

We came to a place where the ground fell away in a deep depression. The others saw a heathland of ling scattered with a few thin birch and feeble pines, and the glint of stagnant water. I saw a beautiful valley, a lightly wooded bowl beneath the azure sky, with the glory of the sun reflected in a series of cunningly placed ponds too artfully arranged to be natural, so that the whole vista shone and glittered like a living thing.

We had scarcely begun our descent when we were surrounded. To me the newcomers were handsome lords and ladies richly dressed in red linen and golden silks, who greeted us with smiles and courteously begged us to honour them with our presence as their guests.

To my companions they were a group of dark men of fearsome appearance, half naked in defiance of the bitter wind, their cruel faces immobile under spiral tattoos. Each had a shock of thick black hair, with two slim plaits dangling by either cheek, and somehow this added to their menace. Moried recognized them at once (as indeed did the others); to him they seemed like goblins, or demons out of Tartarus.

Lleminawg and Gwalchmei drew their swords, but saw at once that it was hopeless. They were too exhausted to fight, and even had they been fresh, Arthur and I were vulnerable. They surrendered their weapons and allowed themselves to be herded down into the great hollow.

'Fhoi Myore,' muttered Lleminawg from the corner of his mouth, referring to the monstrous adversaries of the old gods of Ierne. 'After their defeat by the Tuatha De Danann, the Fomorians fled to their ancient haunts, the seas and isles of Iardomnan. And here they are, cousins, here they are: vile legend come to life.'

'They are mortal men,' said Gwalchmei, 'no more, no less.'

'Your friend does not think so,' said one of the captors, and laughed unpleasantly.

The tattooed men talked among themselves as we descended through the scrub, talked in a strange tongue not even the Hawk – who was learned in these matters – could understand. But whether it was truly an alien language not allied to British, Irish or Saeson, as Moried always insisted, or whether it was simply a dialect of our common speech, so thick as to be incomprehensible, as Gwalchmei later suggested, I cannot say.

They brought us to a rough encampment of leather tents hidden in the lee of a clump of stunted firs. I, of course, was convinced that we were escorted to a great show of buildings worthy to rank with the splendours of Caer Cadwy, an array of halls and sleeping rooms and chambers nestling snugly in the shelter of sweet-scented pines.

To Moried it seemed that these people did not live here permanently. Everything had a makeshift, temporary look, and the very nature of the countryside seemed to confirm his theory, for this was not a land to support life for any length of time.

Nobody noticed Menw was not with us until after we had reached the camp. When they did notice the four of them kept quiet, and prayed I would do likewise if I waked.

They were ushered into the presence of a man with the deadest eyes any of them had ever seen, black holes without a hint of feeling. (And I, I was brought to the throne of a great king resplendent in dazzling raiment of gold, who bespoke me kindly and bade me be of good cheer.)

My comrades knew him for Pedrylaw Menestyr, who had knelt to Arthur by the gate of Caer Cadwy. (And I knew him for the King of All the World, who acknowledges no man his master.) He sat cross-legged, toying with a bone flute on his lap, fixing each of us in turn with his dark gaze.

When he came to me he frowned and spoke for the first time. 'A blow to the head. He must rest. We shall prepare strong medicines for him.'

He gestured and I was led away. Atlendor made to protest, but Menestyr the Cupbearer scowled and said:

'We mean him no harm, not yet. If he does not lie down the blood blister inside his skull may burst and kill him. You can see for yourselves that he thinks himself in some other world.'

'Were it not for that "not yet" I should be greatly reassured,' said Gwalchmei.

'You are the one called the Hawk.' Menestyr stared at him until even he, the fiercest and proudest of us all, was forced to drop his eyes. 'You are blood kin to Arthur. Bring the Magister Militum to me.'

On their arrival the four Companions had set Arthur gently on the ground, then taken up positions around him, one at each of the cardinal points. Now they huddled closer together, refusing to move.

Menestyr sighed. 'No doubt you will sell your lives dearly, but you cannot prevail. Look!' He indicated his followers. 'Still, if it sets your minds at rest, I shall come to him.'

He rose to his feet in a single fluid motion and stepped between Lleminawg and Gwalchmei as if they presented no danger.

'Unwrap his leg,' Menestyr said to Atlendor.

Atlendor studied him for a moment, striving to hold the weight of those dead eyes, trying to read the tattooed man's intentions.

Then he nodded, and unwound the bandage.

The gash was weeping, red and angry, the poison spreading up towards the groin in a series of purple streaks.

Menestyr snapped his fingers and said something in his incomprehensible tongue. One of his followers ran to the nearest tent, reappeared immediately with a small pot and fresh bandages.

The Companions looked at each other helplessly. They had seen wounds like this before, knew Arthur would be lucky to live.

'In this you may trust me,' said the Cupbearer. He grinned wolfishly.

Taking the pot, he smeared a foul-smelling green ointment over the leg, then bound the new bandage into place. The ointment at once soaked through the cloth, giving it a vile greenish tinge.

Menestyr laid his hand on Arthur's brow. The Warlord moaned in his sleep, eyelids fluttering. 'He has gone deep, deep within himself to find his own healing,' Menestyr said. 'There is hope. He is strong.'

He gestured to his followers. 'Take them to their friend. Give them food and drink, let them rest. I shall speak with them later.'

The four gently lifted Arthur and were shown into the tent to which I had earlier been taken.

They found me being fed some potion by an aged crone, a woman with tattoos so faded they were well nigh lost amidst the wrinkles of her face. She cackled at them toothlessly, then pushed me down into the skins of the bed before leaving.

Later they were brought fish and kale leaves, with water. Then they were left to sleep.

I woke the next morning with a great pain in my head. The last thing I remembered was lying among sheepskins on a soft couch, being spoon-fed the finest broth I had ever tasted by the fairest maiden I had seen in a long while. The chamber had been sweet-scented with herbs and rushes, luxuriously furnished in a fashion

I dimly recollected from my childhood. But overnight I had been moved to this dark tent with its mud floor and smell of uncured animal skins and unwashed human bodies.

I must have groaned aloud, because suddenly Moried was bending over me, telling me not to move.

'You have returned to us,' Gwalchmei said from behind him. 'God be praised!'

'I preferred my other quarters.'

Gwalchmei and Moried exchanged a worried glance. Moried sat on the end of the bed – a sorry heap of coverlets, not the soft couch I recalled – and began to explain what had happened. Lleminawg joined him, telling how I had struck my head.

When they came to the meeting with the Hawk, I looked at them in disbelief. 'Cei dead? He cannot be. Not Cei. Not Fair Cei.'

They turned to Gwalchmei and Atlendor for confirmation.

'I fear it is true, cousin,' the Hawk said gently. 'We searched the strand for him, but he was not there.'

'You mean you did not find his body?'

Gwalchmei shrugged. 'No, but then we did not find a dozen or more others. He is gone, cousin, as are they.'

I shook my head, immediately regretted it as the pain lanced through my skull. 'I do not believe it. He is alive.'

Even in my fuddled state I could see them decide to humour me. Moried and Lleminawg continued with their story, describing the deadly march across the deserted isle – if isle it was – and the meeting with Pedrylaw Menestyr.

'And Arthur?' I asked.

'He sleeps, and in his sleep he dreams,' said a new voice.

Menestyr himself entered the tent, accompanied by two younger men who could have been his sons. Atlendor moved aside to allow him access to Arthur, and the tattooed man knelt to examine the wound.

'The worst is past,' he pronounced, then straightened and came towards me. 'And you, I think you too will mend. But you must not exert yourself for several days. Do you understand?'

'Yes,' I said reluctantly, feeling in my bones that he was telling the truth. 'Why do you do this for us?'

He stared at me with the same blank gaze that had nearly ensnared me at Caer Cadwy. 'Because my daughter would not forgive me were it otherwise.'

I think that somewhere inside me I had always known. Nothing else, after all, could really explain his actions: the insane attack upon us in Lindinis, his effrontery within the walls of Caer Cadwy.

'Your daughter?' blurted Moried.

He smiled thinly. 'Teleri verch Afallach,' he said. 'Teleri daughter of Afallach.'

In Ierne, Afallach is a woman's name. In Prydein I have heard it used for men. I do not know whether he was giving us his true name (for Pedrylaw Menestyr, as Degaw of the Creones had told me, is no more than a title meaning 'Skilled Cupbearer') or whether he was telling us the name of Teleri's mother. There again, Afallach could also be a place, the place of apples. (The golden apples of the sun, the silver apples of the moon.)

'She is here?' I demanded.

'Where else would she be, her mission to the South accomplished?' he sneered dismissively.

He stood in the entrance, flanked by the younger men, and addressed us all.

'You have come here bearing arms, fresh from the slaughter of the sea lord Hueil. You are men of violence, all of you, and this is a place of peace, a sanctuary so hallowed its origins are lost. Your master brought you here to watch him undergo a certain testing, and now he lies unable to submit himself to the ritual.'

'Our arrival here is not by any design of ours,' protested Gwalchmei. 'The storm drove us onto your shores. We were shipwrecked, castaway.'

'Not so,' said Menestyr. 'It is not by chance that you are here. It was the Magister Militum's intention to seek me out. It was his purpose all along. I have been waiting for him, waiting ever since I first beheld him in Caer Cadwy and knew he was the one.'

'The one for what?' asked Lleminawg.

'The one to essay the Sovereignty of Albion.'

'Ah,' said the Irishman, as if everything had now been revealed to him. He slipped off his salt-stained cloak and began to chafe his limbs.

'Yet it would seem your master aimed too high,' continued Menestyr. 'For he is disqualified before he starts. And since your master cannot dance the labyrinth, I regret his life is forfeit, and by extension yours.'

From his tone of voice he did not regret it at all. He was enjoying this, playing cat and mouse.

'Forfeit?' roared Gwalchmei. 'If his life be forfeit, why have you taken so much trouble over him? Why the ointment, why the care?'

He was a frightening man, the Hawk, when he was truly angry, and he was angrier now than I had ever seen him.

The Cupbearer's companions flinched away, then remembered their duty and straightened to their leader's side. The air in the tent was suddenly oppressive, close and crackling with menace like the air before a thunderstorm.

'Peace, cousin.'

For a moment none of us knew who had spoken. Then we looked towards where Arthur lay, on a bed of skins.

His eyes were open, calm and reassuring in their strength. They passed across us all, weighing and measuring, then fastened upon the Cupbearer.

'Pedrylaw Menestyr,' he said. 'I thank you for your attentions.'

The Cupbearer seemed disconcerted – I was slowly learning to read the face beneath those hideous tattoos – as if he had not expected Arthur to wake. 'How much have you heard?' he demanded gruffly.

'Sufficient,' said Arthur.

'You cannot dance the labyrinth.' Menestyr spoke flatly, like a man deeply disappointed, and I believe he *was* disappointed in a curious way. 'You cannot even stand.'

'If the lives of my Companions depend upon it, then I can try.' He struggled to rise, teeth gritted against the pain.

Moried and Atlendor with one voice shouted, 'No!' and flung themselves across him, pinning him to the bed.

I had always loved him, ever since I first served him as a page boy when he was a young warrior barely into manhood, but I had never loved him as much as in that moment, when he strove to gain his feet to save our lives though it would cost him his own. One often hears of men willing to die for their commander; a rarer and a finer thing is a commander willing to die for his men.

'Wait!' Gwalchmei cried. 'Wait!'

Arthur ceased and lay still, exhausted by the effort. Moried and Atlendor cautiously lifted themselves from him, holding themselves ready in case he tried again.

'Surely the Sovereign may choose a substitute?' said Gwalchmei.

There was silence while Menestyr considered this, his head tilted to one side.

'And you would be the one?' he said at last.

'If you will accept me,' said the Hawk. 'I am kin to Arthur . . .'

He would have said more, but Menestyr was shaking his head. 'No. I will allow a substitute, but not you, Hawk of the Meadows. This is not your land, nor is it your place.'

Now Lleminawg stepped forward, loose-limbed and easy, a smile upon his face. 'You are right, Pedrylaw Menestyr. It is not his place – and no shame in that, cousin,' he added with a bow to Gwalchmei. 'It is mine, by virtue of my name.'

His voice swelled to fill the tent. 'For am I not the Leaping One, the Bounding One, the Fated One? I am Lleminawg the Dancer, and for this I was born.'

Menestyr smiled thinly, like a man who has achieved his desire. 'Very well,' he said. 'If your Lord will agree.'

Pale and drawn with pain, Arthur stared at the Cupbearer. 'It would seem I have no alternative. Yet remember this, Pedrylaw Menestyr. You are the Guardian of the Chalice, its Keeper not its Owner. It is not yours to grant, nor yours to withhold.'

The Cupbearer's face suffused with blood, visible even through the green tattoos.

'Who are you to speak thus to me?' he hissed.

'You know who I am, and what I am.'

'You are a candidate for the Sovereignty,' he said contemptuously. 'Not the first, and not the last.'

He made to leave, but before he could raise the hanging Arthur spoke.

'Come here!'

The Cupbearer swayed as if struck. I could see him fight the compulsion, tauten every muscle as he struggled to lift the corner of the tent and step through the opening, but he could not manage it. Nobody could have resisted Arthur when he called in that fashion.

Menestyr turned stiffly and went to the bedside.

'Have you forgotten so soon what you saw at Caer Cadwy?' said Arthur. 'I *am* Prydein.'

He was a brave man, Pedrylaw Menestyr, I will give him that. Even now he did not swerve in his pride.

'Many have made that claim, yet few have been found worthy,' he said, and only the lack of conviction in his voice betrayed him.

*   *   *

Later they led us out.

Arthur had lapsed into sleep again, and I needed Moried's support to keep me moving. Lleminawg walked alone at our head, lost in thought, while Gwalchmei and Atlendor carried Arthur on a litter, not daring to let him from their sight now the time of trial was upon us.

We came to a kind of natural amphitheatre set in the middle of low heather-clad hills, and I can only assume that this was a hollow within the greater hollow we had seen earlier.

Our guards indicated positions around the rim, and we stood or sat with the rest of the Attecotti who had gathered there. Looking at them now I saw that they were of many different types, as many and as different as the people of Prydein herself, and that only those who stood near to Pedrylaw Menestyr shared his spiral tattoos and dark skin. I guessed that these, like my lost love Teleri, were his close kin: the Clan of the Cupbearer.

The hollow was a strange place. The sides were sheer, too sheer to climb, and the only route in or out was by a winding path which crossed and recrossed itself at random, its edges marked by low blocks of yellowish stone. These blocks might once have been carved with pictures, but if so they were now so weathered by the elements that the designs had worn smooth, leaving only ghostly traces behind.

'A quarry, do you think?' whispered Moried in my ear.

It was possible, I supposed, though what might have been quarried there I could not say.

I studied the path more carefully, and suddenly saw the pattern. The spiral way wound in and out exactly as Teleri had described it, except that this was within a hollow and not upon a mound. Seven times round it went, a backtracking spiral twisting deviously to the shadowy depths, a maze such as Daedalus wrought when the world was young.

(And at the heart of the labyrinth is the Monster.)

As the path meandered it made eight crossings of itself, and at each of these crossings stood a figure: a priestess in a black cloak wearing a high head-dress. The very bottom of the pit was lost in darkness, but I knew a ninth would wait there, where Lleminawg must go to be reborn.

Arthur slept, and a raven wheeled overhead. A feather fell fluttering from its tail. Lleminawg caught it and put it in his hair, then turned and clasped each of us by the hand. Finally he knelt and kissed the sleeping Warlord on the brow.

'I am ready,' he said into the silence, and took the first step upon the path, the descent into the realm of the dead from which few have ever returned.

'Who comes?' demanded the priestess who stood guard there.

He flung back his head and cried out in a great voice so all the pit reverberated with his shout, and whence the words came I cannot say, but that they were the right ones there was no doubt:

'Am I not a candidate for fame, to be heard in song? Am I not Lleminawg of the Eoganacht Maigi Dergind i nAlbae?'

She drew aside and allowed him to pass, and he danced a full circuit of the quarry wall while the raven circled above, chanting and humming as he went, till he came to the second dark figure.

'Seven possessions to a king,' said she.

'Not hard to name,' said he. 'A sword, a spear, a knife, a whetstone. A mantle of royalty, a game board for wooden wisdom. A chalice. And an eighth possession a king must have: an heir.'

He went on his way, circling the hollow in the opposite direction, till we saw him climbing up past where the first woman had challenged him. Here the third priestess stepped forward to bar his passage.

'Who am I?' she asked.

Lleminawg balanced on one leg while the raven gyred above the hollow. 'Not hard to answer. You are Medb, the intoxicating one.'

'Smooth shall be thy drink from my cup – it will be mead, it will be honey, it will be strong ale,' she said.

He shouted in triumph, and the raven echoed him. Now he ran the outer circuit of the spiral, leaping and whirling, and all present could see the power within him, and none could doubt the rightness of his cause.

Five more questions he was asked, and five more he answered, without hesitation, for they were easy to him though they would have been insoluble riddles to most men.

And at the bottom of the pit, where the shadows lay, a ninth figure appeared. This one was not dressed in black, like the priestesses, nor did it wear their high head-dress.

Instead it wore glittering mail, with a square shield upon the left arm and a helmet of iron upon the head. A mask of silver covered the face, a mask fashioned in the likeness of a snarling boar. In the right hand was a short spear with a barbed blade.

Lleminawg halted, leaped aside to avoid the first thrust. Those of us watching saw that he could not long dodge the spear, not in the confines of the narrow path, and even as we watched he stumbled and seemed to fall, barely evading the cruel blade.

Above us the raven shrieked in anger.

Arthur shifted, growling in his sleep.

Lleminawg below howled like a wolf thwarted of its prey.

In that moment we knew we had lost, failed in our quest, that our champion would soon be slain.

2

'And?' prompted Nai.

Budoc shrugged. 'And shouting, and a great confusion of men running hither and thither. I cannot make sense of it, cousin, for I have lost the key.'

The hermit fell silent, weary with talking. For a while they waited, each lost in his own thoughts, waited for the dusk to thicken so they might stand some chance of escape.

The druid was still snoring, his narrow face contorted in the grip of some dream, his thin nostrils flaring and contracting as he fought for air. His greasy black hair was matted, and the bumps on the shaven wedge that ran from ear to ear seemed more pronounced.

Nai looked at him and shuddered in revulsion.

'Tempting, is it not?' said Budoc, following the direction of his gaze. 'The world would be a better place without him.'

Nai licked his lips. 'Have you broken his powers for ever?'

The hermit shook his head. 'No. He will recover, though his confidence will be shaken.'

'I could do it in the heat of the moment,' said Nai. 'I could do it if I suddenly burst in here and found him. But having watched him sleep for so long . . .'

'I know,' said Budoc. 'I know.'

They lapsed into a companionable quiet again while the shadows clotted in the curves of the hut. Nai assumed the hermit must have a plan, because he himself could see no means of escape. Sooner or later Eremon would wake from his drunken stupor, and when he did what remained of Nai's life would be short and painful.

The sentry outside the door gave vent to a scream of terror. They heard the second guard come stumbling around the building, slipping and sliding in his haste. Budoc laid his ruined hand on Nai's arm, and the two went together to the hanging curtain.

The Scotti were pouring from the huts, staring up at the hillside and wailing. Eremon lay insensible, oblivious to the shrieks around him. Serach appeared, sword in hand, calling for silence. He shaded his eyes and peered through the evening light at the hills behind the fields.

'Where?' they heard him say.

'There!' screamed the sentry, pointing. 'There!'

Serach scowled. Nai saw his lips move; he squinted harder, trying to read what the Irishman was saying.

'Domnuall,' murmured the hermit beside him.

'You, you and you!' shouted Serach. 'Fetch it down!'

The men he had indicated shuffled uneasily from foot to foot. Serach brandished his weapon and roared: 'Fetch it down! Now!'

'The big man!' protested one of the Scotti. 'The big man is loose upon the hills!'

'Go!' bellowed Serach. 'Go or die!' He swung the blade, and the man leaped aside.

'He has lost them,' whispered Nai. 'The heart has gone out from them.' The hermit made no response.

Nai glanced at him and saw the old man's eyes had glazed over. 'What is it?' he said urgently, shaking Budoc's arm. 'Budoc?'

'The Long Man,' said the hermit, speaking more to himself than Nai. 'The Long Man is loose upon the hills.'

Suddenly his eyes cleared and he beamed at his companion.

'Now I remember. I remember . . . everything.' He laughed, clapped his hands, cut a brief caper around the hut, hair and beard flying and eyes sparkling with glee.

Nai stared in bemusement at this transformation. 'The Long Man?' he said stupidly. 'Cei?'

'Yes, Cei, fair Cei!' exclaimed the other. 'It all comes tumbling to my mind.' He slapped Nai's back jubilantly.

The hermit seemed to have lost ten years. In fact, Nai thought absently, if one took away the beard and trimmed his hair, fed him a few decent meals to put some weight on the gaunt frame, he would not look so very old after all.

He turned to the hanging curtain. Serach's reluctant threesome were returning, carrying a pole with an object embedded on one end.

'What is it?' said the hermit, calming down.

'The head of Dovnuall Frych. The birds have gnawed it. The eyes are gone.'

'Gorthyn's vengeance for his father Erfai,' said Budoc. 'A hard cycle to break, the cycle of revenge.'

'How do you mean?'

'Dovnuall kills Erfai. Then Gorthyn kills Dovnuall. Next some kinsman of Dovnuall will kill Gorthyn.' The hermit smiled mournfully. 'It happened in our time too. When Cei was slain by Gwydawg mab Pedrylaw Menestyr in vengeance for what we did upon the Isle of the Old Ones, I could not believe that he was dead and I still alive. I had always thought him so much more complete a warrior than I . . .'

His face was cold in the light that escaped around the edges of the curtain. 'And he died by treachery. Gwydawg the son of Menestyr was never a match for Cei in fair fight. I slew Gwydawg myself, and slowly, toying with him, wounding where I could have killed, forcing him to pick up his sword and continue the fight when he would have flung it aside and welcomed the death blow.'

He sighed. 'In the end I sickened myself. Vengeance is one thing, torture another. Cei was dead, and nothing would ever bring him back.'

'This fight was none of Gorthyn's choosing,' said Nai.

Budoc's expression was still sad. 'You did not have to cross the estuary. For all that the trees sang to you both, you did not have to come. Gorthyn crossed because he hoped Dovnuall would be here.'

'We . . .' Nai shook his head and did not continue.

The Scotti were slowly settling to their rest. The guards resumed their posts, stepping around Eremon who lay curled in the dust, the chalice clutched in one hand, the wooden chest by his feet. Serach made a round of the sentries but did not visit the prisoners, to Nai's disappointment, for he had half entertained some vague idea of appealing to the Irishman's better nature.

Night fell, and with it silence.

Nai was startled from his doze by a thud against the back wall of the hut.

Budoc was already at the entrance, whispering to the guard: 'The druid is worse, I tell you, much worse. Tomorrow your leader will blame us for letting him die. See for yourself if you do not believe me.'

'Enough!' said the guard in his barbarous tongue. 'No need to wake the world. I –'

His words were cut off by the sound of a blow. The curtain parted and Gorthyn lowered the guard's body to the floor of the hut.

'Here, have a knife,' he said by way of greeting, tossing a war-knife and scabbard to Nai. 'British work, not Scotti.'

'It would be,' Nai said drily. 'It is mine.'

'Well, there is lucky then,' laughed the big man. 'What say we cut a few throats while we can?' He nudged the hermit. 'Your Saeson lad. Slit the throats of half a dozen men he did, just sliced them up while I was busy with dear Dovnuall.'

'A youth of hidden talents,' Budoc said solemnly, which made Gorthyn fling back his head and roar with soundless laughter.

'Where are they, Cedric and Eurgain?' asked Nai.

'Safe at the hermit's home with the horses.'

'Is Eremon still out there?'

Gorthyn shook his head regretfully. 'No, he dragged himself inside when it grew cooler.' He turned to the hermit, said more soberly: 'If that fancy cup is anything of yours, I fear he took it with him. He has not let it from his grasp in all the time I have been watching.'

Budoc clicked his tongue in frustration. 'And the chest?'

'That has not moved. Too heavy, I dare say.'

He stopped and looked suspiciously from one to the other of them. 'What is it? You are not thinking . . .?'

'It is not so very heavy,' coaxed the hermit. 'Although of course if you are tired we will understand. After all, Dovnuall was a very strong man, not easy to overcome.'

'And you are not so young as you were,' added Nai, stifling a laugh.

Gorthyn flung up his hands in mute appeal. 'My plan was to sneak down here, silence the guards, rescue you and sneak away again. Now you want me to walk through the middle of the village with a great box on my back. What about giving me a bell to ring as well?'

'The moon is not up yet,' the hermit said confidently. 'They will not see you.'

341

The big man scowled. 'More of your magic?' He jerked his head at the druid. 'What of him?'

'We are not the Saeson,' said Nai.

Gorthyn sucked in his breath, let it out in a hiss. 'No. A shame, but we are not.'

He eased back the curtain, peered into the darkness. 'You make for the trees. I shall fetch the box.'

They crept out, keeping to the shadows of the wall. Gorthyn impatiently waved Budoc and Nai away, so they eased past the crumpled form of the second sentry and dashed for the shelter of the field bank, following (though they did not know it) the route Eurgain's sister had taken in her ill-fated flight from the Scotti.

The carrion eaters had been hard at work among the animal carcasses, and the reek was less powerful than it had been that morning. They walked briskly between the remains, careful where they put their feet, only breaking into a run when they were near the top of the slope.

'Can you truly cloak him from their eyes?' asked Nai as they paused beneath the outer bank with its thorn hedge.

'If he believes it I can,' said the hermit.

They waited until they heard the big man toiling up the hill towards them, then found a gap where they could all slip through the thorn hedge without difficulty.

'One of them looked right at me!' exclaimed Gorthyn as he put the chest on the ground and stretched his limbs. 'Right at me, yet did not see me!'

'It is a dark night,' Budoc said, leading the way into the woods without further comment.

'I am sorry about the chalice,' said Nai after a time. 'I suppose Eremon will take it to Vortepor now all his other plans have come to naught.'

The hermit laughed. 'He can if he wishes. He will receive small thanks.'

Gorthyn, puffing along behind with the box on his back, said: 'Why is the chalice so important? What I saw of it seemed pretty enough in the sunlight, but scarcely worth all this fuss.'

'It is not,' said Budoc.

'But . . .' Nai stopped in his tracks so abruptly Gorthyn almost cannoned into him.

'It is nothing,' the hermit reiterated. 'Oh, it is valuable in its own right, for it is Scythian work from the eastern rim of the world, and very old. But it is not what Eremon thinks. It is not the chalice he was sent to find.'

The youngsters were waiting for them at the hut. They had lit a small fire in the shelter of the hollow, the flames invisible from any distance, and were cooking some of the meat from the village.

Eurgain leaped to her feet at the sight of Nai and Budoc, ran towards them with a cry of joy. She flung her arms around the hermit, hugged him for so long Nai began to think she would never release him.

'I thought you were dead,' she said, over and over again. 'I thought you were dead.'

Ceolric came forward with a shy smile, patted Nai on the shoulder as if he needed to touch him in order to prove to himself that the older man was real, and helped Gorthyn carry the chest the last few paces to the little stone building.

'I wondered if they had caught you as well,' he said softly.

'Not me, boy.' Gorthyn flashed him a grin. 'I could see the Scotti were guarding one hut, so I decided to wait until dusk to find out what was inside.'

Nai's stomach rumbled as he caught the scent of the meat. The others laughed.

'Did we bring anything to drink?' demanded Gorthyn.

'A modest amount of mead,' said Nai. 'In one of the saddle bags.'

The hermit rummaged inside the chest, produced five of the glass tumblers Nai had seen earlier. 'Family heirlooms,' he said with a smile, holding them up to the light of the fire one after the other before passing them round.

They took the tumblers reverently, admiring the heavy green glass while Gorthyn opened the first of the jars and poured out the golden mead. Then they raised their glasses to the fire.

'To the *nemeton* of Porthyle,' said the big man.

'Sanctuary Wood,' echoed the others.

They drank deeply.

Budoc swallowed his mouthful. ' "Sweet, sweet was our mead, but bitter its aftertaste",' he quoted absent-mindedly.

They made the hermit sit upon a log seat beside the small stone hearth and promise not to move, while Gorthyn carved the meat and the rest served the bread and vegetables.

'What will you do now?' Nai asked Ceolric.

343

The youth flushed, his eyes flickering from Nai to Eurgain. 'I do not know,' he said. 'I have not thought so far ahead.'

Gorthyn poked him playfully in the ribs. 'You can come with us if you like. There is always room for another warrior in the warband, and it is not Saesons alone we fight. The petty kings of eastern Britain are prone to dreams of territorial expansion.'

Ceolric gaped at him in astonishment. 'You mean you would take me with you?'

Amused, Nai shot a glance at the girl, but she was busy with her platter of food, pretending not to listen. 'We promised Eurgain she could come with us when she asked us that question. We give you the same promise now.'

'You are our comrade-in-arms,' explained Gorthyn. 'You fought with me against that monstrous hound, and you waited in ambush, doing all I asked of you – and more,' he added, remembering how the Saeson had dealt with the injured Scotti.

He spread his arms wide, grinned at the youth. 'So you are our comrade, and we never desert a comrade. If you want to come, you may. If you wish to stay here, you may. If you want to travel to the lands of Cerdic and Cynric, we shall see you receive an escort for most of your journey. We will not ride away from you in the morning and leave you to starve or be slain by the first bandit you meet. Whatever our failings, we do not abandon our friends.'

'Are we going to ride away in the morning?' asked Nai to cover the young Saeson's confusion.

Gorthyn shrugged. 'Gereint will come by land, not over the water. I had thought we might ride to meet him, warn him of what has passed here. A small troop should be able to drive off the Scotti for good.'

'And what has passed here?' Nai looked round the circle of the fire, at the faces of his friends gleaming with the juices of the meat. 'More to the point, is it finished?'

'We should set a watch when we have eaten,' Gorthyn said judiciously, 'but I do not believe the Scotti present much threat. We have mown them like ripe corn every time we have met.'

'You do not think we should run, run for safety when the moon rises?'

'No!' growled Gorthyn. 'This is my land, and I will not be driven from it. If they wish to fight, let them come!' He brought a heavy fist down on the ground and glared defiantly.

'It would seem we are staying,' said Nai.

For a while they ate in a silence punctuated by the hiss and crackle of the fire. Then the hermit turned to Ceolric.

'Tell me, will others try what your father did, to settle new lands here in the west?'

The youth grunted, struggled with a long slice of meat. 'I would not be surprised,' he said through a mouthful. 'They say one generation was lost at Badon, and their sons at Camlann. Whether that be true or not, a third generation has grown to manhood, and they are land hungry. They look westwards, and they see an emptiness, room for new settlements. I think it will begin once Cerdic is dead, and he cannot live much longer.'

'Ten years since Arthur fell at Camlann,' Gorthyn said gloomily. 'We cannot expect the Amherawdyr's peace to last for ever.'

'There was a man on the ship,' said Ceolric. 'He was at Camlann. In his youth he had sought to serve the Emperor. Though he fought against him, he admired him still, was sorry he was gone.'

'This man fought at Camlann? What was his name?' Budoc leaned forward on his log.

'Garulf. He was a Frisian. He had been here before – to this estuary, I mean – years ago. My father took him on as our steersman and ship's master.'

'Garulf.' The old man pursed his lips, shook his head. 'No, it means nothing.'

'Were you at Camlann, then?' Ceolric asked curiously.

'Who was not? All the warriors of the South fought on one side or the other.'

'We were too young,' Gorthyn said regretfully. 'Barely out of the Boys' House. They made us stay behind and guard the homes. Not that we would have been much good if anything had happened. We hardly knew enough to draw a blade without cutting our fingers.'

'You were fortunate.'

Gorthyn grinned at the hermit, not taking him seriously. 'What? The greatest battle of our lifetimes? You jest, cousin!'

'Have you ever fought in a real battle?'

'Plenty.' The big man was affronted.

'Skirmishes,' Budoc said dismissively. 'You tell me, Nai. What was the largest fight you two have ever been in?'

The dark man massaged the scar on his throat. 'The place

345

where I took this. The day we drove Eremon and the Scotti from their settlements along the River Oak.'

'And how many on each side?'

'Full three hundred for Gereint. Not so many for the Scotti. Perhaps two hundred?'

The hermit laughed scornfully. 'Five hundred all told? There were ten times that at Camlann, and by nightfall most lay dead on the field.'

'Garulf said that if they had known where they were going, they would have turned back,' said Ceolric.

'Wise man.'

Nai smiled, still rubbing at his throat. 'The fight against Eremon was enough. He came close to killing me.'

'He gave you that himself?' said Ceolric.

'I was tired, and I had forgotten how fast he could move.'

'Like his kinsman Lleminawg,' added Gorthyn, watching the old man's face, thinking that if Budoc were indeed Bedwyr then he would have known Lleminawg well.

'The Bounding One, the Fated One. Yes, he was fast.' The hermit looked across the flames at Nai. 'We were talking of him earlier.'

'You knew him?' Gorthyn leaned forward eagerly.

'I knew him. I knew them all. Lleminawg, Gwalchmei, Cei . . .'

'The Long Man,' muttered Gorthyn. 'Cei the Fair. "*A host was useless against Cei in battle*".'

'The chief of Arthur's warriors. By his hand were many enemies overthrown. Who knows, if Cei had lived, perhaps the Amherawdyr might have survived Camlann.'

'So Arthur did die at Camlann?' Gorthyn demanded sharply.

The hermit smiled teasingly. 'Ah, as to that, who can tell for certain? I do not know, though I saw him struck from his horse by a blow that would have slain most men outright. But then Arthur had taken great wounds before, and lived to tell the tale.'

He dropped his voice, spoke so softly the others had to strain to hear.

'Do not say he died, say rather that by the Grace of God, here in this world he changed his life.'

'What difference does it make?' asked Eurgain, who had listened patiently to all this talk. 'You prate on about warriors and Scotti and Saesons, as if there were some difference between them. What good did any of you ever do me and mine? What does it matter whether Arthur or Custennin or even Cerdic rules this land? We are the ones who have to pay for your glory, we are the ones who starve when some lordling seizes our crops by force of arms, or burns our roofs over our heads so that a bard can make a song about how brave he is. We are the ones who are raped and bludgeoned to death, or carried off into slavery, and I tell you, when Dyfyr my sister was being raped it was small help to her to know the men doing it were Scotti and not warriors in the service of Custennin or Saeson pirates.'

The men coughed and shifted uncomfortably, all except the hermit, who reached out and drew her to him.

'It is always on those who live modest lives that the burden falls heaviest,' he said. 'Without them the warriors could not exist, for someone must plant the corn and tend the herds. They forget that, the wolves of war, never having fended for themselves.'

'Never having done a stroke of work in their lives,' spat Eurgain.

The three younger men exchanged embarrassed glances. 'One thing puzzles me,' Ceolric said quietly to Gorthyn. 'Why do you keep calling each other cousin?'

'Because we are members of the same *teulu*. It is a term of affection, a sign of the bond between us. *Teulu* means both warband and family, and thus all the warriors in a *teulu* call their fellows cousin, regardless of the ties of blood.' He took a swig of mead, patted Ceolric on the back. 'You are one of us. You may call me cousin, if the fancy takes you.'

'Thank you,' the youth said formally, spoiling the effect by hiccuping as he held out his goblet to be refilled.

'I shall take first watch,' Eurgain announced suddenly. 'What do you want me to do?'

She rose and stood waiting in the firelight, her hair a mass of tumbled reds and golds, a slim straight figure filled with anger, and none of them dared question her right to stand guard.

'I shall show you,' said Nai.

He led her to a place where she could hide among the bushes and yet keep watch on the path and the surrounding woods.

'What was the message the usurper of Rome sent to Macsen?' he muttered. ' "If you come, and if you come".'

She gazed at him blankly, having no idea what he was talking about.

Nai touched her arm, felt her flinch away. 'If they do come,

347

which they may though Gorthyn thinks not, run back for us as quietly as you are able.'

He hesitated, reluctant to leave, breathed deep to fill his lungs with the night smells, the scent of pines and the tang of the sea.

'Go,' she said. 'I shall not fall asleep, nor start at every rustle of the wind.'

He went.

3

When Nai returned to the fire, Budoc was briefly explaining to the others something of the long tale he had related to the dark man while they were Eremon's prisoners.

'Vortepor of Dyfed?' Ceolric interrupted excitedly. 'Garulf, the man I mentioned who fought at Camlann, was there when the Picts attacked the house in the city. He said he saved the life of the British leader – mab Petroc, he called himself – but the Briton thought he had done it for a piece of silver, which was not so, not so at all.'

'Indeed?' said Budoc with amusement. 'The Saeson boy was on your ship, and still spinning stories, eh? No doubt his tale had grown with the telling.'

Ceolric coloured, looked first abashed and then defiant. 'He was a good man. I liked him.'

'Perhaps age had improved him,' said Budoc. 'When I knew him, he was a lad who chopped and changed his loyalties too freely to be deemed trustworthy.'

Nai busied himself with the ponies, who seemed none the worse for the day's adventures, while Budoc resumed his account, bringing it to the point at which his memory had failed him.

'For years I have been unable to recall what happened next,' he was saying as Nai seated himself beside Ceolric. 'Oh, I had vague images: a sword falling slowly from light to dark; a great outcry of men and women; Menestyr's face contorted with anger . . .'

He smiled across the fire at Gorthyn. 'Tonight you gave me the key, the clew with which to unravel the labyrinth.'

'Me?' said Gorthyn in surprise.

'You. "The big man is loose upon the hills," the Scotti shouted when they found Dovnuall's head. And those are almost the very words that the Attecotti screamed, when they disrupted the solemn ceremony which was about to end in Lleminawg's death at the hands of the figure in the silver mask. "The Long Man is loose upon the hills," they cried.'

'The Long Man is loose upon the hills!'

The cry came from behind us, and was at once taken up by other voices. The crowd shifted uneasily, but before I turned to look (my heart leaping with joy that Cei still lived) I saw Lleminawg run back a few paces, out of the shadows into the sunlight, winning himself a brief respite.

On the hills behind us was a tall figure with a smaller shape beside it, and around them men writhed in the heather.

'Menw went to fetch him,' Gwalchmei said disbelievingly. 'Menw went to fetch him.'

'We should have known it would need more than a little storm to finish Cei,' laughed Atlendor.

He came plunging down the slope, Menw at his heels, and the Attecotti fled before him, scattering like sheep before a wolf: Cei the Pillar of Prydein, the Battle-Bull of Britain, the Upholder of Hosts; Cei the Unconquered.

His fury was upon him then, his hair free and flowing, his face swollen with blood, his eyes glaring, his body trembling from head to toe like a bullrush in mid-torrent, the hero's light dancing around him. He seemed at once more substantial and more luminous than the Attecotti, as if he were real and they were not, as if he alone were solid flesh and they but faded wraiths.

He came to the brink of the pit beside us and gave a great shout. The echoes of it stirred the dust from the walls of the quarry, sent small pebbles tumbling into the depths.

He whirled the great blade above his head, the steel flashing in the sunlight, and hurled it high into the air. It rose, glittering and gleaming, slowed then seemed to hang at the peak of its climb before it faltered and began to descend hilt first towards the shadows, gathering speed as it went.

'Lleminawg!' he bellowed.

The shining sword's fall lasted for ever, beyond the bounds of time, while Cei's shout echoed around the pit and Lleminawg's body surged upward in a salmon leap to snatch the blade from the air, and the masked figure raised its head to watch, mouth wide open in a round O of surprise.

Lleminawg seized the sword, landed catlike on his feet, the

349

impetus pulling him in a circle. He swung and knocked the silver mask askew in a shower of sparks.

(From the corner of one eye I saw a man rasher than his comrades dart forward to seize Cei while his attention was elsewhere: the Long Man struck him, once, with a clenched fist, and he crumpled to the ground.)

The figure staggered, blinded by the blow. The shield dropped and Lleminawg struck again, aiming for the naked neck between the juncture of helm and mail; the figure's head drooped as it tried to shake the boar mask back into position, and the blade caught the iron helmet with a clang. The chin-thong burst and the helm went flying, and with it went the mask.

Long black hair shook free.

She was as beautiful, more beautiful than I remembered.

Dazed, she turned her strong-boned face to the sun while Lleminawg lifted the sword for the final blow.

I was on my feet and screaming, screaming, 'No!'

The raven folded its wings and plunged into the pit. Pedrylaw Menestyr, features contorted with hate, hurled himself at Cei, who caught him and held him one-handed by the throat, legs dangling in the air. Lleminawg swung the sword with deadly force.

Arthur groaned in his sleep as the raven fluttered futile between the champions.

I shouted.

Somehow – and I do not think I could have done it – Lleminawg averted his stroke. The weight of the sword dragged him in an arc, and he fell into a half crouch, his back to Teleri.

She was blinded by the sun, bewildered by the blow which had robbed her of the helmet. In desperation she lunged.

The spear took him in the side, between the ribcage and the hip, the wicked barbs slipping easily into his flesh.

He turned, and in turning tore the shaft from her hands, dashed her to the ground with the flat of his blade.

The spear jutting from his side – he knew it would not come out, easily though it might have gone in – he walked past her into the shadows at the end of the labyrinth, and was lost from our view.

Cei howled, and flung Menestyr from him. The Cupbearer bounced down into the pit like a child's rag doll, rolling and sliding helplessly from level to level, head lolling loose on his neck. The Long Man leaped after him, skidding in clouds of dust to the bottom.

Without Menestyr to give them orders, our captors were at a loss. 'The Lady is dead,' I heard them mutter among themselves. They glanced nervously back and forth from us to the pit, fingered their weapons, mumbled in their private tongue.

'She is not dead,' said Atlendor. (They must have intended us to hear that remark, else they would have spoken in their own language.) 'Lleminawg spared her.'

'And Menestyr our master?' demanded one. 'What of him?'

'His time is done.'

It was Arthur who spoke, sitting up in the litter, his face pale against the bracken with which the interior was lined.

'One last question remains to be answered, and then the Cup of Sovereignty must return with us to where it rightfully belongs. Well have you guarded it through the ages of the world, but henceforth it shall have a new keeper, for Rome has fallen and a new day has dawned.'

Atlendor and Gwalchmei raised the litter onto their shoulders. They seemed to know what was necessary without a word being spoken. Nobody moved to stop them, so they stepped onto the path and began the descent. Moried and Menw helped me to follow, and we wound our way down in a ragged procession into the pit.

I had eyes for nothing and nobody but Teleri. She lay where she had fallen, not far from her father, her long dark hair trailing in the dust. I knelt and turned her over (the pain in my head beating like a hammer with the exertion) and looked again at the planes and hollows of her face. Her eyes were closed, and a thin trickle of blood ran from one temple where the sword had struck her, but her lips were curved in the semblance of a smile.

Whether it was a smile of triumph or disaster I could not tell.

Somewhere far off I could hear voices, and the question I knew must be asked: 'Whom does the Sovereignty serve?'

She was not dead, nor would she die of such a wound, though like mine her head would ache for some days. I held her close, drinking in her beauty, and I think that even then I was saying my farewell.

'Albion, and all those who live within her bounds, whether they be British or Saeson or Scotti or Attecotti or none of these things.'

It was Lleminawg who asked and Arthur who answered, though a chorus of other voices wove with his, and I added mine to them, the seven survivors of our ill-fated foray.

'All hail to thee, Sovereign Lord of Albion!' cried Lleminawg in a great voice. 'All hail, Arthur Amherawdyr Albion!'

Then he was silent, and spoke no more.

And so he was gone from us: the Dancing Man, the Leaping One, the Bounding One, the Fated One. I believe that from the moment we set foot on the island he knew what would happen. *Doomed by the name he had been given at birth* I said, and so he was, yet he went willingly, even joyously, to his fate. He was our sacrifice, our candidate for fame, and when he could have saved himself he held his hand and spared Teleri. He was a better man than I ever was, and a nobler. Scarcely a day has passed since that I have not honoured his memory, for without him we would have failed, and the dream of Albion would have perished stillborn.

Arthur came out from that place with the chalice in his hands, limping as he would limp from this day forward, and it was as if a second sun had risen in the depths of the pit, and the watchers on the rim who had been our enemies, they too hailed him.

'And the woman?' demanded Gorthyn. 'Teleri?'

Budoc closed his eyes. 'She healed, as did I, though the events of that day were never clear in my mind till now. Pedrylaw Menestyr was dead and the Attecotti no longer opposed us, so we rested among them until a ship had been prepared, then took our departure. Teleri remained behind, as was her duty, for she was their High Priestess and they needed her now more than they had ever needed her before.'

He sighed wearily. 'For hundreds of years they had existed to protect the chalice. Now that purpose was gone, for the chalice came with us.'

Gorthyn frowned. 'So Arthur became Emperor?'

'For a time.'

'And on his death the chalice was too dangerous to let fall into the hands of another?'

The hermit nodded.

The big man scowled, poked the embers with a stick. 'So you have the chalice, and would hide it. I can see your not wanting Vortepor to have it, or Custennin, or any other Prince of Britain, but why not allow these tattooed men to take it back?'

He waited for a reply. When none came he raked through the embers and said: 'After all, it was safe enough with them before.'

'Do you really think the man who wrought what the Druid wrought upon the Sanctuary a fit person to have a talisman of such power?' Budoc's eyes were open, angry in the firelight.

Gorthyn shrugged, rebuked.

'Besides, I do not have the chalice. I never have had it.'

'Then where is it?' asked Ceolric.

The hermit shut his eyes again. 'I do not know, not for certain. But I suspect it would be of little use to tell the tattooed men that I do not know – or Vortepor, for that matter. It is not an answer they would accept.'

Nai could contain himself no longer. 'But Teleri . . . Did she intend to kill Lleminawg or not?'

'It was all part of the ritual. She would have driven him hither and thither, then pretended to slay him, that he might come to the heart of the labyrinth as a supplicant neither living nor dead.' Budoc's voice was low, broken with an old sorrow.

'When Cei threw Lleminawg the sword, the fight became real To him she was a masked figure, a threatening stranger. He did not know she meant him no harm. And she struck by instinct, not design.'

He bowed his head in grief, rose uncertainly to his feet. 'I must sleep. Wake me when it is my turn to watch.'

He turned hastily for the hut, but not before they had seen his eyes were filled with unshed tears.

After the hermit had gone the three of them sat for a while staring into the fire, seeing caves and mountains and ships and trees in the flames.

'Is it true?' Gorthyn wondered.

Nai smiled. 'True?'

The fire flickered and the blue flames danced above the red. A log fell in a shower of sparks, flared momentarily bright.

'Their great love,' mused Gorthyn. 'The great love he still feels for her. Would it have survived if they had lived together?'

'Who can tell?' Nai yawned, stood and stretched, tapped Ceolric on the arm. 'You take second watch, wake me for the third.'

CHAPTER SIX

1

Nai woke in the night with a feeling that something was wrong. He lay in the darkness and listened. All he could hear were the snores and grunts of the others. He raised himself on one elbow, waiting, probing the hut with his senses.

A pony nickered, snorted.

He stood, throwing back the cloak somebody had stretched over him. With one foot he nudged Gorthyn.

'What is it?' whispered the big man, instantly awake.

'The horses. Something bothers them.'

Gorthyn sighed. 'Probably just an animal.' All the same the big man rolled to his feet. 'Who is on watch?'

'The Saeson.'

They had stacked their weapons in a corner beside the door. Gorthyn moved silently in that direction, stepping across Eurgain's prone body without rousing her. He buckled on his sword-belt and passed Nai his war-knife.

'Two javelins apiece. Shields as well.'

Nai grunted. His head hurt with the beginnings of a hangover, and his mouth was dry.

'Should we wake the hermit?' murmured Gorthyn.

'Not yet. Let us see first. Perhaps it was just an animal, or the boy coming to the hut for some reason.'

Nai lifted the corner of the skin covering the broken door, creating a peephole.

Outside he could see the dull red embers of their fire smouldering within the circular hearth. He shifted slightly to create a new perspective, and Gorthyn moved uneasily behind him. Now he could see the edge of the hollow, black against the pale sky. He listened, and could faintly hear the crash of breakers on the cliffs.

'Nothing,' he said.

Gorthyn drew a deep breath. 'We had best go out, eh, cousin?' He grinned, his teeth gleaming in the darkness. 'If we are wrong, the boy will think we have no faith in him.'

Nai slipped quietly through the hanging, shield on his arm and spear in his hand. Gorthyn followed him.

The hollow was bathed in moonlight. Their shadows stretched behind them on the wall of the hut, grotesquely mocking their movements.

They waited, listening with all their might, Nai fiddling with the unfamiliar shield, which was one Ceolric had taken from the Scotti and smaller than those to which he was accustomed.

Then they heard the patter of footsteps approaching them, somebody running fast, careless of noise.

Ceolric came into view, sobbing for breath. 'Scotti!' he gasped. 'Close behind me.'

'Rouse the others,' said Gorthyn. 'Quickly!'

Now they could hear more pattering, louder and louder, could feel the faint vibration in the ground. The horses whinnied and stamped their hooves.

'The Trinity be with you, cousin,' Gorthyn said calmly. Nai swallowed, shifted his stance.

'Now!' cried a voice, breaking the silence of the night. 'Take them now, my hearts!'

The rim of the hollow became alive with movement. Spears hissed through the air, clattering against the walls of the hut. Figures came skimming down the slope towards them, weapons gleaming in their hands.

A javelin struck Gorthyn's shield, hung there quivering evilly. He reached across and wrenched it free with an effort, tossing it aside. Then he cast the first of his own spears in the direction of the voice, at the same time bellowing:

'Awake, Budoc! Awake!'

The glowing embers of the fire suddenly flamed high before them, destroying their night vision.

Nai hurled his javelins at the nearest of the charging figures, and, dazzled, drew his war-knife.

'Keep them away from the hut,' shouted Gorthyn. Retreat inside was out of the question: the hut would be burned with them in it.

The two men set themselves shoulder to shoulder before the door, blades in hand and shields raised to protect their torsos.

The Scotti hesitated, and from somewhere behind the ring of shadowy figures a voice called, mocking, unbalanced, its cadences all wrong, speaking British with a hint of the Irish dialect:

'Gorthyn the Strong, Gereint's battle bull. And Nai the Quick, the eagle swooping on the field of war.'

'Eremon?' called Gorthyn.

'Eremon Albanach they call me now, Albanach for my birthing in this island in the lands above the Oak river, the lands which your lordlings stole from us, driving us out onto the seas in bitter warfare.'

'Had you kept the faith you would hold them yet,' Gorthyn shouted. 'You were driven forth for treating with pirates.'

Eremon laughed. Nai picked up a spear and squinted beyond the firelight, trying to find him among the dark shapes.

'You mean we had the wisdom to see what was coming. Do you not know that Prydein, Britannia, is finished? Rome fell a hundred years ago, yet still you cling to your outmoded ideas. And what are you really but dirty little savages aping your betters, a pathetic imitation of your ancestors? Why, they tell me that even the northern Cruithne, the painted people, call themselves Roman now.'

He moved forward, drawn towards the firelight by his own rhetoric, and Nai readied the javelin.

'They say my great-great-grandfather lived in a fine stone house with heated floors and slaves to do his every whim, and slept on a sweet couch and never touched a weapon in his life. But I live on my ship with my crew and put in to land only to do my part in hastening the end, and I sleep on hard ground with a foeman's head for a pillow and a soft slave girl to keep me warm.'

'A foeman's head?' jeered Gorthyn. 'You are brave enough at killing farmers and fishermen, but I had not noticed you were eager to face the like of Nai and me. You leave that to these peasants you have gathered around you.'

Nai threw, but Eremon saw the movement and deflected the spear with his shield.

'Traitor!' growled the Briton in frustration.

'You call me traitor, yet you take a Saeson for an ally. At least I am consistent. All of you, without favour, I kill.'

The firelight flickered on his mail as he came still closer, grinning all the while.

'You slipped away, Nai, without a word of farewell. Not thus were we taught to treat a host when we were children together in the Boys' House.' Eremon's laugh was high pitched and full of mockery.

He came forward another pace, stopped and leaned on his long spear, twisting and turning the shaft so the blade caught the light.

'I will make you a bargain, for the sake of our old friendship. Surrender, and I shall let you go. The boy we shall kill, but cleanly. The girl we take – ' he giggled at the double meaning '– and the old man, the priest or whatever he is, for him I have a special fate, one of which he should approve. As he hurt my druid (who has now recanted his disloyalty) so shall I hurt him. I will nail him to a tree, like his master before him, for the ravens and the crows to peck.'

'Crucify him, you mean?' said Gorthyn.

'Is that what it is called? Crucify. What a beautiful sound,' he rolled the word on his tongue. 'Oh, one other thing. As I said, I will let you both go, but you will each leave behind your right hand. You are both right-handed, are you not?'

'Come down, and I shall send you to join Dovnuall,' snarled Gorthyn.

'What, you do not wish to accept my generous offer?' cried Eremon in mock surprise. 'Well, you were always stubborn. I remember how you used to sulk as a child if denied your own way.'

Gorthyn drew himself up to his full height, feeling the battle fury sweep through him till he trembled in every limb.

'Is it you that is talking?' he said in a great voice that filled the hollow. 'Shame on you, Eremon mab Cairbre! And nothing but shame have you brought upon your line! A loyal man was Lleminawg your kinsman, who was Arthur's Companion: the liberal one, the courteous one, worthy of the trust the Emperor placed in him; loved by his comrades and feared by his foes. When he died all the Lords of Prydein wept for his passing. Who will weep for you, Eremon? Not these your peasant followers, that much for certain!' Gorthyn shook his spear at the Irishman. 'For Lleminawg's sake were you fostered among us for a while, but nothing save dishonour have you brought upon his name.'

'And what good did his name do him in the end, you fool?' screamed Eremon. 'Where is Lleminawg now, and where is your Emperor? Arthur is gone, food for the worms, brought down by lesser men, and his Empire is fallen. Do you not understand, Gorthyn? There are none like Arthur now. If there were I might be his man, like my kinsman before me, but the light has gone out and there is only the darkness, the great darkness spreading across all the world.'

He shook himself, dashed a hand over his cheek where something gleamed in the firelight. 'As to my passing,' he said unsteadily, 'these my faithful companions will mourn me.'

He whistled, and a pair of great hounds came forth from the shadows. He put a hand on the nearest head, and the beasts gazed up at him with adoration in their eyes.

'You talk of the love his companions bore him, yet Lleminawg died alone at the end. What did it avail him then? Where were his brave comrades when he needed them?'

He beat upon the ground with the butt of his spear.

'Where are yours, Gorthyn mab Erfai, now that the hour of your death is upon you?'

Suddenly he stepped back into the night and vanished, the hounds at his heels.

'Ah cousin,' murmured Gorthyn, 'I was too confident of success.'

Nai laughed, the battle madness sweeping over him as it had swept over his friend. 'So, they returned. We shall make them wish they had not.' He stamped a foot, testing the ground, and swung his blade through the air. 'Come on, then!' he shouted, his voice raw.

A man leaped through the flames, his face contorted, knife in hand. Nai rammed his shield into the raider's stomach and slashed his own knife across the man's neck. The Irishman screamed and fell writhing into the flames, the smoke from his clothes and hair filling the air with the foul smell of burning flesh.

Ceolric joined them, wild-eyed, hair tousled, features drawn with fear and desperation.

'Stand behind us,' shouted Gorthyn, hoping the youth would understand what he wanted.

More javelins thudded into the big man's shield, their weight dragging down his arm.

'Their aim has improved!' he said as he flung his second and last spear.

After that the struggle became confused. The Scotti moved in for the kill, trying to swamp the Britons by sheer numbers. Gorthyn and Nai stood their ground, hacking and pushing, using their shields as much as their blades, relying on Ceolric to deal with any who outflanked them.

The fight seemed to last for an age, though it was probably no more than a few moments. At last the Scotti withdrew to the edge of the hollow, leaving the defenders to lick their wounds.

In silence the two groups watched each other, waiting for the next move.

'My shield has shrunk,' muttered Gorthyn. He slid his arm out of the strap, looked ruefully at the hacked remnants of the war-board, and held it ready to spin at the face of his next attacker.

'Stay back,' said Ceolric to Eurgain.

'I have brought you the rest of the javelins,' she whispered, passing out a bundle.

'Is the hermit there?' Gorthyn asked, keeping his eyes on the enemy.

'Yes,' came the answer from the shelter of the doorway.

'Watch the thatch. They made our fire flare as they came in for the first time. It dies now, but they may try to burn the hut.'

'How many are there?' asked Budoc.

'Many,' said Nai.

'But not so many as there were when they attacked the *Sea Stallion*,' said Ceolric.

'They sent those with old wounds in first,' said Gorthyn. 'The next wave will be fresh, and they will give us a harder fight.' He shrugged uneasily, the waiting beginning to tell on him. 'Did you hear Eremon, Budoc?'

'I heard,' said the hermit. 'I heard his offer to us.'

'He is mad,' growled Nai. He spat into the fire to relieve his throat.

'He says the druid is his man again,' said Gorthyn. 'Do you believe him?'

The hermit grunted. 'It could be. If the druid defies Eremon,

359

Eremon will kill him for his treachery.' He paused, added: 'And Eremon made no mention of the chalice, which suggests the druid has not told him the one he holds is nothing more than a pretty cup.'

'So?' Gorthyn said impatiently, his eyes on the hovering Scotti.

'So the druid plays his own game, as he has done all along. I do not think he will come too close while I am here, unless Eremon drives him to it.'

'We should have finished him in the hut,' snarled Nai.

'I need a fresh shield,' muttered Gorthyn.

He tossed the splintered remnant of his old one to the ground. Before Nai could restrain him, he had dashed out into the open and was fumbling with a body lying there, trying to slide the small white shield from an unresisting arm.

'Kill him!' shouted Eremon. 'Kill him!'

A hail of spears flew out of the darkness. Gorthyn wrenched the shield loose and dropped to one knee, sheltering behind it until the worst of the storm was over. Then he raced back to the hut, abandoning the new-found war-board which was heavy with the weight of the shafts embedded in the wood.

'Not wise,' he said with a flash of teeth.

The fire flared again as something was flung into the embers. Dazzled, they squinted against the red light and saw a ring of figures bearing spears and white targes. With the figures were the pair of wolf-hounds, and behind them, capering wildly, the druid in his bird mask, recovered from his fit.

'This is the end,' Gorthyn said calmly.

As the men and beasts swept forward to attack, he began to chant, wielding his sword in time with the words:

> *'I have been where Llacheu was slain,*
> *The son of Arthur, famed in song:*
> *Llech Ysgar, where ravens croaked over blood.*
>
> *I have been where Gwengad was slain,*
> *The son of Cynon, famed in song:*
> *Argoed, where ravens quarrelled over flesh.*
>
> *But I have not been where Medraut was slain,*
> *The well-born one, the scourge of Lloegr:*
> *Camlann, where the ravens were glutted.'*

'Much blood for the ravens this night,' he shouted to Nai. 'And some of it our own!'

A javelin took him in the ribs, and he staggered. Nai turned to help and was himself dashed to the ground by a heavily built warrior wearing mail and armed with a sword.

Ceolric leaped to help, beating on the raider's shield with his knife, trying to win Nai time enough to regain his feet. But a slash from the sword sent his knife spinning, and he too was knocked sprawling.

Gorthyn tore the spear from his side and kept it in his left hand as a substitute for his lost shield. He could not protect the others against the mailed warrior; all his efforts were devoted to fending off a wolf-hound and a pair of Scotti.

The mailed warrior raised the sword above his head. Unable to move, Nai watched it rise. The raider's head came back, and the moon shone full on his face.

'Serach!' screamed Nai, and the raider stayed his blow, peering down at him.

A flash of red light streaked over Ceolric's head and buried itself in the raider's chest.

'Where are you hurt?' cried Eurgain, thrusting the spear home through the mail-shirt.

'Nowhere,' said the youth, reaching forward on his knees to catch the sword as it fell from the Irishman's hand.

Nai struggled upright. He had long since thrown the last of the javelins the girl had brought, and his knife had become blunted on the shields of his opponents. They seemed without number, like the army raised by Yrp of Llydaw in Armorica, who visited the thirty-three chief fortresses of Britain, asking only that twice as many men should leave with him from each fortress as had come to it. And the numbers of that host were beyond counting.

He shook his head to clear it, and drove the rim of his war-board into the spine of the man fighting with Gorthyn.

The big Briton was wrestling with a silver-coated hound, one hand gripping a twist of fur beneath its throat, the other trying to shorten his hold on his sword so that he might drive it home in its body. To Nai it was obvious in the brief glimpse which was all the Scotti allowed him before they were on him again that Gorthyn's great strength was failing, draining away with the blood pouring from the wound in his side.

Then Nai was fighting for his life with three Scotti, any one of whom would have been a fair match even had he been fresh. It was then he knew it was their fate to die here, struggling in front of this stone hut beneath the merciless light of the full moon, with none to carry the tale of their deaths home that they might be remembered in song. The knowledge slowed his arm, and a spear thrust slipped beneath his guard, scoring his ribs even through the leather cuirass, and he fell against the wall of the hut, the stone cold on his back, and saw that Gorthyn had flung the hound aside and was setting about the humans, blood spurting from his left hand. It could be only a matter of moments before he too was finished and they were all dead, their bodies food for carrion scavengers, their heads taken in some heathen rite and laid out for the ravens to peck . . .

The old man comes through the doorway, the length of his sword black and silver in the moonlight, and moving slowly, so slowly, as if he has all the time there was or will be . . .

He floats towards the first of the Scotti menacing Nai and leaves him crumpling into nothing, casually launches a backhand blow that decapitates the second (head and body falling their separate ways to the ground) . . .

Removes himself from the path of the third's sword without appearing conscious of its existence, opens the Irishman's throat in passing with the tip of his own blade (the black beads of blood glittering in the firelight) . . .

And drifts across the white sward to aid Gorthyn, his body dancing to inaudible music, his movements seeming to bear no relation to what is happening around him . . .

Yet every time he comes near an enemy that enemy dies without knowing the source of his death, while the old man continues his leisurely progress across the battlefield, untouched by any weapon . . .

And Nai knows he is watching the last of the teulu *of the Warlord of Britain, the last surviving Companion of Arthur.*

'Though he had but one hand, no three warriors on the same field with him could draw blood sooner than he, Bedwyr the Swift.'

The line ran through Nai's head as he found himself, much to his surprise, sliding gently down the wall and sitting on the grass, watching the proceedings with a sense of detached amusement, wondering why Gorthyn was lying on his face like that (it could hardly be comfortable), why his own vision was blurring and tears were flowing down his cheeks. Perhaps if he closed his eyes he would feel better . . .

2

Eurgain helped the hermit to his feet, feeling the body thin and fragile under her hands, knowing that if she closed her grip she could shatter the brittle bones, wondering at the power which moments before had routed the Scotti.

'They have gone?' wheezed the old man.

She nodded.

The hermit slumped over his sword. In the cold light of the moon his face seemed etched with lines, deep troughs and crinkled whorls, while his white hair and beard were turned to silver. His one sound hand was heavily veined and shadowed where it rested on the wire-bound hilt.

'Are you all right?' Eurgain asked timidly

He managed a smile. 'Exhausted. It is a long time since I last did this. Look to the others.'

She studied him anxiously, tipped her head in reluctant acknowledgement and went towards Nai, who lay huddled against the wall of the hut.

Gently she eased him into a more upright position. He moaned softly, catching his lip between his teeth. Suddenly his eyes came into focus.

'A ministering angel!' he exclaimed gruffly. A calloused finger reached out and stroked her cheek. 'You have been crying. Not for me, I hope, nor that young Saeson.'

He hauled himself to his feet, using both her and the wall behind him for support.

'Gorthyn,' he said, and staggered drunkenly towards his friend's body. She followed, ready to catch him if he fell.

The hermit and Ceolric joined them, and together they rolled the big man over onto his back. The grass where he had lain was slick with blood, black and sinister in the moonlight.

'This was ever the worst part of a battle,' murmured the old man.

'He was your brother's grandson,' said Nai.

'I know. That was how I recognized him. All these years I have garnered news of my kinsmen as and when I might.' He patted Nai's shoulder. 'You guessed then?'

'I guessed. Who else could you be? Some say you died at Camlann, others that you died before Cei. But I never believed it, not of you.'

'Before Cei? I have not heard that tale.' He stared down at Gorthyn's body, his eyes grim. 'I am glad that I knew him, ere his end, my nephew's son. He was a brave a man as his father, and he honoured our line in his life and in his death.'

Dropping to his knees, Nai eased Gorthyn's sword from the big man's death grip. Then he unbuckled the baldric and pulled it out from beneath the body, wiping it clean of his friend's blood. He slung it from his own shoulder, adjusting the buckle so it fitted, and sheathed the sword. As he straightened a movement made him spin round, so that he would have lost his balance had Eurgain not put out a hand to steady him.

'Nai!' breathed a voice. 'Nai the silent!'

It was the mailed warrior, the one she had stabbed. The spear was still in him, the dark rings of mail buckled and broken about the shaft.

He groaned and clutched at the spear shaft. His eyes opened, liquid in the moonlight, and his grey face contorted in a smile.

'Nai,' he exhaled. 'I am glad you survived . . .'

His voice trailed away and his eyes closed.

'Serach?' said Nai. Eurgain knelt and took the man's hand in hers.

The eyes opened again. 'A man must follow his lord . . .' A shudder convulsed the body, and for a moment it seemed to Eurgain that she was holding a claw, not a hand.

Serach groaned. 'He is mad. His crew the sweepings of Ierne. Outlaws and masterless men.' He coughed, choking. 'Who was the man – ' he coughed again '– who took the field after I fell?'

'Budoc. The hermit you held captive.'

Serach tried to laugh. The sound bubbled in his throat. 'He may be a hermit now, but once he was a warrior.' His head slumped on his chest. 'At least Eremon was right about that.'

'Is he alive?' It was the hermit, his hair matted and his face streaked with sweat, the sword still held loosely in his good hand.

Nai nodded.

Budoc pushed the tip of his sword into the grass and rested his weight on it. The pain-clouded eyes shifted to the newcomer.

'You are not a hermit,' asserted the dying man.

'I was, until you and your fellow . . .' He groped for the word, waving his maimed hand in the air. 'Your fellow pirates disturbed me.'

Serach smiled. 'I have heard tell of a warrior with one hand. I always thought it meant literally one hand, you know? But perhaps it was only that one hand was crippled.'

'Perhaps,' answered the hermit.

'Tell me your name.'

The old man blinked at him, combed stiffened fingers through his tangled beard.

'My name was Bedwyr mab Petroc,' said the hermit. 'I was Arthur's man.'

'I was right. I have heard of you, and your lord, and the other, the third great hero, what was he called?'

'Cei.'

'Yes, Cei.' He coughed. 'If I must die, there is no dishonour in falling to one of your comrades . . . even a woman.' His eyes met Furgain's, and one drooped slowly in a wink. He coughed again, seemed to rally his strength.

'Bedwyr . . .' he said, the word turning into a groan, and he was gone.

'When the time comes Gereint or I will take him home,' said Nai, staring down at Gorthyn's body. 'But for the rest of this night he must be safe from scavengers.' He stepped back, his face pale in the moonlight. 'My brother, my brother. If I am still alive at daybreak, I shall weep for you then.'

His voice broke and he bowed his head in silence.

'Let us carry him inside,' said the hermit.

Ceolric lifted the feet while Nai took the shoulders, and between them they brought the corpse to the hut and laid it in a corner.

The Saeson youth found himself almost blinded by an unexpected onrush of tears.

'He was a good man,' he managed to say. 'I liked him, once we had got past the barrier of my father's people.'

Nai shook his head, unable to speak.

Ceolric watched the dark man wrap Gorthyn tenderly in a cloak, like a parent putting a child to bed, then bend to kiss the scarred knuckles farewell.

'What do you plan now?' he asked. 'You spoke as if we would not remain here to guard him.'

'I will have vengeance,' growled Nai, easing the leather cuirass away from his side and probing the slash in his ribs. He winced, and waved Eurgain aside. 'It is nothing, only a scratch.'

'Let her treat it,' said Bedwyr mab Petroc. 'Otherwise the weapon rot will enter it. Is anybody else hurt? I have herbs for poultices. The fishermen were always cutting themselves,' he added, for a moment more like the hermit Ceolric had first encountered.

At his insistence they dressed their wounds, the most serious of them where the spear had scored Nai's ribs, which proved to be rather more than the flesh wound he had claimed.

'I think you three should go,' said Nai through gritted teeth as Eurgain cleaned his side of the encrusted blood which had stuck his clothing to his skin. 'I will stay and meet with Eremon.'

'Alone?' protested Ceolric. 'You cannot mean it.'

'I must.' Nai gasped as the girl probed too deeply, gave Bedwyr a wry glance. 'There is still the druid.'

The old man sucked on one cheek. 'True,' he said, 'though I doubt if he is much danger.'

'He will be a great danger to us if he tells Eremon the chalice is worthless.'

'Yes,' said the hermit thoughtfully. 'And it is possible some of his powers may have returned.' His damaged hand tugged at his beard.

Ceolric watched first one and then the other as they spoke. When they paused he said:

'One thing which has greatly puzzled me. Why are they – Vortepor, Eremon, the druid – so certain you have this chalice?'

'Because somebody must have it, and in their minds I am the most likely candidate. After all, I am the only one of the Seven Companions present when first it came to Arthur who is still alive.'

He pulled again at his beard.

'Besides, among those who survived the slaughter of Camlann – and there were a few of us, whatever the legends say – it was known that Arthur did indeed entrust a certain object to my care.'

He dragged the chest from which he had earlier taken the glass tumblers into the middle of the room, and began to rummage through its contents.

'So that is why you wanted the box,' said Nai. 'I did not think it was simply for the sword.'

'The sword?' Bedwyr frowned, reached deeper into the chest. 'In this box are all the remaining possessions which tie me to my old life. The sword, like the rest, I kept out of sentiment, not thinking I would ever need to use it again. I put it aside after Camlann, when all seemed lost, and I vowed myself to a different sort of existence.' He straightened, shook his head sadly.

'I tried living in a community at first, thinking that I, who had spent all my adult life in company, would find it easier than living alone. But I was too accustomed to command. I could not take orders easily, not from monks who had spent all their lives in seclusion. For years only one man had given me orders, and he was gone. So in the end I left the monastery with the blessing of the brothers and came to the most deserted place I could find, near the sea which I have loved since childhood.'

While he spoke his hands had been undoing a bundle of cloth. At the heart of the cloth was a small copper amulet attached to a leather thong. He held it reverently, displaying it to the beams of moonlight which came through the open doorway.

In the pale luminescence they could see that it was old, very old. The copper had lost its sheen, and verdigris had formed a heavy patina over much of the surface.

'What is it?' whispered Eurgain.

'Eremon and Vortepor were not entirely wrong,' Bedwyr said grimly. 'They were right to believe I had been entrusted with a secret before the disaster of Camlann. But it was not the secret they thought.'

'What is it?' repeated Eurgain.

'My lord Arthur carried this into battle at the siege of Badon Hill, where he won his greatest victory.' Bedwyr smiled quietly at the memory. 'And whether the victory would have been so decisive without it . . .'

Ceolric caught Eurgain's eye and hushed her before she could ask her question a third time.

'This is the tale of it, which you may believe or not, as you please,' said Bedwyr, his voice expanding to fill the hut.

'Half a thousand years ago the Son of God was crucified by the Romans on another hill, outside the holy city of Jerusalem. One of his followers took away the body, and buried it in the tomb he had prepared for himself when his time came. That man, whose name was Joseph, also took a splinter of the cross on which Our Lord had died. As you know, on the third day Our Lord rose again from the dead, and when the time came for his followers to go forth and spread the word, Joseph was among them.

'Now, he was a merchant, and a wealthy man, though he used his wealth wisely and well for the sake of the followers of Jesus. In those days the Romans had not long been in Britain, and Joseph saw in this new land opportunities for both trade and converts. With him he brought the fragment of the True Cross, and after his death it passed from one hand to another, safely lodged inside this copper amulet, always cherished and revered until, at the last, it came to my lord Arthur, and from him to me, the first and last of his followers.'

When he had finished they were silent, Nai and Eurgain lost in awe.

Ceolric alone was unimpressed. He had not understood much of what the old man had said, but he had gathered enough to realize that this was a talisman of power, connected in some fashion with the god Bedwyr worshipped, a god who was dead and alive again, the sort of thing that often happened to gods. What confused him was how the Romans came into the story, for he had always understood they were mortal like himself, and mere mortals do not slay gods. Perhaps he had misheard, or perhaps Bedwyr had got that part wrong.

'What good is it?' he asked, and blushed as the others swung to stare at him. 'Why do you want it?'

'What good is it?' Nai exclaimed angrily. 'What good is it?'

'Why, it is part of the very tree on which died the Young Son, the Defender of Mankind,' said Eurgain, shocked.

'Baldur the Beautiful,' said the hermit. His sad eyes studied Ceolric. 'Against it no heathen magic can prevail.'

Bedwyr slipped the amulet over his head, so it hung in the hollow of his neck.

'We cannot remain here and I will not leave this behind. In a while the Scotti will rally from the shock of their defeat and come again, and this time I think they will overwhelm us. We must try to escape, to join the warband which is coming.'

He turned to Nai. 'We should all go. Let Gereint deal with Eremon.'

'Eremon,' Nai growled to himself. 'Eremon mab Cairbre.' He rubbed at the scar on his throat and shrugged wearily, like a man resigned to his fate. 'As you will. As you will.'

*   *   *

After some discussion it was agreed they should make for the open ridge behind the village by the longer route, staying close to the estuary until they reached one of the streams, then striking out through the woods for the last part of the journey.

They hoped the slaughter wrought by Bedwyr would have taught the Scotti to fear them, but travelling by this circuitous route should lessen the chances of an ambush under the trees.

Before they left the youngsters scavenged the ground for weapons. Bedwyr drew Nai, who had taken a whetstone from his saddlebags and was sharpening his war-knife, to one side.

'It occurs to me that one of us may not survive the night.'

'Only one of us?' Nai raised a sardonic eyebrow, tested the edge of the blade on the hairs of his forearm.

'There is a thing I would ask you to do for me, if you are able and I am not.'

Nai laid knife and stone aside, gave the old man his full attention. 'It would be an honour, my lord,' he said formally.

'The barbarians are on the move again. The petty kingdoms of our people will not hold against them. In the north Elmet, Loidis, Dewr, perhaps even Rheged itself, will fall in time; in the midlands and south the lands of the Severn valley and Calchwinyth of the limestone hills are vulnerable to attack. And eastern Dumnonia, how long will that last once Cerdic's heirs march in earnest?'

'Not long, I grant you.'

'And the wars between our people, between the kings of Britain, show no signs of abating. Small wonder the common folk have little time for their lords!'

'What is it you would have me do?' asked Nai, glancing uneasily about the hollow. He was eager to be gone, to take these people to a place of safety (if one could be found) so he could return and make an end.

'Somewhere in eastern Dumnonia is a house of women, a nunnery. I do not know which house – she will have covered her tracks, as I did, lest she become a pawn in others' dreams of glory.' He ran a hand through his hair, silver in the moonlight. 'I kept the Cross; she kept the Chalice.'

'The Chalice?' Nai frowned. 'You are speaking of the Lady Gwenhwyvar?'

'Yes. After Camlann she entered a religious house near Lindinis, but she did not stay there. It was too dangerous. The widow of the Amherawdyr could have given legitimacy to the ambitions of men like Vortepor.'

'You wish to find her?' By now the youngsters had filled the quivers on the ponies with the javelins they had gathered, and Ceolric was hunting beside the ashes of the fire for his lost knife.

'The descendants of Menestyr, the Cupbearer, will be searching for the Chalice. While there is still order in the east they will not dare attack a holy house, but if the Saesons come . . .'

'I understand.'

'Start with the house of St Helena near Lindinis,' said Bedwyr, moving towards the horses. 'Let it be known you come from me.'

'What should I do if I find her?'

'Protect her. She will know where to go.'

Nai shook his head in puzzlement, shrugged. 'If I live and you fall, I shall seek for her.' The whole matter seemed irrelevant to him, but he was accustomed to people making odd requests before embarking on a dangerous course of action – he had made them himself in the past.

'Please God you do not need to use that,' said Bedwyr, looking at Eurgain.

She had armed herself with a war-knife, a light blade she had taken from one of the Scotti.

'Strange,' she said, cutting the air. 'Having killed once, I shall find it easier another time.'

'As do we all,' murmured Bedwyr, hauling himself up into the saddle. 'God help us.'

3

The moon was high overhead, frosting the turf, limning the branches of the trees, when they left the hut. Bedwyr and Eurgain rode the ponies, Nai and Ceolric walked at their sides, scanning the black shadows and patches of silver light, never certain whether the rustling sounds they heard in the bushes were animals about their business in the night, or something else.

The sound of the sea grew louder in their ears. The land descended to a wooded valley, and there beneath them was a vast expanse of white sand with a thin dark line stretching arrow straight from the trees to the breakers. It was the mouth of the stream beside which Gorthyn, Nai and the girl had passed the night a hundred years ago.

Eurgain screamed.

A great white owl swooped silently over their heads, spooking the horses. It hovered in the air and dropped towards the beach, wings unfurling to their fullest extent to break its fall, and vanished somewhere near the combers.

'There is danger,' Bedwyr said softly, seeming to sniff the night air. 'Be ready, all of you.'

Nai loosened the sword in its sheath and adjusted the strap of his battered shield, wincing as the movement caught the wound in his side.

'What was that?' said Ceolric. 'There! That noise!'

'I know that sound,' said the old man, racking his memory.

By now they had reached the edge of the beach, the place where sand and grass mingled underfoot.

Eurgain started with surprise.

'Who is that?' she said, pointing towards the sea.

Outlined against the pale phosphorescence of the water was the darker shape of a man: a man tapping a sword on the metal rim of his shield.

'Nai!' The cry split the night. 'Nai Still-Tongue! Nai the Silent! Nai mab Nwython! Come down and fight!'

Eurgain groaned with the horror of it. Nai gave a shrug of resignation, drew his friend's sword from its scabbard. The steel glimmered with a blue sheen.

'Nai!' bellowed Eremon, the ring of metal on metal a counter-point to his words. 'Come down and fight. Smooth are these sands and sweet the music of the waves in my ears. This is a goodly place to die.'

'Why should I waste my strength in fighting *you*?' shouted Nai in a harsh croak that made the horses dance. 'Oath-breaker, kin-slayer, what will you give me if I accept your challenge?'

'Are you a merchant or a warrior?' called the other in mockery.

'My blade's edge will answer that, thief.' He hesitated, glanced at Bedwyr. 'Will you grant these my companions safe conduct while we battle?'

The other thought for a moment. 'Why not? Yes, they will be unharmed for precisely so long as it takes me to kill you, cousin.'

'A long while will that be,' said Nai. He turned to the others, kissed Eurgain on the cheek, hugged Ceolric.

'Do whatever the hermit – Bedwyr – bids you. It may be that we shall meet again, if God be willing, but if not, good fortune attend you both all the days of your lives.'

He bowed to the old man sitting straight-backed on the horse. 'I am glad I lived to know you, my lord. May God go with you.'

Bedwyr regarded him for a moment, fierce and unblinking in the moonlight. Then his hands went to his neck and lifted the amulet over his head.

'Take it,' he said. 'Take it, and wear it in my name, and in the name of my two masters, both of whom will come again: the battle emperor of Britain and the saviour of mankind.'

Nai shook his head, but the old man would not be denied. 'You go to defend the ordinary people of Britain against those who would prey upon them, even as my lord Arthur did defend them in days gone by. Take it, Nai.'

'If I fall it will be lost.'

'You will not fall,' said the old man, and so firmly did he speak that for an instant Nai almost believed him.

Reluctantly, Nai bent his head and Bedwyr slipped the amulet around his neck.

'When you have slain Eremon come after us as fast as you can,' said Bedwyr. 'Ceolric and Eurgain may need you.'

Nai started to nod, said: 'I doubt his followers will let me leave.'

Bedwyr shrugged. 'We shall see.'

'Will you fight, Nai?' shouted Eremon, impatient.

He turned, raising a hand in farewell, and they watched him walk across the white sands, leaving black footprints behind him, aiming unerringly for the dark figure beside the waves.

'Come,' said Bedwyr. 'Ceolric, mount behind Eurgain. He has won us time to escape, and we must not waste his sacrifice.'

'Do you trust Eremon to keep his word?' asked the youth as he pulled himself onto the pony's back.

'No. So we ride fast and hard, with our weapons at the ready.'

Bedwyr set as good a pace as he dared, urging the horse through the woodland, trusting it to find its own footing. The others followed, Ceolric clinging desperately to Eurgain, bouncing up and down in the saddle, teeth rattling in his head. From time to time he established a sort of rhythm, began to move in unison with the horse, only to lose it again and find his weight crashing *down* as the pony came *up*, the impact jarring his spine till he wondered whether he would be crippled for life.

Eurgain was crying. She had liked Nai, that fierce and silent man, in some ways liked him better than Gorthyn, who was too bluff and hearty for her taste. None of her family had been much given to talking; day after day spent solitary in the fields or on the water did not create great conversationalists. Nai had reminded her of her clan, her lost family, and now he too was lost. She knew she would not see him again.

They followed the course of the stream for a while, then, when it turned away from the direction they wanted, abandoned it, setting the horses at the slope leading up to the ridge and the open ground.

Two grey figures darted from behind a bush, screaming and yelling. Bedwyr's horse reared, lashed out with its hooves and sent the Scotti spinning into the undergrowth.

More shapes appeared, ghostly in the gloom. A spear hissed past Eurgain's head: she ducked and drew her knife, keeping one hand on the reins, urging the pony on up the hillside.

Ceolric was bellowing incoherently behind her. She heard the rattle of the shafts in the quiver as he snatched a javelin, then she was slashing down at a white face, the blade leaving a dark line across the open mouth, the shock of the impact almost pushing her out of the saddle.

Ahead of her the hermit had drawn his sword, long and wicked in the cold light. It flickered twice, cutting through the shadows; his pony pranced and sidled, trying to wriggle away from this madness, but somehow he was controlling it, despite the slope, despite the broken ground, making it dance in and out of their attackers.

Then he shouted, and it was as if the world had stopped.

The sand was hard beneath Nai's feet, hard and wet. The rush of the waves grew louder. He breathed deeply, preparing himself for the encounter, and tasted salt on his tongue.

His body hurt. It was a mass of aches and pains, not the least of them the wound in his side. He felt old, and weary, very weary.

All around him men stood waiting in a great semicircle. He did not break his step, nor did he look at them directly, though from the corner of his eye he could see the eagerness on their faces.

There was no space in him for fear, only resignation. Everything had been leading to this moment ever since he had wakened on the hillside to find Gereint and Morgant talking of Vortepor's meeting with a man of the Scotti.

In a way he had always known that he would die at Eremon's hand.

The figure before him loomed larger and larger. He turned unthinkingly to draw strength from Gorthyn walking at his shoulder, found only the empty air, and cursed himself for a fool.

'Are you ready, cousin?' demanded the familiar voice.

'I am ready,' he said, raising the battered shield to eye level, taking a firm grip on the sword of his friend.

'Then let it begin!' cried Eremon, charging forward like a bull, seeking to overwhelm him at once.

Nai kept his eyes fixed firmly on the other's sword and shield, avoiding his face. He gave ground, dodging the blows, the blade hissing through the air above his head or by his body.

Once or twice he was obliged to catch a swing on his shield, and the force of the strokes jarred him from head to heel, knocking him back several paces, yet each time he managed to recover his stance unharmed.

'Nai the Quick!' mocked the other. 'Stand and fight, my friend!'

'No friend of yours,' he gasped, teeth rattling from another hard blow to his war-board.

The renegade laughed, and redoubled his efforts.

It seemed to Nai that there was a great weight pressing down upon him, hampering his movements, slowing his responses. Time and again he avoided the Irishman's cuts more by luck than judgement, nearly fell prey to one of his rapid feints. He had been aware Eremon would be a deadly opponent, especially with the sword, but he had not guessed the other was as fast and strong as this.

The sense of oppression grew heavier as he understood how hopelessly he was outmatched.

Suddenly he stumbled. The ground gave way beneath him, and he fell awkwardly, trying to keep a hold on his sword. For a moment he did not know what had happened, and then realized he had been driven against the stream, and the feeble bank of sand had crumbled under his weight.

Eremon grinned at him, blade poised for the death stroke. Nai's heart somersaulted in despair, and he shivered in every limb.

'Come cousin, you can do better than this,' Eremon said contemptuously, and strolled idly away, leaving him room to climb free of the channel.

Tears blurred Nai's vision as he clambered from the clinging sand, so that the mailed form seemed to walk through thick mist. Sweat dripped from his forehead and his breath came in short harsh pants.

He was going to die.

He was going to die at the hands of a man he hated and despised.

All his talk of vengeance was no more than that, mere talk, the impotent threats of an angry child.

When Eurgain's vision cleared the Scotti seemed to have vanished. She could see Bedwyr's lips moving, but could hear nothing, her ears still ringing with the aftermath of that shout. Bedwyr leaned across, grabbed the reins and tugged, heeled his own pony up the hill. She followed, vaguely aware of Ceolric's arms pressed about her waist, of the naked blade clutched in her right hand.

Branches scoured her clothing, whipped past her face. Sods of earth flew up from the hooves of Bedwyr's pony, showering Eurgain with mud and leaf mould as she kept as close behind as she dared. The skirmish and the wild ride purged her of grief. If Nai was to fall fighting Eremon – and by this time he was probably already dead – they owed it to him to make his sacrifice worthwhile.

The horses were lathered with sweat by the time they reached the edge of the woods. Bedwyr called a halt to give them a moment's rest, and Ceolric slid to the ground with a groan of relief.

'What now?' he asked.

Bedwyr cocked his head on one side, listening. 'They do not follow. You are safe, I think. Make for the track leading to Penhyle, and do not turn aside for either man or beast. Sooner or later you should meet Gereint and his men.'

'What about you?' said Eurgain, her voice sounding odd in her ears, which still hummed with the force of the shout.

He took her hand, gently disengaging the fingers from the bloody blade, which he wiped clean on the grass. He kissed her knuckles, returned the knife hilt first while she sat unmoving, not understanding.

'Nai will need help to escape from the crew.'

Ceolric gasped. 'You are going back?'

'I must.'

'But . . .' They both began in unison.

'I must,' he repeated, and turned the pony so it faced down the hill.

'I wish you well,' he said, raising the sword in salute, and was gone.

Eremon had moved to the far side of the beach and was drinking from a leather bottle. While Nai watched he rinsed his mouth and spat, then grinned.

'Ah, Nai, why not surrender to me?' he called. 'We could lead these my comrades, you and I together. Come, what prevents you? Loyalty to your new-found friends?' He laughed cruelly. 'Think what fun we could have with the girl, you and I in the night. Join me! You do not know what it is like, Nai, to bring fire and terror to these ignorant clods in their smelly huts.

'And besides,' he grinned slyly. 'I have the Chalice, Nai, the Chalice of Sovereignty. With it I shall bargain myself a high place in the Council of a new Prydein.'

He tossed the leather bottle to one of his followers. 'I think we shall keep the girl alive for a while, teach her the meaning of pleasure . . . and of pain.' He chuckled. 'She would have been wasted on that Saeson's by-blow.'

Nai licked his lips. The sense of oppression was still heavy upon him. He glanced round at the watchers, some vague and half-formed hope in the back of his mind that this was a bad dream and in a moment Gorthyn would come striding through the crowd to take his place and put a quick end to the Irishman's mockery.

But this was no dream. It was all too horribly real. Eremon's pale and menacing crew were laughing and talking among themselves, laying wagers on how long their leader would keep his victim alive. Behind them was the hideously costumed figure of the druid, dancing and capering in his bull robe and bird mask, the sea breeze ruffling the feathers that hung down his back.

Nai checked his shield. The wood was heavily splintered and it would not last much longer. He slipped it higher up his arm, used his free left hand to massage the scar on his throat, the scar Eremon had given him so many years ago.

His fingers found something warm, glowing in the hollow of his throat.

Bedwyr's amulet.

A fragment of the True Cross, carried by Arthur at the battle of Badon Hill.

Its heat travelled down his numbed fingers and into his arm. (In his mind a great wind blew across an ancient forest, scouring the darkness from the land. Trees tossed and fluttered, whipping the gale to greater force, and their song filled him, a song of endurance, of abiding against the storms of winter for the hope of spring.)

His back straightened. His vision cleared, and he saw things for what they were.

The watching crew, mere untrained peasants, half starved and desperate.

The druid, a superstitious fool dressed in animal skins.

Eremon. Eremon, a mortal man. Quick, but not that quick, not so quick as he had been ten years ago.

The warmth spread from his arm through his whole body. He felt its fire tingling within him. All sense of oppression vanished.

The druid howled with rage, began to chant another spell, made motions of casting something in Nai's direction.

'Too late!' Nai shouted. 'Too late, sorcerer!'

The fire seized him and flung him at Eremon, sword whirling, shield flailing, the pain of his wounds and bruises forgotten, the battle fury full upon him.

Now it was the other who retreated, his expression – Nai no longer feared to meet the mad eyes – surprised, his responses slow. Blood marked his mail shirt where the blade had gashed him.

Nai drove him back into the sea, so his feet were lapped by the moonshadowed foam, a frail lattice of white and cream bubbles that clung like silk to his ankles.

Then Nai halted in his turn and withdrew beyond the reach of the waves. The heat of his anger had passed, and in its place was a coldness to match the glittering beauty of the star-strewn sky, a coldness more deadly than the heat of his rage, for here there was reason.

He stripped the hacked and shrunken remnant of the

war-board from his arm, drew his war-knife and held it in his left hand.

'Come, thief. Let us make an end,' he rasped in his broken voice.

Nothing moved in all the night save those two. Eremon charged forward as he had at the beginning, trying to recapture his advantage. His bulk and power forced Nai to draw back while he watched for his chance, and to the onlookers it must have seemed their champion neared victory, for a roar of triumph went up from them.

But the renegade was panting, and though his blade cut and recut his shieldless opponent, and though the wound across Nai's ribs had reopened and blood was sliding down his side and dripping to the pale sand, Eremon's eyes were afraid.

The once smooth sand was churned beneath their feet, churned in looping patterns that marked how they had battled up and down the beach. Eremon kicked a path through the troughs they had made, planting each foot firmly on the ground, but Nai danced lightly on his toes, his strength waxing as the other's waned.

Eventually the blow came that Eremon, caught wrong-footed, could not avoid. In desperation he countered with his own sword, and the two blades met with a clang.

The sound of the collision ringing in his ears, Nai saw his sword fly from his numb fingers. Eremon staggered off balance, his shield dropping, and Nai gave a yell of triumph and leaped high in the air, the war-knife in his left hand swinging down like a butcher's cleaver over the other's guard, and the two of them fell to the wet sand in a tangle of limbs.

A wail went up from the watchers.

Eremon sighed. He spat sand from his mouth, reached out a hand and probed at the knife in his shoulder.

'I did not think you could do that, cousin,' he said weakly, his face etched with pain.

Nai rolled free of the other, feeling the water lapping at his body as he lay on his side, unable to rise. 'Neither did I,' he said, his voice seeming to come from very far away.

Eremon's mouth fluttered, and Nai leaned close, ignoring the pain in his ribs, trying to catch the words as they formed on the lips.

'Ah, cousin, I am sorry . . .'

The lips moved in a smile as Nai, his own strength failing him, fell forward onto the other's chest. The smile distorted into a final belching gape of agony, and Nai was left lying with a dead man in the foam, his wounds washed by the waves, his body tugged by the undertow.

The pony slipped and slid down the slope. Bedwyr sheathed his sword and clung to its back, ducking under the overhanging boughs, feeling the twigs scrape his hair.

The woods were silent except for the faint stir of the wind in the leaves and the sound of his own passing.

He had uttered a great shout like that on the day he had stood upon the rim of the pit looking down into the labyrinth, and had seen Teleri's long black hair shaking free from her helmet, and had seen Lleminawg, sweet Lleminawg the Dancing Man, his friend, raise his blade to deal her death blow.

With a cold wind whining in his ears he had screamed, feebly, feebly, his thin voice torn away by the blast, and her face (beautiful in its imperfections and more familiar to him than his own) had turned to the sun, like a blind creature of the earth feeling the warmth for the first time.

A sense of terrible wrongness had filled him, akin to what one might feel if when listening to an oft-told tale the end were suddenly and without warning changed, so comedy became tragedy or the brave man a coward: only here the feeling was increased a thousandfold.

The power had pulsed within him and he had given it voice. And in so doing had saved Teleri, but at the cost of Lleminawg . . .

. . . thirty years ago, when he was young and the world was young with him, and Arthur and Gwenhwyvar and Cei and he had dreamed their dream of reuniting the island, Briton and Saeson and Scotti alike, bringing them all together in one great union which would hold within it the best of the old and the best of the new, building upon the foundations Rome had left to create a haven of peace and civilization in a tormented world.

(And they had come so close, so close.)

But somewhere everything went wrong, as they grew grey and weary and lost the ability of the young to dream idealistic impractical dreams and make them come true, as they became caught in the endless sordid round of lesser men's ambitions, as the ancient vicious blood feuds reached up from the depths of the past and dragged them down.

All that remained were the simple things: a Saeson boy and a British girl alike bereft of their kin, going off in the dark to find a new life, maybe together, maybe apart – it did not matter; a warrior with a broken voice, prepared to fight a fight he believed he could not win, so that those two youngsters might have their chance; and an old man on a horse, an old man with a sword, an old man who had thought to live the rest of his days in peaceful contemplation of the mysteries of God . . .

The pony came to the bottom of the slope and splashed across the stream. Bedwyr drew himself up in the saddle and laughed aloud. He should have known that God had other uses for his talents: had the Hawk not warned him?

He reached into his tunic and drew out a leather thong, ran the stiffened fingers of his left hand through his long white hair, caught and pulled the flowing locks back tight, then bound them into place with the string.

In his right hand he took one of the javelins from the quiver, checked it for signs of damage, and raised it high in the air.

Once upon a time this was the way he had given the signal for the charge to the line of horsemen at his back, holding the spear high and motionless to warn them to be ready, then bringing it down in a single swift movement to launch the unstoppable onslaught.

Now there was just him, an old man on a nag the Companions would have scorned as fitted only for the baggage train.

He dropped the spear (blade flashing in the moonlight), couched it like a lance and kicked the pony along the bank of the stream.

They went quickly at first, Eurgain trotting on the horse and Ceolric jogging at her side, her free hand resting on his shoulder. They did not slow to a walk until they were well clear of the trees and halfway up the slope leading to the ridge. Behind them they could hear the rising wind rushing through the leaves, and in the distance the breakers pounding the shore.

When they crested the rise they felt the bite of the chill breeze blowing over the coombes and valleys from the clifftops, bringing with it night scents mingled with the tang of the sea. Here they halted for a moment, Eurgain's legs dangling from the saddle as she swung about and stared down into the dark mass of the forest.

'Will he . . . ?' she asked, and left the rest unspoken.

Ceolric put his hand on her calf, rubbed gently at the tense and knotted muscle.

'I do not know.' He shook his head, repeated: 'I do not know.'

They went on, Ceolric running beside the pony, across the grey-white grass, past the boulders where Eurgain had sheltered with Gorthyn and Nai, following the line of the ridge as it swung to the north-west, catching the occasional glimpse through the trees of moonlight glittering on the waters of the estuary far below.

Eurgain had fallen into a semi-daze, lulled by the rhythm of the pony, when she was nearly shaken from the saddle as the horse suddenly shied, forcing Ceolric to dodge hastily or be butted to the ground. The pony nickered, flung up its head and whinnied full-throatedly, showering Eurgain with spittle, frothing at the mouth, its eyes rolling white and glaring.

'What is it?' shouted Ceolric.

'Grab the reins!' she called as the pony bucked and plunged. 'Get his head!'

Somehow she kept her seat while the horse danced and skittered, knowing that if she came off the animal would bolt.

'Steady, steady,' she soothed, patting the taut neck. 'Gently does it, gently now, my hero.'

Ceolric managed to find a grip on the reins, wary of the great yellow teeth dangerously close to his arm, and together they encouraged the pony away from the bush that had frightened it.

'He's terrified!' said Eurgain, and all at once she remembered.

'The bush!' she said. 'In the brambles! When we were fleeing the other night there was a shape in the brambles!'

Ceolric caught the note in her voice.

'If I let go, can you hold it?' he said, meaning the pony.

She nodded, her face white and tense.

The horse seemed calmer. Ceolric dropped the reins, edged away, ready to leap back if the creature panicked again.

He moved towards the bush, war-knife in his hand (not that it would do any good against the dead), and had he not known Eurgain was watching him he would have turned on his heel and run, preferring to face the Scotti to the thing in the brambles that Gorthyn had described as preventing their escape that first night.

He could see an outline hidden by the scratchy shadows of the trailing briers. He came closer, expecting it to move at any moment, every muscle pulled tight and his grip on the knife so fierce it was bruising his palm.

'Father,' he heard Eurgain breathe behind him. 'Rhodri.'

He summoned all his courage and plunged into the bush, careless of the thorns raking his exposed flesh.

'Rags,' he said, tearing some loose. 'There is nothing here but rags.'

He fought his way out of the clinging brambles carrying his trophies and displayed them to Eurgain.

'Just a few tatters tied to the branches. It does not look as if there ever was any more.'

Eurgain stared at the shreds of cloth. 'No body?' she croaked.

'Nothing,' he said firmly. 'No body and no sign of one. Only these.'

'The druid.' She swallowed, recovered her voice. 'Do you think he could have spelled us, that night?'

'Made you see something that wasn't there?'

'And stopped us from escaping to warn Penhyle of the danger.'

'Yes, I do,' he said, not knowing whether it was true or not, but telling her what she wanted to hear so she would not dwell upon the image of her father hung in a brier patch like a piece of dirty washing.

'Take your tunic off,' she commanded.

'What?'

'We need something to wrap over the horse's head. Then we can lead him past the bush. Quick!' she added impatiently.

'Are horses truly that stupid?' he muttered, and pulled off his tunic, shivering in the chill night air.

They coaxed the reluctant pony round the brambles, Eurgain giving all her attention to the animal and not once glancing aside at the place where the few remaining rags fluttered in the breeze.

Ceolric wiped the worst of the drool off on the grass and dressed thankfully, staring absently along the line of the ridge.

'What's that? Look!' He pointed.

Eurgain followed the direction of his arm.

'It's not Penhyle,' she said doubtfully.

There were lights burning in the darkness, twinkling red embers large and small, too near the horizon to be the little town by the water. The red glows flickered, waxed and waned, sometimes vanishing for a moment then reappearing in a slightly different position, higher or lower against the loom of the land.

'They're moving!' said Ceolric.

They looked at each other. Her face was chiselled in the moonlight, its lines so clean and pure they caught at his heart. His features were blurred by the boyish beard, but still in that brief moment she thought them the noblest she had ever seen.

'Gereint!' they exclaimed as one, and she kicked the horse into a gallop while he raced fleetly in her wake, all weariness gone.

The trot first, the pony stepping well with an easy rhythm, and he tries in his throat the sound the Companions used to make when they charged home for the kill, the deep humming that so terrified their enemies.

It will not come. He coughs and tries again, the noise thin and reedy in his ears, nothing like the awe-inspiring drone he remembers.

(But then he never heard it from a single throat: it always came from the massed ranks of the Family.)

The trot turns to a slow canter through pools of pure moonlight, the black water of the stream flecked with silver, the trees grey and shadowy around him, the spear shaft hard in his hand, the reins cutting into his damaged fingers.

The pony is struggling, the easy rhythm gone, the canter becoming a heavy-footed lumber, puffing and panting, made clumsy by the excitement it has caught from its rider, and he is holding it back on the reins, fearing it may outrun its strength, still making the feeble noise in his throat. But it is on the wrong note and again he coughs and tries another time, and still it will not come, is too high pitched, lacks the depth and power and resonance he seeks.

(What does he expect, an old man alone in the moonlight?)

Above him he hears the croaking protests of the rooks disturbed in their sleep by the heavy thudding of the horse. The wind is soughing in the branches, a lonely sound, a cold sound, and in the distance he can hear the seethe and surge of the sea.

The pony finds its second wind and starts pacing away, quicker and quicker, breaking from a slow canter to a fast one.

The moon-frosted branches and the hoary trunks are flickering past him, and suddenly the drone is rising, rising on all sides, vibrating through his whole body as it did in the old days, and the hooves are drumming and the harness is jingling, and the spear is ready in his hand.

The leaves are trembling on the trees and the humming and the thunder are all around him, and he is not alone, he can feel them at his back, the Companions of the Emperor, as the canter becomes a slow gallop and the beach comes into sight, the hideous drone rising from the warriors and the flutter of wings above as the carrion birds wake and follow like gulls behind a plough.

The earth is shaking and the very air is reverberating (the trees rattling as if they are caught in a winter gale), and Arthur is one side of him and Cei the other, laughing, exultant, and he knows Gwalchmei the Hawk and Lleminawg the Irishman and a hundred others are close behind, the hooves of their horses thrumming and the drone deep in their throats . . .

'Now!' he shouts, howling like a wolf, and the pony leaps forward at full pelt. 'We ride, we ride, Amherawdyr!'

The sands are silver under the white moon, and the Scotti are staring at him open-mouthed. Bedwyr sees everything with preternatural clarity: the ragged clothes, the thin bodies, the way their weapons droop from nerveless fingers. Beyond them the masked druid is thigh-deep in the surf, struggling with a tangled pair of shapes floating in the water, dragging a head up into the air, a knife flashing in his hand as he prepares to draw it across the exposed windpipe . . .

They saw, the remains of the Scotti, saw the dark forest shaking as under a great storm, heard the thunder of hooves and rising above it all a dreadful droning sound that must have come from a hundred, a thousand massed throats, saw the forest burst asunder and the pale horsemen coming for them, their numbers beyond counting, and at their head a lithe figure that hurled a spear with terrible accuracy across the sand straight to the heart of their magic man, their druid, their only hope of surviving in this strange land.

The druid crumpled, the bird mask coming loose and fluttering its own path to the sea.

This was the end.

The Scotti broke, fled screaming, splashing out into the water or running along the beach, anywhere, anywhere at all to escape the vengeance falling on them from the forest.

*   *   *

Bedwyr hauled Nai clear of the waves.

At first he feared he was too late, that the younger man was gone, but then the dark eyes opened and Nai began to cough.

'Amulet,' he whispered when he had caught his breath. 'Druid did magic. Amulet stopped him.'

'I know,' Bedwyr said gently. 'That is why I gave it to you. I thought something of the kind would happen.'

Nai blinked, visibly pulled himself together. 'What are you doing here?' he demanded, his voice much stronger. 'You went with the youngsters.'

'I saw them safely on their road.'

'You came back for me?' Nai struggled to rise. 'Where are the Scotti? Where is the druid?'

'All gone. You lie still and let me see the damage.'

With Nai's reluctant cooperation Bedwyr managed to ease him out of his leather armour.

'At least they have been nicely soaked in sea water,' the old man muttered to himself. 'That will help.'

He rose stiffly to his feet, walked across to Eremon's body in the surf (ignoring the blind eyes of the bird mask bobbing beside it on the waves) and ripped free a number of lengths of cloth.

'This should stop the bleeding,' he said, wadding some and holding them in place with others. 'I have seen worse, though I do not think you will be doing much for a while.'

'What happened to the Scotti?'

'They ran away after I killed the druid.' Bedwyr cocked his head, listened. 'I do not think they will get very far.'

He could hear shouting and the neighing of horses in the distance.

'Gereint?' Nai's voice was fading.

'It must be. I can see torchlight round the headland. They will be here soon.'

'Take the amulet.'

'You keep it. It is time it passed to someone younger.'

Nai shook his head. His voice was very weak now. 'Too much for me. That kind of power – not sure I would use it rightly.'

'It would not work if you did not use it aright,' Bedwyr said softly. 'But perhaps you are wise. Bury it in the Sanctuary grove when you have recovered. Bury it deep, so it will not be found by chance.'

'Pagan,' objected Nai. 'Should be in church.'

'A holy place is a holy place, regardless of what god is worshipped there. And the gods of the woodland sanctuaries were kindly creatures, on the whole. I would not trust a fragment of the True Cross to a churchman. They are an ambitious breed.' He bent and touched Nai's cheek. 'If God wants it to be found, it will be.'

'All right,' promised Nai.

Bedwyr stared along the beach. The lights were closer now. He could hear the splashing as men and horses waded around the headland, the harsh cries as they called to one another.

'I must go. If I stay, Gereint or Custennin will try to make use of me.'

He mounted the pony, gazed down at the wounded man. 'Take care, cousin. God be with you.'

If Nai made a reply the words were too faint to be heard above the susurration of the sea. Bedwyr kicked the pony into a trot, angling away from the approaching lights, knowing that even in the short time remaining before dawn he would not have much difficulty slipping around Gereint's warband.

At the edge of the trees he paused for a moment, looked back. Nai was a dark blur on the pale sands, and the bodies of Eremon and the druid could easily have been lumps of driftwood caught in the surf.

Only the bird mask was clearly visible, caught in a shaft of moonlight as it pitched on the waves, tumbling back and forth with the feathers streaming out behind it. Even as he watched the fabric became waterlogged and it slipped silently beneath the never-resting surface.

He rode on into the forest.

A NOTE ON THE
BACKGROUND TO THE BOOK

∽

The medieval legend of Arthur runs something like this.

Once upon a time there was a great British king or emperor. He defeated the Saxons, Picts and Scots who were in those days harassing Britain, and went on to conquer most of Western Europe. He and his queen, the beautiful Guinevere, ruled this empire from the splendour of his chief city, many towered Camelot, and during his reign there were peace and justice for all. Advised by the magician Merlin, he founded the Round Table, the fellowship of the bravest and boldest knights in all the world. Once the realm was at peace, these knights rode out to seek adventure, and the greatest of these adventures was the Quest of the Holy Grail.

But all ended in tragedy. Arthur's closest friend and champion, Lancelot, fell in love with Queen Guinevere. Too many of the knights did not return from the Grail Quest. The Queen's adultery led to civil war, and Arthur's bastard son and/or nephew Mordred seized both the Queen and the throne. In one last battle Arthur and the few surviving knights of the Round Table defeated Mordred, but Arthur himself was mortally wounded. He was carried away to Avalon to be healed, and he will return to save Britain in the hour of her deadliest danger.

This is the essence of the Matter of Britain, the great cycle of epic stories composed during the Middle Ages, a cycle which reached its finest flowering with Malory's *Le Morte d'Arthur*.

The most important single contribution to the evolution of the Matter of Britain was Geoffrey of Monmouth's *History of the Kings of Britain*, which appeared about 1138. It was Geoffrey who invented the prophetic magician Merlin by conflating two different characters from Welsh legend. It was Geoffrey who related the story of Arthur's conception at Tintagel; Geoffrey who stated that Mordred was Arthur's nephew; Geoffrey who said that after the last battle at Camlann the mortally wounded Arthur was carried off to the Isle of Avalon 'that his wounds might be attended to'.

Later writers added or amplified incidents, or created new characters such as Lancelot and Galahad, but one can see the bare bones of the story in Geoffrey's account.

In creating his *History* Geoffrey drew upon a number of sources – including his own imagination! But one of his sources was Welsh tradition, an often contradictory body of legend. Meanwhile, across the Channel, others were drawing upon Breton tales to create their own version of the Arthurian story.

Much of this material is now lost, although enough has survived to show that there must once have been many variants. For example, Arthur did not always die after a final apocalyptic battle. The *Romanz des Franceis*, by André, dating from the late 1100s, claims that Arthur was pushed into a bog by Capalu, a man in the shape of a monstrous cat, 'and the cat then killed him in war'. This Capalu is presumably a variant on Cath Baluc or Palug's Cat, which some say was slain by Cei.

John Rhys, in *Celtic Folklore, Welsh and Manx*, records a folk tradition current in Gwynedd during the nineteenth century. According to this Arthur and his men chased an enemy from Dinas Emrys in the direction of Snowdon. They were ambushed in a pass between Llyn Llydaw and the summit of Snowdon, and Arthur fell dead under a hail of arrows. The pass is known as Bwlch y Saethau, the Pass of Arrows. He was buried under a cairn where he fell, so that 'for as long as his dust rested there no enemy might march that way'. (Above Llyn Llydaw is a cave where his knights are supposed to lie.)

Wherever possible I have drawn upon those Welsh traditions which did not make their way into the legend as told by Geoffrey of Monmouth and Malory. At times the weight of the medieval version has been too much. I have, for example, kept Medraut as the villain of Camlann, though there is in fact nothing in the pre-Geoffrey sources to suggest Medraut was anything other than a paragon of valour and courtesy. Elsewhere I have returned to the older tales: thus Cei and Bedwyr are the most important of Arthur's Companions in the Welsh stories, and although later heroes displaced them they lingered on in European literature as Sir Kay and Sir Bedivere. Gwalchmei has an almost equally venerable pedigree, and for the other names of Arthur's Companions I have drawn upon the list in the Welsh legend of Culhwch and Olwen.

One major part of the legend I have inverted altogether: Gwenhwyvar the much abducted and unfaithful Queen. Here I have been influenced by the story of Rhiannon in the First Branch of the Mabinogi. This was set down in its present form in about 1060, but – like the Arthurian legend – embodies much older traditions. There is also a particularly obscure Welsh poem which may be a dialogue between Arthur, Gwenhwyvar and Melwas, that *might* – and I emphasize the *might* – support the interpretation I have put upon the legend.

The quest into the shadowy realms of the Western Isles is loosely based on the Welsh poem *The Spoils of Annwn*. This poem is also the origin of the tale told by Teleri at Caer Cadwy, and in both interpretations I have been influenced by Robert Graves's *The White Goddess*.

Christianity became the official religion of the Roman Empire in 337, and other religions were outlawed by 400. Gildas (of whom more later) seems to have believed that Christianity was universal in Britain prior to the coming of the Saxons. This is not true, either in Britain or indeed anywhere in the empire, including Italy itself: despite the ban, pagan practices not only survived but flourished. In Gildas's own day the Church was in decline: its congregations were shrinking, its authority was diminishing, and its wealth was dwindling.

A number of forest sanctuaries or *nemeton* are known to have existed in Devon. The most famous was Nemetostatio, near North Tawton. The neighbouring village of Bow was called Nymet Tracey until the construction of the arched bridge from which it takes its present name, while Broad Nymet still lies between Bow and North Tawton. So far as I am aware there is no evidence for any such sanctuary on the south coast, and Budoc's *nemeton* is entirely imaginary.

So too are the other places in the book. There was indeed a city called Lindinis on the site of present-day Ilchester, but Garulf's Lindinis is not intended to be a reconstruction of a particular late fifth-century city. South Cadbury was refortified at about this time and has a long traditional association with Arthur; my descriptions are adapted from Leslie Alcock's *Arthur's Britain*, but Caer Cadwy is a place of the mind, not a literal reconstruction of an archaeological site.

Constantine of Dumnonia and Vortepor of Dyfed are real people, described by their contemporary Gildas. (What is generally accepted as being Vortepor's memorial stone used to stand at Castell Dwyran in Dyfed, inscribed in both Latin and Irish Ogham.) Cerdic and his successor Cynrig are the traditional founders of Wessex, and as such are neither more nor less historical than Arthur himself. The other characters are my inventions, but I hope are in keeping with the times. The one exception is Teleri – a female bard is unlikely though perhaps not entirely impossible.

So, was there ever any such person as Arthur?

The simple answer is that we do not know, despite the vast amount of ink that has been expended on the subject. If he lived at all, he lived during the fifth and sixth centuries. At that time the Roman diocese of Britannia was dying, and modern Britain composed of the three nations of England, Scotland and Wales was being born. Two of those nations owe their names and their existence to external invaders: England to the Germanic Anglo-Saxons from the east; Scotland to the Gaelic-speaking Celts from the west. Wales of course derives from the native British who remained unconquered in the mountains.

These two hundred years are the most obscure and infuriating in our history. Obscure because nothing is certain; infuriating because we can catch glimpses of names and personalities, yet no more than glimpses. In effect, this is a prehistoric period for which we have one contemporary written source, and in many ways that source has handicapped rather than eased its study. We do, however, know quite a lot about what later generations *imagined* had happened (and it is upon their beliefs and legends that I have based this book).

During the fifth century the Roman Empire in the West collapsed. Rome herself fell to the Goths in 410, and for the sake of convenience we can assume that Britain ceased to be part of the Empire in that year. There is some evidence that the final break actually came from Britain, and that there was a purge of those loyal to the Empire.

By about 600 most of what was to become lowland England was in Saxon hands. Further north, the Scotti immigrants from Ireland were well established in the western regions of what we now call Scotland.

What we do not know is precisely how this came to pass. Should we, for example, think in terms of a wholesale Saxon migration involving men, women and children? Or should we think in terms of small warrior bands mounting a series of successful *coups d'état* in existing regional kingdoms? Did the Saxons come as migrant peasant farmers entering an almost empty land, or did they come bearing fire and sword?

How long did the anglicization of Britain take? Was it more or less complete within thirty to forty years, or was it a long slow process spanning several generations? One recent historian argues that the southern lowlands of Britain were under Saxon domination by the mid-440s – in other words, that there was only the briefest period of transition between Roman Britain and Anglo-Saxon England. Another proposes the very opposite. He believes that the Saxon incursions only affected the eastern part of the country, and that the greater part remained 'Roman' until the period of Saxon expansion in the late sixth century.

Both opinions are tenable. We simply do not have enough evidence to be certain. My own feeling would be that the nature and speed of the settlement varied dramatically from place to place.

In Kent, the archaeological evidence from a series of sites suggests the deliberate early settling of Germanic troops by an existing Romano-British authority, and this would of course fit the later legend. In Northumbria, the evidence appears to suggest a small aristocratic Anglian element ruling over a largely British population. The ninth- to twelfth-century *Anglo-Saxon Chronicle* relates the story of how the dynasty of Cerdic landed at Southampton Water in the closing years of the fifth century and fought their way inland over the next few generations, but the archaeological evidence demonstrates that the origins of Wessex lay in peasant communities along the upper Thames valley dating back a generation before Cerdic's time.

Archaeological evidence offers insights into a variety of cultural activities – such as burial practices, the exchange of artefacts and the use of space within a settlement. What it cannot do is tell us very much about the social conditions – the political system, the language, the beliefs. For that we need written sources.

Our only contemporary written source for the fifth and sixth centuries is Gildas, a British Christian who probably wrote *De Excidio Britanniae*; (Concerning the Ruin of Britain) during the 540s. It is a sermon, a piece of dialectic intended to arouse Gildas's countrymen from the sin and sloth into which they had fallen, with an 'historical introduction' that was meant to establish for his contemporaries that their present afflictions were a consequence of a failure of obedience to God. So by our standards this history is unreliable. Yet it is important, for it forms the basis of every later account, especially that of the Venerable Bede (early eighth century), through which it gained wide circulation. It has also coloured every modern work.

Gildas describes three phases of the Saxon conquest. (To suit his rhetoric the coming of the Saxons *had* to be seen in terms of conquest. The vengeance of the Lord upon the backsliding Britons could scarcely be portrayed in terms of peaceful settlement.)

In the first phase, the Britons have been abandoned by the Romans to their fate. The *superbus tyrannus* (who is almost certainly the same person as the Vortigern of Bede and his successor Nennius) and his counsellors call on the Saxons to help repel the northern Picts. The Saxon mercenaries saw there was nothing to stop them going on the rampage themselves, and duly did so, bringing fire and slaughter to the island. When they had finished looting they went home – presumably to the eastern lands they had been given.

In the second phase, after an unspecified interval, a leader arose among the Britons, Ambrosius Aurelianus, a man of distinguished Roman family and ancestry, to whose standard flocked the surviving Romano-British who recognized his sterling qualities. There followed a period of alternating victory and defeat, culminating in the siege of Mount Badon, 'almost the last and not the least slaughter of the villains'. (Significantly, Gildas does not say who led the British forces at Badon.)

The third phase was Gildas's own lifetime, forty-four years after Mount Badon. Britain now enjoyed freedom from external attack, though it was still rent by internal struggles. Gildas continued his sermon by attacking five contemporary kings: Constantine of Dumnonia, Aurelius Caninus, Vortepor of Dyfed, Cuneglasus and Maelgwn 'the dragon of the island.'

What Gildas said about Mount Badon is open to a number of interpretations. The traditional view, and the one I have used in this book, is that it was an overwhelming victory for the Britons that put an end to Saxon expansion for a generation. But one could equally well read it the other way: it was 'almost the last' slaughter of the Saxons because *thereafter the Saxons were the victors in virtually every engagement.* The battle was memorable because it was the last British success, not because it was an overwhelming triumph.

Again, historians from Bede to the present have assumed that Badon had a national significance. But it is quite possible that it was a local affair, of no great importance to Britain as a whole. Gildas tells us Badon *took place in the year of his birth.* So it was an important event to him. Perhaps all through his childhood, particularly if he was actually born somewhere near the battle site, people reminded him that he first saw the light in the year the Britons defeated the Saxons at the siege of Badon Hill.

What is more (and this is pure speculation), if one adopts Bede's reading of the text – and we should remember that Bede was working from a copy much closer to the original in age than any now available to us – Badon took place forty-four years after the arrival of the Saxons. In other words, the battle of Mount Badon acted as a pivot around which Gildas could hang his history, a central point forty-four years after the fatal invitation to the enemy, and forty-four years before the time at which he wrote.

It may be, then, that Gildas singled out Badon because it suited his rhetorical purposes rather than because the battle was over-whelmingly decisive.

As the reader will by now have gathered, I do not believe that it is possible to construct the kind of narrative history for the fifth and sixth centuries that one can expect for the fifteenth or sixteenth. The whole issue of chronology is too complex to discuss here in any depth, but the very fact it can be seriously suggested that Gildas wrote in 480 as opposed to 540 – a sixty-year difference – gives some idea of how uncertain is our present state of knowledge.

However, if narrative history fails us, it is still possible to adopt an alternative approach. We can identify certain trends within society, even if we cannot identify the time-scale over which these trends took place.

We know that the central political organization collapsed. The capital cities declined in importance, and public building and work came to an end. The ruling elite disappeared and their place was taken by men of purely local importance.

The centralized economy also collapsed. Large-scale trade, crafts and specialized industries, estate management and specialized agriculture, all became things of the past. The British fell back on local homesteads, small-scale cultivation and a barter economy. Many towns were abandoned to the lower classes, and old strongholds were refurbished or new ones constructed. The native population declined.

For our purpose, perhaps most important of all, a romanticized past was created: a Golden Age when heroes walked the earth.

The Roman diocese of Britain crumbled into a number of mutually hostile successor states, some Celtic, some Germanic. The rulers of these new states constructed elaborate genealogies linking themselves to their predecessors. Thus the kings of Dyfed, the kings of Powys and various northern dynasties all at one time or another claimed to be descended from Macsen Wledig, the Spaniard Magnus Maximus who was proclaimed emperor of Britain in 383. (In this context, Wledig means something like 'overlord'.)

As part of the same process, the collapse of the old world came to be viewed in terms of a heroic struggle against external raiders and invaders: first the Picts and Scots, then the Saxons. The tale became personalized and filled with a wealth of dramatic detail. So Ambrosius Aurelianus, the Roman 'gentleman' (*vir modestus*) of Gildas, becomes Emrys Wledig, the forerunner of Merlin, the fatherless boy who reveals to Vortigern the reason for the collapse of his tower on Snowdon. Hengist the leader of the Saxons treacherously slays Vortigern's Council, the three hundred chief nobles of Britain, and holds Vortigern himself to ransom.

By about the ninth century Arthur was firmly accepted as part of this legendary history. Vortimer the son of Vortigern and then Ambrosius had fought against the Saxons with mixed success, but Arthur was the victor in all his battles, the great war-leader who defeated the Saxons for a generation.

And as the hero *par excellence*, the famous victory of Badon belonged to him and him alone.

Early in the ninth century, so the story goes, a certain Nennius decided to write down what he knew of the history of the Britons. Much of his work seems to be a transcription or abbreviation of earlier sources, both British and Saxon, which are now lost to us. The history survives in various manuscripts, some long, some short, the most important of which for our purposes forms part of Harley 3859 in the British Museum. Bound with it – among other things – are the *Annales Cambriae*, or the Welsh Annals, and a series of Welsh genealogies.

The history lists Arthur's twelve battles, a series culminating in Badon. It does not include Camlann, perhaps because it was a list of his victories. It begins:

> *Then Arthur was fighting against them [the Saxons] in those days with the kings of the Britons but he himself was leader of battles. The first battle was at the mouth of the river which is called* **Glein**. *The second and third and fourth and fifth upon another river which is called* **Dubglas** *and is in the district* **Linnuis**. *The sixth battle upon the river which is called* **Bassas**. *The seventh battle was in the Caledonian forest, that is* **Cat Coit Celidon**. *The eighth battle was in Fort* **Guinnion** *in which Arthur carried the image of St Mary ever virgin on his shoulders and the pagans were turned to flight on that day and great slaughter was upon them through the virtue of our Lord Jesus Christ and St Mary the Virgin his mother. The ninth battle was waged in the City of the Legion. The tenth battle he fought on the shore of the river which is called* **Tribruit**. *The eleventh battle took place on the mountain which is called* **Agned** *[or* **Breguoin***]. The twelfth battle was on* **Mount Badon** *in which nine hundred and sixty men fell in one day from one charge by Arthur and no one overthrew them except himself alone. And in all these battles he stood forth as victor.*

This sounds suspiciously like a Welsh battle-listing poem. But how old was it? One simply cannot say. It may have been sung in some form in front of Arthur himself, if he existed. It may have been composed only a few years before Nennius compiled his history. Likewise there is no guarantee that all or any of the battles were originally ascribed to Arthur – he may well have displaced a number of other heroes.

All one can say is that some of the names sound old, that none of the places can be identified with any certainty, not even Cat Coit Celidon (somewhere in Scotland?), and that the legend of the great war-leader, who may or may not himself be a king, had already taken firm root by Nennius's time.

Bound with the history are the Welsh Annals. The Annals have two Arthurian entries, one in year 72 of the cycle, the other in year 93. These may be reckoned as about 518 and 539 respectively. The first says:

> *Battle of Badon in which Arthur carried the cross of*
> *Our Lord Jesus Christ for three days and three nights*
> *on his shoulders and the Britons were the victors.*

The second says:

> *Strife of Camlann in which Arthur and Medraut fell,*
> *and there was plague in Britain and Ireland.*

The text we possess dates from about 1100, copied from a compilation put together in the second half of the tenth century. By their very nature, annals involve a series of entries made at different times, a process of growth not unlike a modern diary where events are entered on a daily basis. Unfortunately we have no means of determining when these particular entries were made, or how old was the tradition on which they were based. Nor are the dates of the entries of any particular significance: they will have been supplied by the chronicler, and in this case were probably deduced from the death of Gildas in year 126 of the cycle.

What we do know is that the association between Arthur and Badon was not universal. The twelfth-century Welsh poet Cynddelw, for example, makes a number of allusions to Badon, but does not connect the battle with Arthur. In contrast, there are plentiful references to Arthur and Medraut at Camlann, which was famous as the most disastrous of the three futile battles of Britain.

So was Arthur a real person?

The evidence against seems at first sight compelling, and certainly I do not believe for a moment that we will find his grave in Powys, as two recent writers have claimed.

On the other hand there is no need to dismiss a character as altogether mythical simply because he keeps the company of myths. The fact that Sir Francis Drake is sometimes said to lead the Wild Hunt is not generally considered to be proof that he never existed.

The case of Ambrosius is even more instructive. It is clear that Gildas's text is part of a wider debate; for some reason his book alone survived. If it had not, we would know nothing of Ambrosius the leader of the surviving Britons. All we would have would be the legend according to Nennius.

Nennius tells the story of Vortigern's attempts to build a citadel in Snowdonia at what was later known as Dinas Emrys: how the masonry crumbled away every night, how his magicians advised him to seek a fatherless boy and sprinkle the building work with his blood, how they found Emrys or Ambrosius, who made the magicians look foolish by revealing the presence of a red monster and a white monster locked in combat deep within the ground. Nennius mentions in passing that Emrys was king among all the kings of the British. Most people are familiar with Geoffrey of Monmouth's version: Geoffrey turns Emrys into Merlin, and the fact he can do so shows what a far cry Emrys is from Ambrosius Aurelianus the Romano-British soldier. Had Gildas not mentioned him, we would have even less evidence for the existence of Ambrosius than we do for the existence of Arthur.

I do not believe we will ever prove the historicity of Arthur, despite the many claims made by various writers past and present. But it is possible, indeed likely, that Ambrosius had a successor. (Gildas says Ambrosius's descendants were still alive in his day, though much fallen from their grandsire's excellence.) If there were such a successor we have to call him something, and we might as well call him Arthur – in precisely the same way as we speak of Hengist or Cerdic as leaders among the Saxons.

When history fails us, myth will have to suffice.

The two texts mentioned on p. 391 are:

N. J. Higham: *The English Conquest: Gildas and Britain in the Fifth Century*, Manchester University Press 1994.

K. R Dark: *Civitas to Kingdom: British Political Continuity 300–800*, Leicester Press 1995.

GLOSSARY OF
PLACES AND TRIBES

            ~

Albany   Roughly, a term for what is now northern Scotland (later applied to all Scotland).
Albion   Earliest recorded name for the island of Britain.
Aquae Sulis   Bath.
Armorica   Brittany.
Attecotti   'The Old Folk'; inhabitants of the Western Isles and western coasts of modern Scotland. I have assumed that they are a confederation of some of the older Pictish tribes.
Badon   Arthur's most famous victory; site unknown.
Bannog   Southern boundary of Pictland; the ranges of hills between present-day Stirling and Dumbarton.
Belerium   Land's End
Blathaon   The northernmost point of Scotland.
Britannia   Roman name for Britain.
Caer Cadwy   South Cadbury in Somerset.
Caer Moridunon   Carmarthen.
Caer Vadon   Bath.
Calchwinyth   'The limestone (or chalk) hills.' The south midlands, including Dunstable and Northampton.
Caledonii   Pictish tribe or tribes from Scottish Highlands.
Camlann   Arthur's last battle: site unknown. I have placed it on the edge of the Somerset Marshes.
Cantware   Kent.

Catuwallawni Major British tribe of the South East.

Celidon, Forest of Great forest in what is now southern Scotland.

Cerdicesora Landing place of Cerdic at top of Southampton Water, near Netley Marsh.

Creones Pictish tribe from north-west coast of Scotland.

Crigyll Westernmost point of Britain, on west side of Anglesey, near Rhosneigr.

Cruithne Irish name for the British.

Dal Riada Scotti tribe. Originally from the area of Antrim in north-east Ireland, some of their number were at this time migrating into Argyll.

Decantae Pictish tribe from Easter Ross and the Black Isle.

Demetae Roman name for the tribe living in what became Dyfed.

Dewr Roughly, East Riding of Yorkshire.

Din Eidyn Edinburgh.

Din Erbin Fortress on eastern side of River Dart, Devon.

Dumnonia Cornwall, Devon, Somerset and part of Dorset.

Dunoding District of Gwynedd.

Dyfed South-west Wales.

Eburacum York.

Elmet Region in and to east of the Yorkshire Pennines, including Leeds.

Gewisse Another name for the West Saxons.

Glevum Gloucester.

Gododdin Kingdom running from Firth of Forth to the Wear in County Durham.

Gwent One of several minor kingdoms in the south-eastern area of modern Wales. Caerwent was its capital.

Gwynedd North-west Wales.

Iardomnan The Western Isles and parts of western Scotland.

Ierne Ireland.

Ingwine A name for the Danes.

Isc, or Ux The Rivers Axe and Exe.

Isca Exeter.

Kelliwig Near Padstow in Cornwall.

Kernow Cornwall.

Lesser Britain Brittany.

Lindinis Ilchester.

Lindum Lincoln.

Llongborth Possibly Portchester in Portsmouth harbour; or more likely Langport in Somerset.

Loidis Area around Leeds.

Londinium London.

Lugi Pictish tribe from Ross-shire.

Mona or Mon, Isle of Anglesey.

Moridunum A settlement on the coast of south east Devon, perhaps modern Seaton.

Narrow Sea English Channel.

Oak, River River Dart in Devon.

Penhyle A settlement at the head of the Porthyle estuary.

Penwith Point Southernmost point of Britain.

Peryddon Gwalchmei's death place: a stream running into the Monnow at Monmouth.

Picts Collective name for tribes living north of the Forth-Clyde isthmus in the land known as Pritdein.

Porthyle An estuary in South Devon.

Powys Kingdom in north-eastern Wales.

Prydein Native name for Britain.

Rheged Roughly, Lancashire and Cumbria.

Sallow Wood Great forest of Selwood on the western edge of Salisbury Plain. It ran north and south roughly along the present Wiltshire-Somerset border.

Sarre Thanet being a true island, this would be the easternmost extremity of mainland Britain.

Saxons, Saesons General term for Germanic invaders of Britain.

Scotti Irish sea raiders.

Severn Sea Bristol Channel

Smertae Pictish tribe from around the River Oykel in Sutherland.

Strathclyde South-western Scotland between the two Roman Walls.

Temair Tara, seat of the High Kings of Ireland.

Ux, or Isc The Rivers Axe and Exe.

Wectis The Isle of Wight.

Ynis Witrin Glastonbury.